Noah's Snow Angel

Gail Knezevich

Copyright © [2025] by [Gail Knezevich]

All rights reserved.

No portion of this book may be used or reproduced in any form or manner whatsoever without written permission except in the case of brief quotations embodied in critical articles and reviews.

This book is a work of fiction. All names, characters, businesses, organizations, places, and incidents portrayed are the product of the authors imagination or are used fictitiously. Any resemblance to actual persons living or deceased, events, places, buildings and products is entirely coincidental

Contents

Dedication	1
About the author	2
Also by	3
Prologue	4
1. Chapter 1	12
2. Chapter 2	24
3. Chapter 3	42
4. Chapter 4	55
5. Chapter 5	67
6. Chapter 6	85
7. Chapter 7	100
8. Chapter 8	113
9. Chapter 9	122
10. Chapter 10	136

11.	Chapter 11	146
12.	Chapter 12	160
13.	Chapter 13	173
14.	Chapter 14	184
15.	Chapter 15	191
16.	Chapter 16	204
17.	Chapter 17	214
18.	Chapter 18	222
19.	Chapter 19	236
20.	Chapter 20	250
21.	Chapter 21	265
22.	Chapter 22	276
23.	Chapter 23	291
24.	Chapter 24	302
25.	Chapter 25	318
26.	Chapter 26	332
27.	Chapter 27	349
Epilogue		357

Dedication

To my soulmate, my husband and the love of my life!
Many thanks to my writer friends Sara Fitzgerald and Kathy Rochell
whom I thank God
are in my life and always make me smile.
Also, a big thank you to Marie Higgins for always making
me beautiful covers.

About the author

Gail Knezevich is an award winning multi-published author of historical and contemporary romance. Filled with adventure and spice. She is the recipient of the League of Utah Writers, Gold Quill award. Writing has always been her passion, and she loves to share her stories and create complex characters who live in the environments she creates. She believes love makes the world go around and of course happy endings.

For more information about her books, you can find them at gailknezevich.com or amazon.com

Also by

GAIL KNEZEVICH

A Whisper on the Wind
A Cactus in Spring
Forgotten Dreams
The Dreaming Box

Prologue

Late July 1878, along the Red Fork of the Powder River.

Death was everywhere.

The smell and thunderous crack of gunfire fractured the early morning stillness and filtered through the small Cheyenne village. But worse than this was the tumultuous screaming of women and children as they ran for their lives.

Smoke from the burning lodges blocked the sunrise and swept across the land. Wind snapped against the skeletal remnants of tepees, creating a rumbling sound that seemed to crepitate the horror of battle.

But this was no battle. It was a slaughter.

The hideous sight was exactly what the hardcore captain Lamar Tamarin ordered to precipitate the horrific scene.

The Cheyenne people never had a chance. It was a one-sided battle. The warriors in the village were old, bone-thin, and completely unprepared. It made no difference to the blood lust that captivated the small regiment of soldiers.

On their captain's orders, Noah Harper was being held captive, tied to a thick pole at the center of the village. Thick smoke floated throughout the encampment and made visibility nearly nonexistent. It wasn't easy even to see ten feet in front of him. Then the swollen eye, broken nose, and split lips didn't help. Even if he didn't die from his unattended wounds, the smoke inhalation would finish him off.

Over the past eighteen months, the men he served with happily followed the orders of their delusional officer. Noah had never been overly liked among his troop. Most thought him a coward because he refused to carry his issued Sharps carbine like the rest. His job was to heal and save lives, not take them. White, brown, and black alike, it didn't matter. Saving lives has always been his highest priority. When he first joined the unit, he thought it would be to help the wounded men in the battle's heat. But this was no battle; it was a massacre he refused to participate in.

For the soldiers however, this was war, and they intended to win no matter what they had to do. And that is why he found himself in this predicament. His only advantage over the others was that he could speak a few words of Cheyenne, thanks to one of the captives back at Fort McKinney. He was able to give some warning, though it made no difference.

As further punishment for his ignoring the orders to kill, he was placed to face the eastern base of the Big Horn mountains. The hot summer sun glared down on him with ruthless abandon.

All around him, a roar of traumatism and unadulterated fear careened in a cacophony of dreadful sounds. The gut-wrenching shouts made by the native people and the intermingled bloodthirsty orders of soldiers all whistled unbridled throughout the encampment. The assault caught many of the native people still sleeping in their beds, causing most of them to flee wearing little or nothing at all. Food, clothing, cooking utensils, weapons, and other essentials were demolished, including most of the meager horse herd. Though a few horses had scattered, no one went after them. It was the human factor that interested the soldier's madness. Not the wild, bony, unshod ponies.

The men destroyed critical cultural items, such as shields, pipes, and unique items, like the sacred ear of corn, which was believed to have great healing powers. All fell into the hands of angry, unforgiving men. What they didn't want for souvenirs, they demolished or burned along with all the lodges.

Still, it wasn't enough.

What infuriated the men most was what they found among the Cheyenne's belongings. Military gear and personal effects taken after Custer's ill-fated attack on the Little Big Horn two years earlier.

Whether these people had anything to do with that battle made little difference to the soldiers; they would destroy, kill, and plunder as many as they could. Even rape had no consequence in all the turmoil. There would be no prisoners. Nothing would be left standing. These bloody corpses belonged to savages and meant nothing to the captain or the men under his command.

Ingrained with their hatred, the soldiers lined up the few bone-thin warriors and shot them where they stood. Only women, children, and the elderly were left. And they were viciously slaughtered, raped, or defiled by scalping or removing essential body parts.

By the time the men mounted up to leave, most of the Cheyenne lodges were ash, destroyed by fire, and any of the few supplies the people had gathered or stored for winter were gone.

Lifeless, bloodied bodies spilled across the ground like a toppled game of Dominos or laid face down in the Powder River. Blood is what the men wanted, and blood is what they got. They were out of control, like sharks drawn to a feeding frenzy.

One of the men stopped and glared at Noah but spoke to the captain a few feet away. "That ought to teach this cowardly slime a lesson! Thinks he's better than the rest of us?"

Noah's head faced sideways. He couldn't see but felt the saliva the man spat run down his bloodied cheek.

Surprisingly, they had left behind his medical bag, although how much good it would do, he couldn't imagine. They had dumped the contents on the ground and either shot at them or stomped on them, sending clumps of dirt or pieces of broken instruments flying onto his already bruised body.

Noah had lost his stomach at least a half dozen times. There was nothing left to vomit except the dry heaves that followed an empty stomach. He felt helpless and filled with the innate horror of what he'd witnessed the men doing. He was trussed up and left to sit in his vomit, facing the blinding sun. Every time one of them walked past dragging a screaming, terrified captive, they spat on him, calling him a coward.

He was no coward but wanted no part in this slaughter. If that made him look cowardly in the men's eyes, so be it. He was not a murderer and never a rapist.

He thought back to earlier. He had believed this was a search mission, but the moment he and the men arrived, he quickly learned this would be a killing spree. Half the men had been nipping at whiskey the night before and were in no condition to make any logical decisions.

He'd joined the Army two months following the Little Big Horn battle, ready to fight for the atrocities he'd been told had happened on the battlefield, how the seventh Calvary had been innocently slaughtered. The unit he served with was ordered to gather what they called the murderous low lives and imprison them or kill them in self-defense. He hadn't been told until later how Custer had given the foolish ego-filled order to charge. They were outmanned, outmaneuvered, and wholly overrun—two hundred soldiers to three thousand, Cheyenne, Lakota, and Arapaho.

But none of what he'd been told of that day compared to what he now witnessed this horrific morning. He had always known some of these men in his regiment were filled with hatred, but until now, he hadn't known where that fury and blood lust would take them. He felt his stomach again revolt.

He'd been attending medical school in the East—his dream was to become a doctor. After being a two-year medical student, he stepped away, always believing he would one day return to his schooling. After serving the first year with this man's army, he was given the position of field medic. An honor, or so he thought. His job was to heal the wounded. Not kill. Of course, the men he rode with did not consider the people of this small Cheyenne village to be human beings. They were savages, and no matter how hard he tried to put a stop to the soldier's hideous behavior. No one would listen.

Noah had turned twenty-two at the beginning of summer and figured he would never see twenty-three. These men would not allow him to live. They couldn't afford any witnesses. He had kept himself still, his head bleeding, and lolled to the left as he watched the last man ride out.

"Hey, what about the traitor Cap'n?"

"Leave him. He's dead anyway or will be soon."

With a wicked blast of laughter, the soldier aimed his carbine at the post Noah was tied to. The wood splinted and cut into his arms and back. It took every ounce of grit he possessed not to move or make any indication he could be alive.

The soldier shrugged, turned his Army-issued horse around on his hocks, and followed the rest of the men from the smoldering village. Through slitted, swollen eyes, Noah watched the men ride out, including the man he thought was his friend. Simon Mason. But even Simon had turned against him. Noah deduced that it was easier for him to go along with others than stand up for his beliefs, which coincided with Noah's.

Until today.

Today, Simon had turned against him.

Hours later, a soft mix of growl and bark came rushing at Noah. Good God, he must have fallen asleep. Standing before him was a half-grown wolf pup partly visible in the haze of wavering smoke. He stood not more than ten feet away. Silently and unmoving, Noah watched the wobbly pup seem to hesitate. The young wolf's fur was matted, burned in places, and full of soot.

Cautiously, the animal began to move forward, baring his teeth.

Great! Noah thought. Even though the wolf was young, there was a pretty good chance the animal's wicked teeth would tear him apart. He prayed the wolf had been a pet rather than a wild animal looking for its next meal. The Cheyenne language has so many different dialects that it could be confusing to know which one is right. He tried his best, hoping the animal would understand. Speaking softly, he lured the pup closer. He might make it out alive if the pup would cooperate.

His patient process worked. The pup happily wagged its fluffy tail, leaped up on Noah, and began to lick his face enthusiastically.

"*Homa'ke ho'nehe,* good boy," Noah told the pup. He began to move his arms up and down at the back of the post, hoping the pup would think it was a game and tug on the rope that held him prisoner.

It worked.

The wolf-dog became excited at the prospect of a game. Playfully, he began to tug on the rope that held Noah captive. He only prayed the rambunctious pup didn't take a hand while he was at it.

Thirty minutes later, the rope was loose enough for Noah to free his hands. He quickly unbound his ankles. The young wolf leaped up in excitement at his new playmate.

Noah stood and stretched. He felt like every muscle and bone in his body had been systematically ripped out. He reached down and gathered what was left of his medical supplies and began to move through what remained of the skeletal camp. He glanced down at the pup, who followed his every step. "How on earth did you escape?"

The wolf remained silent, not even a whimper, as he sat down on his haunches and stared at the tall man. "I guess that's how you did it. Silently," Noah muttered.

He wasn't sure how long he'd been tied up, though he figured all day as he watched the western sun slide like a golden shield behind the mountain. He thought he had seen a few women and children escape into the Big Horn mountains; however, he couldn't be sure in his delirium. But if they had, he felt sure they would return at some point to survey the area and take care of their dead. He had to get out of here before that happened. His conscience inundated him. He didn't like leaving all the dead to the elements, but now he had no choice.

The men responsible for all this had to pay. He had to find a way to get back to Fort McKinney. He would tell his story and resign his commission. He'd seen enough death in the past eighteen months to last a lifetime. This was the worst. Though he had nothing left to vomit, he felt his stomach roll again. The men had been vicious. Everything that had happened here this day had to be told.

As he moved north toward the river, he saw one dog and one wolf lying side by side and a young child with his tiny arms wrapped around the female wolf. They lay before a half-burned tepee still smoldering. All three were dead. "Your family, I take it," he said to the pup. "Well, it looks like it's just me and you." He made a quick tour inside what remained of the lodge.

Within the burned-out remnants, he found two bodies, one of an older boy and the other Noah assumed was his mother. The boy had a hand-made knife strapped to the inside of his leg. Noah carefully removed the weapon and strapped it on himself. At least he wouldn't be completely helpless.

Once outside, he shuffled through what was left of his medical bag. By some miracle, his small container of clean, dried cotton and a small supply of Morphine remained protected. He doused the cloth with carbolic acid to clean and wrap his wounds. He continued to dig through the bag for a small mirror he could use to see his face. Finding it, he saw it was cracked, but there was enough glass left to check his face. His nose and eyes were swollen, and they would have to heal independently. The pain was powerful, but he had to move, and a shot of Morphine would only slow him down; he'd save it until the pain became unbearable. He wasn't sure how long it would take him to get back to the fort on foot, so he started leaving the attenuated remains of the village behind.

The wolf pup eagerly followed.

Chapter One

San Juan Mountains. Late October, 1888

"Get down in the cellar, girl!"

"But Grandfather…"

"But nothing do as I say. We don't know what those men want, and none of them looks trustworthy. Now move, girl!" Elijah Franklyn ordered.

Cora didn't like this at all. Her grandfather was elderly, pushing the other side of seventy. He could use her help. She could fire the old breech-loaded Sharps as well as he could, maybe better; his eyesight had begun to falter. Out of respect for him, she gave herself no choice but to follow his instructions.

Since the age of seven, Elijah Franklyn had raised her and kept her safe after both her parents were brutally killed sixteen years ago. Cora's mother was Elijah's only child from his one-time marriage to a beautiful Cheyenne woman he'd met and married just after the Mexican-American war had finished in 1848.

Their daughter, Ellie, was born the following year. They lived among the Cheyenne for the next ten years. But rumors of a war between the states were taking the forefront. Elijah and his wife decided it was time to move on. The decision to leave was not easy; however, they both felt it was best for themselves and the small village they had lived in. They packed up and came to the San Juan plateau with their ten-year-old child. Away from war and away from civilization.

Cora's father, Calvin Lindstrom, was a white man Elijah met during his later military service. He had friended the young man but had lost all contact with him until years later, when Calvin showed up in the small town of Willowby, Colorado, looking for a place to settle after the War between the states. That was the late spring of 1867.

Elijah had come down the mountain for his yearly supply run into the small settlement of Willowby. Here, he met up with his younger friend from the military. Though the North side won the war, the South was devastated. And it all showed on the young man's face and body. He'd lost one leg severed from the knee down, though he could walk on a wooden leg. Elijah's heart went out to him, and was pleased to know the camaraderie of their friendship had remained as if no time had passed.

Elijah was in his mid-fifties; his young friend had seen his thirty-fifth year. He had lied about his age when he joined the military back in forty-eight. He was only sixteen, one of the reasons Elijah had taken the boy under his wing.

He invited Calvin up on the mountain to meet his wife and their only child, eighteen-year-old Ellie. She and Calvin fell in love almost immediately, even though prejudice still controlled the world. What they felt for one another outweighed the filthy talk.

Once they married, they chose to make their home on the outskirts of Willowby. Calvin was a blacksmith by trade. But hatred caught up to the couple when a group of renegade outlaws dressed as Indians raided the town, and both Elijah's daughter and Calvin were murdered, leaving their seven-year-old daughter Cora orphaned.

When the local sheriff, another man Elijah called a friend, made the long ride up the canyon to inform him of the deaths and his young orphaned granddaughter. Elijah was devastated. He had already lost his wife to influenza five years earlier. Now, a daughter. He would not lose another of his blood. He immediately traveled to town to retrieve his granddaughter.

Cora was grateful the older man had taken her in, mainly because of her native Cheyenne blood.

The attack made People afraid, and they would have taken their anger out on her. It made no difference; she was only a quarter Cheyenne. Her mother was half, and her father was as white as the rest of the people in town. She had been raised as a white child; her skin was nearly as light as the town's people.

But that quarter Indian blood was the enemy's blood, according to the residents. So, Cora lived in obscurity with her grandfather.

As the years passed, she found life lonely in the rugged territory. The only company she ever had was her grandfather. He was a kind man, and she loved him dearly. Still, there were times like this when he could get overprotective.

Obediently, she climbed into the cellar and quietly closed the trap door. She had become used to this place. Anytime there was a possibility of visitors, she was sent down here. "Out of sight, out of mind," Elijah would tell her. It was safer that way. Anyone in the area knew nothing about her, making the loneliness even more difficult.

She listened for her grandfather to cover the entryway with a braided rug she had made out of old rags, a creativity her mother had taught her as a child.

Down here in this small room, boxes were stacked with items that had once belonged to her parents. There were times she came down here to feel close to them. The space was dry and mold-free. Virtually hidden from curious eyes. The floor had been heavily packed and as level as concrete. In fact, over time, it became solid.

To add warmth, she used another braided rug she had made to cover the earthen floor. Eventually, this became her bedroom.

Snow was the enemy high on the mountain, but the worst came in the winter, sometimes starting in late October. Drifts reached as high as ten feet or more, freezing temperatures that could cause frostbite if one wasn't careful. There were days when even making a path to the outhouse was nearly impossible.

But in this hidden room, everything was dry and warm in the winter and cool in the summer. One small window was covertly disguised with makeshift piping to allow airflow. She had a pallet and fur to sleep on, and she discovered linens in the crates that held her parents' things. Even the clothing she needed as she got older and developed into a woman's body. But Elijah wouldn't allow her to wear female clothing. He insisted she dress like a young boy. So, everything remained in their storage crates untouched.

When they rode down the mountain to the town of Willowby for yearly supplies, she always wore a hat and kept her head down and herself bound to cover her maturing chest. As far as anyone knew, she was a boy Grandfather had saved in a snow slide. The sheriff passed away ten years after her parents had been killed. And people tended to move on. There was no one left to know about her. And none who cared to ask about the young boy tagging along with Elijah. He stopped taking her to town in the next few years when it became more difficult to hide her female body or her pretty face.

Cora listened to the angry voices from above. The men were furious and demanded to know the whereabouts of one they called Noah Harper. She had never heard of this man.

"Listen, old man; we know he lives here on this God-forsaken Mountain somewhere. The government wants him. He is dangerous. Was responsible for a lot of death, and we are here to bring him in."

"I'm telling you I never heard of him, and I've lived up here for nigh onto forty years."

"He's lying, Cap'n. Just shoot the bastard. Look at all this friggin' Injun stuff hanging about. He's a low-down sympathizer," the captain's intransigent right-hand man, Hyrum, informed him.

Elijah held his Sharps close to his side and cocked the lever into place. The rifle was ready to fire. He didn't like killing people, but there were times when it became necessary.

However, Elijah never got the chance to pull the trigger when the leader fired his Colt revolver. Elijah grasped his chest and crumbled to the cabin's floor. "Search the place!" The captain ordered the men.

They spent the next several minutes searching the small space. "Ain't nothing here. It looks like the old man lived alone."

"Come on, Cap'n, we have been searching this area for months, and winter comes early this high up. It's already as cold. as a witch's tit! This is the first human we've seen in weeks. Noah ain't nowhere to be found. He's probably dead. We ain't heard nothin' about him in years," said Charley, one of the original riders in the unit the captain had commanded back in seventy-eight.

Captain Lamar Tamarin glared at the four men surrounding him. "He ain't dead. I would know it if he was. And I'm never going to forget what the bastard did! Or how I ended up spending two long years of my life in prison thanks to the turncoat. He is going to suffer long and slow when I kill him!"

"We were all court marshaled, Captain. You weren't the only one who's had losses or has lived with the consequences." Simon Mason, another original rider, popped up. "For the past eight years, we've been searching and coming up empty-handed." Simon briefly lowered his eyes, though he couldn't admit what he was feeling and how he was damn glad they had never found Noah; he cleared his throat and added. "Don't you think it's time to let this go and allow us all to move on?"

Captain Tamarin gave Simon a menacing look; he'd doubted Simon's loyalty for some time now and was furious with him. He lifted his gun and pointed directly between Simon's eyes. "Put up or shut up, you yellowed livered coward!" Then he swung the weapon to include Charley, Hyrum, and Earl.

Hyrum wasn't about to stand here and let the bastard threaten him; he reached for his gun so quickly that no one even saw the movement until it was pointed directly at the captain. "I can end you all right here right now. I don't give a shit if we ever find this Harper. This is your revenge. I am only here for the pay and the fun. Don't you ever point a weapon at me again!"

Tamarin ground his teeth together. It wasn't the first time he'd questioned hiring the short-fused man. One day, Hyrum would rue the day he had ever threatened him, but for the moment, he needed the kind of man Hyrum was. He lowered his weapon.

"None of you sonofabitches," Tamarin growled. "None of you will ever understand what it feels like to be sent to prison for something you were taught was the right thing to do. Killing a bunch of redskins nobody wanted around is what my orders were. I was taught from the beginning that there is no good injun except a dead one! It has been my motto from the beginning, and I'm certainly not alone in the thought. But because some dog-faced politician got a moral stick up his ass, I paid the highest price. And now I want that Injun lover Harper to suffer no matter what the hell it takes. If none of you want a part of this, pack up now and get out. I can always hire others to take your place, and you know I will."

"Now hold on a minute, Cap'n, I never said anything the like. There's another mountain to check up north," Charley informed them. "It would be like the bastardly coward to stay in the area where all this began—hiding in plain sight. We never searched the area along the Red River or the surrounding towns, figuring he wouldn't be stupid enough to stick around. Maybe he's not stupid but smart as a fox."

"I agree. Let's head out. Spend the winter in Cheyenne sure as the Devil tempted Eve; there ain't nothing here to find," said Hyrum, sneering with disgust. I'm itching to have me a woman."

"Hell, Hyrum, you are always itching for that," Charley laughed.

"You got that right," Hyrum snickered.

In frustration, Simon threw his hands up and left the cabin to join the other three who waited outside. A place he would have stayed had Tamarin not ordered him to go with him and the other three into the cabin. As he left, he overheard Charley say, "What about the old man? He certainly is an Injun lover and might still be breathing?"

"Forget him," the captain barked. "Burn the place down with him in it! Nobody will miss the old coot, leastwise any of us."

"Too bad he didn't have a woman. Even a squaw is better than nothing," Hyrum spit.

Everyone ignored him.

"I see a couple of containers of paraffin stored in the cooking area. Get it and spread it around," Lamar ordered.

Charley nodded. "This thing's gonna go up like a tinder box."

"That's the point; now get to it."

Cora quietly lifted the wooden plank hiding the cellar and peeked out from under the loop in the rug when she heard the men leave, slamming the front door.

She watched in horror through a window to her right as one of them splashed paraffin outside the cabin walls. Though the flammable liquid oil had little odor, Cora knew what the men were using. They were going to burn the place down. Two men used a pine branch, wrapped cloth around the tip, and dipped them into the oil bucket. Once they were lit, the material swiftly ignited. One was tossed onto the front porch, the other on the roof. Immediately, flames shot up, licking at the dried logs. All the men, including the ones who waited outside, rode away from the cabin in less than a minute, hell-bent for leather.

Cora pushed the rug aside, lifted the planked doorway on the floor, and climbed out of the cellar. An icy blade of fear raced up her spine, causing her heart to do triple beats. She crawled across the floor to reach her grandfather's side. He was moaning in excruciating pain. Blood bubbled from a hole in his chest. She grasped him beneath his arms and dragged him through the back entrance and away from the cabin. It was not a simple task; she was small-boned but had strong arms and legs. She had him outside and away from the blaze in only a few moments.

Cora glanced back at their home. Tall flames shot skyward and leaped across the roof line created by pine resin. In seconds, she knew they would engulf the cabin and collapse the roof.

"Girl, forget about me! You need to leave!" Elijah muttered in a gurgling whisper when she had him out of harm's way.

"Grandfather, I won't leave you. I can help," she pleaded. "You know I can. You've taught me well."

"No, you can't; there is no help, Cora. I'm dying. You must save yourself. I want you to take Sugarloaf and visit my friend about five or six miles north. He lives at the base of Sandcove Narrows."

"Friend?" This was the first she'd heard of any friend who lived that close to them.

"His name is Noah Harper. He is a man of medicine. Those men are looking for him; he's in danger and needs to know. He can protect you."

"I can take care of myself," she countered. "I don't need this old friend of yours."

"You can't against men like those four. And Lord knows how many more were outside and out of sight. If you don't do this and they return, they will do unthinkable things to you! Hurry before Sugarloaf's lean-to is destroyed. A medal cash box is in the corner beneath the harness and saddle wall. Dig it up and take it with you. It's all I have to leave you. Now get moving."

She didn't like it, not one doggone bit. But he was right. His wound was beyond anything she knew how to treat. Maybe this man her grandfather spoke of could help. No matter what, she couldn't leave her grandfather lying here alone.

She glanced around the property. There had to be something she could do. She could use the travois and harness it to Sugarloaf. Get her grandfather on it and pull him to Noah Harper's cabin. Grandfather did say he knew medicine. With anticipation giving her courage, she lowered her gaze to tell the older man about her idea. His eyes were open and glazed. He stared sightlessly toward a cloud-infested gray sky.

"Grandfather!" She nearly screamed and shook the elderly man for a response.

Nothing.

Elijah Franklyn had gone to his maker.

"Damnation and hell's fury." Cora cried, tears slipping down her cheeks.

She took the next couple of hours digging a grave. The ground was partially frozen, so the grave was shallow. She wrapped the old man in one of Sugarloaf's horse blankets, pulled his body inside, and covered everything with dirt and stones.

Tears raced down her face. Her heart was broken. This man whom she loved was the only family she had. She respectively murmured a few words from the bible she had memorized. The Bible was one of the many books she and her grandfather owned. They both loved to read. One of her favorites was The Count of Monte Crisco, a romantic, adventurous tale of a falsely imprisoned man. He escapes with the help of an inmate who tells him of a hidden treasure on the Isle of Monte Crisco. The story was beautiful—the kind of adventure she would never experience.

The fire had run its course thanks to the crisp, moist air. It was going to snow. Years ago, they had cleared the land around the cabin of vegetation and other fire hazards. A monthly precaution one needed to take while living up here on the mountain. The chore was tedious but necessary. They made a rock firewall with a thirty-foot circumference out from the cabin. Protection is always the number one priority. The surrounding forest had been saved, and nothing had been destroyed. Even the lean-to had survived. But the cabin they'd made their home was another story. The roof had indeed collapsed.

Cora began to shiver now that the laborious burying had been done. She looked over to the charred remnants of the cabin. She had to rummage through the debris to see if she could salvage anything. Hopefully, the storage in the cellar room remained untouched. She needed her heavy calfskin coat lined with thick sheep's wool and her snowshoes to strap onto her boots if she ended up on foot. Both things were near the rear entrance.

She didn't have time to check out the cellar or dig for some cash box her grandfather had spoken of before he died. Maybe after delivering the message, she could return and start to clean up this mess. She retrieved her coat and clip-on snowshoes.

She had to get moving before the storm struck, making the pass impassable. Sugarloaf was getting old and showing the signs with his arching back, deteriorating teeth, and graying hair. Cora was surprised the old beast still lived. But right now, he was all she had, and she needed him.

She brushed her muddy hands on the damp trousers she wore, bit her lip, nearly drawing blood, and went to work collecting what she could to fill her valise, but most of her things were in the cellar. They would have to stay there for now.

With the meager things she'd gathered, she loaded them onto the old horse. By then, it was early afternoon. She debated whether she should wait until morning but figured it would be wiser to move now. If the snow started, she could be trapped indefinitely.

She had been lucky to salvage her warm coat and a heavy knit cap. Another thing she had made for both herself and her grandfather. Thank the Lawd he'd had the foresight to keep her mother's knitting and sewing items.

She lifted her grandfather's old-time piece and his long Bowie knife and stuffed them inside the travel bag. The rifle was buried under debris; it would have to stay there until she could return. She figured if she was lucky, she had maybe six or seven hours left of daylight to head up to the base of Sand Cove Narrows. It should be enough time if this weather allowed it.

Quickly she snapped the overlapped cover of her bag and urged Sugarloaf forward. Slowly, they left the charred cabin behind. She was probably insane even attempting this, but as she turned and took a final glance at the cabin, she knew she didn't have much of a choice. Curiously, she wondered about this man her grandfather called friend. The men who had shown up were looking for him and said the law wanted him. Was he dangerous?

But if that were true, and he was, why would her grandfather have been so insistent she make the trip?

Damnation! She prayed he knew what he was talking about. God only knew she did not know Noah Harper.

Cora and Sugarloaf plugged along as they followed the path on the north side of their cabin. The narrow trail climbed up and around a hilly, rocky section and through an umbrella of pine, leafless aspen, and thick gamble oak.

Thousands of dead leaves and debris ushered forth on the ground caused by a breeze and Sugarloaf's hoofs. She hunkered deeper into her coat. Hoping against hope, she would find what she sought at the base of the Sandcove Narrows. She and the horse continued forward.

Chapter Two

A small one-room cabin was nestled high on a plateau in the San Juan mountains and hidden from view. The route to get up here was steep, filled with craggy U-shaped terrain and dozens of box canyons. Rarely did people find their way this far up. According to the guidebook Noah purchased years ago when he first arrived, the mountains bragged the highest, most jagged summits in the continental United States. Twenty-eight peaks ranged from nine to fourteen thousand feet.

The surrounding forest was situated along the Continental Divide, often called the nation's headwaters, because all water flowed either west to east or vice versa, filling natural lakes and streams and eventually dumping into the San Juan River, which flowed toward the Pacific Ocean.

Noah loved it up here. He loved the solitude, especially knowing his family was safe a thousand miles away. He stood on a precipice overlooking a small, pristine meadow covered in a fresh blanket of snow.

As if rebelling against the elements, everything sparkled like millions of diamonds, even though the sun was well hidden behind storm clouds and the towering evergreen trees lining the quiet meadow.

The snow had been coming in hard for the past two hours. As usual, everything remained peaceful. He took another sip of his morning coffee. His half-breed wolf, Loka, moved toward him and sat steadily at his side, watching and listening. But all that changed in a fraction of a minute.

Loka growled.

Noah snarled.

The silence shattered.

A crackling sound of timber reverberated through the air and reached the man and his wolf.

Irritation filled Noah as he watched a small figure looking more like a kid riding a half-dead horse. They broke through the tree line and began to move across the snow-filled valley. Both horse and rider plugged along, leaving behind the crackling of heavily laden pine and twisted gamble oak.

A massive storm was breaking over the top of the Handies Peak. Fat flakes were already falling in a steady flurry. And the fool kid would get caught smack dab in the middle of it.

Continuing to stand on the edge of a hill that flowed into the valley about five hundred yards from his one-room cabin, he became rigid as he watched the snow pick up and swirl like a dust devil in the wind.

Who the hell was this idiot? And why, in the name of God, was he moving in this direction? From what he could tell, whoever it was appeared to be a young boy. Was he lost? Whatever he was, he sure moved at a turtle's pace.

Loka, whom he'd had since the massacre on the Powder River, gave him a nudge. Unconsciously, Noah reached down and gave his friend an affectionate rub between his large, pointed ears. "What do you think, Loka? Should we find out what the fool wants?"

Loka gave a short howl. They'd been together for ten years, and he was the only real company Noah had. He knew he would probably be dead if it hadn't been for the young wolf's help. He was about a six-month-old pup back then, but the rambunctious fellow freed Noah from the mess his troop had left him in.

The two of them had been joined at the hip ever since, and thank God for that. He had been wounded and in a lot of pain after what the soldiers had done to him and was horrified at what they'd done to the Cheyenne village. He reached down and again scratched Loka between the ears. He would never have survived the journey to Fort Mckinney had it not been for Loka.

Noah had tried to stop the carnage, but all he got for his trouble was a near-death experience. He still held the scar along the left side of his jaw, though not as visible thanks to the stitches he received at the fort. And unseen because of the beard he'd grown since coming up here on the mountain. A very long beard that hung nearly to mid-chest. He certainly looked like an old, scraggly mountain man.

Noah continued to watch the fool down on the plateau. The horse let out a misty whinny. The sound carried up onto the ridge where he stood. Seconds later, the animal collapsed. The young boy toppled with the horse and laid face down on the snow-covered ground.

"Christ on a crutch!" Noah hissed and raced back to his cabin, retrieved his snowshoes, clipped them onto his boots, grabbed his medical bag, and started down the hillside to the flat valley below. Loka was right behind him.

Cora couldn't move, couldn't breathe. The way she fell from the horse had forced the oxygen from her lungs. Still gasping, she reached over to touch Sugarloaf. Was he dead? The poor beast had given everything he had.

Unwanted tears began to seep from her eyes, freezing as they flowed down her cheeks.

Finally, after a few seconds, her breath returned. She rolled to her side. The valise she'd packed lay unopened about five feet away.

Son of a gun; she was so cold. She felt like an icicle. She couldn't feel her toes or fingers even though both were covered with gloves and footwear. Tarnation, what was she going to do?

She had no idea how far they had traveled. But here is where they ended. She was going to freeze to death out here and be as dead as her grandfather. More tears crested, and they felt like fire when they hit her cheeks. She helplessly groaned.

A sliding crunching sound came from her rear. Oh God! Now what? Would she have to contend with the wild animals? Though she hoped bears were in hibernation, there were wolves and other predators who existed. The thought of getting eaten alive was more terrifying than freezing to death.

The sounds were getting closer. She heard a male voice tell something or someone to stay. Was the male voice speaking to her? She was paralyzed with fear. To make matters worse, she was so cold that she could no longer move her legs.

"You okay, kid?"

Now she realized the animals weren't the only thing she had to worry about. Sweet Lawd, she should have stayed in the burned-out cabin. She remained silent, never making a sound or movement.

"Shit!" she heard the voice repeat the curse and knew he was squatting down next to her. He gently nudged her and felt his fingers move about her neck. "Well, at least you're not dead." He rolled her to her back.

What she saw as she squinted at him was the most frightening thing she could recall ever seeing—some snow creature. She had heard about these strange beings that roamed the forests and mountains for years. And now she was alone with the one. He was covered from head to toe in fur. A hood made of the same material ensconced its head. But it was his hairy face that frightened her the most. She screamed. Everything went black.

Noah would have laughed had the situation not been severe. He knew he looked like a hairy monster. He lived alone with only his wolf for company. He couldn't remember the last time he had taken a razor to his face.

He carefully lifted the boy and pressed his frozen cheek against the fur clothing he wore. Noah thought the child was almost pretty as he gazed down at it. Long dark eyelashes rested on high-boned cheeks—a very feminine mouth. The upper lip had a perfect bow shape, and the lower was full. The kid's appearance gave him an eerie feeling, making his heart pump wildly. Under any other circumstance, he might think this kid was a girl, but that was utterly crazy; there were no females up here on the mountain.

What the hell was this person doing up here alone? Whatever the reason, the kid couldn't be more than twelve. The time for guessing could come later. He needed to get him up to the cabin and warm him up. Frostbite was a killer, but he wouldn't know if that was the case until he warmed the child up and checked his hands and feet.

Halfway up the hillside, Noah switched the young one he had been cradling over his shoulder. He needed his hands accessible if he was going to make it to the top without slipping. Loka was investigating the brush-filled landscape, darting around with excitement. He must have spotted a rabbit. "Get him, boy."

Loka chuffed, sounding like a steam engine, his way of approval, and in only seconds, the wolf ran up the hill with a mouth full of wild snowshoe, a rabbit known for their large feet, which were shaped like snowshoes.

When Noah reached his cabin's front door, the rabbit lay on the stoop with barely a mark on him. Supper for tonight, he thought with a smile, though the smile couldn't be seen through all the hair on his face. He pushed the door open, carrying his human bundle inside.

He heard a slight moan from the child over his shoulder, then only the crackle of fire inside the firebox of the old rock fireplace. He laid the boy down on the only bed. Grabbed extra bedding from a storage cupboard in the corner of the room and quickly, carefully adjusted the kid on his back.

The child's cheeks were a bright red from the cold, and his outerwear was icy wet. These were the first things Noah removed. The child was trussed up like a bloody turkey. Some binding wrapped around his chest, and Noah wondered if he had been hurt, maybe a busted rib.

He loosened the thick cloth from around the boy, and at the same time, he pulled the stocking cap from the kid's head. Soft, silky, ebony hair slipped free and hung in jagged cuts to mid-neck.

This boy had a beautiful neck, long and feminine. Again, he wondered if this was a young girl instead of a boy. He looked at the chest where the loose binding had covered the kid. *Christ on a crutch!* Noah almost felt like fainting himself.

This was no boy. And by the looks of her, she was no kid either. She was slender though curvy, with a small waist, lovely shaped hips, and breasts that could fill his hands. *A woman's breasts!* He couldn't help it, he stared.

It had been a long time since he'd seen such a sight. Who was she? And what the hell was she doing on the mountain all alone? Not for the first time since finding her, he wondered where she had come from. He'd lived up here alone for eight years and had never heard of any females residing in the area, yet here she was all alone. Things like this didn't happen.

Her underclothing beneath the binding was still dry, believe it or not. He left them on her. For whatever reason, she was hiding the fact she was female. Her ribs were unharmed. Noah furthered his exploration. Her small feet and little toes were pinker than usual and icy cold, which explained the coloration. Her delicate hands were the same, he noticed when he removed her gloves.

He took turns rubbing her feet and hands with his own hands to bring the circulation back and warm them up. Finished, he carefully wrapped her in blankets and rested her head on a pillow. She was as snug as a bug in a rug. Her shortened hair fanned her face and neck like an angel's halo. A snow angry. He could imagine her body making angels in the snow, and the thought made him smile and reminded him of home.

He couldn't take his eyes off her. For several lucid moments, he studied her pretty face. Softly arched brows matched the color of her silky hair and curved delicately above her closed eyes, framed with long, lush eyelashes brushing the soft skin below her closed lids. On closer inspection, he realized the lips he had studied were plump and sultry and just about the most kissable mouth he could ever remember seeing.

Christ on a crutch, it had been far too long since he'd laid with a woman, not that he'd laid with many. He was only eighteen when he joined the Army and still a virgin. But from that point forward, there had been some ladies of the night.

The woman was young, though he'd never been good at guessing age. Hell, look at himself. He looked much older than his thirty-two years, thanks to all the facial hair covering him from his upper cheek to his lower neck and flowing down to his breast muscle.

He wore his usual winter clothing. Furry outer coat and leggings, which enveloped him from head to toe. He probably looked like a dangerous snow creature to her, such a delicate little thing. No wonder the poor thing fainted when he'd moved closer. He didn't think he would ever forget the look of shock and fear when she glared up at him with such vast, beautiful eyes. The color of deep topaz. *What the hell was he thinking?*

He quickly stood as if his very thoughts would set him afire. Grasping the snowshoe rabbit Loka captured, Noah moved out to the back slab, where he skinned and cleaned the long animal. Within an hour, the rabbit was in the cast iron stew pot with onion, carrot, dried mushroom, and potato. This would be the last of his potatoes and carrots. He carried the heavy Dutch Oven to the fireplace and hung it from a trammel above the fire to cook. The scent of added spices filled the cabin with a delicious fragrance within the next hour.

A whimper came from the bed on the other side of the room. Noah peeked over his shoulder to check on the girl. Loka lay on the bed, curled up next to his patient. Noah smiled at the homey sight. Smiling was something he rarely did. But as he watched the girl cuddle closer to Loka's warmth, he found the picture of them pressed together made him do just that.

For a brief second, he wished it was himself she canoodled up too. *Nope, it wasn't going to happen. Hell no!* He'd never really thought about how lonely it was up here on the mountain; after all, it had been his choice to leave civilization behind, but now, as he looked over at this attractive young female who had her arm wrapped around his wolf's midsection Noah wondered if it had been a mistake not to mingle at least once in a while with other humans. Or to take an occasional woman to his bed.

He hadn't even tasted liquor until he'd joined the Army. A babe in the woods, his older brother Amos would have said, when alive. Noah had two brothers, both years older than himself. Both were killed about thirteen miles east of Brownsville, Texas. One of the last conflicts before the Civil War came to an end. Noah was only nine years old at the time. He had been a surprise birth to everyone. His mother was in her forties and figured she was done having babies.

Neither of his parents approved of him joining the Army. He was their only living heir, but Noah had made his mind up, and they wouldn't dissuade him. He had two sisters who could indeed take over the farm. Looking back, he wished he had let them talk him out of joining. Years went by without contact. He didn't even know if any of them were still alive.

He had avoided everyone connected to his past life when he decided to become secular and made this life-changing decision. He'd made a lot of enemies when he testified against the men in his unit. The horrific carnage they had left behind in seventy-eight on the Powder River could not go unpunished. It was one thing to gather prisoners for relocation but something entirely different to senselessly murder, rape, and pillage. The men had become the very thing they claimed to hate.

Savages.

No, they had to pay for the cruelty. Noah knew at the time he would put his own life in jeopardy. But to live with the memory and what he knew happened firsthand, he could not let the perpetrators go unpunished.

Maybe that made him a coward, but he believed that it would have been more cowardly to say nothing.

He turned back into his rugged kitchen. Rugged was right, and he felt embarrassed for the first time since coming here to live this hermit life. Only the bare necessities. Fine for his needs, at least he thought so. But what the hell would it look like to a woman? He had only a few tin dishes and utensils, his cast iron frypan, and a Dutch oven.

Christ on a crutch, he chastised himself for even having thoughts of what a woman would think. It made no difference what she felt about his meager life; she wouldn't be staying here. This little feminine fluff would be gone as soon as he figured out where she had been headed. That, of course, was the mystery. There wasn't anyone around for miles except for his friend Elijah, who had made it pretty clear he lived alone. And he lived in the opposite direction.

Damnit, so where was she going? He sure didn't need any woman hanging around up here, getting in his way, causing trouble. The problem was that his traitorous body seemed not to want to cooperate. He grabbed a large spoon and viciously began to stir the stew.

While the girl, *at least that's how he would think of her,* slept on his bed with his traitorous pet, he began to make biscuits. They would taste good with the stew. He laid them in the cast iron skillet and stiffened when he heard her voice.

"Are you a man or one of those hairy mountain Yeti's?" Cora nervously asked and glanced around the one-room cabin. Like the home she and her grandfather shared, this place had a planked floor, and she could imagine some of the braided rugs she had made to keep the floors warm as they lay across the bare wood. The place was neat and clean. The bed she laid on had a pristine, masculine smell of wood and musk.

There was a small counter for prep work and a dry sink with a metal bucket inside. One glass paned window was above the sink where pots of lush herbs rested on the sill. Open homemade shelving adorned the walls from the back door to the end of the counter.

On each was an assortment of at least two dozen jars filled with dried herbs. A mortar and pestle that he must use for grinding them sat center stage.

The only heat in the cabin came from a large stone fireplace. To the left of this on the hearth was a rectangular medal container standing upright and she guessed he kept water heated inside. The odd thing looked to hold about eight gallons.

A tiny potbelly stove was tucked in the corner beside the small counter, but it didn't look like he ever used it. He was doing his cooking in the fireplace which served as the only heat in the cabin.

Inside the brick firebox was a cast iron Dutch oven that hung from a trammel and released steam, giving off a wonderful scent that made her belly growl.

A small, rounded table with two chairs sat near the sink and counter. But what lay beyond outside she couldn't see with the door closed. A second window was on the wall beside the bed, more significant than the other above the sink.

Where the devil was she? And who was this crusty-looking personage puttering around the inside of the fireplace and stirring a pot where the succulent smells she had detected came from? She swallowed and asked again. "Are you a man or a snow monster?"

Startled, Noah jerked around. Her eyes were wide, and not for the first time, he noted they were as pretty as she was. No, they were more; they were mesmerizing, soul-searching. They were stunning, filled with warm tones of golden amber, reminding him of a dark topaz crystal; however, at the moment, they didn't look happy; they seemed more filled with intense terror than anything else.

Cora realized she had her arm wrapped around a large dark gray animal. A wolf or dog, she wasn't sure. But he seemed friendly enough. But this tall man, who must reach over six feet, was something else. What that might be, she couldn't imagine.

He was dressed in what appeared to be furry hides on his bottom half, a blue plaid flannel shirt with suspenders attached to a wide leather belt that held up his furry pants. Also attached to the belt was a rather large knife tucked inside a beaded sheath. Similar to what her grandfather wore.

She wondered if it was Cheyenne. Her grandfather's scabbard certainly was.

The man's feet were covered with fur boots and looked like he'd made them himself. The hair on his head was thick and wavy, a combination of chestnut brown and deep red highlights, though on the long side and hung to the top of his broad shoulders. He looked clean enough. But tarnation, he was the hairiest man she'd ever seen. She wondered if he was just as hairy beneath his clothes. Like she figured a Yeti would be.

She looked across to him. He had the bluest eyes, a deep cerulean blue, and they were transfixed on her. Mercy! Who was he? And what in tarnation was she doing here with him and this wolf-dog who seemed to guard her closely?

As if understanding her wonder, Loka leaned down and licked the hand she had curled around his stomach. He yawned, showing off very sharp, pointed canine teeth, a long wolf-like snout, and bright yellow-gold eyes. She carefully lifted her arm from the animal, who let out a soft, almost silent plea that sounded more like a howl. Tarnation, he indeed was a wolf. But how could this be? A wolf was as wild as the land on which she and her grandfather made their home. For the third time, she asked the stranger if he was a man or a snow monster.

Noah cocked his head sideways, never taking his eyes from her; not only did her face have the look of an angel, she had the musical, slightly husky voice of one.

"I'm a man," he told her gruffly. "You were in some trouble, and I couldn't let you die."

Cora detected a wealth of sadness in his voice and felt ashamed for her abruptness. "I apologize. I didn't mean to insult you," she said.

"You didn't; I know what I must look like to you." He turned his back on her and moved back to his cooking pot. "I've made some rabbit stew; should be done shortly. Are you hungry?"

The man said no more as he turned away, but Cora carefully watched him as she heard the clang of a Dutch Oven lid as he lifted it to check the cooking food and give another stir.

Pulling the blanket higher, she pushed herself to a sitting position. The wolf exited the bed and moved to the man crouched over the heavy cast iron pot and sat down on his haunches. The animal sniffed the aroma of cooking food. She also enjoyed the delicious smells as they filled her senses and made her belly growl for the second time. Forgetting to hold on, the fur blanket that covered her slipped down to her waist.

Tarnation! All she wore was the underwear she'd donned yesterday. The binding she wrapped around herself each morning was gone, and only the old camisole was left to cover her bubbies, and an old pair of cutoff longjohns was left to cover her bottom half. Horrified, looking at her near nakedness, she cringed. Lawd in heaven, her grandfather had never seen her this undressed, not since she was a child.

"Where are my clothes?" She choked out.

"They are drying over there in the corner. They were frozen and wet. You were already freezing. I didn't want things to get worse for you. I was worried about frostbite. But you remained modestly covered at all times if you are worried."

"I see," she nervously replied, pulling the fur higher to her neck and placing her hands beneath. "Thank you, I think," she whispered, and the remark caused heat to color her cheeks.

"What were you doing up on this mountain alone?" He asked.

Cora turned to gaze at the low flames and red-hot coals dancing and smoldering inside the large fireplace. He added a couple more pieces of wood, which quickly caught. He seemed furious about something as he dropped the iron potlid with a clang.

Instead of answering his question, she asked one of her own, "What happened to my horse, Sugarloaf?"

"Is that what you called the poor wretched beast you rode?"

She swallowed. "He was old; he'd been with us for as long as I can remember. But I needed him to take me and my belongings up the canyon to Sand Cove Narrows. Is he dead?"

"I'm afraid so. While you were asleep, I cared for his body and brought your satchel up here. But you haven't answered my question. What are you doing up here and very much alone, and what do you mean he has been with us? Who is us?"

Again, she ignored the question, keeping her eyes averted from him and on the cooking pot and the biscuits he lined in the frying pan.

She was so used to keeping her identity secret. Her grandfather had insisted, especially when she began to develop female assets, as he put it.

He had done the same thing with her mother until her father met up with Elijah, and he brought him up here, where he met her mother.

The two of them fell in love and married. Shortly after, her mother became pregnant. She and her father moved to the town of Willowby and lived in harmony for the first seven years of her life. A harmony that ended when tragedy struck. Both her parents were killed, and with nowhere else for her to go, her grandfather brought her to his cabin, where she had lived ever since in secret.

"My Grandfather sent me to find a man called Noah Harper. Do you know of him?"

Did he know him? Hell, he was him. "Who's your grandfather?" he barked. Damnit, no one was supposed to know of his existence. It was dangerous for him and anyone who knew the truth of who he was. There was only one other person he had ever shared this information with. He'd met the older man eight years ago when he first got here. He was a recluse, just like Noah wanted to be. A mountain man who'd lived here most of his life. He helped show Noah survivalism, how to hunt with bow and arrow, trap, save the hides for clothing, what plants he could eat, and much more.

The older man repeatedly shook his head in amusement regarding Noah's pet wolf. But the two got along very well. After the first two years, Noah made enough money from the furs; he'd tanned thanks to the older man's teachings.

Once a year, Elijah Franklyn would take the furs to town for trade and purchase supplies with the money. Noah shared the profits with the mountain man. He had other money tucked away from his time with the Army that had been placed for him in the First National Bank of Cheyenne in Wyoming, but he had never touched any of it. It was too risky, considering he wanted his identity to be kept a secret to protect his family.

After the initial meeting and survival lessons, the older man's visits were narrowed down to once a year when he brought Noah's supplies up to him. He certainly had no granddaughter that Noah was aware of. He lived a solitary life just like Noah did. "Who's your grandfather?" he snarled.

Cora jumped at the tone in his voice. Not only was this man an ugly hairy beast, but he was also mean and ornery.

"Elijah Franklyn," she answered, but her voice was so low Noah had to strain to hear her. Loka chose the exact moment to return to the young girl. She reached for the wolf and gently petted his long outer fur guard along his neck. She had learned long ago this was the fur that protected the soft, downy underlayer. Loka moved closer so as not to miss a single stroke. Cora obliged.

"You mean Elijah Franklyn, the old mountain man?" Noah barked.

"Yes," she barked back.

"Loka!" Noah ground out and tapped his hand against his furry buckskin pants. "Cease!"

The wolf ignored the command and licked the girl's face more readily. *What a bloody traitor the wolf was. Or was Noah acting like an ass?*

"I've known the man for several years, and he never mentioned anything about a young kid living with him."

"He kept me secret when my body started to change. And I'm not that young. I'm certainly not a goat, either. Now it's your turn; who in tarnation are you?"

Noah couldn't help the smile he felt coming on, but his hairy face covered the expression. No, she certainly wasn't a goat. And she certainly wasn't a kid. Hell, she was a very pretty young woman, and when he had removed her outer clothing and the binding strangling her chest, he knew for a fact she was no child. She had lush curves that affected him more than he cared to admit.

For the second time this morning, he angrily thought, he shouldn't have remained celibate over all these years. She still clung to the blanket as if it were a lifeline.

"You can call me Jones."

"Well, that's better than Snow Monster, I suppose."

He grunted. "How old are you? Twelve, thirteen?" He snapped with irritation, his cerulean, blue eyes giving her a distinct perusal.

Cora felt the snap of disapproval in his question. She knew she was small-boned and of an average height, but she certainly wasn't a child. "Grandfather and I would have celebrated my birth next February. That is if we would have celebrated. He wasn't much on celebrating. I will be twenty-two."

"Christ on a crutch!" Noah damn near choked. "He kept you hidden all these years?" He nearly shouted, and Loka looked up and gave a slight growl as if to urge Noah to show some respect.

"Well, he had his reasons. Sometimes, he would have to leave me alone when he went down the mountain for supplies. He said it was safer for me to stay behind and unseen. He said too many men would begin to notice me, which would endanger me. Mostly, I didn't mind. I have my room down in the cellar. I love to read when I don't have chores or before I go to sleep. Do you like to read, Mister Jones?"

Noah turned away again; he felt the threat of a smile. "Umm yeah, I like to read when I have time." He remembered when he cleaned out his things back at the fort. He had at least a dozen books, which he kept with him over the years.

A loud cracking sound from outside resonated inside the cabin. Cora jumped, and Loka stood at attention, sagging the bed in the center. Noah grasped his rifle from the wall, shoved his arms into his furry coat, and moved out the front door without a word. The wolf leaped from the bed, following close behind. "Sweet lawd almighty!" Cora choked out.

Chapter Three

Cora shuttered when she heard the horrendous racket outside, more of a dragging and crashing sound. She wondered if the roof was about to collapse and cave in on her. She didn't have time to ponder when another loud thump at the front door made the foundation rumble. What the devil was he doing?

She was about to stand up to check, but seconds later, the snow-covered man swung the door open with a bang, carrying an arm full of firewood. When he stepped back inside, the wind gusted around him like an icy tornado, bringing a blast of frigid, blustering snow. Quickly, he dumped the wood in a large bucket on the hearth, slammed the door shut, and dropped the latch in place.

Without looking at her, he snarled with irritation. "The storm's coming in heavily and overwhelmed a branch, knocking it to the roof. I got it off. But this storm has become a blizzard and will probably last for days. Now I got to figure out what the hell I'm supposed to do with you?" he grumbled and pulled his coat off, hanging it on the hook by the back door. "Of all the rotten luck. I sure didn't need this, damn it to hell."

She glared with dismay at the man. "I was wrong when I thought you might be nice. You're not. You are a cranky old snow monster. And for your information, you don't need to do anything about me. Just give me my clothes and valise, I'll be on my way. I told you I need to find Noah Harper."

The man gave her a look of shock along with irritation. "What the hell for? Are you out of your mind? You can't go out in this stuff. You nearly froze to death only this morning. Do you want to die, you silly little fool? Shit!"

"Must you cuss every other word?"

"Look, lady, I already saved your life once, and I ain't in the mood to do it again," he snarled, curling his lip. However, the thought of tending to her again was tempting. But it was the last thing he needed. He had nothing to offer any woman, let alone this one.

"Does all that hair on your face keep you warm?" She innocently asked.

"Huh?" Self-consciously, Noah combed his fingers through the thick beard that hung down his chest.

"I can shave it for you if you have a mind. I used to do my grandfather's all the time, especially when it got to itching. Does all your facial hair itch? It looks to me like it would. Maybe critters live in there."

He sneered down at her without apology.

She quickly decided this snow creature might be the orneriest man she'd ever known; however, she ignored his distasteful grimace and instead studied his eyes. He had the most brilliantly colored blue eyes, and they reminded her of a clear summer sky or a translucent crystal of the deepest sapphire.

Tiny crow's feet cut into the corners of those eyes, and attractive dark brows arched above, making the color of his determined gaze remind her of the blue flame of fire. Long, thick black lashes handsomely sheltered the upper and lower lids. But tarnation, the rest of his face was ugly as sin. How could a man stand all the facial hair? She glanced back up at him. He was still wearing a sour look, at least what she could see of it.

"Really," she started. "I could barber it for you. Never once did I cut my grandfather. He said I had a gentle touch. We didn't have a mirror for him to look at himself like you do on the backside of the door."

He grasped his beard, running his fingers through it. "Christ on a crutch! Do you always talk this much?"

"I never really thought about it," she replied, "but maybe I do." She lowered her gaze to her hands, still gripping the furry blanket to her chin. When she chanced an upward glance, she felt her heart hammer inside. Those mesmerizing eyes she had been so intent on studying now held a subtle change. For an instant, she thought she detected a smile when they briefly lit up.

"Well, you do," he gruffly stated, turning away with irritation. He picked up a narrow log he'd just chopped and shoved and shoved it inside the firebox. Her gaze followed the action. Again, as earlier, her stomach growled. She had not eaten anything since yesterday. She had traveled all night, not daring to stop. And now it was dark outside and snowing to beat the band. Thunderation, how long had she been here?

Noah heard her stomach the moment he straightened and noted her perplexed expression. He leaned down and lifted the Dutch oven's lid, grasped the spoon he'd been using, and stirred the contents for the umpteenth time. "I take it you are hungry. This is about done. I'll just put the biscuits on to fry."

"Thank you," she whispered. "It all smells wonderful."

He said nothing as he moved about the sparse kitchen area, grabbed the cast iron frypan where the biscuits he'd prepared waited, and placed it on the coals beneath the Dutch oven.

"Where is your outhouse?" Tarnation, but she needed to go.

"Outback."

"Could you hand me my clothes and turn your back so I can put them on?" That's when she remembered her binding was missing. In a panic, she hissed. "What did you do with my binding?"

"Your clothes are still damp. I'll hang them closer to the heat when I get the food dished up. As far as that awful binding, you don't need to keep strangling yourself with it. I already know you are female; he barked unnecessarily. "Here use my coat, he snatched it from the hook and shoved it in her hands. "Your boots are on the floor beside the bed."

Cora's cheeks blazed. She supposed he was right; she hated the restriction the bindings gave her. "I have spare clothing in my valise. Could you hand it to me, and I will get changed?"

Noah swallowed; shit, he was acting like an angry old grizzly. The poor little thing was embarrassed and ashamed of her womanly body. Did she wish she was a boy? He didn't think so; she was far too feminine in looks and actions. "I'm sorry, I should not have said that." He walked over to her travel bag, where he had placed it on top of his trunk, lifted it, and handed it over. "I'll step outside while you get dressed."

"You don't need to. I can dress under the blankets. As you said, there is a blizzard going on outside. If you turn your back, I'll be dressed faster than you can say my name."

"I don't even know your name."

She smiled. "I know. But I will be fast."

He nodded and turned his back to her.

"My name is Cora. What is yours, it certainly isn't Snow Monster?"

He could hear her wrestling with her clothes. "People just call me Jones."

"Jones?"

"Yes."

"That isn't your real name, is it?"

He didn't answer.

Beneath the covers, she removed her soiled underwear and pulled on her clean long johns. Her heavy socks came next.

As she grew older and developed, she separated the boy's underwear into two pieces, top and bottom. The alterations made it so much easier when she had to use the outhouse. No longer did she have to strip down naked every time she had to go, especially in the winter months. Just the thought of being nude in the outhouse made her shiver.

The bindings came next. She had worn these for years ever since she had grown bubbies. She began to wind the cloth about her chest. The material was stiff and very uncomfortable to wear. She hated how it made her feel. But her grandfather had always insisted she hide herself.

But on second thought, her grandfather was gone, and Jones was right. He already knew she had bubbies, and this binding seemed stiffer than usual. She would wash them and use them when her monthly curse came. She tossed the bindings down. A beet red flannel shirt came next, and she quickly buttoned it. Finally, she tugged on her buckskin trousers. Grasped her rope belt and tied it about her waist, sat down and pulled her boots on.

"I'm ready," she announced.

Noah swung around and immediately noticed the bindings lying unused on the floor. He could see the outline of her breasts. He quickly lowered his gaze. He led her through the cabin to the back door. "It's about twenty feet ahead. Be careful. The snow is coming down heavily."

He wrapped his coat around her shoulders and instructed her to push her arms through. She did and tightly wrapped the heavy material around herself. The oversized coat hung down to her ankles, but lord, it was warm, and she could smell his essence. There was a delightful scent of musky leather and pine as she cuddled down inside.

"It's nice to know you can be kind, Jones. Thank you." She rushed outside and headed for the outhouse. Loka glanced up to Noah, then dashed outside, following Cora.

The traitor! Noah thought for the hundredth time but couldn't help smiling as he watched the shapely little woman, though very modestly covered from head to toe with his heavy coat, race toward the squat little building. Even in her baggy clothes, he knew what was beneath, and Damnit to hell, she looked good enough to taste. For the first time in years, he was enjoying the company. He waited for her and Loka at the door.

When she returned in a bluster of snow, Noah held the door open for her, noticing her cheeks were a beautiful rosy red. Her topaz brown eyes seemed to sparkle like a warm whiskey toddy, giving her a delightful sheen created by the cold. Christ on a crutch, he was aroused. He glanced at himself in the clouded shaving mirror he kept nailed to the back door and scowled at himself. She was correct; he looked like some hairy snow monster. Maybe he should shave.

"My goodness, Jones," Cora said in a rush as she returned. "You have some of that medicated paper for wiping. It was wonderful. My grandfather and I used leaves and old newspapers; even once, I used a corn husk. Tarnation, that was nasty."

Noah did not reply; maybe he had retained a little of civilization. *A corn husk! That certainly was nasty.* "There's a bucket of water in the sink; it's heated, and you can wash your hands."

"Thank you, I will."

They shared the rabbit stew and the flaky biscuits. Even Loka got a large serving. Noah wished he had a better setup for sharing a meal. The table and two chairs were scarred and rickety. They belonged to the previous owner, who died years ago.

But now, as he looked down at the worn-out furniture, the ancient reading chair in the corner, this table, and two rickety chairs, he felt like the old hermit he had personified for years. Long ago, he gave up living in a polite society. As far as the world knew, he was dead or had disappeared to some unknown, invisible place, never to show his face again.

Now, however, and for the first time in a very long time, he felt his solitary life crowd in on him and stick to his spirit like pine sap. He had always planned to build an extra room for sleeping and an attached water closet and revamp the furniture, but since he had no one to worry about except himself, he never got around to it. And Loka well he could take care of himself, always had. A large part of him was still wild. Come spring, he would work on changing the living conditions.

What the hell was he doing? He chastised his ridiculous notions.

But the thoughts continued to sneak in and propel firmly through him with tiny pinpricks of conscious regret.

Noah stood, took the empty bowls, and placed them beside the sink. He poured water from a pitcher inside the bucket and then added the heated water he kept close to the hearth. He began to wash the dishes when he felt her step beside him, take the clean dishes, and begin to dry. He could feel her heat, and it was making him tingle.

"I have more water heated. We can use it to wash ourselves; the water is hot. You go first." But when he noted her blush, he quickly added, "I'll give you some privacy. I need to make a trip to the outhouse. Ten minutes will that be enough time for you?"

"Thank you, that would be fine," she whispered, praying it would be. She needed to wash, but she nervously wondered how much clothing she should remove to do it.

He pulled his coat from the hook and pushed his arms through the sleeves. "Do you need some soap?"

"I have my own, but thank you for offering," she shyly smiled.

Noah nodded. "Don't worry about emptying this bucket; I'll take care of it when I get back." With that said, he left through the back door. Once again, Loka followed.

Cora hurried over to her valise and removed her long-sleeved nightgown. Nothing fancy for sure, but it would help keep her warm. She quickly stripped down to her long johns and pulled the warm flannel nightgown over her head. She grabbed her soap, toothbrush, and homemade cleaning powder and moved to the heated water bucket. She began cleaning herself and quickly realized it wasn't easy with all these clothes on but reached beneath them and began to wash. She had just finished up when Noah returned with Loka in tow. "I still need to brush my teeth," she told him. "I'll just step outside for a minute so I can spit, and you can have some privacy."

"Here," he handed her a small tin filled with water and an empty jar. "You can rinse with this and spit into the jar. No sense in freezing your as... butt off doing it outside."

Tarnation, she had never spit in front of anyone before. She gave him a pink-cheeked look.

"It's alright, I won't watch. And leave the jar and cup on the counter. I'll use them when you're done."

She nervously nodded, quickly brushed, rinsed, and spit into the jar, then placed it on the counter. "Do you want me to heat some more water for you?" she asked.

"I cleaned up outside; I just didn't take my brush and cleaning powder with me."

"I see, so what you are saying is that it's alright for you to go out there and freeze to death but not me?"

He angled her a side look. "I'm used to it, that's all."

"And you don't think I am? I have lived up here most of my life, and..." *tarnation*, she dropped the subject and moved to the bed.

Noah glanced at himself in the mirror. *Christ on a crutch*. He was indeed disgusting. Maybe he would cut and shave come morning. He finished with his teeth, emptied the rinsing jar into the wash water, quickly carried the whole shebang outside, and dumped it. When he returned, she was already tucked in bed. He knew she was awake, but he pretended not to notice. Tomorrow morning, he would have to fill the water tank. But at the moment, it was colder than a witch's tit out there.

He laid a bedroll out for himself on the floor before the fire. Cora was using the only bed. *Cora*, he liked the name; it felt musical, like her voice. "Good night, see you in the morning." He quickly climbed beneath the blankets, blew out the lantern, stripped down to his underwear, and turned on his side away from her.

"Jones?" he heard her whisper.

At first, Noah didn't answer, forgetting he'd told her to call him Jones. " What is it? Are you cold? I have extra blankets."

"Oh no, I'm very comfortable. I just wanted to thank you. I know I would have frozen to death like Sugarloaf if you hadn't found me. However, I must head out as soon as this storm eases up. I promised my grandfather I would find Noah Harper."

"Why did your grandfather want you to find him?"

"He was worried about his friend, and the message was for him only. And he didn't like leaving me alone. I told him I would be fine. But he made me promise, said this Noah person needed to know what happened at our cabin. But how I got so turned around and ended up here, I don't know. Then I never ventured out this far, not even when we went hunting. We never came up this way. And when the years piled up on him, and his eyesight faltered, we stayed closer to home."

Noah remained silent for a while. "What if I told you I'm Noah Harper? Would that frighten you?"

Silence.

Noah turned to look over at her and realized she'd never heard a thing he'd said. Cora had fallen deeply into sleep. Once again, Loka was curled up next to her.

The Bloody traitor!

Captain Tamarin, Lamar to most people because he hated the name of Carol that his father had stuck him with and chose to use his middle name. Lamar was once a highly respected officer in the United States Calvary. Now he found himself as far from being respected as a gutter snipe in the slums of Chicago.

After two years of being locked up inside Fort Leavenworth, a military institute, he was only known as an ex-inmate. As further punishment, he was Court-Martialed in front of his entire fort.

Lamar still wore the emotional and physical scars that came from the onslaught of insults he received when he was cornered and beaten inside Leavenworth. All of this he blamed on Noah Harper.

He was the one who caused all of the misery he had to endure while in that prison. When he got his hands on him, the coward would wish he'd never been born. No one would stop him or get in his way. If they did, they would pay a steep price, just like the older man on the San Juan had.

And just like the dozens before him.

"Goddamnit!" He bellowed, causing the men he traveled with, including three who had once served under him, to stiffen. They all knew when he was in a bad temper, you didn't argue. Well, that was except for Hyrum Raintree. He would say and give his opinion whenever he felt like it. But Hyrum wasn't in the saloon, at least at the moment.

Lamar downed his whiskey in one huge gulp and slammed his glass onto the scarred bar. He'd spent the morning with one of the gals upstairs, hoping it would calm his bad mood.

It did not work.

He was furious. Noah Harper was slicker than a babe's snotty nose. For the past eight years, the bastard had hidden himself so well that no one could locate him.

Lamar poured himself another shot of whiskey. Even the silver-haired barkeep was anxious around him. Thirty minutes ago, the middle-aged man left the bottle on the bar and moved away with a nervous tick that lifted the corner of his mouth.

Lamar thought of the old mountain man up on the San Juan. He was a stubborn old fart. He claimed he'd never heard of Noah. Bull shit! Lamar knew when a man was lying. Once again, Noah had found an ally.

Under normal circumstances, he would have just beat the friggin' hell out of the older man to get the answers he wanted but not this time. He let his temper get the best of him, and it irked the hell out of him. He should have controlled himself at such a pivotal moment. Over the years, he'd become efficient with his Colt. However, some of his men were far better marksmen. But Lamar liked to think of himself as a cut above. He drew his pistol before the old goat could fire and sufficiently ended his tirade.

And he ended any information he could have beaten out of the older man.

There were times Lamar knew he should learn to control his temper, but it had been a struggle since he was a boy. His father had taught him everything he needed to know about a temper frenzy using his thick barber's strop. Or an ax handle he kept in the woodshed. "Boy, you gonna learn to obey me, or one of these days I will kill your dumb ass" Lamar could still feel the whack of the strop or ax handle. His father even once broke his arm using that ax handle.

Now, he used all the same tactics his father had taught him when he signed up with William Quantrill and his hoard of fun-loving heathens. They rode and pilfered throughout Missouri and Kansas in search of sympathizers. Hell, he fit right in—a group of pro-Confederate guerillas who vowed revenge. While serving, he even rode with Jesse and Frank James; everybody knew what field of endeavor they chose after the war. Hell, he liked those two wildings.

Lamar grew up on a small farm in Ohio. The son of a sodbuster. But that fact made no difference to any of the men. He fought with them, prowled with them, raided up a storm, and killed more than he could count.

He loved the chase. He certainly had an excellent teacher for his cruelty. His sonofabitch of a father was a damn good instructor when it came to meanness. Lamar learned very quickly farming wasn't the life he wanted. He killed his old man when he was only sixteen, then headed out on his own.

First, he rode with Quantrill and later the Calvery, gathering the filthy Red Skins. Every time he killed, raped, or plundered; it was his father he saw in his mind's eye. And now he was on the hunt again. He'd get the traitor, Harper, he had no doubt. Rip the bastard from limb to limb for the cowardly turncoat he was and still is.

"Hey, Cap'n, the boys are ready to head out. We ought to make it to Fort Collins and the Horsetooth Mountains the day after tomorrow. The place is a haven for men who want to stay hidden, says one of the men I've been playing poker with. It is a great place to live in obscurity like old trappers and mountain men. It sounds just like a place that coward Harper would go. Certainly, worth checking out."

But was it? Lamar still wondered if Harper was hiding in the San Juan mountains. He emptied his shot glass with one swallow. He stood, hitched his pants up, and glared at his underling. "Let's go!"

Chapter Four

The next several days were spent in a pleasant camaraderie. Cora loved to talk, and Noah found that he enjoyed her little antidotes more and more. He still hadn't told her his real identity.

He was the first to wake on the fourth morning. He hadn't been sleeping well and spent most of the night watching Cora sleep. She was so pretty. Those eyes of hers could see clear to his soul. She was not his usual type of woman, but then, he didn't have a type.

Any woman he'd spent time with were saloon girls, and that was only to ease a physical need and stifle some of his loneliness. Even that tiny release hadn't happened for years. Admit it, Harper, *you are lonely*.

He'd been hibernating for too damn long. But he knew the men he'd testified against would never give up the chase. Especially Captain Lamar Tamarin. He'd been sentenced for his leadership and punished with two years in Leavenworth while the rest of the men in the unit were set free with only a court martial to live with. And Noah knew most of them didn't give a damn about that.

They were the only ones to be free. Noah had chosen this life, but it was not freedom, not when he lived in the hell he created.

The first light of day hadn't appeared yet, and Cora was still sleeping. Noah quietly got up and went through the cabin to the back doorway. He thought of the girl's surprise when she found the paper in the tiny toilet facilities. She had been so delighted, and for some odd reason, he didn't take the time to analyze; her reaction pleased him. Stupid probably because, sure as eggs are eggs, she couldn't stay here; he had nothing to offer a woman.

Why had old Elijah sent her up here to him? Again, he glanced over at her before stepping outside. She had taken his advice and not wrapped herself in the bindings. Now, he could see her breasts rise and fall where the fur blanket fell. The movement became so sensual with each breath she took he started to feel that itch again and quickly turned away. Quietly, he stepped outside and made the twenty-foot walk to the outhouse.

A natural light created from the snow sheltered the ground, glistened off the massive evergreen and leafless aspen, and helped give a filtered light inside the outhouse.

After he finished his business, he returned to the cabin, grabbed two medal buckets from the back porch, and headed to the one-story spring house for fresh water.

Filling the water reservoir connected to the old firebox took two trips carrying two buckets at a time. He stoked the fire, placed the last bucket on the trammel, and heated the water for a spit bath. He grabbed a clean shirt, pants, socks, and a pair of long johns, taking them into the kitchen and placing them on the washboard counter.

When the bucket of water was heated enough, he put it in the sink, stripped down to his long johns, which he dropped to his waist, and began to wash himself. When it came to his lower half, he glanced over to Cora. She still slept. He lowered the bottom half of his underwear to his ankles, stepped out, and washed his lower half. He had fibbed last night and hadn't bathed outside. Too damn cold, and this morning he felt downright filthy. He would have to change his bedding.

He quickly finished washing and redressed in clean underwear and buckskin pants that rode low on his hips. His longjohns were unbuttoned and off his shoulders and arms, where they gathered around his waist. He might look like a fierce old snow monster, but at least he'd be clean.

He knew keeping the body frequently washed was healthy. According to his medical training before joining the Army, bathing was the best way to keep disease away. Brushing his teeth was another. The bathing and teeth-cleaning ritual he did each morning and evening would help him stay that way. He received a lot of criticism from the men in his unit about his daily rituals. He tried to convince them of the benefits, but it all went in one ear and out the other. They thought he was nuts. Many of them would go a month before bathing. Only his friend Simon listened. But Simon joined the others in the end and turned on him.

But this scraggly beard he'd let grow was a whole other story. *Christ on a crutch* he needed to get rid of it. She was correct; the damn thing was itchy and possibly filled with God knew what. He glared at the mirror, and the reflection that stared back at him made him realize how far he'd let himself go. No wonder she had fainted when she first saw him.

Before completely dressing, he did something he rarely did: he studied himself in the small square-foot mirror nailed to the backside of the rear door. Not understanding why he was doing something so foolish, he left the top of his underwear resting on his hips and reached for his folded shaving razor and a pair of sheers.

He cut the excess hair from his cheeks, jawline, and neck. *Damn, he'd really let himself go.* Once he finished trimming the excess hair, he soaped his face and began to shave, though he opted to keep his mustache. After all, even back in the day when he shaved, he always wore a mustache.

He almost didn't know the face staring back at him. The look made him look much younger.

Cora clandestinely watched him through thick black lashes and squinty eyes. He was naked from the waist up. He reminded her of a swash-buckling pirate. He was much younger than she'd first thought. He certainly was not some old mountain man. Lean muscle, broad shoulders that met with an upper back that tapered down to a narrow waist and slender hips. He certainly would not be considered muscle-bound like a wrestler she had seen in a picture book, but he was well-defined, tall, and strong like a towering pine.

When he turned his profile to her, checking himself in the small mirror, she realized his front was also symmetrically pleasing. Not one ounce of flab touched his body. His stomach was flat, though rippled with muscle. Deep nut-brown hair caressed his breast muscle and lowered to a gentle V and swirled in a silky pattern around his navel and moved further down in a narrow line below the waistband of his pants and the loosely hanging long johns below his hips. Though his lower half was covered in buckskin, she knew instinctively he had solid and muscled legs. She noted the roped muscle filling his biceps and forearms. Tarnation; she could see his male nipples tighten like hers did when she was cold.

Was he cold?

Well, of course, he is, silly goose; he's practically naked, she reprimanded herself, yet she couldn't drag her vision away from him.

The rugged masculine plains of his face showed inherent strength. He had a squared jaw with a slight dimple that suggested stubbornness yet made his lips look full and generous, though a thick, soft-looking mustache mostly hid the top one. He was one of the most attractive men she had ever seen or could even imagine.

She wanted to touch the silky softness of the mustache that seemed to beg for it. But what drew her even more were those jewel-like sapphire eyes, so deep blue and penetrating, filled with a mixture of mischief, spirituality, and sometimes sadness. The look was heart-stopping. If a man could be beautiful, he definitely was.

Cora swallowed anxiously and licked her lips. She could feel heat fill her entirety. *Sweet Lawd!* He was even more handsome than any descriptions of male characters from one of her adventure novels. He was perhaps seven or eight years her senior. *Calamity!* she hissed silently and yanked the blanket she'd used up to her neck. She was practically naked! Long johns and her nighty certainly didn't seem enough.

Noah heard her rustling and turned in her direction, seeing the bright red in her cheeks as she nearly strangled herself with the blanket. He quickly pulled up his long johns and fastened them, grabbed his clean flannel shirt, pushed his arms through the sleeves, and tucked it inside his pants. *Christ on a crutch!* How much of him had she seen?

She looked so damn pretty with her wide, sensual, topaz-brown eyes. A look that reminded him of liquid coffee spilling onto a white saucer. She was embarrassed. Again, he wondered, how much of him had she seen?

"Thunderation, Jones!" she blustered. "You are a young man and very handsome. I...I thought you were old and ugly! But criminy, you're not ugly at all! And here I am, improperly dressed. You must turn your back so I can cover myself."

He smiled, emphasizing the handsome crinkles at the corners of his devilish eyes. They somehow seemed bluer. She ruminated about that when he discreetly searched her face. She felt like a specimen under a microscope. Thunderation, he seemed to look straight through her, right down to skin and bone. "Please turn around."

He chuckled. "Ah honey, you are so modestly covered I couldn't see a darn thing even If I wanted to." *And hell, he wanted to!*

But she was powerless to stop the flash of heat that burned throughout her. She again noticed that delightful dimple in the center of his chin. She watched that fantastic mustache curl slightly when he smiled, enhancing his good looks even further. He had a thin scar along his jaw, adding mystery to his good looks. No, nothing could detract from his powerful, rugged beauty.

Without another word, he returned to the mirror, watched her stand, and quickly removed her nightgown. He had to grin. Beneath the night clothes were long johns. In seconds, she stepped into pants. A blue plaid shirt came next, and she tucked it beneath the waistband, making her breasts even more pronounced as the cotton material clung to the soft, round shapes. He couldn't help gazing at her in the mirror's reflection even though he knew it wasn't right to do so.

He also knew it wasn't right to have the risqué thoughts he was having. Damn, but she was so pretty and sensual. Even with her ebony hair that was cropped shorter than most women, he found it gave her an innocent pixie appearance. The silky strands hung in soft, shiny waves around her face to the middle of her neck. Part of her disguise, he knew. She was, after all, supposed to be a boy. She fooled him when he first saw her lying face down in the snow. And even for a brief moment back at the cabin, tightly bound as she was across the chest. She had a delicate structure. She stood maybe five foot five, possibly an inch more, but he knew he stood more than half a foot taller.

He silently watched her hastily sit down, pull her socks, and boots on. She was unaware he could see every nuanced curve of her body and all her angelic, lovely features.

"Okay, I'm decent. You can turn around now." She moved to the window above the sink and by the door and looked outside. Heavy snow continued to fall. She needed to head out and complete her journey. She had to find Noah Harper. "How long do you think this storm will last? I need to be on my way."

"It depends. You should know as much as I do; you've lived here longer than I have."

"Well, I can't stay around here forever. I need to find the man my grandfather sent me to find. That isn't you. You are much too young."

"Why did he send you out to find a stranger? Alone and knowing this storm was coming on?"

"He didn't know the storm was coming; he was already gone when it hit. He told me I had to warn Noah Harper, and he was adamant about it. Grandfather said he was a good man, and nothing was left back at the cabin for me. He said I couldn't be alone, which I think is hogwash. But grandfather insisted I go. It was my last promise to him. I couldn't break my oath."

Loka began to whine at the door. Noah opened it, and the wolf ran outside. The action reminded Cora she needed to use the outhouse. "I need to use the facilities."

"Facilities, huh?" he said with a sideways grin. "By all means," he held the door open for her. "I'll fix us all something to eat while you do your business. I assume you are hungry."

She nodded and raced outside.

"Be careful. It's slick out there," he shouted to her retreating, shapely back. No sooner had he given her the warning than she slipped, landing hard on her rear. He practically leaped out the door and raced to her. In seconds, he had her in his arms. "Judas H Priest! Are you alright?"

"I ah..." words became stuck in her throat when she felt him dust snow off the underside of her britches. "Please, Jones, put me down. I'm about to wet myself."

He carried her to the outhouse in just a few steps and deposited her at the door. "I'll wait for you out here."

She wondered if his shoulders and arms got tired from carrying a burden. He had to haul her up here the other morning from the shallow valley when she'd fainted, then went back down to get her fallen things, collected all the wood they burned the previous night, buried her horse, and lastly took care of the fallen tree branch.

She nervously glared at him. He was so tall and strong. He had strength in places she couldn't even imagine. "Mister Jones, this isn't necessary and certainly not the first time I've taken a tumble." With that said, she threw the door wide, stepped inside, and slammed it shut. The only light inside came from the splits in the narrow slats that made the walls. She was breathless. Never in her life had a man, including her grandfather, ever touched her in such a way.

Noah stood outside the wooden doorway and waited for her to emerge. God, she was a sweet little thing, and he was a friggin' lecher for thinking the things he was thinking! He needed to get his improper thoughts together. This was an innocent girl, not some soiled dove.

Inside the darkened outhouse, Cora sat on the wooden bench and shockingly realized she had started her monthly curse. She had brought nothing out here with her to protect herself from the leaking blood. Tarnation, what was she going to do? She needed her padding, and everything she had for protection was packed in her valise.

Ten or more minutes passed, and she still hadn't appeared at the door. Had she fallen down the lavatory? "Are you alright?" Noah asked worriedly.

Cora felt tears gather in her eyes and drip through her lashes. This was a personal thing; she wasn't sure how to reply.

"You didn't fall in, did you?" *Judas!* She was so tiny that she might have slipped through the circular opening.

"Umm, no!" She didn't have a choice. She had to ask for help. "Could you bring me my valise, please?"

For a moment, Noah felt paralyzed before it dawned on him that she had probably started her monthly flux. He knew of the feminine curse; he had a mother and two sisters. Then, there were the anatomy studies in school before the Army. But hell, he had been away from decent women and even women of the night for so long that he just hadn't thought about the things their bodies did.

"Jones, are you still out there?"

"Sure, I'll be right back," he answered.

With relief at not having to explain her predicament, Cora gratefully listened to Jones's footfalls crunch against the frozen snow.

Only minutes later, he was gently knocking outside the entrance. She opened the heavy wooden latch, cracked the door by less than a foot, and reached her hand out to retrieve her carpet bag. "Thank you," she said in a mere whisper and quickly shut the old wooden door. *Well, so much for not having to strip down to her birthday suit.* She would need to change everything.

Noah barely heard her and detected her tears of embarrassment. He could hear some rustling that seemed to go on for an eternity, then quiet before she opened the door and came outside wearing entirely different clothing. She clutched her bag against her chest. Her cheeks were a blazing red.

"I once had two sisters," he started by way of explanation. "So, I understand some of what you are going through. It's just part of nature, and there's no need to be embarrassed." Her cheeks blazed further. *Christ on a crutch!* He should have just kept his mouth shut. He also knew how emotional the female could get during this time of the month. "Forgive me. I didn't mean to upset you."

Cora tried to give him a small smile, though avoided meeting his face. Mercy, the difference between all the facial hair he once sported and now all shaved, except the attractive mustache on his face and his thick wavy chestnut hair on his head, caused her to catch her breath. And now he seemed to understand the ways of a woman's body. And this predicament, more than anything, embarrassed her all the more. But somehow, she sensed that a part of him was embarrassed as she followed him back to the cabin. "Thank you, Jones," she repeated.

He cleared his throat. "Certainly, no problem. I'm glad I could help." He nervously fiddled with the collar of his shirt.

Not only was he the most attractive man she had ever seen or imagined, but he was also sensitive to her feelings. She couldn't stop the fluttering inside her stomach. She had wanted to die a thousand deaths when she had to ask for help. She considered herself brave, but to have him witness her shame as he had and still put her at ease was something she never thought she would see from a man. She gathered her pride as she returned up the pathway, walking more carefully than when she'd come down.

Later in the afternoon, the sun came out briefly and poured through the window on the west side. "I need to go check my traps while the sun is out. Will you be alright if I leave you here alone for a while?"

Well, of course, she would be alright. She had become accustomed to being left alone when she lived with her grandfather. Although she loved him dearly, he never had been much of a conversationalist. "I would be fine, but if you don't mind, I want to join you. I'd like to see where you've laid your traps just in case I run into one when I'm alone on my journey. The last thing I must worry about is getting caught in one."

"Your journey! You can't be serious. This sunshine is only a lull in the storm. Looking to the north, you will see those thick, heavy gray clouds moving in. More snow is on the way."

"Needless to say, I need to be on my way. As I told you yesterday, I need to find this Noah Harper fellow and give him the warning."

"A warning about what?" Jones grumbled.

"Information for his ears only. This was my last promise to my grandfather before he died."

"So, what you're saying is he sent you on this wild goose chase to give a message to someone you've never met."

"Yes."

How were you supposed to go about that?"

"He gave me directions, and I would have been fine, but I got turned around and missed the base of Narrows Canyon when it started snowing heavily. I couldn't see more than five feet ahead of me."

"I suppose that was very admirable of Elijah, but to send a young woman out into this wilderness country was very foolish indeed."

"Now, wait a dog gone minute; he didn't make me do anything," she defended. "There was nothing left of our camp. The cabin was burned to the ground. The only possible things worth saving were in my cellar room, and I didn't have time to clear the debris and get down to get anything more than what I brought. It's why I must deliver the message, return to the cabin, and begin to make repairs."

"What really happened down at your grandfather's cabin? This has more to do with something other than your grandfather's passing, Cora. Why did your grandfather believe he needed to warn Noah Harper? You need to tell me!"

"Why would you even care? The message is for Noah."

He placed his hands on top of her shoulder. The top of her head reached just beneath his chin. He towered over her, forcing her to look up at him. "I care because I told you a bit of a fib."

She gave him a comprehensive look of nervous amazement, making the mixture of amber in her brown irises swim more closely to the surface.

"A fib? What kind of fib?" she exclaimed.

"I am Noah Harper." He admitted with exasperation.

Her pretty face filled with alarm.

Chapter Five

"What did you just say?" she sputtered with stupefaction. This man couldn't be Noah Harper. He had been a friend of her grandfather. He should be an elderly person. Not this healthy, well-built man who glared down at her with such intensity. He was far too young. Far too masculine and unquestionably far too handsome. And she suddenly felt her nerves begin to fray.

Perdition, he knew she was a woman. If what this man said was true, what had her grandfather been thinking when he sent her up here? Did he think she needed a mate now that she would be alone? Thunderation!

No, this man who loomed above her was not the old mountain man called Noah Harper. Couldn't be! Could he? *Hell's fire!*

Though Cora had to admit, at first, he had appeared to be the old one and had reminded her of a terrifying snow monster. He had to be lying! Thunderation, this younger man who stood above her could not be her grandfather's friend! There was no way!

"You can't be Noah Harper. He is an old man like my grandfather. You are young, you are too..." she couldn't finish. This whole thing was unequivocally the most insane notion.

"I am too what?" he demanded.

Her cheeks flamed. In all her twenty-two years, she had never imagined meeting a man who could make her pulse race. Take her mind to places it sure as heck shouldn't go. This was some insidious dream she could not wake up from.

"A liar!" she finally choked out. Shame clung to her like a maggot drawn to spoiled food, and the feeling became unbearable. But was he lying, or was she lying to herself? She couldn't stop the words that flew from her mouth. "A downright despicable liar! Even if it's true, I don't understand why my grandfather felt such worry for you. You certainly can take care of yourself."

"Thanks to him," Noah admitted. "I met Elijah when I first got here on the mountain. I had a similar experience to yours, getting caught in a horrific snowstorm. He saved my life. He would travel back and forth from your place to here for months. He taught me much about the area and many survival skills. I was a greenhorn."

Cora thought back over the years and counted how often her grandfather had gone off alone. He had said he needed time to think and be by himself. Was this what he was doing? Helping his friend? She studied Noah's face as he spoke.

"Many years ago, another man lived up here alone. He built this cabin and went by Jones, which worked for me. It was a name I used when I left the Army. He and your grandfather became close friends over the years. But Jones passed away about sixteen years ago, probably around the same time you came up here to live." Noah paused and studied the confusion on her face but quickly started again.

"This property belonged to him and sat vacant for years. I like it because it is secret and obscure, far from any other people. As you know, there are very few human factors up here. And those that do live this far from civilization also live apart from each other like you and your grandfather do. This Jones fellow lived off the land. Elijah knew the old man would not want this place to fall to ruin, so he made sure what belonged to Jones would now be mine."

Cora had never heard any of this before.

"I owe your grandfather a debt I never thought I could repay. And now I figure sending you up here is part of that debt. He didn't want you to be alone. And I suppose he didn't want me to be alone either." He released one of her shoulders and wiped a lone tear down her soft, pretty angel face.

"I'm sorry he never told you about me, but it was my secret to tell. I have things in my past that no one needs to know about. There are people who want me dead. Elijah respected my circumstances. I suppose that's why he never told you about me or told me about you. But now you say he had a message for me. A message he felt I needed to know. You need to tell me, Cora."

Another tear fell down her cheek. He gently wiped it with the pad of his thumb. "Please, Cora, tell me what your grandfather said. Our lives could very well depend on it."

Cora wanted so badly to believe him, but her grandfather had kept her in the dark about so many things she had become very paranoid over time. She never would have come here at all had she not promised him on his dying breath. Oh, mercy's sake, she didn't know what to do. She stepped away from Jones' gentle touch.

Noah moved to the enormous old trunk by his bed. He lifted the lid and rummaged around inside for several seconds. Finding what he sought, he lifted a thick leather pouch from the trunk and walked to the lone table in the sparse cooking area. "Come take a seat and open this," he said with sadness. "Then you'll know I truly am who I say."

Cora glanced over to the folder and back up to his face. The alluring charm of his blue sapphire eyes studied her. Maybe she should believe him; his eyes seemed to speak the truth.

She sat at the table, and with shaky fingers, she unwrapped the folder and removed its contents. There were photographs of a happy family: a mother and father and three children—one boy and two girls who were mirror images of each other and looked to be the same age.

"My parents, me, and my twin sisters, Alley and Maddie. They are two years older than me. I was just the right age to tease them. By the time this picture was taken, both my older brothers had been killed in the war."

"I'm so sorry about your brothers. That war took a lot from many." Cora glanced back at the picture and couldn't help but smile at the mischief she saw in the young boys' eyes. He began to speak again.

"You can't see it, but I'm holding a frog behind me. I had planned to tease my sisters with the thing until my dad caught me holding it. He wasn't pleased with me. I got my bottom smacked several times for that one."

Cora grinned; she could picture that little boy playfully teasing his sisters. She had often wondered what it would have been like to grow up with a family and siblings surrounding her, brothers and sisters, mother and father. Now, the way everything stood, what family she had was all gone. "Identical twin sisters. Oh gracious, that must have been so much fun." Carefully, she set these pictures aside and looked at the rest.

A beautiful farm filled with horses, cows, and chickens. The very thought of fresh eggs every morning made her mouth water. Rolling hills and large fields surrounded a two-story farmhouse and barn. Rounded stacks of golden hay were piled high in the hundreds throughout the pastures. How wonderful it must have been to grow up this way. The closest she had ever come to seeing anything like this was in her imagination and descriptions inside books.

Books her grandfather would buy when she would accompany him on his yearly trip to town.

Later, they became thick novels when he began leaving her behind at the cabin. Though she'd had a few years of schooling while living in town, her grandfather furthered her education. He taught her almost everything she knew. He'd continued her reading and writing. As a young man, Elijah once taught school.

The Mexican-American War changed everything for him. It was years before he went back to teaching. When he finally started educating young minds again, he opted to give lessons on the newly established Indian Reservations. This was where he met Cora's Cheyenne grandmother, and they were married. But too soon, war came again. He was called to serve once more. This war was very different; it pitted brothers against brothers—fathers against sons. Elijah wanted no part of it.

He had served his time and had no desire to fight again. During this period, the native people were mostly left alone because most of the Army had been called to arms to protect the nation. However, all that changed once the turbulent times of the era came to an end. Following the war and the insurmountable raids on native villages, Elijah, his wife, and his young daughter made their home in the San Juan Mountains. Cora turned her thoughts back to Noah.

"What a wonderful life this must have been. Why on earth would you not want to return to it?" She gazed at him; sadness washed through his eyes and over his handsome face.

"I had no choice; they would have been placed in harm's way if I returned."

Cora wasn't sure how to respond to his words, and she was pretty confident he didn't want to talk about it or the danger. She continued to go through his things. She lifted out a small rectangular box and removed the lid. Inside was a decorated badge with the emblem of the Maltese Cross. "What is this?"

Again, his expression was despondent, but she sensed he needed to discuss it.

"Back in seventy-eight, I was a medical officer while serving in the army. I was barely twenty and still believed in honor and the goodness of man's heart and soul. I was given that medallion, so all knew I was a medic."

She passed her eyes between the medal and his sapphire-blue gaze. "This is an honor then?" She reverently ran her finger over the shiny brass cross.

"At the time I received the badge, I thought so, but during the following year, I saw so much carnage and thoughtless killing perpetrated by the men I rode with I no longer believed in the honor this was supposed to give me or the human decency it implied.

"The last campaign I served on. My Captain ordered us to attack a peaceful Cheyenne village. Everything was destroyed, and the death and the bloodshed left is something I shall never forget. My training was to help anyone who needed medical attention. But these Cheyenne people were being slaughtered, and my captain would not allow me to help. His philosophy was. The only good Indian is a dead one. There was no provocation for this unwarranted attack. The people were primarily elderly, women, and children. Only a few warriors lived among them, and they were of middle age. They were hauled outside the village and lined up before a firing squad and shot. I protested, but the men were mindless and furious. It was like watching an out-of-control mob at a hanging."

Noah paused for several moments and glanced toward the window. These memories were horrendous and continued still after all these years to attack his sleep. But he started the tellin he might as well finish in spite of the shock he knew she must feel listening to him.

"I was told if I refused to take orders and help with the slaughter, then I could just die with the natives. I was tied to a post at the center of the village and forced to watch helplessly as the men raced through the collection of tepees, murdering, raping," Jesus he felt the sick taste of chunder moving through his throat but forced himself to finish the sentence.

"The men who still lived were mutilated and there wasn't a damn thing I could do about it. The attack came while the Cheyenne still slept. The mission was to capture and take prisoners who would be placed on Reservations. Instead, the men in the unit went on their killing spree and forced me to watch."

Cora gasped covered her mouth and swallowed so hard it made her cough. "Oh, mercy, how could men behave as such. Lawd Noah, is that how you got the scars on your face?" She quietly studied a tiny scar that split across one eyebrow and along his jaw.

"Yes, but not from the raid; it came from the men who tied me to the post because I refused to help in the carnage. They thought it entertaining to strike me each time they passed. I was a bloody mess by the time they rode out and left me.

"How did you escape and live to tell the story?"

Noah gazed down at Loka, curled up next to her feet in protection mode. "My wolf." He told her.

Shocked at his answer, Cora reached down and petted Loka's thick ruff, moving her fingers deeper into the underfur. "Dear Lawd!" she stammered, never taking her hand from the wolf.

Loka glanced up at her with large golden eyes, made a sneezing sound, got up, and moved to the back door. Cora quickly stood, opened the door for him, and returned to her chair and blew out the air she hadn't realized she held; this was unbelievable. "Loka helped you?"

Noah smiled, turning the brilliance of his sapphire eyes on her.

A tickling began to move from her belly up and down. *Tarnation,* how she loved his smile; it lit up his entire face and made him sparkle.

"To this day," he started. "I don't know how he survived all the carnage left in the village but thank God he did. He was only a pup, three or four months. I made a game out of my tied hands. Little by little, Loka pulled on the knot until it came loose, and I could finish the rest of the way and free my ankles. He has been with me ever since."

She grinned, "Thank goodness he wasn't the big bad wolf like the one in the story of Little Red Riding Hood. He might just have eaten you instead."

Noah laughed, reached out, and cupped Cora's chin. A dainty chin connected to a beautiful face. He couldn't believe he had ever thought of her as a young boy. This little angel was a delight. "Sometimes, when I look at you, and your eyes light up in a glow of brown and amber, I feel a bit like a bad wolf."

Whether it was her innocence in the way of a man and woman or something else, she quickly changed the subject and said, "I saw a wolf in a picture book once, and his eyes were a beautiful blue-gray, not as blue as yours, but your eye teeth do look a little sharp. But you wouldn't eat me, would you, Mr. Jones?"

She quietly watched his full lips curve upwards, emphasizing his chestnut-brown mustache. She couldn't help but wonder what it would be like if those lips touched her own.

She shivered at the thought; she had never been kissed before. Not by a man on the lips. Sure, her grandfather had pressed a few on her cheek when she was much younger, but that certainly didn't count. She thought about the couples in her romantic Jane Austin novels. She felt a fluttering sensation inside.

Noah's sky-blue eyes twinkled when he whispered, "I don't know. You look pretty tasty to me," he teased and caressed her lower lip with his thumb.

"I do! She said, perplexed. "I never thought I was much to look at, what with my shorter black hair and light brown skin. I've seen women in pictures; they all have long golden-colored hair and milk-white skin. Taller and more sophisticated than me, all dressed in their finery. But my grandfather insisted I keep my hair short and dress like a boy. But oh, to be able to wear one of those beautiful gowns. I guess I'm downright foolish. I never go anywhere. What difference would it make."

She glanced over at him. "Men like long hair, don't they? And lily-white skin?"

Noah realized this little angel had gratefully taken the awful memories from him. He couldn't help it; he chuckled. She was so damn delightful. "Do you ever stop to take a breath from talking?"

Her pretty face blushed. He knew that was not the first time she'd been told she was talkative. It must have been tough on her to stay sequestered. Then again, he had kept himself secluded as well. He also knew Elijah was not big on carrying a conversation—many grunts or nodding even when they played cards.

"I'm sorry. I guess I talk a lot. Forgive me," her cheeks still held the attractive pink flush.

"I didn't say it bothered me. I rather like listening to you." *And Christ on a crutch, he loved looking at her.*

"I don't think my grandfather would agree with you. He was constantly telling me to hush or read a book. I love reading; it lets me go to exotic places I will never see." They were seated at the square oaken table across from the large stone fireplace. She quietly studied him. He epitomized every handsome hero she could imagine or had ever read about.

She found it difficult to look away now that all the facial hair and furry skins covering him were gone. She felt compelled to study his very male physique and how beautifully proportioned he was. His light blue shirt enhanced his sky-blue eyes, wide shoulders, and broad chest. His forearms rippled with muscle as they rested on the chair's back, and his long legs enticingly straddled the worn seat.

The sight of him as he watched her sent a wave of unfamiliar thoughts and feelings through her. The only thing separating them was the old, scarred oak table. *Gracious,* but it was nice to have someone to talk to. And someone who listened. Her heartbeat pounded like a crazy hammer inside her chest. What was she going to do? Some tiny voice told her she could trust him. Tarnation, what would it be like to kiss him?

She knew a little about kissing; she had read enough romantic novels. Not understanding why, she wanted him to kiss her. She needed to know what the touch of his lips against hers would feel like and see if he was wondering the same thing. So, like an idiot, she asked the absolute craziest thing. "Does your stomach sometimes feel like dozens of butterflies are flitting inside you when you look at me? And do your palms ever itch to do some exploring?" *Tarnation,* she was losing all her faculties. How could she even think a thing like that? She felt such heat fill her.

Noah swallowed heavily. "Whatever do you mean?"

"Ah, I don't know. I was thinking about kissing and exploring the wonderful feelings. Do you ever think about kissing Mr. Jones?"

Did he ever think about kissing and exploring? Christ on a crutch! He thought of it every time he looked at her. "Please call me Noah. If I ever wanted to kiss you, I would like you to call me by my birth name. If you still don't believe who I am, keep going through that binder. My identification is in there with my picture."

Seconds later, she held a billfold and freed his Military identification. The papers certainly proved what he had been telling her. Noah Harper, Medical Assistant. He looked a bit younger, but there was no denying this was Noah.

"Not a doctor?" she asked, looking over to him.

"I joined the Army before I finished schooling. They referred to my position as a Medic. However, that day in the village, I was the only person with medical experience. Our regular doctor had been killed a week earlier. I had been assisting him for about a year and knew enough to care for minor injuries, even simple surgeries. Broken bones, bullet removal, stitching, and so forth."

"But why do you stay up here alone? Especially since your service was over, why didn't you return to your family? Don't you miss them?"

"I do, very much. My sisters are probably married by now and have families of their own. I can't endanger any of them." His expression became distant.

"You see, at first, the unit that left me behind thought I was dead, and that's what my family had been told. Once I was free from my shackles, thanks to Loka, we made our way across the plains and into Fort McKinney. The journey nearly took two weeks, which is why everyone thought me dead, and my unit clarified the story of my death by returning with my horse and rifle, both covered in my dried blood."

"But your body? How did they explain that away?"

"They told the commanders I had been tortured and burned by the Cheyenne, which is why they attacked the village."

"And they believed them?" She asked with shock.

"At first, yes, but when I showed up with my side of the story and what I had witnessed. They saw things differently. I was released from my commission. But before I left the fort, I was asked to stay on and testify against the men I had ridden with. It was probably one of the biggest mistakes of my life, but I felt obligated to tell the truth, and I agreed.

"There was discord among our country's leaders led by public outcry. This wasn't the first time something like this had happened. It was decided the men had to pay for all the atrocities that had occurred that day in the Cheyenne village. You see, the politicians in Washington needed to know the truth about the massacre, what led up to it, and how things could have gotten so out of control. I felt it was my honor and civil duty to testify. I was wrong.

"It took just over a year to get any justice, and that basically was nothing, even with two others who finally broke down and agreed with my testimony. Both were killed a couple of months later. Only one man paid any price: my Captain, Lamar Tamarin. He was already being held for his crimes. It was directly after the trial he was sent to Leavenworth and vowed he would hunt me down. Make me pay and anyone else who thought to help me, especially my family. Which I'm sure is why the other two who confirmed my story were killed.

"Lamar organized several men to track me down while he was in prison and would join them as soon as he was release from prison. By then, most men in our unit were nothing more than a rag-tag bunch with questionable morals and ideals. The captain became their leader. For the next year, I could stay a few steps ahead of them. I took every precaution to protect my family. I could not put them in danger for a decision I had made.

"That's the reason I told my commander to erase my background from the military records and to inform my family I had been killed. This was all for their safety. If the captain had found out about them, he would have killed them just as he planned to kill me.

"The men were relentless in their search. Left no corner unturned. They traveled from place to place, town to town, searching for me, leaving death and destruction in their wake." Noah briefly looked away. A deep sadness touched his eyes and turned his mouth into a straight line.

"After two years of running," he began again. "I couldn't take all the deceit and lies I had to live under. But most importantly, I couldn't endanger those who had helped me. I was sick of what my life had become. That is why I chose to leave civilization behind and came up here. In many ways, that wasn't very smart. Reading about it and living it are two entirely different things. But thankfully, I met your grandfather. So, there you have it, my life in a nutshell."

Cora stood at that moment, came around the table, and wrapped her arms around his shoulders, leaning against his muscular back. "I understand why my grandfather was so adamant about warning you. For two years as a young man, you waited, ran, and hid to protect your family; then, you imprisoned yourself up here for the next eight years. You must get very lonely."

"Actually, I have come to love living here. I enjoy the seclusion and peace. I certainly don't need any pity; these were all my decisions. Loka and I make out nicely. But right now, that is not the important thing. Tell me what happened at your cabin and what your grandfather wanted me to know. Lives could depend on it."

She felt his tension, quickly released her hold, and returned to her chair. "You are right. You need to know. I have never seen men like them before. We rarely get visitors living out here as we do. Grandfather ordered me into the cellar. I didn't want to hide away. I'm an adult; I could have been helpful. I shoot as well as he does. He wouldn't listen. He was always so protective of me, so I lost the desire to argue further when he ordered me down into the cellar I went. The men were very close by then. From my room in the cellar, I could hear the front doorway being kicked in, followed by a lot of shouting, though I couldn't understand much in my hiding place. But I heard enough to know my grandfather was in danger. I couldn't stand not knowing what was happening. I climbed the stairs from the cellar to the main floor and peeked through the trap door and a loop in the rug left from the opening. There were four of them. One was referred to as Captain though no name went with it. He was ugly-mean and completely unreasonable."

Noah's face heated with anger, and he knew what was coming as Cora continued.

"My grandfather was brave but never so much as he was that morning. He stood proudly before the men holding his large bore Sharps carbine. He kept the rifle pointed at the one they called captain."

"Did you hear any other names?"

"No, but this captain argued with one of the men and ordered him out of the cabin, calling him a coward. I never got a good look at him, but he seemed relieved enough to leave. Other than that, I only heard your name. They were looking for you. They told my grandfather you were dangerous, wanted by the government for killing innocents, and they were here to take you into custody. But my grandfather stood steadfast and never wavered in his convictions. He told them he had never heard of you. The leader was furious, and the other two followed suit. Never have I seen such horrifically dangerous men. They never gave my grandfather a chance."

Noah silently cursed. How did the bastards know where to come looking for him? No one knew he was up here except Elijah. And now he was dead. He felt like the worst kind of slime. But the old man trusted him enough to send this sweet little angel to him.

Cora sensed his anger and guilt. This isn't your fault, Noah. They would have killed him anyway, even if he had never heard of you. They were out for blood. Of course, when my grandfather told me to find you, I questioned him about what those men said about you being wanted and a dangerous killer. But grandfather assured me it was all a lie. You were a good man. You needed to know what happened here."

"Damn, this sickens me," he shook his head with remorse. "Neither one of you should have ever been put in danger. Elijah was the only friend I've had since coming up here. I would have died all those years ago if it hadn't been for him. And now you've lost him because of me. God! Honey, I am so sorry."

"But we have each other now."

Yes, he had this sweet little angel. She was filled with tenderness and a healing soul that touched him in a way he never thought possible. But he couldn't keep her though he would make damn sure he would protect her no matter what it might take, even if only for a short time. "Please finish," he urged.

She nodded. She wanted to reach out to touch his hand but held back. "Like I said, Grandfather told them he had never heard of you and ordered them to leave. They...they...only laughed, called him an Indian lover."

Noah could see her eyes fill again.

"You see, we had a lot of Cheyenne mementos from my grandmother's people hanging on the walls. He was so proud of all these things, given to them as wedding gifts. But these men only showed hatred. Before my grandfather could pull the trigger, the one called captain drew his revolver so fast my grandfather never had a chance to fire. Then he laughed when the deed was done and ordered the other men to burn the place to the ground. They left the cabin after that, but not before they set our home on fire." Cora's tears could not be held any longer.

Noah was tempted to go to her but stayed quiet and waited for her to speak again.

"The cabin was coming down fast. Flames were already reaching the sky. I opened the trap door and climbed out. Grandfather was bleeding heavily. I dragged him outside beneath an old Douglas fir and raced inside to salvage what I could. I knew he was dying, but I refused to give up. I wrapped him in a blanket and tried to make him as comfortable as I could. But he knew he wasn't going to come out of this alive. That's when he told me to go to you. I thought, in all his pain, he had lost his mind. I had never heard of you before this day."

Noah's heart sank. "It seems we have both had our crosses to bear. I should have just died that first week I came up here, and none of this would have happened."

"No!" she cried. "Never say that. Those men would have killed him anyway. You know that too from what you've already told me."

He stood from the table and walked the length of the small cabin. Guilt furrowed deep inside him. He briefly stopped and turned his attention back on her. "When this storm lets up, though, it doesn't look like it will anytime soon. Would you like to go back down and see if anything can be salvaged? We could bury Elijah."

"I already did that. Though I could not dig very deeply because of the frozen ground."

"Good God, you did this by yourself?"

"Of course, I couldn't just leave him lay there for the wildlife to tear him apart. But that is why I got such a late start getting up the canyon. Poor Sugarloaf, he tried, but the journey was just too much for him. You saved my life just as my grandfather saved yours. If I didn't say so before, thank you."

"Well, just the same; when this weather clears up, I want to check out your cabin or at least what's left."

"I suppose you are right. I did hurry as I got ready to leave."

Loka scratched at the door, and Noah moved to open it. The wolf joined them carrying a fat rabbit in his mouth."

"My goodness!" Cora exclaimed. "He's quite a hunter. And he shares."

Noah grinned. "Between Loka and my hunting, neither of us has gone without eating."

"Does he ever get anything larger than a rabbit?"

"He's got a deer or two. He even tried to wrestle a bear once and got banged up pretty badly. I stitched him up and used disinfectant and sterile bandages; it took nearly a month to heal. I think he learned his lesson and never returned hurt like that again. He's a good hunter. Between us, we have enough meat to last all winter, which is especially helpful when we are snowed in sometimes for months. Another thing I'm grateful for is what the real Jones left behind when he passed. There is a shed out back for storage, a smokehouse, a spring house built over the stream, and even a makeshift sled that Loka can pull."

"Grandfather and I didn't have a wolf, but between us and Sugarloaf pulling the travois with the meat, our hunting kept us well-supplied for winter. A stream runs a couple hundred yards from the cabin, so we could also have trout. I'm good at filleting."

"The upper part of that stream runs north of my cabin. You are right. There are a lot of rainbow trout in it."

She nodded. "We also smoked a lot of them. I even grew a small garden in the summer months. We have discussed getting some chickens in spring for the last few months. I guess now that's not going to happen. There won't be any trips to town." She watched Loka drop the rabbit on the floor and glance up at both of them. Cora could have sworn the wolf smiled. But quickly, he returned to the door and gave a low growl.

Cora's heart began to slam against her chest. Tarnation had those murdering scoundrels come back.

Noah snatched his rifle above the fireplace mantle and followed Loka.

Chapter Six

Cora got up to follow Noah and the wolf. "Stay here and drop the door latch the minute I get outside," Noah ordered, stopping her progress.

His voice made her jump, but she didn't argue and unwillingly did what she was told, but she didn't like it. No, not one bit. Her grandfather did this to her all the time. He would have never said a word if she'd been a boy.

He made her dress like one but always treated her like a dad-blamed girl. She returned to her chair, pulled her feet onto the seat, and wrapped her arms around her knees.

Minutes later, she heard the gunshot and bit her lip so hard she could taste blood. She couldn't just sit here and do nothing. She leaped from the chair, grabbed her coat from a hook on the wall, pulled the fur-lined hood over her head, and stepped outside. One of them could be hurt. She made it no farther than the stoop connected to the back landing when she saw Noah and Loka come around the side of the outhouse.

"I thought I told you to wait inside," he shouted over to her, but the words weren't angry.

"What happened? Thunderation! I thought it might have been…"

"It's alright, Cora. It was just a mountain lion. I shot only to scare him off. What happened to your lip? It is bleeding."

She released the breath she didn't realize she was holding. Fear and anger accosted her. "You scared the devil out of me! She angrily turned her back on him and stepped back inside. "Hell's fire!" she hissed, tore her coat off, and replaced it on the peg.

Noah followed her inside, Loka at his back. He immediately saw her fear and her anger. It's alright. They are known to show up occasionally, especially during the snowy season. Didn't you ever see them down at your grandfather's place?"

"Yes, but you could have said something! Hells Fire! With what's been going on and what happened, I thought, damnation, forget what I thought."

He replaced his rifle above the fireplace, turned back to her, and, in a couple of steps, he pulled her into his arms. His warmth and gentleness nearly undid her. However, she refused to cry.

"I'm sorry, Cora, honey," he breathed against her ear. "I guess I'm so used to not having to explain myself. When Loka hears different sounds, usually wildlife, I head out with my rifle. It could mean food, or it could mean something wild that is after my food supply. I didn't stop to think what my action might do to you," he apologized. "But if it's any consolation, my guess about those men who showed up at your place is they are long gone, at least for now.

"Our winter storms will keep them at bay. They are bloodthirsty, alright, but not stupid to continue the search in this weather." He leaned back, holding her at arm's length. "Take a seat. I have some salve for your lips. He quickly reached for one of the jars on the open shelves and brought it back to the table. Carefully he applied the medicine. "Am I forgiven?"

She looked up at him. His sapphire eyes were just about the bluest things she'd ever seen. "I suppose," she relented.

He smiled and capped the jar, returning it to the shelf. *Christ on a crutch. She* felt so good when he held her in his arms and rest his chin on the top of her head. He had been away from the female persuasion for too long. She was slender, but perfectly curved, and though she wasn't a large-breasted woman, what she did have were young and full. They would fit in his hands. Hands that wanted to caress. He shook the thought from his mind for all the good it would do him.

Cora stood and leaned in closer. Her pulse skipped a beat. So did his when she rested her cheek on his breast muscle. "Thank you."

He lifted her chin and lowered his head, touching her lips gently. When she didn't object, he slipped his tongue out and lightly bathed the soft outer skin, tasting the sweet taste of salve he'd just put on her.

The sensation was utterly foreign to her, and she immediately stiffened and stepped back. "What are you doing?" Her face lit up like a ripe tomato.

"I'm kissing you. Haven't you ever been kissed before?" Well, of course, she hadn't, he realized. Living as she did with her grandfather, never seeing anyone.

"No!" she nearly choked. Is that how a man and woman do it? With wet tongues."

Noah grinned. "Well, it's been a while for me, but that's how it's done. But I won't do it again if you don't like it."

Cora cocked her head to the side, sending her cropped, ebony hair askew across her cheeks. The silky strands framed her face. She blinked in fascination as she watched the different expressions on Noah's face. Was this one of the reasons her grandfather had sent her to him? She voiced her thoughts aloud. "Do you wish to mate with me?" she bluntly asked.

He nervously cleared his throat. How the hell did he answer that? "You have a beautiful mouth that reminds me of a shiny bow. I just wanted to kiss you."

She leaned into him again, lifting up on her tiptoes, and pressed her lips against his. Her tongue touched him. "I like the feel of this; it gives me butterflies in my belly. You must kiss a lot of women. You are quite good at it. And you have very nice lips as well."

He released her, feeling his own flush. "It has been a long time, but I have kissed a few ladies." He remembered his first kiss with a neighbor girl just before he entered the Army. She was the one who showed him how to use his tongue. And he also remembered a few soiled doves he'd spent a night with while on a twenty-four-hour pass from the Army and then a few more over his years of hiding. She changed the subject, thank God!

"I can skin the rabbit Loka caught and prepare it for cooking. I used to do it all the time for my grandfather. We could roast it inside your Dutch oven. It tastes delicious that way—tender, juicy, and browned."

Noah grinned, "I know it does; I've done it myself that way. How about we prepare the rabbit together."

"Alright," she smiled at the prospect. He was different from her grandfather, who would never have offered help. And besides, she liked the idea of working together. The warmth of his body seemed to emanate from him.

They worked side by side, and while skinning the rabbit, she showed Noah a few simple tricks to make the work easier, like taking the rabbit fur and gently pulling toward the rabbit's head. "It's like peeling an upside-down banana," Noah said, using his hands to pretend he was removing the thick yellow skin.

"Banana? What is that?" I read something about them in one of my books but never got the concept."

"It is a long, narrow, yellow fruit; you peel the skin off in strips, then eat the white soft fruit beneath. They are delicious."

"Maybe one day I will try some. You know this is really nice working with you and nice to have someone to talk to," she told him. "The skinning I usually do by myself. It's the first thing my grandfather taught me, living as we did. When my mother was alive, she taught me how to cook. By the way, you keep a spotless and well-organized cabin."

Noah warmly smiled. "My mother also taught me cleanliness is next to Godliness. He turned back to the work. "Would you like to keep a rabbit's foot?"

"Whatever for?" she asked, perplexed.

"For good luck, of course. I'll show you how to preserve them."

"Good luck, you say?" she lifted one brow and beamed enthusiastically. "If that's true, we could use some good luck."

He reached up to one of the shelves, brought down a bottle of rubbing alcohol, poured it into a bowl, and submerged the severed feet inside. "We'll leave these here for about forty-eight hours, then clean them well and dunk them again in a mixture of borax and warm water for another twenty-four hours. After this, we will clean them up again and hang them to dry. It takes about a week."

"Then what do we do with them?"

Once they are dried, we string them, and you can wear them like jewelry, attach them to your clothing, or keep them inside your coat pocket. Remember, they are for good luck, so you'll want to carry them with you," he grinned. One for you and one for me."

Eagerness filled her amber-brown eyes. And those lips of hers that he found so damn intoxicating curled up in a delicious smile; seconds later, they turned down in concentration.

"I wonder why grandfather didn't do this?"

"From what I knew of your grandfather, he didn't believe in luck. But as a boy, I grew up believing."

"I want to believe too." She looked up and again met his eyes, so blue and filled with a boyish playfulness. "You don't have a frog behind your back, do you?"

"Huh?" Then he chuckled. "You mean like in the picture of my family?"

"Yes, just like that."

Noah continued to grin. "Nope," he placed his hands palm up on the table and watched her satisfied expression. There certainly weren't many people in this world that something this simple would please them. Cora was absolutely delightful. She, indeed, was an angel filling his lonely days.

The feet were preserved in the liquid two hours later and set aside. The rabbit was skinned, and the fur was curing. Cora cut the rabbit into pieces and placed them inside the Dutch Oven with a bit of lard and seasoning, lowering the heavy lid. That evening, they sat down to share the fresh meat and biscuits that Cora had made this time.

"Back at my grandfather's cabin, I had a store of potatoes, onions, and carrots. Maybe they survived. When we do get the chance to return, we can check them. If unharmed by the fire, we can bring them up here."

"That would be great. Don't get vegetables often; when I do, they run out quickly."

"I plant every spring. I also have a stash of seeds." She quickly told him.

In the next several days, heavy snow surged through the mountains, leaving an icy thick blanket of white covering the land in high drifts.

The heavy weight caused all the surrounding pine boughs to hang nearly to the ground. The Shortstem Beardtongue and San Juan Gillia that circled the cabin resembled vast mounds of snow dwellings. Igloos Cora remembered reading about it in one of her books.

She missed her books. They got left behind when she hurried to find Noah Harper. A man she had thought at the time was an old man. But instead, he was strong, nicely put-together with muscle and height. Deliciously handsome. The soft lines that sprouted from the corners of his eyes and mouth only added to the persona of his good looks. And whenever Cora looked at him, she felt an unnatural tingle run through her whole body.

Over the days and nights that followed, they grew a strong bond through the hours they spent together. Though there were times she didn't think about what had happened to her grandfather, he was always in her heart.

Outside, the wind howled and blew through the treetops, sending more snow. The mounds of icy shrubs grew even higher. Looking outside, they knew they would be stranded here for several more days, maybe weeks. The outhouse door was covered halfway up with snow.

After supper, they headed outside to clear a pathway. Just tramping outside to relieve himself was okay for him, but Noah knew he couldn't expect Cora to do the same. It wouldn't be fair. She needed some privacy.

Noah made his bed on the floor close to the fireplace each night. He had given up his feather tick, the only bed in the cabin for Cora.

A couple of reasons for the sacrifice: he didn't think sharing the bed would be intelligent, he was attracted to her and began to think of her as his little angel. And secondly, he still, after all these years, continued to have the haunting nightmares of blood and death in the Cheyenne village. He would wake up in a cold sweat, and sometimes, the blankets would be twisted around his legs.

God only knew what he might do if she slept beside him. But even with all these emotions he suffered, he still believed that exposing the horror of that day was the right thing to do. Those men should never have gotten away with the massacre they had instigated.

That's exactly what happened anyway. Only one went to prison. The rest were court marshaled and dishonorably discharged from the Army. And every one of them lived for revenge against him.

He undressed to his skivvies and crawled into his bedroll, lifting the bedding over him. He briefly listened for Cora's even breathing. When he knew she was asleep. He rolled to his side. He was bone weary. The two of them had worked hard all day, keeping the pathways clear, chopping and hauling wood for heat during the day and night.

They also hunted for edible vegetation. There was a lot up here, even in the winter, if one knew where to look. What he didn't know Cora did. Cattails and their roots could be used for stock, rose hips, wild onions, garlic, chickweed, and barberries. They made a good team. What one didn't know, the other did. Noah was more familiar with medicinal plants than Cora. However, she did know some of the healing herbs you could use for tea.

The storm finally let up late in the afternoon, almost a week from the day it had started. If the weather stayed clear, they would make the five-mile trek down to Elijah's cabin in a few days and see what might be salvaged. Cora had only brought the bare minimum with her. But said there were other things they could get back up here using the sled he'd told her about. Loka was strong and would help pull significantly when the snow hardened, which made traveling over it easier.

Dozens of things pushed through Noah's mind as he laid in his bedroll that night.

He was due a good night's sleep just as the pretty little snow angel in his bed did. She was a hard worker and very knowledgeable of this way of life. It was a hard life here in the backcountry. But she never complained. Was she as lonely as he always was? Indeed, she was. The first indication was that she liked to talk, which made him smile. Noah was increasingly drawn to her each hour he passed in her company.

But he shouldn't think that. He was no good to anyone. He'd been on his own for too long. He had to shut his mind down. He needed sleep. Not once in the past ten years had he gotten a good night's sleep. Maybe tonight he would. At least he wasn't alone. He closed his eyes. His mind slowly slid into the dreams that would forever haunt him. At some point, he must have dropped off to sleep because the next thing he felt, he was being caressed with a cool cloth against his face.

In the early hours before dawn, Cora was shocked awake by loud shouting in the darkness of the cabin. She quickly sat up and glanced at Noah, restlessly moving to and fro. For a brief time, she watched him. He was having what appeared to be the worst kind of nightmare. She felt a strong pull to go to him and comfort him. Was it attraction or a simple concern? How could she know? He shouted out again.

Something was undoubtedly wrong. Noah was thrashing back and forth and kicking his thermal-covered legs about. He was yelling out to people seen by only him. There was a mixture of anger and fear. Let them go," he shouted. "Stop this bloodshed. They are supposed to be prisoners, not murdered or torn limb from limb. And look at what they are doing to the women. And the children. Dear God, captain, stop the men. These people are human beings!" On and on, Noah screamed out. "I'm a medic, for God's sake! I can't abide by this with good conscience."

"Noah, wake up. You are dreaming." She spoke to him from across the room. He didn't seem to hear her.

She got up and moved to the sink, poured some water from the pitcher he kept on the counter, moistened a cloth, rung it out, and raced to his side.

Gently she ran the cool material over his face and neck. His skin was warm and damp from sweating. He began to moan and then stopped moving as he fell back into sleep.

This time, more calmly. She couldn't help but reach out and caress the silky smoothness of his mustache covering half his upper lip. These lips had kissed her a week ago, giving her such a foreign fluttering through her body. Lips she would like to feel against her own again. But he hadn't touched her since that first kiss.

"It's alright, you are just dreaming," she whispered with concern. She leaned down and touched his face, mouth, and chin with her fingers. She was utterly fascinated with him. She moved down his neck over his shoulder and across his masculine chest muscle so well defined, his nipples were hard against her fingertips. She couldn't help it; she leaned in and touched his lips with her own, letting her curious tongue touch him as he had toyed with her.

And *sweet Lawd*, she liked what the simple touch did to her. She was so enthralled with what she was doing that she never noticed when he opened his eyes and quietly watched her. The moment she did, she pulled back, feeling her cheeks flush. His eyes were like the most precious jewels, matching the sparkle in the fireplace's light.

"What are you doing, Cora?" There was no shock in his voice, no anger, just the simple question.

"I...I, oh my. You were having a bad dream, and I was worried about you. I read something about how you should wake a dreaming person with a gentle touch." Embarrassed at getting caught in her exploration, Cora pulled her hand away and sat back on her heels

"So, that's how you wake a person, with a soft touch that rouses and a sweet taste of their lips? I rather like it."

She pushed herself up onto her feet and stood. She felt the heat of getting caught. "It must have worked. Here you are awake. Was it a horrible dream? You were shouting and pleading with someone."

Noah barely listened to her; he was still caught up in the nightmare, but even more so in the touch of her lips and tongue.

"Umm, sorry if I disturbed you."

"You didn't."

"I was just worried about you. But I'll leave you be," she shyly whispered. "It is still a couple of hours until dawn. You should go back to sleep." She started to move back to the bed.

"Cora?"

"Hmm," she turned back to him.

"Come here."

When their eyes met, a vaguely sensuous light passed between them—a cerulean blue intensity and a topaz-brown filled with curiosity. He was smiling up at her, and she caught the beauty of his lips in the firelight and shadow casting golden highlights in his mustache. He was so handsome, and Cora felt transfixed in magical fascination.

When she reached his side, he took her hand and gently pulled her down next to him. "That had to be the nicest way anyone has ever woke me up."

He pulled her closer to his warmth. "You're shivering, are you cold?"

"Umm, no," Cora felt more alive than ever. Was he going to kiss her again?

That's precisely what Noah wanted to do; he couldn't remember ever wanting to do anything more or with any other woman. He watched her full lower lip quiver, and in seconds, he captured her angelic face between his hands and pulled her down closer to him.

Cora slightly lost some of her balance and fell against the length of him when he kissed her, and the moment his lips touched hers, an intoxicating heat filled her. The intensity further ignited her when he separated her lips with the gentle force of his tongue. She could taste him, and she felt like she might just have died and gone to heaven. She moved softly against the hard length of him. The warm, corded muscles of his chest, arms, and legs gave her a euphoric feeling. She knew little about the male anatomy but understood something was happening.

The juncture between Noah's muscular thighs brushed against her. She liked the feel and pressed tighter against his body.

Christ on a crutch, he felt the arousal, fire his sex. But he swore he would not touch her in any other way. She was innocent. But it wasn't easy to ignore his growing electrification as the lightning-hot streaks of need moved through him. She was kissing him back, making the most erotic sounds he'd ever heard. He wanted her, all of her, but for now, he would only make love to her mouth inside and out.

Cora didn't fully understand what was happening to her body, but tarnation, the pleasure she felt when her nipples rose against her nightshift and brushed his powerful chest. She felt his hands move through her hair. She copied his movements in the kiss and through her hands as they caressed his scalp and funneled through his wavey chestnut hair.

"Oh Cora, you are the sweetest thing I have ever had the pleasure of kissing," he whispered against her moistened lips and deepened the kiss. Their tongues explored, made love, and sent ripples of desire through them both. He could feel the hardened tips of her breasts as she pressed against him. He left her sensual mouth and trailed his lips and tongue along her jawline down the silkiness of her neck, then back up to the hollow beneath her ear, where he gently pulled the small lobe into his mouth.

She cuddled even closer with an innocent abandon that only served to ignite him more. He leaned up and watched the beauty of her innocent expression culminate across her extraordinary face. She was so precious, but he knew he needed to end this right now before he took advantage of her willingness to allow him further access. He wanted it to be unique if they ever joined their bodies as one. Special for both of them. He quickly released his hold on her, and with a gravelly voice, he said, "You better go back to bed and get some sleep."

How was she supposed to sleep after what he had evoked in her body? She remembered, as a child waking from a bad dream, how she sought out her parents for comfort. She saw them cuddled together with soft movements that rustled their bedding. She was so captivated as she stood at the doorway and silently watched them. Though she couldn't hear what they whispered, she felt their love and closeness.

Is this what they were doing? She wondered. Were they the same beautiful things she had just done with Noah? As she thought about it now, she knew instinctively that what they did was much more and wildly different, and she couldn't stop watching them as she stood in the doorway. Moonlight spilled through the room, causing her mother and father's shadows to play against the wall.

Her parents were unclothed and moving with each other. Cora must have made a sound because her parents quickly realized she stood in the doorway. A rustling sound took place as the covers were pulled up tighter. "What is it, sweetheart?" her mother asked as she gathered her robe, slid her arms through the sleeves, tied the sash around her waist, and slid from the bed. "Did you have a bad dream?"

No, what she witnessed that night differed significantly from what she and Noah had done. Now, she wondered what it would be like if she and Noah were naked in each other's arms.

"Noah?"

"What is it, honey?"

"I liked what just happened."

"So did I, but you better get some sleep." He was still stiff between his legs, and he feared if she came back to him, he would scare the living hell out of her. "But you need to go back to bed and get some sleep. I will see you in the morning. If the sun comes out as I expect, we can head down the canyon to your grandfather's place and see what we might salvage."

"Okay," she whispered, feeling his loss as she moved away. In the next moment, Loka raised his head, arched his back, and stretched, pushing his large paws forward. He yawned, straightened, and moved toward Cora and the bed, where she climbed back under the covers. With a slight thud, he plopped back down on the floor between her and Noah and quietly went back to sleep.

On the other hand, Cora found she couldn't rest. She continued to think about the magic of what she and Noah had done. Her body still tingled.

So did Noah's. He had never wanted a woman the way he did right now.

Chapter Seven

Long shadows from the east stretched across the snow and sparkled like the finest jewels leaving bright rays to dance through the lone window above the old dry sink. Noah was already up filling the wood box.

Cora climbed from the bed, removed her nightgown, grasped her pants and the flannel shirt where she'd left them on top of the trunk, and quickly pulled them over her long johns. "I'll get some coffee started she said as she stepped into the rustic kitchen area. "I've been meaning to ask why you don't use this little potbelly stove in the cooking area?"

He glanced at her from over his shoulder. "It needs a good cleaning out, and I just never bothered. Didn't need it with the fireplace."

"I see, but it would be easier than preparing the firebox for simple things like a coffee pot or the frying pan you use for biscuits. If it's alright with you, I'll clean it up sometime this coming week."

He gave her that smile she loved looking at. "That sounds like a good idea, but I'll help. God only knows how bad it is. I've never used the thing." He added wood to the firebox and placed the medal grid over the coals.

"Are we still planning on heading to my grandfather's cabin today?"

"Yes, as soon as we eat something. I double-checked the old flatbed sled to ensure the snow blades worked properly. We should take it if there is anything worth bringing back here. Loka is powerful, and he can help us pull it. All and all the contraption is pretty light weight."

As if in answer, Loka let off a howl, sounding like approval.

Cora smiled over to both Noah and Loka. "I just gathered what I could reach and what I might need. But I didn't go through much. I'm hoping there might be something worth saving in the cellar. Most of my clothes, dried goods, and books are down there. Too much debris covered the latch door, hiding the steps to the cellar. I didn't dare take any more time sorting through anything. The hour was growing late, and I needed to keep my promise to my grandfather, find you, and give you the warning."

"And nearly kill yourself doing it. That still irritates me. But on the other hand, it sounds like you wouldn't have been any better off if you'd stayed."

"I am used to this weather, being out in it one way or another for the past sixteen years; I just wasn't planning on the blizzard or Sugar Loaf collapsing. I thought I could make the trip faster than I did. The sun was still out even though there were a few flakes. I just convinced myself it would fizzle out. I guess it wasn't very intelligent. I could have spent the night in the lean-to and headed out in the morning."

"And still froze to death."

"I would have stayed warm enough," she defended. "Sugarloaf was out there and hay to cover on the cold ground. I would have stayed warm enough. But the truth be told..."

"You were afraid those men would come back."

She met his gaze, a cross between blue ice and fire. "Partly, but mostly, Grandfather was adamant I should go immediately. In fact, he would have thought I wasted time just burying him. Despite that, I couldn't leave him in the open for the wildlife to tear him apart for food."

Noah nodded in understanding. She was a brave little thing, no doubt about it. Thankfully, he had been out on the hilltop to see her struggle. Had he not been, she most certainly would have frozen to death. He smiled briefly when he thought of how she had reacted to him that early morning. Thought he was a snow monster.

They finished the rabbit they'd roasted last night for breakfast and cleaned up dishes and the cooking pot. Within thirty minutes, they left, pulling the sled behind them. Noah's pocket watch said it was still relatively early, just past seven. Loka blazed the trail ahead, sticking his long nose in shrubs and snow. Fortunately, the path they chose was not as steep as the one she had used coming up here. Loka was strong, but Noah didn't want his friend to get hurt, so they would all pull and push whatever they could rescue back up the mountain.

By mid-morning, they arrived, and the place was in ruin. If it were ever to be used again, the cabin would have to be rebuilt entirely. The first thing they did was clear the boards and other debris scattered across the interior so they could lift the trap door. A dusty, smokey smell wafted up, and Cora sneezed.

"When all this collapsed, it probably created a dust bowl. If we're lucky, the things left here are still dry and useable," Cora told Noah and began moving down the narrow stairway.

"Hold on, Cora. You don't know what has been stirred up; let me check first."

But she was already at the bottom shouting up. "Looks like almost everything survived. It's dusty and a little smoky-smelling, but everything looks fine," she sneezed again, then twice more.

"Damn it!" Noah grumbled and followed her down with irritation. "You should have waited for me. This whole place could have crashed down on you. That was a fool thing you did!"

"Sorry, I'm just used to doing things for myself. But as you can see, everything is fine."

"Still, you should be more careful."

Loka chose that moment to stand at the opening leading down to the cellar and began sniffing at everything in sight. He also sneezed and started to take the narrow steps down. "Stay!" Noah shouted up, but the wolf ignored the order and kept coming.

Noah stared between the wolf and the woman with frustration. "It would seem I have two free spirits on my hands that refuse to listen."

Cora grinned and began to rummage through all the items. She opened a bin filled with onions, potatoes, and carrots. She poured them together inside a burlap bag and handed them to Noah. He climbed back up the rickety stairway. It was truly amazing the old thing had survived. He took the sack out to the sled. Next came a bundle of clothing also stored in a burlap bag. "Will there be room for some of my books," she asked when he returned. "And there's all this bedding. Needs to be washed; however, it is usable."

"Sure, I can also use it to pack some of this stuff. But the books only take a few. We don't want to make the load too heavy to pull. Take only your favorites."

Cora grinned. "They are all my favorites. But I will only take a few. Would six be alright?"

"Sure, that should be fine. I have a few books in the shed outside; you might like them. Let me see what you have; I may have some of the same."

Cora handed him the stack of six, and he quickly looked them over. "These two I have. He lifted them from the pile and handed them back to her. Why don't you grab two different ones."

The two he handed back were Mark Twain's The Adventures of Huckleberry Finn and Robert Louis Stevenson's Treasure Island. "I must admit I haven't read them for years. But like I said, I have copies back at my cabin."

"Rereading them is like visiting an old friend you haven't seen in ages." She told him with seriousness. And he knew it was her only entertainment. She returned them to the crate where she had stored the books and grasped two others: Jekyll and Hyde and The Scarlett Letter.

He gave her a look of surprise. "These are good ones, and I have wanted to read them. Especially this one, he held out Jekyll and Hyde. You have good taste in reading."

"They were the only ways I could have adventure and romance. I also have a collection of Shakespeare's plays. I loved Romeo and Juliet," then she made a scowl, "but must admit I hated the ending when they died." She reached back into the crate and pulled three smaller books of poetry, Keats and Oliver Wendell Holmes, also William Wordsworth. "Do you like poetry?"

"Bring them."

"But that will be more than six."

"They are small. I will carry them in my backpack. "I also like poetry."

Cora grinned with excitement and added them to the stack he held.

"Have you ever read Mary Shelley's Frankenstein?" he asked, meeting her smiling lips. After years of loneliness, he finally began to feel some of it dissipate further. He really liked this pretty angel the old mountain man had sent him. She was weaving such a sensual and binding cord inside him, a feeling he thought he had long ago given up on.

"No, my grandfather said it was too frightening for a young mind."

"Yet he let you read The Strange Case of Jekyll and Hyde?"

She chuckled and placed two fingers against her lips as if she were telling a secret for his ears only. "He didn't know I had it. The book was my father's, and I kept it hidden amongst my parents' things when I first came here to live. But I didn't read it until much later."

Noah grinned at her expression. "Well, I have a copy of Frankenstein if you would like to read that."

"I would love too!"

She handed him the blankets and a pillow next. "You've given me so much, and I've been using your only pillow. This way, we can each have one. I have a washtub for laundry and a washboard. I never asked what you use to wash clothes, but you always smell nice and look clean. I need a good scrubbing, and I'm out of clean clothes," she added.

"I have these things back at the cabin. I should have offered them to you. Forgive me."

Her topaz eyes sparkled bright with pleasure. "I should have just opened my mouth and asked. It is me that should be sorry. I always did the clothes washing. Mine more than Grandfathers because…" she stopped herself, her cheeks rimming with deep pink, almost red.

"Because you are female. I understand." He reached out and caressed her cheek with his gloved hand."

She lowered thick ebony lashes against her cheeks, hiding the sparkle of the tears she fought to hold back. She swallowed and whispered, "Thank you."

"Ah honey, I should have thought of all this two weeks ago. I've been alone for so long, I didn't think." They made their way back up the stairs, each carrying a load.

"At the time, there wasn't much to be done for it," she admitted, continuing their conversation. "We had to wait to travel. The weather only let up yesterday. I washed out my underthings in the bucket you keep below in the cabinet beneath the sink while you were outside a couple of days ago, working in the shed and smokehouse. Which reminds me, we probably need to fill the water reserve when we return."

"Already did while you were sleeping. Now, we should start back to the cabin. It will be slower going up than it was coming down, especially with the load."

She glanced up the trailhead they'd used to come down here, a much easier way than she'd chosen when she first came up the canyon. "Do you think Loka will be able to pull all this stuff? Maybe I should leave my books behind."

"He'll be fine. However, there may be a few spots we'll need to help him by pushing. But take your books, they aren't that heavy, and as I said, I love to read too. And I look forward to reading yours."

"Oh, Noah, you are so wonderful." She threw her arms up around his neck and squeezed herself against the length of him.

He wrapped his arms around her, pulling her tight against him, and for a few seconds, he could feel the softness of her breasts even through her heavy clothing. *Judas* he wanted to kiss her like he did last night. Instead, he stepped away. "Is there anything you want from the lean-to? It appears pretty much unharmed?"

She remembered her grandfather's cash box. "I will go look inside; she handed him the sack with her vanilla and lilac scented soaps, the only feminine things she had, her extra homemade toothpaste and a couple of new bone-handled toothbrushes, an oval-shaped hairbrush, and a handheld mirror.

She was thankful and amazed the mirror's glass had not cracked. She glanced back at the burned-out shell of the cabin, a home she'd had since she was seven. "It's kind of like leaving a dear old friend behind," she told Noah, looking over her shoulder at what had become her sanctuary.

"I spent much of my time in the cellar room when I wasn't helping grandfather. He wasn't much of a talker, but he did teach me many things, including my love of reading." He was once a teacher, you know. It is how he met my Cheyenne grandmother." She hoped it didn't shock him to know she was a quarter Indian. He said nothing, only smiled with that handsome mouth. "Did you want to check out the lean-to?" he reminded her.

"Do you think we will come back down? If we do, I can look through it then. I know my grandfather was always puttering around out there. But right now, we already have a heavy load."

"Sure, I don't see why not."

Cora was relieved; though she genuinely liked Noah, she wasn't sure she was ready to share the secret of her grandfather's cash box. And right now, it wasn't necessary. They wouldn't be going to town to spend any of it for months yet. They worked together, tying everything onto the sled and hooking Loka up to the harness in front. "Some of these things we can store in the shed. I cleared space when I knew we'd be coming down here. We can pull things out as we need them."

She nodded in compliance. "I didn't ask this morning, but did you make this travois sled?"

"No, it was on the property when I moved up here. It had belonged to the old man Jones. I often use it in the winter when Loka and I go hunting."

"Well, it's wonderful. I hope Loka can pull it without too much trouble."

"Like I said, we definitely will have to help him in the few spots where it's a bit steeper."

The way back up the canyon took them two times as long to travel as it had to come down. By the time the three of them reached the cabin, all three were worn out.

After they released Loka from the harness, he ran through the trees at the rear of the cabin and disappeared. They quickly began to unload the six-foot bladed travois. The extra bedding, dehydrated vegetables, dried meat, and her personal items were brought into the cabin, along with Cora's books and extra clothes. A few of her gardening tools were placed inside the shed. Noah also had his supply, so he packed only the ones he didn't already have.

"In the spring, I will plant a garden with the seeds I've dried from last year's growing season," Cora announced with a smile and handed him the bundle. "I made a garden every year for grandfather and myself."

"I have a garden, and I plant many medicinal herbs. Pretty much anything we need if either of us is ailing, even including medicine for Loka if he needs it. You are welcome to share the space, and I will help you enlarge it if you like." *What in the world was he talking about in terms of a future?* She had been cloistered for years. She needed to taste what life would be like outside this dreary lifestyle. He couldn't do to her what Elijah had by keeping her out of sight.

Cora's topaz eyes widened with knowledge. "You made some medicines for my grandfather, didn't you?"

Noah smiled, *Judas*. She was pretty. "His payment for always bringing me supplies when he made his journey to town."

"You never went down the mountain with him to the town?"

"Never, I felt it was better that no one knew I existed."

"But nobody would have known who you were, not with all that Yeti hair on your face."

He chuckled, "I did not want to take any chances. As I've told you, my family's lives could have been put into jeopardy if people knew I was alive."

Not for the first time, she realized how lonely this life must have been, which gave her even more understanding of why her grandfather had sent her to him.

Noah seemed to know where her thoughts were taking root. "Yes, I sometimes get lonely, but it didn't matter. I couldn't take the chance of being exposed. I wanted my family to stay safe and away from the decisions I had to make. Your grandfather is the only one who knew of me. As I've told you, he saved my life. He understood my circumstances because of his reasons for living up here. I only saw the town once, and that's when I first arrived.

"I stocked up on what I thought I would need. I packed a mule and made my way here. I was foolish and had no idea what kind of task this would become, and I nearly died. My mule certainly did. I almost made my death a reality on that first day up here. If it weren't for Elijah, like I told you before, I never would have made it in one piece. Thanks to him, I became self-sufficient. He taught me to trap for food, tan the hides, and other survival techniques. I was pretty green. I only knew how to hunt for meat with my rifle, skin, and butcher for storage. Something my father and I did together when I was a boy. Every season we went until I left home to join the army.

"It's true I got lonely sometimes, but I had Loka and the yearly visit with Elijah. But in all that time, he kept you a secret. He never talked much about himself." Noah shrugged as if none of it mattered. "How about we get this stuff in the shed for now."

The shed was more extensive than it appeared from the outside. It was very organized, with a wall of shelves for gardening tools and another with wood planks stacked neatly from floor to ceiling. He carried in the few boards he had recovered from her grandfather's place and placed them on the floor in front of the planks already there.

"I didn't know you grabbed some of these boards she said, surprised. It's like having a part of my home up here."

"Thought we might get some use out of them. I have meant to build an attaching washroom on the back of the cabin."

Cora got excited, "you mean maybe have a tub to wash in?"

He smiled. "Something like that."

She began to check out other things inside the old shed. A guitar case hung from a peg on one of the walls. Dust covered the case, and Cora moved toward it. "Do you play?" she asked as she ran her hand over the leather case, leaving finger marks in the dust.

Noah looked in her direction. "I haven't touched it in years. I don't even know why I held onto it. Should have sold it."

"I'm glad you kept it. Everyone needs some music in their hearts. The sounds and rhythm fill the soul with pleasure. My grandfather played the harmonica a lot in the winter. And my father, when he was alive, used to play an old fiddle he had since he was a young boy. My mother and I would dance in the parlor while he played. Sometimes, if his wooden leg didn't bother him after a day of wearing it, he would dance with us, and we'd hum the music."

Noah thought of the first two years after the testimony he had given at the trial, how each man had issued death threats not only against him but his family. It was the threat against his loved ones that sent him on the run. Night after night, to earn a few coins, he had played inside one saloon or another where there was no piano for the customers to listen to or dance to. The tips he received helped him to survive. He could never go home. His loved ones could not be hurt because of his decisions. He watched Cora and realized at some point, he would have to let her go for the same reason.

"I once had a friend who could play a harmonica. Many times, we used to play together. But when I first came up here," he explained. "I had so much to learn just to survive. I figured I had better things to do with my time than sit around and play. After a while, I just forgot about it."

"Please, Noah, do bring it into the cabin."

He smiled at the pleasure he saw brighten her face. "Well, I need to tune it up. I haven't touched it in a very long time. I can't guarantee I'm any good."

"Just to hear the sounds would be so wonderful. Besides, I'm told once you learn, you never forget."

"Noah smiled. "We will see about that, but I'll take it inside. You might be sorry."

Her exotic eyes glittered like a thousand heavenly stars. "I will never be sorry."

He changed the subject, "I have something else I can bring inside for you and me to use." Noah moved to a corner of the shed and lifted a heavy tarp from an oddly shaped, hollowed-out chair-like apparatus.

Again, her eyes went wide with interest. "Whatever do you do with it?"

"You take a bath in it. It's called a hip bath."

"But I don't understand," she said with confusion.

He chuckled. "You fill this bowl-like section with hot water and sit inside to wash your body. You can lean against this sloping back," he ran his hand down the back end, "and let the water flow over you."

"Oh, my goodness. Just the thought of submerging myself in such a wonderous way is marvelous."

"Would you like to try it?"

"I definitely would. Gracious to sit in a tub of hot water and clean my whole body sounds like the most heavenly thing ever. Especially in the winter, when it's so cold to bathe in the creek, I must carry the old washtub down to the cellar."

"We'll set it up in the corner by the fireplace. I'll make some covering so you can have some privacy."

"Please, let's do it." She remembered the precious soap she'd squandered over the years when her grandfather brought her some from town. She had to make it last all year. This would be heaven, she decided.

Noah grinned at her excitement. "He lifted the lightweight copper tub and carried it to the cabin. Once we get it inside, we'll give it a good cleaning."

They no sooner got the tub inside when Loka returned carrying a grouse hen.

"Where on earth did you find that?" Cora asked, breathless.

Loka dropped the hen onto the floor, looked up, and gazed at them with his soulful golden eyes. Then hustled back outside.

"I wish I knew where he finds them, especially in the winter, but occasionally, he shows up with one. One of these days, I'm going to figure it out. It sure would be nice to have some eggs."

Chapter Eight

Six dangerous-looking men sat inside a social club in the sprawling city of Cheyenne, Wyoming, filled with lavish homes and state-of-the-art buildings. Cheyenne had become one of America's wealthiest towns thanks to the railroad and the cattle boom. The population was over eleven thousand. There were over ninety saloons and gambling halls, brothels, and tents that housed over four hundred prostitutes.

The place was indeed up and coming, and also a place where it would be easy to hide in plain sight, especially for someone who didn't want to be found.

The men were playing a game of five-card draw and swilling down whiskey and beer by the boatload. It was nearing midnight, and Captain Tamarin was bored. He tossed his cards on the table, finished his shot of whiskey, and growled to the rest of the men that he was calling it a night.

This town had been nothing but a waste of time. They'd spent weeks looking and questioning shopkeepers and ranches before reaching this city. Not one person they had questioned had ever heard of Noah Harper. Even when Lamar and his men used torture, the people claimed they'd never heard of the man. They were quickly disposed of. They could never leave witnesses.

Sick of hearing the same things from any of them, he and his men began dropping people like swatted flies. They were liars, every stinking one of them. He knew somehow that they had helped his nemesis, Noah Harper.

The turncoat was like trying to catch a greased pig squealing and jostling around an enclosed pen. The captain supposed the coward could have changed his name and appearance. The younger man had been handsome, tall, lean, and muscularly built. Not someone most people, principally women, would easily forget.

He was also educated and well-read. Lamar remembered that before the man turned traitor, he would entertain the men in the evenings with tales from books he had read or his talent for playing the guitar. None of that excused what the bastard had done following the Indian village's well-deserved raid.

With his knowledge of medicine and rank of sergeant, Noah turned on the men with a righteous indignation he had no right to feel. Those savages had to pay for the horror of Little Big Horn, especially when some of the men had found items that had been taken from the battlefield.

Items that had belonged to soldiers. Sabers, rifles, and horses wearing the military brand. That told him and the men this village and the inhabitants had been there. His interpreter, a sly forty-something man hired for the right price, turned from the Indian he had been interrogating and hurled a derogatory glance at Lamar. "He says they traded for the stuff, but I don't believe him."

Neither did Lamar. He knew Injuns always lied. "Shoot him!" He turned with disgust.

The interpreter grinned with delight and sent a bullet between the old man's eyes. They all continued their bloody rampage on the village with blood lust and no remorse. They were revenging their lost comrades. Nothing would keep them from destroying these filthy sub-human animals. None of them would be left alive. Only one man had objected; that man was Noah Harper, the Indian lover.

The few places from Denver to Cheyenne yielded nothing—a bunch of no-account sodbusters with run-down ranches and farms. The idiot owners were in just as bad of condition as that old man back on the San Juan. Lamar figured he did all the losers a favor by killing and burning them out.

He'd started this search with a dozen men. Only seven men remained; they were the bloodiest of the bunch—except Simon Mason. And if he didn't straighten up, he would be easy to get rid of.

Two of the men had been killed by a young boy at the beginning of this search. He had hidden in the barn. He was a damn good shot. He began to pick the men off one by one. But luckily, the kid had only been able to get two. Lamar had the kid taken out with a bullet through the brain before any more damage could be done.

That was when they began to burn down the places they came to when no one had any answers. Never leave witnesses.

Within the next four years, three more of his men moved on. One of them had fallen for a thieving whore in Cortez, who liked robbing her drunken customers. She had quite a nest egg hidden away and offered to share it with the lowdown bastard who called himself Jonah. That was the end of him. Another headshot for both of them, and the money was in Lamar's pocket.

"Hey, darlin'!" a well-endowed, brassy redhead shouted down to Lamar from the open-railed hallway. A dozen doors lined the wall behind her. "You look like you could use some good news and maybe company. Why don't you bring that bottle you've been nursing and come on up? I have some information that might interest you, and then we can have a real good time with each other afterward; what do ya say, handsome?"

"What kind of information?" Lamar growled at her, dragging the words out with an interminable lack of enthusiasm.

She peered down at him over the rail, showing a great deal of cleavage. "The kind you've been looking for," she answered. "So why don't you come up and listen to what I have to say? Then we can continue what we started last night."

One of the men riding with him reached over and clapped him on the shoulder with a lascivious glint in his eyes. "If you don't want to, I sure as hell do, captain. She's the best beaver in the place."

Lamar gave him one of those looks that said don't touch me. Find your own entertainment. "Dolly's mine," he sneered.

She had promised him last night she would talk to a few girls working here for the past ten years. He was sure Cheyenne was one of the places Noah Harper had hidden in plain sight. He wasn't in Denver, Dodge City, or any other town; he and the boys had searched over the years. Not even as far away as San Francisco. Maybe, just for once, he would finally get lucky and get some solid information.

He quickly poured a half glass, downed the contents, stood up from the poker table, and scraped his chair across the dusty wooden floor, then grabbed the whiskey bottle, and headed upstairs.

Dolly grinned and walked with a pleasing strut down the hall to the room she always used. By the time Lamar got there, she was half-naked and sprawled across the bed. Her large nipples painted a delectable scarlet as she fingered herself into hardened tips.

Lamar stared at her with boredom as he stood just inside the doorway of Dolly's room. "Look, I don't need none of that," he flung his hand with a pointed finger in her direction as she lay sprawled across her bed, naked for all intents and purposes. "Jesus! Put something on, and tell me what information you have?"

With pouty lips, she crawled from the bed and stuffed her arms in the sleeves of a satiny dressing robe, then tied it at her waist, leaving a good deal of cleavage and shapely legs exposed.

Her expression turned sour as she glared at him. Lamar was a man she certainly wouldn't call handsome. He had a stern face. His mouth was a straight line of pure meanness, his eyes were a shallow brown color, and they never showed any delight. He was not tall, but mid-range at about five foot ten. He wore a dark blue mid-thigh army jacket with brass buttons and yellow-gold rectangular patches on his broad shoulders. Dark blue pants with a yellow strip running along the outer legs. He had knee-high boots and a black hat, which he rudely refused to remove.

All of his clothes had certainly seen better days. But the worst thing about the man was he packed a punch of meanness that would send most men on the run, especially women. Dolly certainly did not want to get on the man's cruel side. He'd been known to beat a woman near to death if he didn't like what she performed sexually or how she spoke or looked. But Dolly could deal with some meanness because he always paid very well for her services.

"Then right down to business." She said, watching his scowl. "My mistake for thinking you wanted more."

"Just get to it, 'cause I'm getting bored real fast."

She nodded her compliance, "Sugar Moran, one of the girls who has been employed here for the past ten years, claims to remember the man you are dead set on finding. Everyone called him the Gee-tar Man. And Sugar was sweet on him, he..."

"Goddamnit! Get to the point! I ain't got time for all the bullshit. Get this Sugar and bring her here. She can damn well tell me herself."

Dolly swallowed deeply; he was in one nasty mood. And as far as she was concerned, he could take the meanness out on Sugar. Dolly had a night's worth of work coming, and she didn't need a messed-up face to do it. She stepped past him and went to find the other woman.

A very short time later, an attractive blond in her early thirties entered the room. "Dolly says you asked for me. She began to undress; he stopped her by shoving her backward, slamming her hard against the bed's footrail.

Anger began to fill her; she would get back at Dolly for this. "Look, ass rub," she hissed. "I don't let a man do whatever he wants to me, and getting the hell beat out of me is one of them. If you want sex, then let's get to it. But if you're looking to put me inside the Doc's office for cuts, bruises, or broken bones, you can turn around and get the hell out of here.

"This establishment is for card playing, drinking, or spending an hour or two to have pleasure with me or one of the other girls, but we sure as hell do not go for any of the rough play it appears you are looking for. It just ain't going to happen. So, tell me, soldier man, what do you want?" She dubiously watched his demon-like eyes turn to slits, and his cheeks flushed with fury.

"Is that right? You lousy good-for-nothing whore!" Lamar knew he needed to get his temper locked down; otherwise, he wouldn't learn a damn thing, and beating the hell out of this woman would only bring more attention to himself. But as it turned out, he could see nothing but the red blaze of anger.

He glared at her better-than-thou expression. He doubled his fist and slammed his meaty hand into her cheek, bloodied her lip, and hit her jaw so hard it sent her flying against the wall. "Now quit all this bullshit. Don't matter a hill of beans to me what this piss-poor establishment's rules are one way or the other. Who the hell is this man you call Gee-tar Man? And don't even think about lying, or I'll flog you so well you won't be able to see for the next month of Sundays."

He grasped the front of her dress, yanked her up against him, and breathed his whiskey-tainted breath across her face and growled. "According to the other whore he used to come here and play music. Where the hell is he now?"

Sugar wiped the blood from her swollen lip and lifted her hand to her reddening jaw. She was used to dealing with good-for-nothing bastards like this madman. It came with the business. "Well, now, I ain't seen him for about eight years or more. I couldn't say where he went. Could be dead for all I know."

"Did he ever indicate where he was headed when he left?"

"Nope, he just got up and left one day. I spent a few nights with him off and on. He was a decent man, very handsome and polite. That kind of clientele we rarely see, more of a kind like you," she said, giving him a look of revulsion. She needed a cold pack on her lip.

"For a few months, he showed up on Friday and Saturday and played his six strings. He was good. The cowboys who patronized this place back then looked forward to his playing. He could do fast-dancing music or ballads. He helped business while he was here. The cowboys could pay the girls for a dance and a drink and head upstairs if they'd a mind to, which most did. The Gee-tar Man also did well with tips. Coin after coin would be dropped in his hat. A hat very similar to yours. But if he was ever a soldier, he never said. There was a sadness about him, though he rarely talked about himself.

Lamar knew she spoke of Noah Harper; he had no doubt. "And he never said where he was going?" He asked again. This was the first good lead he'd had in years. She lowered her eyes, knowing it would probably be her worst nightmare. She wasn't about to tell this monster anything that would get the Gee-tar Man in trouble. He was one of the very few men who had treated her with kindness.

"Like I said, he didn't talk much about himself."

"You're a liar!" Lamar bellowed loud enough to be heard downstairs. He slammed his fist with deadly force once again into her cheekbone. "Let's try this again and with the truth!" he demanded, pulled a knife from a sheath on his hip, and placed the tip just below her deep green eye. If you want to keep that eye, you'll start talking."

Sugar wasn't stupid; she knew when she was beaten. Gee-tar Man was good to her, but he wasn't worth her being scarred for life. Again wiping the blood from her split lip and cut cheekbone, she began on a wavery note. "One night, after several drinks customers had purchased for him, we talked a little when we got to my room. He mentioned he might like to explore the southern part of Colorado or Utah—some Spanish named mountains. I never heard of them. At any rate, I can't remember. In this business, it's better to forget."

"San Juan Mountains?" Lamar demanded.

She thought for a moment. "Yeah, I think that's right. What do you want with him?"

He ignored the question. *Shit!* He shouldn't have been so quick to kill the old man. The information he received last fall in Eldorado was correct. With winter in full force, he and the men would have to wait till late spring to head down there. This was one of the snowiest winters he could recall.

He lowered the knife blade down to one of her breasts, piercing it enough to draw a drop of blood. "You sure?" Sonofabitch, he was having a devil of a time holding back his temper. He was a man who asked questions and expected answers right away and couldn't stomach all this pussy footing around.

"I'm not sure about anything." Sugar whimpered, her courage leaving her destitute. "But I've told you what I remember. That was eight years back. This life has been lucrative, and I would like to continue without scars. And like I said, most times it's better to forget."

"If you got as close to him as you say, did you ever notice he had a scar that ran along his jawline?" He pushed the knife's tip a little harder into her soft flesh.

"No, I did not. He had a beard that was well-trimmed, but it covered the lower half of his face. Now, please let me get cleaned up and continue working."

He'd gotten more information in the last ten minutes than he'd received in years. This saloon had to be one of the first places Harper had gone to hide after the trial. A Goddamned trial that had sent him to prison for two years and got all of his men court marshaled.

He reached into his pocket, pulled a ten-dollar golden eagle free, and tossed the coin at her. Without another word, he left the room and headed back downstairs. Now, he and the men could make plans and end the miserable traitor's life once and for all.

Chapter Nine

Noah and Cora placed the cleaned hip tub in front of the fireplace and close to the door, which would make it easy to drag outside to empty.

Noah then fashioned a screen using some lumber stored in the shed. They would lay a sheet over the frame for privacy. After heating the water, he helped her fill the oddly shaped tub. When they were finished, he said, "You go first, and while you are bathing, I will refill the water reserve and remove the feathers and clean the hen."

Cora did not argue. She wanted this one treat, and the sooner, the better.

"Sorry, we can't fill the tub more than halfway. If we do, it will overflow, but once you get in, the water will rise around you and give you plenty to wash with, even to soak a little."

"Alright, just sitting in hot water to clean myself is the best gift I've ever had. Nothing is going to spoil this."

Three buckets of water later, the tub was filled halfway. Cora raced around the screen Noah had fashioned to retrieve some of her clean clothes. She went through the sack of things that had once been her mother's.

There were three different dresses. A blue gingham, a pink floral filled with roses and white daisies, a pale-yellow muslin with a lacy yoke, and matching puffy sleeves. She wasn't sure how well they would fit; her mother had been a little heavier in the chest, but that could have come from having a child.

Cora had read once that some women became fuller after giving birth. Although she had been a young child the last time she'd seen her mother, she realized things tended to look much more prominent to a child.

None of that mattered; She felt electrified and joyful. The last time she had worn a dress, she was only seven. Right now, she wanted to feel like a woman; no matter what she might have to do, she would make the dress work. And she hoped Noah would be pleased by her transformation.

Her only downfall would be her bluntly cut hair. Tarnation, she wished her thick ebony hair was longer, like the ladies in her books, but grandfather had always insisted she give herself a cut every spring. By then, her hair hung down and brushed her shoulders. She drew a sigh. Maybe by this coming spring, there will be a pleasant change. Her hair grew reasonably fast, and it had been months since she had taken the shears for a cut. Right now, the thick strands reached mid-neck and delicately brushed her cheeks. But it was ragged and unevenly cut.

She dug further through the sack of her mother's things. At the bottom, she found a beaded hair clip wrapped in tissue. Cora grinned with excitement; she had forgotten her mother even had this. A Christmas gift from her father, the last holiday they'd ever spent together. Both parents had been killed the following year, and Cora's life had changed forever. She clasped the clip in her hand, hoping to use it if her hair was long enough. Oh, how she hoped so. She wanted to look pleasing to Noah. She quickly returned to the screened-in tub, taking the hair clip, brush, mirror, cotton chemise, and the blue gingham dress.

Noah was out back, plucking the feathers from the wild chicken. She tested the water with her index finger and was pleased it was nice and warm.

They were beginning to lose daylight, but the fire in the large rock fireplace should be adequate for lighting and warmth. She quickly stirred the fire—the small area filled with light.

Laying her items on the stone hearth and away from the flames, she removed her boy clothes and climbed inside the tub. The minute her body slid into the water, her bubbies reacted, and the tips became hardened buds. Bending her knees, she scooted down low using the slanted back of the tub and submerged her head. When she sat back up, she grasped her precious soap and began to scrub her hair. The scent of vanilla and lilac filled the cabin, and she gloried in the clean scent.

Noah immediately caught the sweet smell of her bath the moment he stepped back inside the cabin. He could hear her splashing and the few sighs of pleasure coming from behind the screen.

His body had an automatic response as he thought of her nakedness. What the hell was he going to do come spring? As soon as the signs of warming and the first growth of mountain flowers, he knew he would have to let her go and take her to town. She needed to begin a new life away from this secluded place and away from him.

Christ on a crutch! he cursed. He was already halfway falling in love and beginning to think of her as his own. He struggled to turn away; he shouldn't be looking. But then his pants tightened even further when he noticed the feminine silhouette spill across the white makeshift curtain as she leaned against the slanted back of the tub.

He could see the shadow of soft, plump breasts and hardened nipples as she ran the soap over herself. How he longed to caress her. The tightness in his pants became unbearable. He thought of the kiss they had shared last night and realized he wanted her even more now than he had after tasting her beautiful mouth.

How on earth would he be able to take her to town come spring? The thought was depressing, agonizing. He had been so alone with only Loka for so many years. And now, having this pretty little angel around made him long for more. Hell, he needed more.

Maybe that's what Elijah had in mind all along. She had been such a Godsend for his isolated existence. He liked her company; they had many things in common. God, help him! He wanted her to stay. But how in hell could he ask her to stay and share his life when this was the first time in sixteen years she would have freedom? He had no choice but to live this way, but she did.

"Is that you, Noah?" she asked the obvious.

Noah swallowed back his thoughts and teased. "Nah, it's Loka."

"Very amusing, but then I guess if I ask a foolish question, I'll get a foolish answer," she laughed. "I'm almost finished."

"Take your time; I'll cut the bird up for frying."

"Imm, fried chicken, gracious, that sounds so good. I'm hungry, are you?"

"Starved," he answered, unable to take his eyes off her silhouette. The hunger he felt was for much more than food." He wanted to make love to her. He should do the gentlemanly thing and let her know how much of her, even in shadow, he could see. But hell, he wanted to see. And what she didn't know wouldn't embarrass her or *cause her to cover up.*

But the view was torture for Noah.

This was heaven; Cora felt she could laze here for hours. But of course, if she did, the water would be too cold. Noah would probably also like a bath. She lathered her skin and began to use her hands to scrub herself.

She should have seen if Noah had a washcloth. She had found his two towels but didn't look for anything else. She was so excited to take a bath. After about ten minutes, she stood from the water, carefully held onto the copper lip, and climbed out. First, one shapely leg, then the other. She pulled the soft hemp towel from the hearth warmed by the fire and swirled it around her nakedness. The towel was soft and toasty on her skin. First, she dried her hair and then her body.

Noah had a perfect view of her profile. God, he wished it was him drying off her beautiful body.

She stepped into a pair of pantalets and then shimmied into something that fell to her ankles. It did nothing to hide her shape or curb his imagination. Next came what looked like a dress, and he vaguely wondered where that came from. Then he remembered some of the clothing that had belonged to her mother. Items they had brought up this morning when they took things from her grandfather's cabin. She wanted so much to be the female she had been born to be.

And he wondered if she wanted him to notice she was a woman. Too late for that, he smiled; he already knew she was. And if she dressed to please him, she would get what she hoped for. He was pleased as punch. He silently watched her hold what he figured was a hand-held mirror and brush and begin to run the bristles through her shortened coal-black hair for several moments.

"Noah, are you still out there? It's awfully quiet."

"Yeah, I'm here," he slammed the cleaver he held against the hen's neck with a thunk on the cutting board. A few more chopping sounds, then he asked. "Do you need me to step outside for a moment?" He kept his eyes fixed on the hen as he chopped once, twice, and again.

"I'm dressed." She drew the curtain slightly open and peeked out. He was bent over the cutting board and concentrated on the hen. Another loud chop. His cheeks were a rosy red, and she hoped he didn't have a fever. She let the curtain fall back in place and checked herself in her tiny hand-held mirror. She had done all she could. The butterfly clip held her hair, leaving a few wavy wisps tickling and framing her cheeks. It would have to do. Her hair just wasn't long enough to do much more.

Noah felt like a heated stove when he heard her fully draw the curtain open and step out from behind, holding her skirt up to display the prettiest little toes and feet he'd ever seen. He quickly turned away and again focused on the hen.

"Are you all right?" she asked with concern. He looked like he had a fever. Sweat trickled down his neck and dotted his forehead. She quickly walked to his side and reached out to touch him.

He jerked sideways. "I'm fine," he snarled. Then he saw the hurtful expression on her face and the slight waver of her lower lip. Just because his body was out of whack didn't mean his words and mind had to be. "I am, just a little on the warm side." Hell, more like the hot side of hell after watching her shadow from behind the curtain. "Sorry, I barked. You look very pretty. Is that one of your mother's dresses?"

She met his very blue eyes and shyly smiled. "Yes, for the first time in years, I feel like..." she gulped, "a woman."

She definitely was a woman. *A woman who stirred his blood like no other ever had.* For the umpteenth time, he thought of the kiss they shared last night. *God forgive him; he wanted to be wrapped within her so much that* he hurt. These thoughts he kept to himself and smiled up to her from his chair. He glanced from her to the tub, now exposed by the open curtain. "I usually wash up down at the creek or in the kitchen using the sink in the winter." At the moment, he wondered if a dip in the ice-cold creek was just what he needed.

"Don't be silly. You will enjoy the tub. Although you are tall, it might not fit all of you like it did for me."

"I have used that kind of tub before. You are right. It is cramped, but it feels good to sit in hot water. My legs hang out at the end, but I can reach them to wash."

"I've got water heated for your bath; I can finish the cutting while you bathe."

"You'll ruin your dress, and I'm almost finished." The thighs, wings, and legs were already removed. He used the cleaver, split the breast, stood, took all the cut meat to the sink, and placed them in a bowl for washing. If you want to clean these, I'll take the tub outside and dump the used bath water. When I'm finished bathing, we can store the tub outside on the stoop by the door and under the overhang.

"All right." She timidly glanced down at herself. "I guess it was pretty silly of me to put this on. I just wanted to..."

"To feel pretty, and you are." He answered for her as he washed his hands. Reaching for one of the large sheets of hemp cloth, he tore it in half, "Come here and turn around."

She looked at him with surprise but did as he asked. He wrapped the material around her tiny waist and tied it at the back, covering the lower half of the dress. With the second piece of cloth he'd torn, he fashioned a triangle to let it flow down her front and tied a loose knot at the rear of her neck. "This should protect the dress."

"But now you won't have a clean towel for your use."

"I'll just use the one you had and hang it over the frame we made. It will dry soon enough next to the fire."

Cora felt a tingle when he touched her, and goosebumps formed as his fingers lingered. She wondered if he would kiss her again. Oh Lord, she wanted him to. But he didn't; instead, he dragged the tub out on the stoop and dumped the water. A couple of minutes later, he pulled the tub back in and went to get himself clean clothes, soap, and a washcloth. In the meantime, Cora refilled the tub with heated water. "I got the Dutch oven ready to place on the trammel.

He lifted the pot from her hands and hung it in the firebox.

Cora watched him step inside the small alcove, hang the heavy cooking pot, and close the curtain.

Silently, she listened as he undressed, then splashed the water as he climbed into the tub. The sounds sidetracked her momentarily, and she curiously wondered what he would look like naked. Tarnation! she chastised herself. What the devil was wrong with her? She blocked out the sounds of his bath and instead listened to the meat sizzle along with the cut potatoes, onion, and carrots as they began to cook inside the Dutch oven.

She glanced at the curtain he was behind and watched his shadow dance against the sheet as he climbed from the tub, careful not to splash water onto the floor. She found she couldn't keep her vision off him. His shadow against the curtain showed how beautifully built he was. Tall, lean. Broad shoulders, well-defined biceps, triceps, and long, powerful legs.

When he turned away from her, she could imagine the V shape of his back and how it trailed down to a narrow waist, hips, and buttocks. When he bent to retrieve his clean clothes, she saw the part of him that made him a man. This was something she had never seen before. But she knew the intimate portion of him would join with a woman. She drew a breath and clamped a hand to her breast when he began to cover himself with his clean longjohns. She felt the heat in her cheeks rise and yanked her vision away as he finished dressing.

Once again, the shadows played against the wall of material. Her heartbeat drummed inside her chest when she stepped back and foolishly realized that if she could see his delightful shadow across the sheet, how much had he seen of her reflection on the curtain?

Her cheeks heated.

"Damn, woman, this smells good."

She jumped like a child caught in mischief and nervously chuckled, trying to push her embarrassment aside. What was done was done. It was too late to change anything, but her next bath would be in daylight. "That's what my grandfather always said, excluding the part about calling me a woman. In many ways, he still thought of me as a child."

"I will never think of you as a child, even though I thought you were a young boy when I first found you. Guess that was pretty stupid."

"Not really, it meant my disguise worked."

He pushed the sheet aside and stepped out.

Cora gave him a side glance. He was clean-shaven, his mustache trimmed, and he smelled heavenly of washed man, a masculine musky scent that immediately stirred her already active imagination. Anything she cooked could never match his intoxicating scent; he was beautiful and gave her a dancing sensation deep in her stomach. She smiled as he stepped closer, not touching but only inches away. She sidestepped, pulled the curtain free, and folded it. She then went to the Dutch oven, lifted the lid, and flipped the meat and vegetables.

While she finished up, Noah drained the tub for a second time. "Tomorrow, I will devise a draining system for the sink; it will save time from dragging the buckets back and forth."

"That would be nice, and while you do that, I will do laundry out on the porch. I don't know about you, but I need clean clothes from top to bottom. Like this dress, the ones we brought back from the cabin still smell smoky. I was probably foolish putting the thing on; it needed washing."

"I don't know about that. You look so pretty and have such a wonderful scent of vanilla and lilac. I hardly notice anything else."

Her cheeks pinkened as she returned to the Dutch oven, removed the lid, and scooped out the meat and potatoes. She placed them on a tin plate and carried them to the table. Noah had reserved and separated the gizzard, liver, and heart from the grouse hen, which she quickly added to the vegetables on a plate for Loka. He immediately gobbled them up when he returned to the cabin.

Both she and Noah sat down at the table, and in a short time, their food quickly disappeared.

"The meat is tasty. What did you do with it to make it taste so good?"

"Rosemary, garlic, and a few other spices, which I dried last fall and brought up here from my grandfather's cabin. And some salt."

"Well, it's wonderful. Thank you."

They both cleaned up and occasionally found a reason to touch each other.

When Noah returned from dumping the dishwater, he said, "About the laundry, it's too damn cold outside to do it. So, if you wait until tomorrow afternoon, I will devise a draining system for the sink and cut a larger opening so you can wash the clothes inside the cabin and drain the water when you finish. We can use the bathing screen to hang our clothes before the fire. And in the spring, when the weather begins to simmer down, I'll build a clothesline for us." he paused.

What the hell was he doing? There could never be an *us*. He was making plans as if she would always be staying with him. Come spring, the only thing he should be thinking about is how he would have to find a way to take her down the mountain to town. She deserved a better life than he could ever give her. The way he had lived these past years, he knew it wouldn't be safe for her to stay. God, he felt like horse dung.

"That would be nice," she said, interrupting his depressing thoughts. "But if you knew how to do all these things, why haven't you done them? Noah, please don't feel you have to do them for me. I'm quite used to roughing it."

"I do this for both of us." Judas why the hell did he say that? He just been thinking about taking her down the mountain, but he couldn't stop himself.

"I just figured the time had come to use some of my knowledge. If anything, Cora, you inspire me. You see, I learned to do many things while living on my family's farm. Plumbing was only one of them. Unlike this place, we had an indoor washroom fixed with a regular tub, sink, and commode. I helped my father build a large kitchen. The house had four bedrooms, a parlor, and a huge fireplace. With Loka and me alone, I guess I never saw the need. Seems I gave up a lot of stuff. The spring house was already here. I cleaned it up for drinking water and to keep meat and other perishables fresh until I could dehydrate or smoke them."

"Had you given up on life that much?"

"It wasn't a matter of giving up. I didn't think I needed much. Never thought I would be sharing..."

"With me?" she interrupted.

"Or with anyone. Loka and I don't need much, but if I fix things up it will benefit all of us. And I should have done it long ago."

"I see, but Noah, please don't feel you need to do it for me. I am used to doing things independently and don't need much either."

But he wanted to give her everything, even if it was for just a short time. *Judas!* He wanted to pull her into his arms, kiss her sweet mouth, and travel over her face to the soft skin of her neck, the hollow below her dainty ear, and so much more, but he knew he would struggle to let her go if he did. It was best to keep his distance even if it hurt.

Cora thought he might kiss her like last night, but he moved quickly away, as if he might catch fire if he touched her. A sadness like thick molasses flowed through her. Maybe she was just so inexperienced she hadn't pleased him.

"We better head to bed and get some sleep. This time of year, daylight is so short, and we have much to do tomorrow." He stepped further away.

"I thought we might read for a while.

He looked over at her. There was a forlorn look in her topaz eyes, which made them look liquid in the dim light of the cabin. Ah hell, it wouldn't hurt to read for a little while, and it might give him something else to think about besides kissing, touching, holding, and loving. "Alright, would you like to read Frankenstein? But then maybe that isn't such a good idea for bedtime reading. It might give you nightmares," he grinned.

"Hardly," she grinned back. If I could handle Edgar Allen Poe's The Pit and the Pendulum in my cellar room, I can read Frankenstein without a problem." Besides she told herself, the scariness of the story might keep her mind off Noah's beautiful lips, the silky softness of his mustache, or his tongue grazing gently over her skin. And especially the press of his wonderfully masculine body against her own. "Would you like to read Jekyll and Hyde?"

"You surprise me all the time, you know. I can't believe you've read Edgar Allen Poe. How in the world did you keep that from your grandfather?"

"Like Jekyll and Hyde, the book belonged to my father. Grandfather never knew I had it. The story was frightening when I first read it. The horror of one man's impending death after being sentenced for heresy during the Spanish Inquisition. How the poor fellow had a mental breakdown as he made a choice of being thrown down a pit with bloodthirsty rats or having the sharp edge of a pendulum swinging back and forth, coming closer and closer with each horrific swing that would eventually cut him in half." She shook with repugnance.

"Yes, it was disconcerting, to say the least, but the man was saved at the end. However, I did not bring that one. It's one story that stays with you long after you finish. I will probably never reread it."

"Well, I'll take Jekyll and Hyde. Noah needed the distraction as much as she did.

She moved toward the small stack of books on the floor by the bed, lifted the one he requested, and handed it to him. "Here you go," she said.

Noah, in turn, rummaged through his pile, pulled out Mary Shelly's Frankenstein, and handed her his copy. "Tomorrow, we'll make room inside the trunk for your few books and mine. Or better yet I'll build some shelves for the wall above the bed."

"That would be nice, thank you."

She made herself comfortable on the bed by lying on her stomach, resting on her forearms and elbows. She crossed her legs at the ankles. Then, she began to turn pages and read from the open book.

Noah propped the pillow she had given him, lit the small lantern, and opened his book. After about an hour or so, he heard her yawn. When he leaned up to glance over, he saw her ebony head bob up and down, then plop down against her pillow with the book lying against her face.

He stood up and went to her, moved the book to the top of the trunk with a bookmark to save her place, and lifted the quilt over her. He blew out the lantern, pressed his lips against her cheek, returned to his makeshift bed on the floor, and set aside his book. Loka gave a big yawn, stretched, and leaped up beside her. In her sleep, she reached over and cuddled the wolf.

Noah didn't know how long he lay awake, wishing he was Loka spooning with his angel, but he must have drifted off at some point. The next waking thing he saw was morning sunlight as it streamed in through the window on the east. Cora was already up, the bed made. He could hear her make her way back from the outhouse. Snow crunched beneath her feet.

Noah quickly got up and pulled his pants on. He was buttoning his heavy flannel shirt when she stepped back into the cabin. Her ankle-length coat was sprinkled with snowflakes. *Christ on a crutch,* her smile was as pretty as a breath of spring. How on earth was he going to send her away?

Chapter Ten

Simon Mason watched his captain leave the soiled dove's room. She was one of the more popular girls in this place. They had already been in Chyenne for the past month, and now that winter was here, he figured they'd remain at least until spring. They had all taken the train from Denver, convinced they would once again find a clue where Noah had disappeared.

Simon thought back to the day they'd left the old man dead on the San Juan. And the unnecessary killing. The plan had been to keep after him for answers, but the captain, as usual, lost his temper. He'd killed that old mountain man, never getting the information he sought. Shoot first, then think about the consequences later, which were always the captain's thoughts. They burned the place down with the old man inside and rode off.

Simon was one of four men left, including the captain, who had participated in the original massacre back in seventy-eight. He had also been a friend to the young medic Noah, the only one in the unit who'd stood up to the captain.

Simon never wanted any part of the destruction or the death and blood either, but he had long ago admitted he was a coward and had turned on Noah just like every other man that day. Even when he saw Noah's sadness and betrayal, Simon ignored it and just kept riding with the captain and the other men, never looking back.

Things changed after the first few years, and now he was inundated with horrendous regrets. Too much killing and pillaging, even rape, over the years to keep track of the bloodlust. He carried enough guilt to sink a battleship. Besides, it was much too late to turn himself in. At least, that's the excuse he told himself to ease his conscience over the years. He could not help Noah and keep his own life. Things were different now. Maybe death was the only thing that would ease his guilt.

He didn't stay with the captain because he agreed with what happened that day. No, he hated what had gone on. Hated the frenzy of madness, yet he had taken part in it. A part he knew he would regret for the rest of his life. They were supposed to take prisoners. Captain Lamar Tamarin didn't want prisoners. He wanted them dead. Every last one of them. Old ones, young ones, and the women. God, the women trying to save their children.

The ground was drenched in blood where all the bodies lay along the banks of the Powder River. The women were saved for last. Raped multiple times and then slaughtered. He was every bit as culpable for the bloodshed, maybe not for the raping, but for the rest. He was one of the men who lined up the bone-thin warriors and shot them to death.

It's too late now to wish he'd stood with his friend.

He hadn't; water under the bridge now and forever.

Instead, Simon found himself just as wrapped up in the hellish behavior as the rest. Noah was the only one who refused to participate in the debauchery. He wanted to help those who were dying. No one listened.

They beat him and tied him down, forcing him to watch all the horror, then left him to die alone.

But Noah didn't die.

Simon was genuinely grateful Noah had escaped and made it back to the fort in one piece in the company of a wolf. Noah was half dead when he returned. But that wolf was something to see. Course, the men took shots at the animal, but he got away, not to be seen again. He often wondered if Noah and that wolf ever met up again or if one of the bullets had killed him.

Simon's shame and cowardice kept him from ever looking Noah in the eye the day he returned to the fort. None of them did. The captain had threatened each of the men in the weeks following to keep their mouths shut or suffer the consequences.

Captain Tamarin had a lot of importance in the day, not that he still didn't, but Simon knew if he ever turned on Tamarin, he would be a dead man or hunted down just as Noah was being hunted. Nearly eight years now starting with the release of the captain.

They were wasted years as far as Simon was concerned. The search, ordered by the captain even before leaving prison, had taken its toll on many men after the first few years. These last men he'd hired were the worst.

Simon thought back to the original twelve they had started with. Most just ran off because they were sick of the lifestyle. Not so much the killing but the nomadic way of living. Though none of them got the freedom they sought. Eventually, the captain caught up to them and either shot them for desertion or hung them. These last men he'd picked up were a mix of renegades, Comancheros, or just plain bloodthirsty tyrants. Only himself, Charley and Earl were left of the original men. But Charley and Earl had become as sadistic as the others. They all called Lamar, Captain.

Simon felt like the lowest human being for even being associated with them. He knew it was wrong to stay, but he did anyway. Cowardice made a man do many things. But Simon had his fill of it all.

He'd left a pretty gal he'd fallen for after the first year of the incident. But he left her behind anyway and followed the captain. By doing so, he'd given up any normal life he might have had. About a year later, he learned she had married and probably had a couple of kids by now.

Lamar made his way over to Simon's table. The man's stern, unattractive look said nothing of his thoughts. No anger or pleasure, maybe some determination, but you never could tell when it came to the captain. "Gather the men," he ordered with no room to argue. "We're heading back toward the San Juan. There's a small town with little law about halfway there. We'll stop and wait out the worst of the winter, then ride south again. The old bastard lied. Harper is up in the San Juan somewhere, and this time, we'll find the traitor. The bastard will pay!

Simon choke back the bile he felt fill his throat.

Cora glanced at Noah and smiled as he buttoned his shirt and straightened his collar. "You are up. I hope I didn't wake you," she said, quietly shutting the door behind her. "It's a beautiful morning. The sun is out, and the snow sparkles like a fairy's wand has sprinkled her magic dust over the mountain. It's so nice to see, especially when the winters are so bitter and cold up here. Seeing such a serenely beautiful beginning of the day is very agreeable. Each time I step outside, I feel like I'm entering a new world."

She watched him grin.

"I'm doing it again, aren't I? Yammering on and on. I'll make a fresh pot of coffee and another batch of biscuits. Maybe the next time we go down to my grandfather's cabin, we can tear apart the beehive oven we used for baking, and I will make bread. Maybe a pie or two. Do you like pie, Noah?"

Noah chuckled; the little angel never stopped talking. But he loved how it filled his lonely heart. "An oven? I don't remember seeing anything like that."

The oven is out back behind the lean-to," her lips curled in a pleasant smile.

"Trying to hall that kind of heavy load up the pass would be near impossible. I'd say we make drawings of the design. It's been a long time since I've tasted homemade bread, and I definitely love pie. Some wild raspberries and blueberries grow all over the mountain in the spring. Even wild strawberries."

"I know we had them grow around our cabin, too," Cora told him. "I can use them for pie and make some berry jam when they come in season. How does that sound? One day, I would like to plant a couple of apple trees. Wouldn't that be wonderful?"

Noah couldn't help it. Even after thinking about not getting too emotionally involved with her, he said, "Sounds like heaven."

Cora loved making him happy. She quickly started the coffee, and soon, the cabin filled with the delightful scent. "Today, I will work on cleaning out the pot belly stove. The flat top will make a good place to cook smaller items, like the coffee pot and the frypan for biscuits."

"I'll check out the stove pipe to ensure it is still in good working condition while you clean the inside. But at the moment, I'm going to take a trip to the outhouse, and I'll be right back," he told her.

She nodded and began mixing the biscuit dough and sectioning it in the Dutch oven. They were baking when he returned to the cabin.

"The coffee is almost done," Cora said with a smile.

"Great, I don't know if I mentioned it, but you make the best-tasting coffee."

"That's one thing my grandfather would have agreed with you. However, it did take the first year I lived with him to learn the right amount to add."

Noah inclined his head, grabbed his guitar from the case that leaned against the wall, moved to the table, and took a seat. He drew the instrument across his lap and began to tune it. "What kind of music do you like?"

Her sultry eyes sparkled. "Any kind!"

"Good. There are a lot of songs I know, but many that I don't." He began to tune the guitar using the tuning pegs as he moved down the fretboard, tightening the strings. The sounds went from low to high as he shuffled his fingers up and down along the strings at each frat point.

The beautiful sounds made Cora feel giddy. She began to step side to side, back and forth, as if she were dancing a fast-paced waltz.

"You like to dance, do you?"

She swung around; her cheeks were flushed. "I don't remember much; it's been years. But I remember my mother and I moved about the parlor in a box-like configuration, and dip and bough it would make my father chuckle. We held one another by a hand and gripped the other's shoulder or waist. It was more of a hug, but we had fun as my father played his fiddle. What about you? When did you learn to play? And did you dance also, maybe with your sisters?"

Noah continued to run his fingers over the strings while his opposite hand and fingers pressed the upper strings. He returned to the tuning pegs if it didn't sound right. As his head remained bent down, working the steal strings, memories swam through his mind as he softly spoke.

"I learned to play from my father," he told her, still checking the sounds. "As a boy, the guitar always fascinated me, so he taught me to read music and all the different cords. Took some time not only to learn but to toughen my fingertips. But once I got the logistics, I played all the time. Many evenings, we played together while my mother and sisters danced around our parlor, much like you and your mother.

"Sometimes, either my father or I would play a solo while the other danced with the ladies. It's been a long time for me as well. But the guitar playing I did for years. Even in the Army, I would play for the men in the barracks or at night when we made camp.

"When I left the military, I continued to play in different towns at dance halls while the patrons and the girls who worked there would dance. It gave me spending money and places to stay. Though I never remained long, I moved frequently from one town to another. The last place I played was in Cheyenne, Wyoming. That was eight years ago. When I left there, I headed south and stopped moving around once I got here."

"Dance halls?"

This time, his cheeks flashed red. "Um, yeah."

"Is a dance hall a place where couples go to dance?"

How did he answer that without tripping over his tongue? He nodded with hesitance and finally responded to her question. "They are also called a saloon. Men would go to play cards or drink and spend time with the night gals. A saloon is where you could do all three."

"Grandfather said they were no place for a lady. The women who worked there were called strumpets. But he would never tell me what that meant."

Christ, on a crutch, how the hell did he explain that one? Damn, sometimes he had such a big mouth. "In all the books you've read, have you never come across a description of a lady of the night? You know, like a Courtesan."

"Oh my!" She covered her lips. The Coffee pot on the grate in the firebox hissed as the dark caramel brew bubbled onto the hot coals. She turned back, grabbed a pot holder, and lifted the hot vessel off the heat. "Did you spend time with these Courtesans?"

"Would your opinion of me be lower if I said yes?"

"No, I understand you were lonely, just as some men were in my books. So, you did spend time with them." She filled two tin cups and placed them on the table, trying desperately not to look at him. He would be able to see everything in her heart, especially her fear.

He set the guitar aside and silently watched her. He knew she was embarrassed. "Look, Cora. I'm sorry if I upset you. Please forgive me." He studied the brilliance of her topaz eyes as they peeked through thick, dark lashes. Seconds later, she sat across from him and sipped from her cup. Afterward, she fidgeted with her fingers, giving the impression she'd rather be anywhere else as she uncomfortably wiggled in her chair.

Judas, what an idiot he was; he never should have opened his mouth. "I did once in a while. I got lonely, and a few of the ladies offered me comfort. I was a lot younger, and on the run, there were just some days I needed comfort. I didn't live as a monk if you were wondering."

"Is that why you haven't kissed me again because, in my foolish innocence, I offered no comfort? You see, that was my first kiss. I have never known a man." She felt a tear take flight and begin to cloud her vision. So, I'm sure I shocked you with my inexperience and gave you no comfort. I guess I am a stupid fool."

All this time, he thought he was protecting her from his essential male nature and knowing he would have to let her go in the near future. But apparently, by trying to shield her from his physical response, he had inadvertently hurt her feelings. "No, Cora, your kiss was special, and I... well, I didn't want to take advantage. Or frighten you. You certainly aren't stupid or foolish. I have been impressed with your intelligence and your friendship from the beginning. Inspired by your fortitude, your love of life." Then he grinned. "Hell, I think Loka likes you better than he does me.

"But Cora, you have lived a cloistered lifestyle with your grandfather. He kept you hidden for years. You've never lived a life among other people. Good people, not like me or like those men who came to your cabin. Despite all that, you have learned kindness and trust. Your love of reading is wonderful, and now I learn you love music too. Dear God, you are one of the most naturally pretty and intelligent women I have ever met. I like talking to you and spending time with you. Never think I'm not attracted to you because I am. I just..."

"Didn't want to mate with me," she finished. "I understand, and I feel very foolish for thinking otherwise. Books were and are my friends. As I've said, my grandfather wasn't much of a talker unless he tutored me in school learning; even then, it was minimal. I know you are just trying to be kind. I also know I'm not much to look at. I'm just some undesirable, backward girl who dressed like a boy for years. Tarnation, Noah, how on earth could I have thought any differently? You had a life once. You've been with other women who pleased you, a pleasure I'm sure I wouldn't begin to know how to do." She stood up and moved to the sink.

He swallowed so hard he nearly choked on his coffee. What had he done? He had never once thought the things she was saying. She nervously rinsed a cloth and began to wipe the counter, scooping up crumbs only she could see. She moved to the fireplace, lifted the Dutch oven lid, and quickly removed the biscuits. Damnit, he cursed himself. He stood and moved up behind her and gently placed his hands at her waist, cradling her before he turned her around.

"Don't! Please don't pity me," she cried. "I never should have let my imagination control my thoughts and feelings. I have nothing to offer an educated man like you. You're a white man, and I'm part Cheyenne. I created a life of fantasy through my books. So please leave me be. I don't need sympathy. I know very well what I am."

She moved to step away, but Noah would not release her. "This is too important. You will listen to me."

Cora's heart felt like it would leap from her chest. There was something different in the deep sky blue of his eyes.

And it was not pity.

Was it desire?

How the devil would she know? Her grandfather was right; she should have stayed as a boy. "I should have stayed that way." She didn't realize she said this part aloud until she saw the look in his eyes. He looked angry as he huffed out a breath. She shivered despite the warmth coming from the fire.

Chapter Eleven

"Stayed what way?" Noah demanded, giving her a look of blue fire.

"A boy!" she blurted out.

Noah's concern turned to what seemed like an all-knowing smile. "That would have been very difficult to pull off, Cora. You have the most feminine curves, the softest skin, and a mouth only a man can dream about kissing. Remember, I took care of you the first day. I was, for a better word, aroused by your beauty, you are, beyond a doubt, very desirable." He watched the light in her eyes begin to flicker. God she was beautiful.

"Hell no, I don't feel sorry for you. I'm as emotionally and physically stirred up as you are. Secondly, you have given me such joy these last few weeks. A joy I never thought I would or could ever feel again. He released her waist and lifted one hand to caress her warm cheek. "I enjoyed kissing you more than any other woman, and that was my problem. I wanted your touch so much that my mind and body craved more. You are innocent and young, and I repeat, the last thing you are is foolish! I just did not want to frighten you. Or take something from you that can never be mine. You need a life off this damn mountain."

"What are you saying? I'm not a child, and I am not that young! I'm a woman," she said indignantly. "And my life up here is what I know. I have no desire to go anywhere else. Especially now that I felt the magical things inside my body when you kissed me the other night. Maybe I'm not supposed to have such blasphemous feelings. Maybe it's a sin, or something is wrong with me, and I shouldn't feel what I do. Maybe only those night ladies you saw feel such things, and only they can..."

"Good God, no! Those women are the ones who don't feel the magic. They are with so many men night after night that they've learned not to feel anything. Most want to get their money and be done with it. Knowing that I make you feel those wonderful things pleases me more than you know."

He moved from her cheek to her mouth and caressed her with the pad of his thumb, then pressed her against him and lifted her to his mouth. He could feel her heartbeat hammer against his chest as he deepened the kiss. "You have such a beautiful mouth. Any man would want to kiss you. That was a truth Noah realized he didn't like. He felt a heady stream of jealousy scream through him. He selfishly didn't want anyone else to kiss her.

Christ on a crutch! He wanted her for so many different reasons. As she pressed her body against his and he heard the soft whimper of arousal escape her lips, he slipped his tongue out and began to bathe her outer lips. "Open your mouth for me," he whispered. "Let me taste you."

The words sent such an incredible warmth through Cora that she couldn't help but do as he asked, and when their tongues met, her body reacted to the deep, growing fire within her. She pushed closer to the feel of his hardened length as he pressed enticingly against her softness.

There was such an incredible rush of pleasure crashing through her body. Tarnation; she never wanted the physical or the profound emotions they stirred ever to disappear. She needed and wanted all of it. All of him. But was it wrong? Then she didn't care. She lifted her arms, clasped her hands at the back of his neck, and gently moved her fingers through his thick, wavy, chestnut hair; it felt like velvet to her exploratory fingertips. And when she heard his aroused moan, she felt a kind of power she'd never felt before. He liked her touch. This knowledge sent her emotions soaring.

Noah lifted his mouth and gazed into her desire-filled topaz eyes. God, she was precious.

The silky softness of his mustache brushed across her heated skin when he smoothed his face against hers and then returned to her lips. For the first time in her life, Cora felt wanted, and filled with profound need when their lips, tongues, and bodies began a sensual dance. He unlocked something in her heart, and her body. The idea sent her spirit soaring.

She knew about desire and how it affected a man physically through her reading, but she never knew the effect it would have on her. But he said it was natural and that the women of the night didn't experience the things she was feeling. Was this what her parents felt the night she quietly watched before her mother noticed her standing in the doorway? *Sweet harmony,* she hoped that was true because this warmth and pleasure that was singing through her body felt like the soft, thick flow of sweet honey, and the sensation gave her such a hunger she wasn't sure she would ever get enough.

His lips and tongue were the most perfect aphrodisiac in the world. And when he tasted her, mated with her tongue, the inside of her cheeks, lips, and the warm, wet sensuality of her. She followed his lead and returned his kiss, tasted him. She felt her body react. Her breasts began to swell against the cotton bodice of the dress she wore, and she sighed against his moist mouth as her nipples rose to heightened awareness. She wickedly wondered what they would feel like if he touched or kissed her there.

God help him; Noah wanted to touch her body, cup her breasts, and suckle on her nipples. Reach down between her thighs and caress the sweet honey of her femininity. Mate with her as she had said. No, he wanted more. He wanted to make love to her in every way, know every inch of her body. Be one with her, fill her with himself. After several minutes of kissing, his logical mind finally leaped to attention. He knew he could never let her go if he physically loved her all the way. She had to experience real life away from this Godforsaken Mountain. He could offer her nothing, only his love, and just love was not enough.

The devil take him, but the last thing he needed was to fall in love, but sure as the sun rises that was what was happening to him. He quickly realized he was as vulnerable as she.

He released her mouth and took a step back. Her cheeks were flushed with desire, igniting him further. It would be so easy to undress her and take her to bed. Instead, he murmured against her moist lips. "Does that tell you how much I enjoy kissing you?"

Cora's legs felt limp, like a stretched piece of rubber that had lost its elasticity. Her lips were slightly swollen, and she instinctively knew they looked like they had been thoroughly kissed.

"Another thing, my sweet angel," he continued. "I have never kissed anyone the way I just kissed you. Not even that neighbor girl I told you about. That was only a drop in the bucket compared to what you and I just did. He noted the shock and questions in her eyes and smiled down at her. "Really!" He truthfully admitted. "Never."

She gave him a nervous half-smile and took a step back. "Well, that is the second time for me. And this last one was more powerful than the first kiss you gave me."

Noah changed the subject. "Can we have our coffee and biscuits now?"

"Yes, I think that would be a good idea. And Noah, I have no objections if you want to repeat what we just did." Without another word, she turned to get the plate of biscuits and carried them to the table where they could enjoy them together.

After sharing the hot drink and the food, Noah began inspecting the stove pipe. She was correct; the kiss was more powerful than the last one. He could still feel his arousal pressing tightly against the front of his pants.

Cora moved over to the bed with the sack of clothes she'd brought from her grandfather's cabin. It's funny how she never thought of it as hers. It was always his.

She began to sort, separating underthings from regular clothes made for a boy. She glanced down at herself and the dress she wore. Even this hadn't been hers, merely a hand-me-down from her mother. She really had nothing feminine of her own. And hadn't since the day she came up here with her grandfather.

Even her ugly hair was made to look like a boy. The thick braid she'd worn as a young girl had been chopped off, leaving what was left to look like a Dutch boy haircut with short bangs. It was how she imagined Huckleberry Finn's hair was in the story beneath his straw hat.

Her grandfather had always insisted she cut it every spring, just as it began to look girlish. She had tried to argue with him. She was a girl. No one would see her; why couldn't she look like a girl? And when she began to develop as a young woman, she had to bind herself up. He told her one never knew when they might have someone wander into their camp. But tarnation, she hated it.

Lawd, she wanted so much to look pretty for Noah. Again, she looked down at her meager things. Only a couple of pantaloons and two chemises. One she used as a nightgown. Both were threadbare after years of use.

She needed material to make new things. She had some cloth to make shirts back at the cabin, but foolishly, she hadn't brought any of it up here. The material and patterns once belonged to her mother. She had planned to sew them during the winter while she and her grandfather mostly stayed inside. She should have stashed the cloth with her other personal items.

She could have fashioned the cotton into new underthings, maybe even a dress or two if only she could get the material. The majority of these items lying on the bed needed a good washing. Most everything was dirty or smoky smelling. Even her mother's things smelled of smoke.

"Noah?"

He poked his head around the pipe. "I'm almost done."

"I wasn't asking. I have a small trunk back at the cabin I used to keep my clothes in. We didn't have room for it this time, and I was wondering if we could get my trunk when we go back down to check out the beehive oven. I have nowhere to keep my clothing or my extra material and patterns. I don't have much, but what I have I would like to keep clean by storing them inside my trunk like I used to do and like you do inside yours."

Hell, what was wrong with him? He should have thought of that himself. "If this weather holds through tomorrow, we can head down first thing in the morning. If not, after I fix the draining system, I'll get busy with the shelfs above the bed, we talked about. There is enough wood in the shed. I can make you one. How does that sound?" he asked, then strategically changed the subject. "I wonder where Loka got off to?"

"He followed me out to the outhouse earlier and waited for me. He ran off into the woods when I returned to the cabin."

"He has become quite protective of you, hasn't he?"

"I guess he has, and frankly, it is kind of nice."

"Even though he still has a wild side, he is a good judge of character," Noah added with a smile before returning to his work.

"I know he is," she agreed. "After all, he loves you, and I know he would protect you with his life," she smiled dreamily.

"Yes, he would and already has. The day we got to the fort all those years ago, some of the soldiers took shots at him, and he ran off. I was afraid I would never see him again. But there he was waiting for me when I resigned my commission and made the promise to return and testify. Clear as a raindrop on the tip of my nose, he ran to me once I was clear of the fort. We made camp for the next couple of months while awaiting the trial to get underway. When the legal proceedings were finished, we left together."

"That's a miracle."

"I thought so. He has remained a good and loyal friend over the years. Anyway, back to your trunk; if we cannot retrieve it, would you let me make one for you? I actually made my own."

"That would be a great idea. The one I had is also homemade. My grandfather made it for me when he first brought me to his place. So, we won't need to return to the cabin until spring. It is already early December, and one never knows when the weather could drastically change, especially this time of year. It could be sunny in the morning, then turn to a giant snowstorm by early afternoon. I'd hate to get trapped down there with no shelter. It was bad when I came up here that first day. I'm lucky you found me, even though I thought you might be a Yeti," she giggled.

"And I thought you were a young boy, so I guess we are even," he chuckled and crawled out from behind the stove pipe before disappearing outside for about twenty minutes. When he returned, he came in with black metal sheeting squares, which he cut and used to reinforce the stove pipe in several places.

"This pipe should work properly if you want to check the inside of the stove. While you do that, I've designed a draining system for the dry sink. In the next hour or so, he used a hand drill with a brace and auger bit to crank out a hole in the bottom of the sink. He then ran some tubing from the hole to the outside and fastened everything down.

He grabbed the bucket he'd filled earlier with water and poured a third down the drain. Immediately, the liquid emptied outside. It worked perfectly. He stepped out onto the narrow porch and brushed himself off, removing the loose dust from the stove pipe and the drain, and put his tools away, stepping back into the cabin.

"I also fashioned a plug to hold the water," he was saying when he stepped back into the cabin but came to a dead stop as he watched Cora pull her head out of the stove's opening. She was covered in black soot from head to toe.

"Oh good, as soon as I finish this, I'll start on the laundry," she said when she stood up and turned to him, catching the amused look on his face. "What's so funny?" She looked so comical that Noah couldn't help but snicker. You'll probably need to launder yourself before you start that."

"What do you mean?"

Noah took the mirror from the back door and handed it to her.

"Oh, my lawd!" She started laughing. "Well, I guess you're right. Tarnation." Self-consciously, she wiped her face with equally sooty hands.

Noah laughed all the harder. "You can do laundry tomorrow."

"I can do both. Besides, I have run out of everything. Why should I put it off until tomorrow when it can be done today? I'll wash me up first. After all, you worked on fixing the stove pipe and building a draining system all morning. The least I can do is our laundry."

"All right then, if you are sure, I'll gather the clothes, but I can do my own. They are much heavier than yours."

"Don't be silly, my grandfather's certainly weren't lightweight."

Noah's eyes brightened. "Okay, then tomorrow we will see what the weather's like. If it's good, we'll head down to your grandfather's first thing in the morning. I'm itching to check out that oven, the thought of fresh baked bread and pie makes my mouth water."

Cora dipped her head and hid a grin. "I'll just check out this sink and wash up. If you want to collect your laundry, I'll get started. When she finished cleaning herself, she gathered her clothes, brought them to the sink, and moved the privacy screen before the fireplace to use as a clothesline. Her cheeks heated when she remembered how she could see Noah's silhouette on the curtain when he was bathing.

Noah stepped outside and returned in a few minutes with the washboard. "The soap is in a metal container in the cupboard below the sink."

"And your dirty clothes?"

He walked across the cabin, and in a laundry bin by his trunk, he dumped out his dirty clothing and placed it on the floor next to hers. "I hope you know what you're getting into. My clothes get pretty dirty, what with my traps, gutting, and skinning."

"Mine can get just as bad. Trust me. Look at me right now. No one would say my cleanliness is next to Godliness. Thank goodness I used some of my raggier things. I think these are quite ruined."

He started chuckling again, "I think you are right."

"Haha! Why don't you check out the job I did inside that stove and see if you think we can use it."

He bent down and looked inside. The inside was spotless. No wonder she was wearing all blackened soot. "This looks fantastic, honey. You did a great job. I'll put some wood in and fire it up. Later, if you are up to it, we can walk up the hill and check out my traps. It's been a few days."

"Sure, like I said, it is a nice day, and fresh air sounds glorious. And I feel like I've been lazy since coming here. I'm used to doing almost everything myself. Grandfather struggled with his rheumatism a lot in the winter. Somedays, his joints would swell up something fierce, so I learned to do most of the lifting and checking traps. I also did pretty much all of the butchering. It was nice the original Jones who lived here had so many helpful items like wood, and pipe."

"I collected many of the supplies in the shed over the years myself. When Elijah went to town on his yearly supply run. He would pick up the things I needed and gather lots of scraps that many had tossed out. I suppose Jones, who inhabited this place, planned to do some upgrading here and there but ended up passing before he got the chance. He must have had a mule or horse at one time; there are still remnants of an old corral that I intend to fix. Elijah was going to get me another mule this spring, but..."

"He was killed."

Noah nodded, "I will miss him. He allowed me to stay hidden. Hopefully, enough time has passed, and I can make the trip myself. It's been eight years since I've seen the town. If I'm lucky, no one will remember me, or at least not care.

"Grandfather said it has changed a lot. People come and go. Businesses close while others open. They have a General Store now, he told me. And next year, they will build a hotel for when the railroad comes through."

That thought made Noah a bit nervous. That meant more people, but he said, "No matter where a body goes, there is always progress. Good for some, not so good for others."

"Noah, if you do go, I would very much like to go with you, please."

He glanced over to her. She was giving him the excuse he needed to free her, but for now, he would remain silent and keep it to himself. "Tell you what, if I go, I will take you, but if anybody asks. We will tell them we are new to town, and you are my wife. Would you agree to that?"

"Yes," she answered with excitement. How wonderful it would be if only that were true, she thought.

After the laundry was done and hanging over the privacy rack before the fire and a quick lunch of smoked venison and hot coffee, they went outside to check traps. Loka was waiting on the stoop. When the door opened, he dashed inside and ran to his water trough. Cora scooped up the leftover meat and vegetables and placed them in a bowl for the wolf. It was gone in seconds. "I guess he was hungry and thirsty." Cora chuckled.

"He's always hungry, probably why he hunts so much."

Ten minutes later, all three left the cabin and went through a forest of tall ponderosa and Douglas fir. Most of the branches were laden with snow. Everything was beautiful, pristine, and snowy white.

"I really hate traps, Cora admitted as they checked the first one, which was empty. "I would rather just shoot dinner. It's less of a struggle for the animal, and it's over much quicker. I hate to see an animal suffer. What if Loka got trapped in one of them?"

"I don't like them much either. But it has given me enough fur for clothing and some money off the pelts over the years. My traps are snares, not conventional steel traps. Steele traps can injure the animal, not to mention ruin the fur and, often, the meat. Loka is gentler on them than any steel trap would be. And as you can see, I don't use them. I use robe snares that snap the neck, instant death. Basically, they are for rabbits or squirrels and occasional raccoons, and up a little higher by the stream, there are a few beavers. It takes large quantities even to make a hat.

"That's basically what my grandfather did. I would worry about Loka getting caught in one, though. He is much taller, and the snag would not be strong or high enough to break his neck. He could be caught for a long time. And other animals might get to him."

"Loka knows to stay away, though he has occasionally chased a few into my traps. He alerts me when he does by giving off a howl to let me know he has trapped one and to alert any larger game to stay away. I made sure he was well-trained, though still give him the freedom he needs for the wild. I have had him since he was a pup, like I told you, and he is the one thing that kept me alive when I left the village."

He reached over and squeezed Cora's gloved hand. Her smile was the most beautiful thing he'd ever seen.

The following three traps were also empty. "As you can see, I'm not very good at this. If it weren't for my rifle and Loka, I would have probably starved to death and lived naked," he gave Cora a side look of amusement when he noted her pink cheeks and lowered eyes. Let's head back to the cabin."

As they began to move back down the trail, they heard a loud rustling and crashing noise about twenty yards to the east, just beyond a narrow clearing along the rocky slopes. Noah held his index finger to his lips as he watched the surprise on Cora's face. Loka took off toward the sound. "I'll bet it's a buck," Noah whispered and lifted his breech, loading Sharps from his back to the crook of his arm, moving toward the clearing.

They heard Loka's growl, and the closer they got, they could see a four-point buck trapped against a rocky wall. Loka was making sure there was no escape. Noah raised the rifle to his shoulder and gazed down the gun's site with his finger on the trigger.

Cora's heart began to pound inside her chest. "Don't hit Loka!" she ground out between her teeth. But she didn't need to worry. Noah was an excellent shot, and Loka was extremely wise.

The wolf sensed their arrival and slightly backed off. Noah fired before the deer had a chance to run. The animal dropped straight down, and Loka began to do his excited growl and bark mix. He danced around the body. "We'll have meat for the next few months and much to do. You know it's funny, while in the Army, I did not carry a gun because I was there to heal, not kill, but since coming up here, I have frequently used my rifle."

"To survive out here, you need one," she added.

"So, I've learned," he grinned down to her.

They each grasped a side of antlers and began to drag the carcass down the incline and toward the cabin.

Halfway there, the sky turned a dark gray, and snowflakes tickled Cora's nose and lips. She stuck her tongue out and caught several.

"Looks like we won't be going down to Elijah's cabin any time soon," Noah stated.

Cora lowered her head in disappointment. "I'm afraid you are right. You got me excited about making fresh baked bread and pie."

"Do you think you can remember how he made it?" Noah asked.

"No, dagnabit, it was already made when he first brought me here.

Noah crooked a brow at her scrunched-up expression. "You might want to straighten your face up, honey; you wouldn't want it to freeze that way."

"Huh!" she huffed, perplexed. "Do you think we could rig some kind of rack for the inside of the stove and use that for an oven?"

"Hmm, maybe; let me think and see what I can come up with." He looked over to her and winked. "Ah huh, I think I see your frown turning upside down."

Cora giggled.

They continued to pull their heavy burden of meat over the snow and down the hill to the cabin.

Chapter Twelve

The early winter storm moved on; a tease Mother Nature often gave in the high country. The sunny weather held and continued through the next couple of days. They decided to make the second trip down to Elijah's cabin. It was mid-morning when they arrived. First, Cora retrieved her small trunk. She packed some more books, this time a collection of Shakespeare. A couple of romance stories, including Mansfield Park, Persuasion and Emma by Jane Austen.

They tore through the outside storage and retrieved sacks of flour, cornmeal, yeast, a small container of sugar, and all the dried meat that was still edible. She also had yarn stored that she placed in her trunk; she could use this to make warm socks and caps. There were only a few patterns for shirts and a couple of dresses, all out of date, but that didn't matter. She was excited to make new clothing for both herself and Noah. Over the years, she had become quite efficient with needles and threads.

While Noah hauled the dry goods and the stored vegetables and placed them on the travois, Cora deposited her trunk on the ground. She would let Noah organize the way he wanted. He was particular about how he packed, and she understood.

She remembered the cash box her grandfather had told her about the day he died, a secret she had pushed from her mind. She wasn't sure she should tell Noah about the money. She knew he was nervous about keeping her here with him, and what was in this box would give him a reason to leave her in town and out of his life. She couldn't stand that thought but knew she needed to get the box. The money could mean everything to both of them.

They both agreed that tearing down the oven was impossible and too heavy to drag back to the cabin. So, Noah grabbed his sketch pad and began making drawings of the large oven. While he did this, Cora made her way to the lean-to. Everything was as she had left it after saddling up Sugar Loaf. She moved to the corner where a few stacks of hay and other tools were used for the care of the mule and began to dig for the hidden cash box. She found what she was looking for about two feet down and lifted it from the ground.

The box was heavy. "Tarnation!" *The thing must weigh at least thirty pounds if not more!* She lifted the lid. There was a note on top and beneath it a lot of money. Where on earth did her grandfather get all this cash? She let that thought go and began to think of all the things she and Noah could get with this money. The thought only lasted a few seconds when her doubts began to filter in.

She quickly slammed the lid down. What if Noah used this money to persuade himself that she was better off without him? There was that note on top with a possible explanation. No, she would let sleeping dogs lie, as the saying went. She dropped the box back into the hole and began covering it with dirt.

"Hey Cora, I've finished my drawings. I'm not sure we can replicate the oven. I may have to design my own. I also found your grandfather's Old Sharps rifle. Do you want to take it with us? Believe it or not, it is still in good shape. Why didn't you bring it when you went looking for me?" Noah stepped inside the lean-to and watched her drop something into a hole and try to cover it. "What are you doing?"

Cora swung around with a guilty look and began to stand. He was holding the rifle in his right hand.

"What are you hiding?"

"I'm not hiding anything, then her conscience got the best of her. She simply could not lie to this man. Instantaneously, she broke down and told Noah. "I'm digging up something my grandfather hid and told me about before he died. Oh, Noah, please don't use this to abandon me in town when we go."

He gave her an odd look, "I would never abandon you. I believe you would be better off and able to make a good life for yourself. You don't deserve to be stuck here with me. No hope. No future. So again, what was buried in the ground?" He was starting to sound a bit miffed. And the fear built stronger in her heart.

"My grandfather's cash box. He asked me to take it with me when I searched for you. But I had no time. I needed to leave immediately if I were to find you before nightfall. Then I got caught in that snowstorm, and the whole thing slipped my mind. Even when we came down here the first time, I didn't think about it. However, this time, I remembered, but now I wish I hadn't."

Noah lifted one quizzical brow in a manner that reminded her of a squashed question mark. "I see; what's in it that's got you so skittish?"

Once the container was again pulled free, they both carefully lifted the lid and looked inside. Dozens of silver dollars, a large bundle of stacked paper money filling the medal box, and a note addressed to Cora just under the lid. Noah pulled the note free and handed it to her.

She quickly unfolded the paper and began to read aloud.

Cora, my dearest granddaughter,

I know this life we live has not been the easiest for you. But I felt you should know if anything happens to me, this money will help tide you and Noah over. It is my life savings. I never trusted banks. This is all money I have earned over the years. Noah is an intelligent man, and whether he will admit it or not, he is also a lonely man, just as you are a lonely young woman. For this, I am sorry. I know life has been hard on you pretending to be a boy, but I thought it was the best way to protect you. I have no doubt you and Noah will be good company for each other. You both deserve the best. Use this money wisely when the time comes. I love you, sweetheart, more than you could ever know. And I am sorry I did not express this while alive. Forgive me,

Elijah Franklyn, your loving grandfather.

With tears in her eyes, Cora refolded the note and placed it back inside the box; she was never quite sure the older man truly loved her. There were times he could be so stern and showed very little emotion when it came to her, never a hug. She often wondered if she were nothing more than a burden to him. After all, he had always been a loner, especially since her grandmother had passed away and then her mother and father, the reason she came to live with him.

But he must have loved her. He taught her many things over the years. How to be self-reliant, how to hunt, process the meat, and work with hides. He always made sure she had all that she needed. And now, after reading his note, she knew he loved her in his own way. And he wanted her and Noah to be together. This last part made her wildly happy.

"This money belongs to you," Noah said with conviction. He lifted the box as if it weighed nothing, carried it out of the lean-to. He separated the coin from the paper to lighten the load, placed them in a gunny sack and tossed the medal box aside.

Cora followed him, but she was so scared Noah would use this as an excuse to take her down the mountain to town and leave her because he believed she would have a good life without him. Why couldn't he realize there was no life down there for her? Not without him.

That evening, after returning to the cabin, the snow came. A storm that lasted for the next three days and laid another six to seven feet across the landscape.

The money was not spoken of again, though the atmosphere between them was as cold as the weather. Finally, on the evening of the third day, the sky cleared, allowing a parade of stars to cover the night sky. A quarter moon hung like a lopsided teeter-totter.

Noah was busy at the table as he'd been the last few nights with paper and pencil trying to design an outdoor oven.

Cora could no longer take the silence that had fallen between them. "How's the plans coming?"

"I think I might have figured something out."

"Really?"

"He chuckled; "just cook it in the Dutch Oven."

"Oh, you," then she chuckled. For the first time in days, the mood had begun to lighten. "But you know that isn't such a bad idea; I should have thought of it myself. And now that we have flour to work with, I could even make a pie or a fruit cobbler. We absolutely should try it."

Noah continued to jot figures down. Like her, he was tired of the silence between them. Over the last several days, he had wondered if she was afraid that he would steal the money and leave her with nothing. The thought made him angry, but the light in her eyes this evening dissuaded the thought. What she was afraid of, he realized, was that he would take her to town and leave her so she could make a new start without him, which is exactly what he had been thinking. She would be better off without him.

This money could give her a head start. He would ensure she was set up, maybe with her own house, a job at the General Store, or even the library. She loved to read. She would make a great asset to the town.

Though he knew it would be the best thing for her, the thought broke his heart. Judas, he had gone and fallen in love with her. The thought of her making a life without him gave him such a depressing feeling. And worse, the idea of another man ever laying a hand on her shot a jealous rage through him that funneled deep inside. After supper that night, he pleaded sleepiness and went to bed without another word.

Sometime after midnight, he began to shift wildly on his pallet. He shouted incoherently, kicked his covers off, and moved his head in a frenzy of back-and-forth movements.

Cora jerked awake and frantically glanced down from her higher perch. Noah had kicked off his covers and lay only in his long johns, which were scrunched up to his knees. His feet were bare, his toes curling inward. Quickly, she crawled out of bed, went to him, and gingerly reached out. The last thing she wanted was to startle him. His skin was cool to the touch where he'd kicked the covers off, though sweat glistened along his neck, and his long johns were damp. "Wake up, Noah," she whispered. "You're having a nightmare."

The movement continued. He was not responding to her words or touch; he began to shiver. Quickly, Cora adjusted the legs of his underwear. He had such strong legs—long and muscular with a soft feathering of chestnut hair. She straightened the covers and lifted them back up to his waist. Again, she whispered, "Noah, you are having a bad dream. Wake up."

He moaned and rolled to his side, kicking the covers free again. This time, when the covers slipped down, they exposed the back flap of his long johns, which was wide open, and the more he moved, the more the opening exposed his naked backside and his bottom. *His naked, manly bottom.*

Cora felt the heat slide through her. She had never seen a man this uncovered. A fine silky fuzz of soft gold protected his exposed skin and moved up toward his lower back, where it stopped and met smooth, muscled, tanned skin. She was so tempted to touch him. She drew her breath in with fascination. With all the skin and muscle of his lower half, she found she couldn't take her eyes off him. He had smooth masculine hips and *sweet heaven; the* crevice that separated the manly cheeks fascinated her.

She blew out a bubble of air she didn't realize she still held. The heat turned to fire, burning her from head to toe. She was so tempted to turn him on his back to see what his front might look like. But she didn't need to turn him because, in the next few seconds, he rolled on his own.

His long johns were loose and loosening further when he started thrashing once again and moaning. *"Captain, please stop what you are doing! Stop the men! We are supposed to be taking prisoners. This is slaughter! And what they are doing to the women! Have a conscience, sir! I want no part in this. It's wrong. Dear God, women and children!"* Noah held his hands up to his face in a protective move. Pain clouded his expression before he quieted once more.

Cora couldn't be sure, but she instinctively felt the dream changing. And now the dream was about her. "Ah, little angel...please, *I don't...*"

Don't what she wondered. He was in some kind of mental pain, and Cora again tried to soothe him with her words and touch. But tarnation she was having a difficult time removing her gaze from his nakedness, and now his man parts were exposed. She squeezed her eyes shut. Sweet heaven, he was so beautiful, but she couldn't think about this now; he was under emotional strain from whatever this dream was. She quickly covered him up again.

The last time a cool compress worked, she stood up, raced to the sink, moistened the cloth, quickly rung the excess water out, and returned to his side. Gently, she wiped the cloth over his face through his wavy hair and neck, down to his shoulders, where more of his skin was exposed. She loosened the buttons on the front of his underwear and spread the material aside as she carefully moved the moist cloth along his chest.

Silky dark chestnut hair curled around her fingertips when she continued to move over his breast muscle, his hardened male nipples, and down to his navel, where another soft swirl of chestnut hair surrounded the small indentation. From there, a narrow line moved down, flared out, and protected the bass of his male parts. Cora gaped in horrified fascination; she also had the same kind of protection for her lower female parts.

Noah gave a very different kind of moan as she touched, caressed, and bathed him. His narrow hips began moving against the innocent onslaught of her hands. He was now fully awake and fully aroused, but the moment the cloth brushed the tip of his sex, he knew he needed to stop her while he could. God all mighty, she was burning him alive, and the angelic smile on her lips when she moved closer to his sensitive organ made his heart jump. He became filled with sexual flames that scorched and smoldered through him. "Umm, Cora, what are you doing?"

Cora jolted up and yanked the hand that held the cloth away; oh, *tarnation, he was awake. She gave him an embarrassed glance. The deep blue of his eyes reminded her of the hottest part of a fire, but* there was something more; he was enjoying her touch as much as she enjoyed giving it to him. "I ah, she sheepishly mumbled. "You were having another nightmare, and taking the cloth to your skin seemed to help last time."

"I see," he grinned, "but it would seem you were a bit bolder this go around."

Damnation and hellfire that was exactly what she had been doing. She was about to take the cloth she'd been using down the length of his man part. She had been mesmerized watching how his body reacted to her touch, how he grew down there.

Cora quickly stood, dashed to the sink, and dropped the cloth with a splat. How could she ever face him again? Tears formed, and desperately, she tried to choke them back. "I'm sorry, I didn't..." she heard him climb out of bed, refasten his longjohns and pull his buckskin pants on. In seconds, she felt him behind her, and the part of him that brought her curiosity to the forefront was covered, though pressed tight against her backside.

"You aren't the only one who is curious; don't be ashamed."

"I just never knew... how your body...or how you react and grow!"

"Didn't anyone ever explain what happens between a man and a woman?"

"Not really; I got an idea when reading some of my books, though the descriptions were basically non-existent. And once I spied my parents..." she paused briefly. "It was an accident, of course, and I couldn't see their body's reaction. But they loved each other. They were playing some games. Covers were moving and sounds I had never heard before." She couldn't look him in the eye. What must he think of her? But she continued.

"The following morning, when I asked my mother if what happened between her and my father was how babies came about, I watched her cheeks burn red. And the only answer she gave was that I was a little too young to know. She suggested I wait until I got older. But I never got the chance. She and my father were killed a few days later. It was uncomfortable asking my grandfather, who never volunteered any information. So, no, I don't really understand."

"Do you remember how you felt when we kissed?"

Cora's cheeks turned a delicious apple red as her mother's face had done all those years ago. "Yes, but I didn't understand what was happening to my body."

"Do you think you could explain it to me?"

"I liked it very much."

"But how did it make you feel?"

"My body did funny things; things I was afraid it wasn't supposed to."

"Ah, honey, your body did exactly what it was supposed to."

"But I still don't understand. I felt achy between my legs in my secret parts. And my bubbies…" she reached up to cover herself.

"They are breasts."

"My breasts," she corrected, "felt like they were growing, and their tips hardened like when I get cold, but I wasn't cold; I was hot, wanting, oh, tarnation, I don't know. Something more."

"It is similar to what a man feels when he is excited. He gets hard down there."

She lowered her eyes, looking at the floor. "But that doesn't explain all this wanting something more and the aching I feel?"

Noah turned her around and ran his fingers along her soft cheeks and over her lips. "I feel all those things too, little angel. It's our minds and body's way of naturally telling us they wish to join. That's why I get hard, and you get achy and moist. Our bodies are reacting with need, preparing us to fit together."

"You mean mating?"

"I like to call what happens making love. Kissing, touching, and finally intercourse." Noah felt a little strange explaining lovemaking to her. And God help him; he wanted to make love to her. Keep her for only him.

And he had the distinct feeling she wanted the same thing.

But it couldn't be. He couldn't ruin her for another. Another! His mind cried out with pain. How the hell could he let her go to another?

"Would that be adultery if you and I made love? And would we be shamed like the woman in The Scarlett Letter?"

"Neither of us is married. So, no, it is not adultery. But it can be frowned upon when two people are not married. The Bible calls it fornicating."

"But you fornicated with those women of the night. Does that mean you could go to hell?"

"Hell?" he thought for a moment. "Well, I don't know, maybe I suppose," he glanced down at her. "What I did might be called wrong by some, but I don't think it was worthy of a trip to Hell. I didn't cheat anyone or hurt anyone. It was simply a service I paid for. It was purely physical, and no emotion or love was involved."

"I see. And that makes it all right?"

"No, sweetheart, that is also frowned on. As I explained, our bodies have needs, and maybe men have a little more than women. Sometimes, a man's thoughts can make him hard. Women seem to have more control, though I believe they enjoy the act as much as men if they are in love. And I believe that is why God made the human race the way we are. If men and women did not enjoy the love-making part, there would never be children. The earth would be empty." He gazed into those mesmerizing eyes of hers.

"I had been on the run for nearly two years. I needed human comfort, and those women were willing to give it to me for the right amount of coin. But it never was love. And it never was like the feelings I have for you."

"You have feelings for me?" She asked with surprise.

Noah gulped; he hadn't meant to say that, but now that he had, he murmured, "Of course I do. What man wouldn't."

She ignored the last part. She didn't care what any other man might feel. Only what Noah felt. "I have feelings for you too. I want to kiss you, touch you, mat...make love with you. To know what our physical connection of love would be like. I would like to have your baby. Oh, Noah, but not any man, I want only you."

Loka scratched at the door to go out. Noah continued to study Cora's beautiful eyes, the slight quaver on her lips, before he opened the door for his wolf. When Loka ran outside, Noah turned back to Cora. "I have nothing to offer you. You would be better off moving down to town. Use your grandfather's money to make a life. Meet someone who can give you all the things you need."

"I don't want a life without you. I need you. I love you. Can these people in the town give me you?"

"Ah, honey, how can you know what you feel in your heart? You've never really experienced what life could be. It would be best if you had a chance to see what the other side is like. I've lived up here like an old hermit for years."

"The other side of life?" she nearly screamed. "By that, do you mean like those men who killed my grandfather? No, thank you! And who's to know the feelings I have more than myself," she lifted her hand to her chest, and tears filled her eyes. "If you don't want me or feel the same way, I will learn to live with it. I will make out by myself back at my grandfather's cabin. Now it makes sense why you haven't wanted to speak to me these past days."

Her heart was breaking; she stepped away from him, slipped her boots over her woolen socks, grabbed her heavy winter coat from the hook by the door, and practically tripped as she ran outside. Quickly, she followed the path Loka had taken. Noah didn't want her; now, part of her just wanted to climb into a hole somewhere and stay there. She pulled her coat tighter around herself. Tarnation, she still wore her night clothes. What was she thinking? But she couldn't go back. She couldn't stand to see the sympathy or regret shine in the blue sapphire eyes.

Chapter Thirteen

For several moments, Noah stood motionless, glaring at the closed door Cora had just slammed shut. She said she loved him. He hadn't heard words like that since the day he left home so many years ago. And those words came from his family. Was it possible she could love him? He remembered the way she had intimately touched him during his repetitive nightmare. And how she continued touching and exploring, not realizing he had awakened. But love, how could she know? She'd never been in love.

And neither have I, he silently told himself. He had been in lust, but love had nothing to do with it.

Realizing he'd just been standing in the same spot while Cora was out there, feeling rejected, he yanked on his boots, tore his coat from the rack by the door, grabbed his pack and rifle, and stepped outside.

With the cold air blasting him in the face, he briefly wondered if she had grabbed her snowshoes. Or had she been so upset that she had just run away. God, how could he ever forgive himself if anything happened to her?

There was no sign of her or Loka. The cold air blew with icy ferocity burning his skin. Another storm was coming. What was the little fool thinking? She could freeze to death. He grabbed his snowshoes, where he had left them hanging on the chinked log exterior, and beneath the shallow overhang, he quickly clamped them on his boots. In minutes, he followed the tracks she'd left behind. They were quickly disappearing. And his heart felt like exploding.

Cora moved through the thick cluster of pine that surrounded the cabin. She jammed her fur cap with ear flaps lower on her head, shoved her hands inside her coat pocket for her gloves, and found her rabbit's foot. She pulled it free, grasped it, and shoved the soft furry foot inside her glove. She would need the good luck it was sure to bring her.

Her snowshoes flapped against the ground, so glad she'd had the foresight to grab them. Tears flowed down her cheeks, freezing almost immediately on her face. She didn't care. She had just given her heart to Noah, and he tossed it away. Tossed her away like yesterday's garbage. *"Experience another life,"* he had told her. There was no other life for her.

She'd lost her parents, her grandfather, and now Noah. Then maybe Noah's loss wasn't right. She'd never had him to lose. How could she have been so stupid to think any man would want her? She was a quarter, Cheyenne. Her skin was golden-tanned, not the ivory white of the ladies in her books or the women who lived in Willowby. Her ugly black, cropped hair didn't help. She had lived as a boy for so long, and even though her hair had grown, it was still ugly and boyish. She shivered. Yes, she was ugly and stupid.

And so very foolish!

He said he had nothing to offer her. Well, hellfire, she had nothing to offer him. Why would he want to keep her? Her grandfather told her that white people were afraid of the Indians. *Tarnation!* Why hadn't she thought about that when she confessed her love? She probably scared the devil out of him.

Loka burst through the snow-covered brush, stopped, and looked up at her, bumping her legs and giving her a barely audible whine. Cora leaned down and petted him between his pointed ears. "Well, I guess you like my company," she told the wolf. "Why don't you show me where you found those grouse hens? And I'll roast one for us, though she didn't believe he understood her or would take her to the hiding place; it was nice not knowing she wasn't alone after all."

Loka turned and ran ahead. What the heck, she thought, why not follow him? Time seemed to stand still as she moved behind Loka. How much time she had no idea. The path was rocky and thickly tree lined. But he led her to a deep overhang of rich red sandstone. There was a firepit off to the side. She glanced up at the sky; the snow was coming down heavier. At least this overhang would give her a little cover. She shouldn't have been in such a hurry to race out of the cabin, allowing her emotions to guide her.

Christ on a crutch, where the hell had she gotten to? The path and footprints he tracked quickly disappeared in the icy wind and snow. The little fool was going to freeze to death. What the hell was she thinking running off like that? And where the hell was Loka?

He whistled for the wolf to come.

Nothing.

"Cora!" He shouted, "Come back!" *God in heaven, what had he done to her?*

But only the howl of the wind answered him.

Visions of a frozen woman crashed inside his head and lambasted him with guilt. Was Loka with her? Had she fallen and hurt herself? She was such a trusting, gentle soul, and he had just trampled all over her heart. She said she loved him. Wanted to make a life with him. Have his babies. Hell, he wanted the same things, but more importantly, he wanted what was best for her, and letting go was best. At least it was best for her; why couldn't she see that? *But she wants me. She says she loves me.* "Cora!" he shouted out again.

No answer.

Noah searched for the next several hours. There was no sign of her. Where could she be? Had she returned to Elijah's burned-out cabin? That's where she threatened to go.

Maybe, but these tracks he followed led in the opposite direction. Again, for the umpteenth time, he whistled for Loka and shouted her name, but there was no response from either of them. The wind was growing more intense and louder. There was nothing more to do than keep moving in the direction he started hours ago.

<hr>

"This little nook is cozy and gives us a little cover. Is this where the hens stay?" Cora wondered aloud. If it was, there was no sign.

Hellfire. She was hungry. She had let her blasted emotions guide her this morning and raced out of the cabin with no plan, no food, and not appropriately dressed. She only grabbed her boots and coat; it was a last-minute decision to grab her clip-on snowshoes hanging on the outside wall next to Noah's. Luckily, she kept her gloves and stocking cap in her pockets. Beneath it all, she only wore her night shift. Tarnation, she was an idiot. No wonder Noah didn't want her. She was just a stupid Indian girl. She squeezed her rabbit's foot.

Cora shook her head. She had no time to feel sorry for herself; she'd gather wood and make a fire. She might starve, but she would at least be warm. No time like the present. She moved back outside and began to collect wood. Loka disappeared, and several minutes later, he gave his gentle howl bark. She turned back to glare at him. He was standing inside the alcove's entrance. "What are you going on about?" The wolf moved toward her and nudged her leg.

"What?" she gave him a look of irritation.

Was he trying to warn her about something? Nervously, she followed him back beneath the overhang and glanced about. There was enough wood to start a fire on the dry, sandy floor about five feet away. All of it was piled near an old firepit. A firepit she hadn't noticed in her haste to get out of the wind, but obviously Loka did.

"Where did you get this wood?" she asked with bemusement staring into the pit. She moved closer, knelt down, removed one glove, and reached out. "And it's dry, too. My goodness, you are such a smart fellow. How grateful I am that you are with me. Is this how you helped Noah in the beginning?" Loka cocked his head sideways and looked like he might answer. But Cora knew if he did, she would be shocked and probably pass out. Then she laughed at herself for such a silly thought.

She placed her bundle of damp wood on the sandy floor next to the small fire pit. With her ungloved hand, she reached inside her pocket and pulled out a piece of Quartz chert and a char cloth. Another thing she always kept in her pocket. One never knew when you might need it. She could use this for fire-starting.

Others had stayed here before, though she believed it had been a long while since they had. She didn't really know why, but the thought made her feel welcome. She wondered if Noah knew about this place. Maybe he had been one of the people who'd stayed here when he'd first come up the mountain.

She pushed the thought aside and adjusted the dried kindling in the pit. Rubbing the quartz against a char cloth to create friction was a chore she had often done. Within a few minutes, a flame started. She blew on it to keep it going and slowly added more wood. Now, to figure out what to eat. But she had no tools to skin or trim and cut. She knew better than to run off halfcocked as she had. Even if Loka caught something, she could not butcher it. Within minutes, an adequate blaze formed.

Nearing nightfall, Noah realized he'd been out here all day. Snow fell heavily, covering everything, including himself. Where was she, and where the hell was Loka? Then he smelled smoke as the wind blew it downhill. The smoldering scent was coming from the old outcrop of sandstone cut into the mountainside from wind and water for thousands of years. She would get a piece of his mind if she were up there. *Or he would hold her and never let her go.* And he knew it would be the latter.

He moved up toward the familiar overhang.

Cora curled up on the floor next to Loka and the fire. Thankfully, the wolf's fur as he nestled down next to her helped keep her warm. For the hundredth time, she chastised herself for being so impulsive. Was Noah looking for her, or was he just relieved she'd run off? She felt her accursed tears threaten but stubbornly refused to release them. She would go to sleep. Worry about food and what Noah may or may not do tomorrow. And where she would go from here.

Noah found himself outside the overhang. Cora and Loka were huddled together next to the glowing fire. He knew it was probably hard for the wolf with all his winter undercoat, but Loka was protective and would never leave her side. She clutched one of the rabbit feet they had made weeks ago.

His heart swelled with love as he silently watched his two favorite beings. Loka sensed his presence, lifted his head, and carefully watched with big, golden, all-knowing eyes. He did not move from Cora. Her arm was lovingly wrapped around the wolf's midsection, and her head rested against his furry rib cage.

Noah quietly stepped closer, and once he reached the two of them, he lowered himself to a laying position next to Cora and pulled her back against himself so her head rested between his shoulder and upper arm. Instinctively, she moved her body closer, pressing her bottom to the front of his pants, and gave a soft sigh.

He briefly wondered if she would make such sensual sounds if he did make love to her. Just thinking about the risqué thought aroused him. And the more she pressed against him, the harder he got, but try as he might, he couldn't talk himself into moving. He just reached around and tucked his hand beneath the swell of her breast and tried to breathe normally. He realized the delightful curve of her body fit so well against him when she snuggled closer.

The three of them lay this way until dawn. Loka and Cora were sound asleep, him wide awake, torturing himself.

But at some point, he must have drifted off.

Vivid light created from the snow glistened through the tall pine and leafless Aspen and into the opening of the alcove. The snow had finally stopped sometime through the night. The temperatures dropped to freezing. Cora was so comfortably warm that she didn't want to move. But Loka did, lifted himself, and disappeared outside into the trees. Funny, she still felt warm, as if he had never left her. Wait! Someone was wrapped around her.

Her heart rapidly danced against her chest. She jerked up and scooted away. When she felt safe enough, she turned and glared at the intruder with fury, lighting her topaz eyes. "Hellfire!" she shouted. "Who... Noah! What the devil are you doing here? You scared the Dickens out of me!"

"Sorry, but you and Loka were so peaceful; I didn't want to disturb you."

"So, you decide to crawl into bed with me instead!" She leaped up and took several steps back.

Noah laughed so hard that tears came to his eyes. "Bed? What Bed? Dirt floor, no covers, no pillow unless you want to call Loka or my arm a pillow."

"Well, it's where I slept last night, and if I want to call it a bed, I will!"

"Guess you can; it isn't much different than the one I sleep on in the cabin, leastwise as far as floors go. Frankly, that pallet was very nice the night before last when you petted me like Loka."

Her pretty face blazed with red. "Ooo, you!" She picked up a piece of dry kindling and threw it at him.

He quickly reached out and caught the stick, then stood up and went to her.

She squealed, taking several steps back.

Loka bounded back inside the alcove, sat on his haunches, and moved his head back and forth between the two of them. Then, bored by the whole thing, he made his wolf sound, laid down on his belly, and placed his head on his front paws away from the firepit. His eyes were still watching this ridiculous human display.

Noah stood before her, tossed the stick aside, reached out, and pulled her into his arms. "I'm so sorry, Cora, if I made you feel so unwanted, that you felt you had to run away."

She lowered her eyes.

He cupped her chin and raised her face to meet his dark sapphire eyes. "I do want you, but I also want you to have a life. Staying up here with me will be no life. But I will wait till spring to see how things go for you. If you still wish to stay with me at that time, I would be honored to have you as my wife."

A tear trickled down Cora's cheek. "Do you mean it, Noah?"

"I do." He tugged her softness against the hard contours of his body, lowered his mouth, and covered her sensual lips with such a crushing intensity that he could feel her reaction through their heavy clothing. Using his tongue, he separated her lips and slid inside the warmth she always offered him.

There was no doubt in his mind. He didn't want to lose her. He was in love. She had come into his lonely life when he most needed her. He would have to take a chance, a leap of faith, and pray things would work out even if it meant he'd suffer pain and lose her forever. He lifted his mouth from hers and whispered, "Will you come back to the cabin with me now?"

"On one condition."

Noah grinned, "And what might that be?"

"That you understand. I am a grown woman who knows what's best for me. I've lived in these mountains longer than you have. My grandfather taught me everything he would have taught a grandson. I can survive on my own. What do you think I did when I was left alone while my grandfather went to town to restock for the coming year? He would be gone for a month." She met his deep blue eyes. "The only desire I have of going down to Willowby is if I am there with you and can stay with you."

She could see the argument flicker in his expression, and she knew where it was coming from. "Yesterday, my foolish decision to run away may have convinced you differently. But yesterday, I let my emotions control me. It won't happen again. And if by chance it does happen, I will not take flight, no sir, I will stay and fight. Do you agree to my terms?"

Noah studied her serious face and gave her a quick grin. *Christ on a crutch,* she was so pretty, even more so when she got stubborn. "I agree," he answered, praying he could keep the agreement. He quickly extinguished what was left of the hot coals in the fire pit by covering them with dirt. Snow began to drip from the trees, forming sharp-edged icicles that hung nearly to the ground and added to the miserable temperatures. Many inches of snow had been added overnight. It was deep and frigid.

He handed Cora her snowshoes. She quickly clipped them on. He gave her a quick kiss. "Let's head out. I need some coffee, and I don't know about you, but my stomach thinks my throat's been cut. I'm nearly starved to death." Noah took her gloved hand inside his own and led her out of the alcove.

Taking a different path, he led her down through the thick line of trees along a trail that got them to the cabin in just over an hour. Loka quickly followed. "Jeez," Cora said, glancing at the wolf, "you devil, you led me around the long way. I suppose you left markings so Noah could follow."

Noah's lips curled in an ironic smile, and he chuckled despite himself. "No, this big furry troublemaker did not leave any tracks. It was yours I followed.

Chapter Fourteen

The small town of El Pueblo was situated on the confluence of the Arkansas River and Fountain Creek. Spread out over a semi-high desert and close to the front range of the Rocky Mountains. The town was founded on the fur trade decades ago but eventually became a supply town for nearby ranches and farms. It boasted a saloon called Lucky's. Inside, Captain Lamar Tamarin and his men lazed away in the late afternoon, waiting for the evening entertainment. He glared outside through the batwing doors, studying the dusty street.

Next door to the saloon was a boot repair shop, a Post Office, and a bookstore. To the right was a law office, and further down Santa Fe Avenue was a slaughterhouse and a General Mercantile, selling fresh produce, canned food, dry goods, and some clothing. At this time of year, in December, the Rocky Mountains to the west were covered in snow.

Lamar figured there would be about two or three more months of boredom as they waited in this town. With disgust, he looked away from the street and returned to his poker game. They had decided to bypass

Denver to wait out the winter and traveled further south to this tiny town. He was itching to go back to the San Juan mountains and capture, no, not capture, kill the no-account bastard, Noah Harper.

Lamar sat with his back to the wall and glared outside through the doorway again. A few people milled about on the wooden walkway, but most people were headed home for supper or to spend time with their families. Some would pile into the saloon looking for drink and entertainment. It wasn't the worst nor best town they'd stopped in while on this mission of revenge and profit. El Pueblo was small and unassuming, the perfect place for him and the boys to hold up. There was no law to speak of, just a young man, more boy, who knew about as much of the law as a thimble full of water did.

The environmental conditions were perfect for waiting out winter. The natural habitat boasted various trees, including Siberian Elm, Mulberry, and Tree of Heaven. This tall, leafy, fern-like growth sprouted up in alleys, yards, and along the street. Anywhere there was a free space, the damn things grew and obstructed walkways, yards and served to block the view along the street. Tree of Heaven, right? It's more like the tree of Hell. But then, this time of year, they looked more like spindly naked soldiers reaching their arms out to a cloudless sky.

Pine, spruce willow, and jagged rock hugged the Arkansas River and flowed through the high desert plateau next to the town. If Lamar were a settling man, this would be where he'd like to stay. Build himself a cabin along the banks of the river. But he wasn't. He had revenge on his mind and a traitor he wanted to wipe from the earth. The thieving he and the boys had done over the years since he'd been released from prison had made him a wealthy man in his own right.

He traveled with a set of the rowdiest bunch he could dig up. Only three of the men from the original twelve remained. However, one of them, Simon Mason, was turning out to be more of a pain in the ass than anything else—a hindrance. And one of these days, Lamar would ensure he was rid of him.

What was left of his men were entertaining themselves inside Lucky's. The scarred bar was at least twenty feet in length. Stools lined up before it. A massive picture of a nude woman hung above the bar, surrounded by mirrors decorated with Christmas garland, red candles, liquor bottles, and shot glasses intermingling with the worn-out decorations. Several round tables clogged the midway. He and the men had come across this town a couple of weeks ago, and the saloon made their stay easier.

Lamar sat at one of the round tables with four other men. Two were his men, Sean and Eric. The other players were cowboys who lived outside of town on one of the numerous ranches. They played a game of five-card stud. Charley, Earl, and Hyrum, the last man he'd chosen to hire and ride with them, sat at the bar, sweet-talking one of the red-haired floozies. Another man, Jacob, a joker who liked to hornswoggle the soiled doves by not paying for their service, was upstairs with a plump yellow-haired gal who called herself Dixie.

Simon sat alone in the corner of the room, looking like he'd lost his best friend and would rather be anywhere but here. Lamar gave him an unpalatable look as he watched the man lift a bottle of Old Crow whiskey, the same one he'd been nursing for the past three hours and pour another drink. For the life of him, Lamar wondered why he kept the useless bastard around. Over the past few years, the man had begun to irritate the hell out of him. With disgust, he turned his attention back to the poker game.

Minutes later, all hell broke loose.

The ruckus caused every man in the place to glare at the stairway. Jacob, who looked as if he hadn't seen a wash tub in a month of Sundays, came barreling down the stairway, taking two steps at a time. Halfway descended, he leaped onto the banister with a peel of laughter and rode the rest of the way down to the floor. Dixie, who closely followed behind Jacob, began screaming obscenities. Her backless slippers clicked wildly on the stairs in her rush to catch up to the man who had just robbed her. In her right hand, she toted a small handled boot gun.

"Jesus!" Lamar swore vexingly as he watched his man finish his ride on the outer handrail and hit the bottom with a thud. His laughter was so high-pitched and boisterous that the sound scraped the nerves of everyone in the place. So much for a quiet town to hold up.

"Somebody, stop that sumbitch!" Dixie shouted and fired a shot from the pistol she brandished, blowing a hole in the floor close to Earl's boot heel, who in turn continued to laugh and skedaddle across the unpolished floor toward the batwing doors.

"The good for nothin' sumbitch owes me five dollars, and I aim to get it!" Dixie informed every man in the place with an ugly snarl as she continued to chase Jacob.

Simon glanced up from his whiskey and over to the captain with distaste. God, how he hated all this. For the umpteenth time, he questioned his sanity when sticking himself with this lot of deadly losers. Just thinking about the things he'd done or witnessed in the last decade made the whiskey curdle in his gut.

"Looks like Jake has gone and cheated another whore, Earl, who'd been stationed at the bar, chortled. "Goddamn Capn' he ain't worth all the trouble he gives us. His ma should have dropped him on the head when she brung him into the world."

"Shhhhhit!" Charley, another of the captain's men, pontificated with amusement. "I done think she did! The man is as mad as an old hoot owl stuck in a tree with no wings."

Dixie leaped from the bottom stair and quickly reloaded, continuing to follow Jake as he weaved in and out of tables. "I'm gonna kill you, sumbitch! Nobody cheats me!"

Everyone could still hear Jake's hideous laughter when he raced around the corner and slammed through the swinging doors. Dixie was right behind him. The pistol she continued to hold was cocked and ready. She fired again, taking out a chunk of wood on the left side of the batwing door. She pushed through, leaving them to swing at a crooked angle, and followed Earl along the boardwalk.

Two of Lamar's men at the bar reached for their holstered six-shooters. His other two men at the poker table shoved their chairs back and pulled their sidearms.

Simon continued to sit and take another sip from his glass. This was nothing new; Jake was always causing trouble, especially with whores.

Lamar held up a hand to stymie his men. "If the fool is gonna act like one, then let the harlot shoot his ass."

A shot echoed outside and filled the inside of the saloon—a slight breeze filtered through the swinging doors, filling the room with the acrid smell of gunpowder.

Minutes later, Dixie reentered the saloon, blowing the tip of her pistol as if she were Annie Oakley herself. Then, she wiped the weapon down with the hem of her frilly frock tied at her ample waist. "That takes care of that!" she snickered, shoved the cooled pistol inside a garter on her thigh, and glared over to the barkeep. "Just gave ya another one to clean up, Boone. He's lying face up and pushing daises around the corner at the top of the alley."

Boone grinned, "Looks like these damn fools ain't never gonna learn they can't cheat our very own flower of the west."

"You got that right, honey," she winked at him, returned to the stairway, and moved her impressive hips on her way up.

None of the men inside the saloon knew that Dixie had already raided the cowboy's leather purse, but the barkeep knew. Each time she did it, she would share the spoils with him. He moved out from behind the bar and stepped outside. No fundamental law existed in town, so most folks handled problems themselves.

Once Dixie reached the upper landing, she turned and stared down at Lamar, knowing he was the one in charge, but quickly included all of them. "Okay, now which one of you, sumbitchs, is gonna pay me for what your buddy cheated me out of."

Not wanting to stir up any more notice, the captain gave Simon a resentful side look. "Take care of this," he ordered.

Simon reached into his pocket, pulled a shiny silver coin free, and tossed it to the woman.

Dixie caught the coin one-handed and placed the shiny disk between her front teeth to check its authenticity. Satisfied, she made her way down the hall, her lush hips swaying with her movements. Then, changing her mind, she turned back, leaned over the rail, and shot a look of invitation down at the remaining men. In a husky voice, she asked, "Who's next!"

Not one man moved. She chuckled, swung around, and continued along the upper hallway, her harsh laughter following her.

"I think it's time we moved on," Simon uncertainly suggested to Lamar. "Our faces are now well known in town." Simon watched the captain's face turn sour. He had to be the most unpredictable man Simon had ever known. No one ever knew how he would react from one day to the next.

The captain glared back at him. "If I wanted your opinion, I would have asked. Now shut up, mind your business, return to the hotel, and gather our stuff. We're moving out. I've grown bored with this place. Lest you'd all like to end up the same way as good ol' Jake." All of this was said as if it were the captain's idea, not Simon's.

"No sir," several men replied at the same time.

"Good. I hear Colorado Springs to the west is an up-and-coming place to be. The railroad runs through it now. Plenty of entertainment for the men. And it gets us closer to the San Juan and Noah Harper. If the weather holds, we will start the hunt again in a month or two."

Without another word, Simon left the saloon. As each day passed, he felt more and more regret. He needed to stop his cowardly behavior, get out of this mess for good, and find a way to warn Noah.

Chapter Fifteen

Snow flurries continued off and on as November turned to December. Cora and Noah stepped back into their routine of sharing chores, reading, and playing the guitar in the evenings. There was no more discussion of Cora being left in town to start a new life away from Noah.

The temperature had risen a few degrees. It almost felt like an early spring day. Icicles dripped and sprinkled down from the eaves on the cabin and outhouse. But they both knew the weather would not last.

Cora's love for Noah grew stronger each day. Somehow, she would convince him he needed her as much as she needed him. It seemed like her grandfather had known this all along. And now that they had the money, they could use it to restock their meager supplies, do some needed repairs on the cabin, and maybe even buy a wagon and a mule.

They'd be as comfortable as two bugs in a rug.

"Would you like to dance with me this evening after we finish supper and clean up?"

"But we won't have any music. You can't play the guitar and dance with me at the same time."

"Watch and see," he beamed. "It's a surprise, and I have it all planned out," he gave her a mischievous grin. His deep blue eyes glistened enticingly as he gathered their plates and utensils and took them to the sink and the hot, soapy water Cora had prepared.

Eagerness filled Cora when she followed him, grabbed a cloth, and wiped down the table and small counter. She loved surprises. And this surprise came so close to being like a Christmas gift that she felt the magic glide through her like warm liquid. "Did you celebrate Christmas when you lived at home with your family?" She asked and dropped the cloth into the hot, soapy water; another thing they had brought up from Elijah's cabin was a box of soap flakes. She quickly took over washing the plates while he rinsed and dried.

"Sure, didn't you and your grandfather?"

"No, he wasn't into celebrating the birth of Christ or any other holiday for that matter. But when my ma and pa were still alive, we did."

Noah noted the sadness in her eyes. "Well, let's fix that. Tomorrow, we can head out and get a small tree. We can decorate it with dried berries and paper angels. I have some parchment paper in the bottom of my trunk. Would you like that?

Her thick, dark lashes shadowed her high-boned cheeks, and he could see her eyes fill with emotion. How had he made her so sad? This was supposed to make her happy. "Ah, honey. I didn't mean to upset you. We can forget the Christmas tree."

"You are wrong. You didn't upset me; you gave me joy."

"But your tears?"

"Tears of happiness," Cora swiped at the moisture on her cheeks and smiled. No one had ever wanted to please her as much as Noah seemed to want. "To celebrate Christmas for the first time in over sixteen years is like a miracle, a gift so powerful that only you could give me. I'm not sad but delighted. Thank you."

She quickly dried her hands and stepped closer to this gentle, handsome man who wanted to make her happy. Without further thought, she stood up on tiptoes, threw herself against his lean, strong length, and wrapped her arms around him, lifting her face with a shy smile. Their lips were only inches apart. Seconds later, she pressed her mouth against him, feeling the tickle of his soft mustache against her lips when she drew him closer and helped him deepen the kiss.

She was the first to break the kiss and step away.

Noah gently pulled her back and dropped his head to meet her lips again. The heat of his tongue bathed the velvet, moist skin of her lips, then slid inside, tasting, loving, and drawing the beauty of her to comingle with his own heat.

Cora ardently returned the passion. Her tongue danced to the invisible music they were creating; it was the first kiss they had shared since leaving the alcove nearly a week ago.

His hands slid over her back, caressing her. Moved to her ribs and gently brushed the side of her breasts, where her nipples responded and turned to hardened nubs. She curiously wondered how it would feel if he completely cupped their fullness.

Softly, she cried out when his hands moved lower to her waist, then down to the curve of her hips, where he tugged her closer. She could feel his stiff maleness press against her belly, and she sighed against his exploring mouth.

"God, how I want you. Never want to let you go, my sweet angel," he moaned with arousal.

"Oh, Noah, I want you too. And I don't ever want you to let me go."

"I have never felt such lack of control," he admitted. "Let's slow down and have the dance I promised." He caressed her lips with his thumb and crossed the room to retrieve his guitar. Nervously, he strummed a few cords. *Judas!* He was shaking like a boy who'd just had his first kiss. Then again, the kiss he shared with Cora had nothing to do with being a boy. He was sure he would regret what he was about to do. Already his pants were so damn tight in the front. He held the guitar in one hand. "Come over here, face me, and put yourself tight against my body."

Cora felt her heartbeat quicken, and excitedly, she did what he asked.

Damn, but he was a glutton for punishment! Noah thought when she enticingly pressed against his bulging pants and pressed her breasts just below his chest muscle. *Hell, she fit him perfectly.*

He forced himself to ignore the reactions of her shapely front side, lifted the guitar strap over both their heads, and snuggled the instrument to rest at her back midway. Holding the instrument's long arm with his left hand, he positioned his fingers to the upper frets while the other hand poised in front of the sound hole. Instantly, he began to strum the strings. "All right, now wrap your arms around my back and hold on. "Do you know the song Camp Town Races?" he asked, stringing the guitar and whirling her around the cabin.

Cora giggled and started singing.

"Dee Camp Town ladies sing this song, doo-dah, doo-dah! De Camp Town race track five miles long, oh doo-dah day! I come down here with my hat caved in, doo-dah, doo-dah! I go back home with a pocket full of tin, oh doo-dah day."

They both laughed and sang the chorus together. *"Gonna run all night! Gonna run all day! I'll bet my money on a bob-tail nag. Somebody bet on the bay!"*

They danced and stumbled through the rest of the song's verses as they moved around the small room. It wasn't easy, nearly impossible, to play his guitar and hold her, but Lord, how much fun they had. He played a couple more raucous tunes. And they swirled and dipped until they were both breathless.

Loka howled and jumped onto the middle of the bed, turned in circles, and eventually plopped down on his belly and gave his unique mix of howl and bark as he watched the two humans sway and step.

Laughing and breathless, they finally came to a stop. Cora gazed up at Noah. "That's the most fun I think I've ever had. Oh, thank you!"

He lifted the guitar strap over their heads and carefully laid the instrument across the tabletop. He turned back to her and tugged her into his arms. He lowered his mouth, giving her a full-bodied, deep kiss, using his tongue in the most erotic way, tasting her, loving her as he moved across her lips, inside her mouth.

Cora readily reciprocated, matching his movements in all the ways he had taught her the first time he had kissed her. Lunge for lunge, taste for taste. Neither could keep their hands stationary as they moved over muscle and feminine curves. Cora's heart skittered wildly in her breasts. *Would he caress her there? Lawd God,* she wanted him, too. She also wanted to touch him and pushed provocatively against the length of him.

With an unbridled need she didn't understand but couldn't let go of, she unbuttoned his shirt and then his long johns. She pushed the cloth aside and moved her hands over his exposed skin and the soft, silky tuft of chest hair entangling her fingers. He was so beautiful. She moved her hands down over his chest, his belly, and lower to the waistband of his soft buckskin pants. His raw masculinity was pressed against her belly. He was thick and hard, just like he had been the night he had his nightmare when she'd explored him, thinking he was still asleep.

"Umm, Noah," she purred seductively. "Remember when I gave you the sponge bath after your nightmare?"

"I'm unlikely ever to forget," he breathed against her ear and tugged the lobe inside his mouth, wishing it was her breasts and puckered nipples.

"Well, you are growing right now like you did that night. And I love the feeling of you pressed against my belly. May I touch you?" Her fingers began to dip inside his waistband.

Christ on a crutch!

He couldn't speak when her fingers brushed the tip of him through his long johns. But he tried. "Did you mean what you said to me?"

"I mean whatever I say to you. But what in particular are you asking me?"

"That you love me,"

"Yes, I love you. I feel like I always have and know that I always will. And Noah, I would like you to touch me too," she continued. "I feel such a delicious ache between my legs. Do you want to touch me?"

So much for trying to control himself! His face felt warm, hell; his whole body felt on fire. He brought her exploratory hands up and kissed her fingertips. "I do, honey, but if we try to relieve ourselves, we could find ourselves in one heck of a dilemma."

"What do you mean?" Then she lowered her head, resting her forehead against his powerful chest. "You don't want me the way I want you."

"Oh God! I do, but we should wait. We both agreed to give ourselves till spring."

Cora stepped away. Her face was flushed with desire, and her expression echoed what was happening inside Noah. The temptation was burning him alive.

"I see, she whispered.

"No, you don't. We both need to know this is what you really want. Hell, Cora, you have never been with a man. If I take what you offer and it isn't right for you, I will have ruined you. And I don't think I could live with myself for taking advantage."

"Take advantage, and please ruin me because I will never want another man the way I crave you."

"You are not going to make this easy, are you!"

She sighed. "You made this decision. I told you at the alcove that I would not change my mind. I want to be with you like you said you wanted to be with me. But if you only said that to get me to go back with you, then so be it. But you will be the first and last man ever to touch or kiss me. I could never stand another's touch. Ever! I learned a long time ago there is only one thing a white man would want me for. That was proven when I was fourteen and the last time my grandfather took me to town and why he never took me again. I should have known better than to throw myself at you."

"Did some man hurt you?"

"They never got the chance; my grandfather aimed his rifle at both of them."

"Both of them?" *Christ on a crutch!* "And you were only fourteen?"

"Yes, they held up their hands and laughed, saying they didn't know the squaw belonged to him. After we left town that day, Grandfather explained that some whites think that the only good Indian is a dead Indian unless that Indian is female. Females got used up, raped and beaten, and treated like slaves. My Cheyenne blood made me a target.

"When I was a child still living in town, the other children teased me because my mother was a Halfbreed. That is why she taught me at home. And that's one of the reasons my grandfather took me up here in the mountains. I used to pretend I was the girl in the story of Heidi. Of course, I didn't read that particular book until after a few years of living here. It wasn't published until 1880, but it was one of the books my grandfather brought me from town. I was fifteen or sixteen at the time."

"Hell!" Noah swore. "He shouldn't have told you all white men are like that. He loved and married a full-blooded Cheyenne woman. He should have known better."

"He didn't say all white men, but there were many. Like the soldiers you rode with."

Silently, Noah watched her eyes fill. She was correct; he nearly died trying to defend a Cheyenne village, though it didn't do much good. They were all murdered anyway. And now he could never go home because he had to protect his family.

He just wasn't sure he could put this little angel in peril. She didn't even look native. True, her skin was a light golden olive, but her features must have taken after her white father and grandfather. He certainly didn't know she was Cheyenne until she told him. Then he thought she was a young boy. Maybe he was just blind. Blind and in love.

He pulled her into his arms and pressed her tightly against him. "God knows I want you. I want you to be my wife. But Cora, I have had some experience and know what I want. I need to know if you want the same thing. There really are good men in the world. Men who want someone as sweet and loving as you are to share their life with. I'm certainly not the only man." He was failing in his endeavors and losing control over the argument. Hell, he didn't want anyone else ever to touch her.

"I thought you understood," Cora began thoughtfully, "how I felt when you found me in the alcove. I don't want anyone else. I love you and want to be with you. I...thought you might feel the same way I do. Was I wrong?" She turned away.

He gently grasped her upper arms and turned her back to him. "You have not been listening to me, honey. You are the most desirable woman I have ever met. I want you so much that only thirty minutes ago, I was willing to compromise you," he ran his hands up and down her arms.

"And thirty minutes ago, I wanted you to compromise me as you say, and I still do."

"Ah honey, you are everything I have ever wanted. You make me laugh; you make my life complete. You plain give me life! A life I never thought was possible. I figured I would just always be alone. Die alone. Never know what it was like to fall in love or have that love returned. Then, out of the blue, here you come, filling me with dreams, with life. You are my companion, my friend who brings me such joy, and most importantly, you have saved me from myself, teaching me to love for the first time in a very long time.

"Maybe it is time for me to stop hiding and come out into the open," he admitted. "Face my demons and have a life. A life with you and any children we make together. Someday, I want to see my family back in Nebraska and start anew. Ah, Cora, I do love you. And that gives me the courage to dare to try anything." He clicked his tongue to get Luka's attention. The wolf immediately vacated his spot on the bed and ran outside when Noah opened the door. "You spoil him you know, letting him sleep on the bed. Now, back to what we were discussing."

"Like the courage to make love to me?" She teased.

"Are you trying to seduce me?"

She giggled. "Maybe if I knew what that word meant."

Noah grinned, in the most sensual way, "entice me?"

"Then yes, I am! Is it working?" She took a step back, cocked her head sideways, and continued to meet his look with a mischievous sparkle in her gaze.

His blue sapphire eyes were filled with a mixture of desire and amusement. "Yes, you little spitfire, it is working, and I think I'm about to..." he took another step closer. "Break every rule I set up from the moment I found you near frozen on the snow-covered meadow. And..." he paused and swallowed, "all this pent-up emotion scares the hell out of me, but God help me. I want you with a powerful yearning."

"You don't have to be afraid of me. I will be gentle," she beamed with a seductive upturn of her lips.

The smile reminded Noah of the impish look Loka would give him after getting caught making mischief. Cora's topaz eyes sparkled with the same unabashed look, and her lovely mouth stretched enticingly, filling her face with overwhelming beauty. He took another step closer.

The backside of Cora's thighs bumped the side of the bed, and she plopped down, making the ticking of straw and feathers rustle.

Noah moved another step. He pulled his shirt up and out of his buckskin pants, then over his head, and tossed it onto his sleeping pallet. Next, he sat on the edge of the bed and removed his boots and socks. Lastly, he swiftly released the front cording of his pants, slipped them down over his hips, and pushed them down to the floor, where he stepped out of them and kicked them over to join the shirt he discarded.

He still wore his long johns though the top section was unbuttoned. The material was tomato red and soft. The slit covering his hardened sex was partially open. Cora's eyes riveted directly to it, but quickly, her vision lifted. He was taking another step. Directly in front of her, his muscular thighs surrounded her hips. Placing his arms and hands on either side of her on the bed, he leaned over, inclining his head toward her face. Her lovely eyes were wide with jeweled brilliance.

His lips were only inches from hers. "Should I continue?"

Cora gulped in a short breath and nodded.

"Good," he whispered and moved across her lips. "God knows I don't want to stop."

The moment she felt his mouth brush her own, she wrapped her arms around his neck and pulled him closer.

It wasn't enough for either of them.

Noah gathered her into his arms, scooted her back on the bed toward the middle, pressed her down against the rustling mattress, and crawled up to lay beside her. He lightly pressed his mouth against her lips.

The kiss deepened, and Cora could feel his male hardness pressed against her seconds before he gently lifted her, placed her over the middle of the bed, and lowered himself partially over her. He was back at her mouth. His tongue entered her and began to explore. She gave him a soft mulling sound when he lifted his mouth and brushed his tongue over the outside of her lips, then along her cheek, jawline, neck, and back up to her lips. His fingers began to tug the buttons at the front of her pink flowered dress.

Again, she gave a muted sigh when he slowly released the buttons. He was going to touch her in the place she longed for him to caress her. She pushed against his hands when they brushed her feminine softness. This time, he gave a subdued muffle. "You want me to touch you here?"

Cora felt breathless. She had no words, or if she did, they wouldn't come out, "Immm..." came her muffled affirmation.

Noah released the last button and pushed the dress front open. She wore a cotton chamise with narrow ties, which he quickly untied, pushed aside, and exposed her naked flesh. "You are so beautiful," he whispered.

His hands gently massaged her, bringing her nipples alive. Before Cora could register this wonderful feeling, he was capturing one nipple inside the warmth of his mouth, bathing her with the heat of his very mobile tongue.

She arched her body up, pushing herself further into his mouth. Languidly, he took advantage and suckled her.

"Oh, Noah, this feels so…"

He lifted his mouth and murmured against her wet skin, "Amazing because you are." He pulled her nipple back into his mouth. For several moments, he bathed her and gently scraped his teeth across the hardened tip before he switched to her other breast and repeated the process.

When he finished kissing her breasts, he felt her hips begin to gyrate against him, and he carefully slid the dress and chemise down to her waist, where he lifted her hips and pulled the remaining material free of her body. All she had left to wear were her pantalets. These he left for the time being. He caressed the soft inside of her thighs. Slowly he slipped his hand up to the underside slit between her upper thighs and moved his hand inside the cotton material, cupping the silky curls and then sliding his fingers between the feminine folds.

Cora groaned at the sensation and squirmed. "Oh…tarnation! Noah, what are you…." She didn't finish when his fingers moved back and forth over the swollen bud of her pleasure center. She was moist. Her body begging for more attention. Which he gave her using his thumb and fingers to slide over her responsive inner skin, velvety soft and very moist.

Something was happening inside her. The sensation was so intense that she couldn't help but cry at the pleasure spilling like warm honey. She ground her hips against his hand and the mattress.

Noah knew instinctively that she was nearing her first climax, but he wasn't done. He slipped a finger inside her, and again, she cried out, a breathless beat of fulfillment. He leveled himself up, kissed her bare belly, dipped his tongue inside her navel, and returned to her breasts.

Her eyes were closed, and the expression on her face was pure bliss. "Cora, honey, your body is ready to accept mine. Do you want me inside you?" *Dear God, he hoped so!* "The first time will bring you pain, but you will enjoy all the sensations afterward." Thank the good Lord; his father explained all this to him many years ago. Noah had never taken a virgin before. And God help him he didn't want to hurt her.

"Yes, please, I want you inside me. My body has been telling me I need more. "Please, Noah, love me."

He removed her pantaloons, then his long johns. Slowly, he covered her body with his own warmth. She was so moist with arousal. He prayed she was ready for him.

She clamped her hands on his buttocks and naturally widened her legs so he could enter her.

The moment he did, her lips pinched tightly together, and her topaz eyes widened with awe or shock. He wasn't sure.

Chapter Sixteen

"Are you all right? I'm told this will hurt you the first time I make love to you; I must penetrate your maidenhead, and I've just reached it. God knows I don't want to give you pain, but I'm also told when I break through the gift of you, the feeling will be pleasurable for you. Are you still sure you want to take this to the next level?" Noah was so damn nervous he didn't want to hurt her, and he knew he would. He just prayed he could stop if he had to.

He was ready to explode. His mind was thinking one thing, but his sexual organ was on a completely different track, especially when he felt her sensual movements beneath him igniting him further.

"I want you to love me the whole way. I want to know what it is between a man and a woman who love each other. To feel you inside of me. To be a part of you. I want the beauty of your love and the closeness of our bodies. Only with you, Noah."

He kissed her deeply and carefully continued to enter her. She was so tight. Taking an inch at a time, he moved so painstakingly slow. Again, he asked. "Are you all right."

She smiled at him. "I'm fine. I love the feel of you, but I thought there would be more of you. This doesn't hurt at all."

"There is more of me, honey. I'm just trying like hell to slow down." He moved another inch or two. In seconds, he burst through her feminine barrier. He leaned down and took her lips, bathing her with his tongue. She was like satin and creamy velvet. For a few seconds, he felt her stiffen and give a small cry. He stayed where he was, allowing her body to adjust to him; all the while, he continued to kiss her, moving his hand between them and cupping the silkiness between her legs, finding the passion knob, caressing her with his thumb. She began to gyrate her hips.

"Ahh, Noah, I feel you deep inside me, and you feel so good."

"And you are sure I'm not hurting you?"

"Maybe a little at first. But I am alright, really."

"Then you need to know there is more of me to share with you." He kissed her. "Are you ready?"

I'm ready; take me to heaven."

"Heaven, huh? I think it's me that's in heaven, little angel." He moved deeper within her with an in-and-out motion. He felt his release coming, but he wanted to hold back, but when she began to meet him with her own thrusts, he lost the strength to curtail himself. It had been so long since he'd had a woman, and Cora's body enveloped him with the most beautifully tight fit he had ever had. He felt his climax spill inside her. And God only knew he wanted to reciprocate the beauty back to her. Still, inside her, he used his fingers to massage the creamy inner folds within her and over the sensitive knob of her sacred place.

Cora began to moan with pleasure as she thoroughly enjoyed what his hand and fingers were doing. A burning inner fire of wonder cascaded through her body. She felt warm and tingly everywhere, but especially between her legs where his fingers were bringing her magic, along with the sensation of him still being lodged within her. She moaned with pleasure.

This feeling was nothing compared to what she felt earlier when he kissed her, though close when he suckled on her breasts. This was far better. She clung to him. Oh, Noah, is this what I am supposed to feel? I never imagined..." she couldn't finish; she released her climax. The feeling was so potent; there was nothing in her life to compare to the physical pleasure he was giving her.

"Ah honey, let me feel your body respond to me," he whispered against her mouth. Her moistness mingled with his own and covered his fingers and the palm of his hand. Lord God, she was so beautiful.

She cried out with a shutter of satisfaction. "Oh, my stars, Noah. Is this how you feel? So delicious. So wonderous," she shuttered and softly moaned a cooing sound that touched him in a way he had never felt before.

"Yes, and I'm still feeling those things right now." He was still hard inside her and, with a few brisk movements, took a deep breath and whispered against her mouth. "I don't know if my feelings are the same as yours, but you make my insides dance for release. Our bodies fit so well together. I don't think I will ever get enough of you. God, my little angel, you hug me so perfectly."

He felt her release and listened to her moan of pleasure. In seconds, he again spilled his seed within her and was amazed he could, especially so swiftly after the first time. After several minutes, he began to pull out and heard her sigh as she caressed his back and buttocks, over his hips and upper thighs, and then between his legs.

"Ummm, you need to ummm... your body needs to rest, and so does mine. Aren't you sore? Next time, it will be easier and not painful. We don't need to rush...ah..." he moaned as he slowly pulled out all the way.

Her fingers lightly brushed against the intimate length of him. Wet from their commingling.

"I'm not sore at all," she softly murmured. "Are you?" Then she noticed the sprinkle of blood. "Oh, no, but you must be hurt. You are bleeding!"

He smiled and moved slightly to his back, pulling her close to his body. "No, sweetheart, the blood came from you when I pushed through your maidenhead."

She blushed, "gracious! That's from me. I had no idea."

"Your maidenhead is a soft piece of tissue, and when it breaks, it slightly bleeds like a small cut. You only have one, and once it is broken, it never returns."

"How do you know so much?"

"When I was growing up, my father explained all this to me, as I'm sure his father explained. It is a precious gift a woman can give to a man, telling him no one has been there before him." Noah wrapped an arm around her nakedness and tugged her bottom close in spoon fashion between his hips and upper thighs. Then he moved his arm and hand across her belly.

Cora used his other arm as a pillow, resting her cheek against the muscled upper portion, snuggling closer. "Thank you, Noah, for a wonderful night. Eating homemade bread and honey, dancing, and mat...making love. I could never want more. I love you so much."

"Trust me, little angel, it was wonderful for both of us. But there is still the worry those men who are after me and killed Elijah are still out there. For now, they know nothing of you. But if they return here, all that will change."

"Are you suggesting I dress like a boy again? My hair is finally growing, and I really don't want to smash my bubbies."

Noah reached up and caressed her breasts, "I would never do that to you again, and I do love caressing you here." He filled his hand with her breast. "But we need to figure out something. I don't have a cellar here for you to hide in." he felt her shiver from cold or fear; he wasn't sure. He pulled the blanket up over them both. "We don't need to decide anything tonight. We'll figure out something in the morning. How does that sound?"

Cora pushed tighter against his arm, "tomorrow morning," she repeated.

Noah kissed the top of her head, "Let's get some sleep. The sun will be up in a few hours. And we have a lot to do if you still want me to cut a Christmas tree. In a couple of weeks, it will be Christmas Eve. I don't have a gift for you."

She giggled, "I think you just gave me a gift, and it's the best present I ever got."

He grinned back and pulled her beneath him. His lips made sensual pathways across her face to her mouth. I guess we gave each other a gift." He kissed her deeply, and a robust, sensual light passed between them, leaving a smoldering flame to ignite inside their bodies. Tongues massaged, explored, and made love as their naked bodies had done a short time ago. After several minutes, Noah felt himself grow with hardened desire again.

He reached between them and molded her breasts inside his hands, splaying his fingers over and over across her extended nipples. He was about to move his mouth down to exchange with his fingers when they both heard the scratch at the door. "Damn," Noah muttered.

Loka wanted in. Noah slid out of bed and padded naked across the floor. The moment he opened the heavy wooden entrance, the wolf-dog leaped inside, bringing a burst of icy air with him. "You have miserable timing, my friend!" Noah growled.

Loka ignored Noah and made his way to his water bowl. He drank his fill and then turned to jump up on the bed, but he discovered Noah had beat him to it. The wolf glared, whined, gave a growling bark, turned in circles, and plopped down on the floor near the warmth of the fireplace that still danced with flames. He gave another dissatisfied growl before laying his head on his front paws.

Both Noah and Cora chuckled. "Ooo, your feet are freezing, Cora complained.

"So warm me up."

"Noah!" she screeched when he ran his bare foot up and down the calf of her leg. "Where's your socks?"

"On the floor tucked into my boots. Want me to get them?" he teased, continuing to rub the bottom of his foot against her leg. "You are warming me up just fine."

She reached around and swatted his behind. "Tarnation! You are even cold back here."

"Uh-huh," he released her leg, turned on his opposite side, and pushed his fanny up next to her warm belly. "You sure are nice and toasty. You feel so good.

This time, she reached her arm around him and huddled closer. I guess I'll warm you up." She let her hands slide down his belly across his hips, allowing her thumbs to inch closer, closer to his arousal.

Yup, he was getting toasty warm, alright. He was also hardened with arousal and began to wiggle against her pelvic bone the moment her fingers brushed the tip of his sex.

"Noah Harper, I thought you wanted to sleep?" She felt his smile before she saw it, and she kissed his back, making designs with her lips and tongue. And delighted when she felt him shiver. Not from cold but sexual heat. In moments, he turned around and gently pulled her beneath him; quicker than he could say his name, he was inside her, slow at first, then faster and deeper, so much for giving her more time.

※

In the following two weeks, the temperatures plummeted about thirty degrees. They had not seen any more snow storms, though they both knew it was only a matter of time. However, right now, sunlight shot through the evergreen trees, bare Drumond, willow, and alder. The lower temperatures made January very cold, though snowless.

They celebrated Christmas, and as Noah promised, he cut a small pine tree. They decorated it with dried berries and paper angels. A few angels were crooked, and they teased each other about who may have cut the worst of the lot. None of it mattered; they had a splendid holiday.

Cora hydrated some of the dried wild berries and baked them a pie. They danced, sang, and made love long into the wee hours of the morning. It was a wonderful Christmas gift they were delighted to give one another.

Following the first night of lovemaking, Noah disassembled his pallet on the floor and shared the one bed with Cora every night. He wore his woolen socks to bed, though the rest of him was as naked as the day he was born. Cora didn't mind; she was fascinated with his very masculine, rugged, lean body, and she enjoyed petting him whenever she got the chance.

Daily, they took turns using the hip tub, one inside while the other stayed outside with a sponge and soap. They washed each other's backs, fronts, hips, legs, and sensitive parts. There were so many sensitive spots to explore, and they quickly turned the whole experience into a game that guided them back to bed and more love-making. They were happier than either one had ever been or ever imagined they could be.

One evening, Cora pulled a colorful cord from her clothing trunk, wrapped it around Noah and her wrists, and tied them together. When she was finished, she announced they were now man and wife in the Cheyenne way. Of course, there was more to the ceremony in reality; there was no family or friends around, and there was no horse to ride throughout the village and share their happiness with loved ones. But they were both content and so much in love they were joyful with the ceremony they made up.

That night, when they made love, they experimented. Noah began to undress Cora slowly, and she had never felt more loved or fulfilled when he caressed and kissed her, honoring her body. She did the same for him. The taste of him went through to her soul. A fire only he could build or douse.

With a soft, crooning sound of pleasure, she wound her arms around him. Wanting everything he gave her. And he gave of himself and to her with overwhelming tenderness.

His kisses turned deeply sensual, igniting heat that roared through her body. She became dizzy with the taste of him and the slow delivery of his tongue inside her mouth, against her breasts, and lower across her belly, to the sensitive insides of her thighs. She thought she would explode when he reached the juncture of her womanhood. He pushed the soft curls aside and worked through her warm folds. He was kissing and tasting as he went. He was driving her crazy with the most intimate kisses.

The moment he buried his mouth into the hot, sensitized folds of her and ran his tongue back and forth over her insides, she found she couldn't breathe. *"Sweet mercy!* Noah!" She muttered incoherently, yet in the same instance, she lifted her lower body to his mouth, getting closer to his exploration. Neither could get enough of the other. Never in her whole life could Cora ever have imagined such pure, unadulterated ecstasy. The rapture was so foreign she didn't know whether she was coming or going. "Noah!" his name was wrenched from deep inside her. "What are you...ah...."

"Shh," he whispered against her moist skin, never stopping the movements of his tongue or lips. "I just want to love and kiss every last inch of you. This is the first time for me, too. You are so sweet. Just let me love you."

Cora couldn't speak; the things he was doing to her silenced all but the soft moaning of pleasure. She couldn't have said a word even if she wanted to. And she didn't want to. Noah was giving her such heavenly euphoria. She was on fire, and just like every time they made love, the intense heat of climax plunged through her.

When he lifted his head to gaze at her, she wore the dreamiest sensual look he had ever seen. And he knew her body was experiencing an exploding fulfillment. The physicality and emotion of it pleased him.

Slowly, he began to move his body back up the length of her. His erection brushed against the satiny heat of her pubis and pelvic bone. "You are so beautiful, my little angel. He trailed his tongue up along her breasts, taking a nipple deeply into his mouth, and listened to her moan, making his own erogenous zones fill with uninhibited pleasure. He placed his hands beneath her bottom, lifted her, then entered her, slow then urgently. No woman had ever felt so good, and he knew without a doubt that none ever would again, not after having the perfection of his little angel.

Instantly, she wrapped her legs around his midsection and relished the feel of him when he moved inside her.

January flowed into February, colliding into March with a vengeance of a roaring lion as storm after storm moved through the mountain. But none of it mattered to the lovers. They were the most glorious times of their lives.

And in itself brought numerous gifts.

Chapter Seventeen

Three hundred miles away on the eastern slopes of the Rocky Mountains, facing the vast plains of Kansas. Signs of spring were beginning to show. Miles of range grass flowed undulating in the breeze across an open valley resembling ocean waves. Wildflowers cropped up here and there across the land. Four people, two boys, a man in his mid-forties, and a woman in her early thirties, were standing over a piece of farm equipment shaking their heads.

This was the picture Captain Tamarin and his five cohorts saw as they rode onto the land early in the morning. The sun had just crested Pikes Peak. For a moment, they watched as the shabby-looking farmer, dressed in shirtless, worn-out coveralls, and a woman wearing equally worn-out clothing, issued orders to two young boys.

"Sodbusters," Hyrum spat and gritted through tobacco-stained teeth. God, I hate dirt farmers and the way they stink up the land with their pigs and friggin' goats!"

Lamar glared over to the man with amusement. "If it weren't for them, this country would have no produce to sell at market or hay for the horses you ride."

Hyrum shot a long stream of brown juice. "Makes no friggin' difference to me. I hate vegetables, the smell of pigs, and what the hell do you do with goats? And there's still plenty of grass for the horses. Sheet!" He spat. "I'd just sooner shoot the mud-caked sod busters than not. I hate um!"

"You may get the chance if they refuse to give us the information we want," Lamar said with an irritated laugh. He needed these men, but there were days when he felt like shooting all of them himself.

Hyrum spit another stream of spittle that looked like the color of dried cow dung as it splattered on the newly tilled ground.

The two young boys were out in the pasture working with an old wooden plow attached to a massive Oxen. It appeared they were experiencing a breakdown. The cast iron parts added to the cutting blades looked like they'd come loose, clanging and rattling as they bent over, trying to reattach them.

Hyrum and the others watched with humor when the farmer pulled off his sweat-stained hat, swatted his upper thigh, and raked his right hand through his damp hair. He moved across the half-plowed rocky pasture and headed for a dilapidated-looking barn. His wife quickly followed him while the two boys began to unhitch the Oxen. The woman appeared younger than they first thought. Women didn't last long with this kind of life.

"I sure would like a piece of that!" Hyrum gave a pleasurable snort of lustful innuendo. Sure, as shit I would."

The worn-out farmer heard the ruffians before he saw them. He came around the corner of the barn to get a better look, his wife closely following. The men were all riding frisky horses across the prairie toward the barn. The horses they rode were probably stolen. All six riders looked like a rough bunch as they galloped, kicking up plowed dirt clods as they moved. That was the first sign that made the farmer's heartbeat race. The second was he knew without ever being told these men were mean, brutal and out for trouble. "Get into the house!" he ordered his frightened wife. Get the rifle."

"Oh, my Lord, Johnson, what do they want? Are they here to rob us? Or worse?"

"Whatever they want, it ain't good. That's trouble riding toward us if ever I saw it. Now hurry, woman, and go around the back way."

It did no good. One of the men stopped in the barnyard through a cloud of dust. He slid from his mount and went after the woman. Once he had her, he dragged her over to the captain. "Well, looky what we got here. I want the first dibs. She's kind of pretty."

"Martha, don't fight, honey. Do as they want!" the farmer shouted in panic. He was unarmed and defenseless."

"We got questions for you," Lamar growled. "Give us the answers we want, and no harm will come to you or yours."

The farmer knew whatever questions these men spoke of had nothing to do with directions or anything that could be interpreted as innocent. But he asked anyway. "What kind of questions? We wouldn't have many answers. We live out here, mind our own business, and rarely have company. If you are looking for the nearest town, it is about twenty miles south of here, called Silver Spur. There ain't nothing more I can tell you. Please tell your man to let my wife go."

Hyrum, who held Martha, just laughed and spit. He continued to grip the woman's arm. "Hot damn, Lamar, ain't she just a live one."

Then he glared at the farmer. "She ain't goin' nowhere. He pressed her tighter against the length of him and ran his tongue over her face.

With a satisfied grin, Lamar glared at Johnson. "We were told the person we were looking for rode this way a few years back. He played guitar in many saloons as he traveled from town to town. He may have decided to stay here and might even be one of your neighbors. His name is Noah Harper. Ever heard of him?" Lamar asked with malice.

Johnson became even more uneasy. He indeed had met a traveling guitar man, a drifter, several years ago when he and his oldest boy first came to the area. But the guitar man he knew went by Jones. And he distinctly remembered his talent with a guitar. Played most every night in the town's only saloon. They got to know each other as strangers have a way of doing. In fact, it was Jones who invited him to the town's spring dance that first year. Jones would be accompanying a minor quartet of musicians.

It was one of the happiest nights Johnson had experienced since losing his first wife three years prior and where he met his current wife, Martha. He had been trying to raise his son alone and make enough money on his farm to support them. Martha was pretty, sweet, and willing to marry him to help raise his young son. After the first year, they had a child together. His son from his first marriage turned thirteen a month ago. The boy he and Martha shared would be eight by summer's end.

But Johnson decided that none of this mattered to these hooligans. He would not stay silent to protect this Jones fella as long as his family were in danger. He looked up to the man who seemed to be the leader. His expression gave nothing away. Everything inside Johnson told him his life and the lives of his family were about to come to an end—especially the way the scroungiest one was man-handling Martha by yanking her up against his filth.

Johnson licked his lips and nervously glared at Lamar. "There was a drifter I met 'bout eight or more years ago, called himself Jones, not Harper. But I couldn't say if he was still in the area. Now I told you everything I know. The townspeople may know more. Like I said, we stay to ourselves. Please let my wife go."

"Hmm," Lamar looked doubtful. This wasn't the first time he'd heard the name Jones. "I think you are lying. You know where this Jones is?" he glanced over to Simon, who had dismounted and anxiously shuffled his feet in the dirt. The bastard had turned out to be such a yellow-bellied coward. But for the moment, he needed him. He was one of the original riders, and Simon did help keep some of the others under control. He looked back at the farmer. "I'd start talking, or my man over there holding your wife will take his fun with her."

"No! I've told you all I know," Johnson shouted with panic. "Let Martha go!"

"So that's her name. Hyrum lasciviously groped the woman between the legs and laughed.

Lamar kept his vision on the farmer and shouted out to Hyrum. "This here, farmer says, don't hurt Martha. What do you think, Hyrum?" Lamar joined in the laughter, not realizing the opening he gave Hyrum.

There was no reply.

Simon, Lamar and the farmer glared over to Hyrum for an answer, but he and the woman were gone.

"My wife!" Johnson cried out in fear. "What has your man done with her?"

"Hyrum!" Lamar shouted.

No reply.

"Son of a bitch!" Lamar gave Simon a look of abhorrence. "Go and get him!"

Simultaneously, they all heard the blood-curdling scream of a woman. And all three ran for the barn.

The rest of the men remained saddled and laughed. "Looks like Hyrum's gone and got hisself some tail."

"The ugly horn toad!" said another.

"True, but also one lucky horn toad."

Martha's dress was torn open on the top, the bottom half was wrapped around her hips, and her legs were painfully spread while Hyrum tried to shove himself inside her with a vicious forward motion as he clamped onto one of her breasts. "God damn!" he spat. "She's as dry as an old prune. She's gonna scrape the skin off my rod."

"Get off her!" the farmer yelled. "Can't you see you're killing her?"

Hyrum just laughed.

Lamar leaned down, grabbed Hyrum by the collar, and hauled him off the woman. "You're done."

Hyrum grinned as he looked down at himself. He'd already sported a mess all over the front of his pants.

"Guess I am at that," he grinned.

Lamar swore and cocked his Army Colt. He shot Martha between the eyes. When he heard the farmer's caterwauling from behind, he turned and did the same to him. "Christ! Hyrum, you're such a stupid bastard. I swear, one of these days, that's gonna be you laying there bleeding. And it will be me doing the shooting!"

"Clean this up!" Lamar glaringly ordered Simon, noting the distress on the younger man's face. "Find those two boys, kill them, and bury them all deep!"

But Simon stood frozen to the spot. He was going to toss his stomach.

"Christ, sake, you yellow-bellied coward! Wake up and get your ass out of your head and take care of this."

The two boys in the pasture heard the gunshot. Wide-eyed and fearful, they ran into the barn from the back entrance, pulling the ox behind them. "Ma, Pa..." were the last two words they spoke. Two quick shots from Lamar's Colt, and they both lay dead in the barn's corridor. The old ox clomped all over the bodies before he turned and shuffled back outside.

Lamar kicked Simon in the rear, sending him spilling across the bloodied farmer. "Now bury 'em!" He ordered with repugnance, grabbed Hyrum's arm, and angrily yanked him from the barn. "And when you are done with this mess," Lamar said over his shoulder, "meet us in Silver Spur!" He shoved Hyrum forward, who still laughed. "Mount up, you sonofabitch!"

"What about Simon? You gonna leave him here alone?" Earl, one of the mounted men, shouted out.

"Damn right. The coward ain't got enough guts to go on alone. He'll meet us."

The moment Simon heard the men ride out, he began dragging the bodies out of the barn and toward the lone cottonwood at the top of the shallow hill where a small cemetery stood. This would be the last thing he would ever perform for Lamar Tamarin—even if escaping meant losing his life. At this point, dead or alive didn't much matter; he'd be free. He glanced down at the four bodies. These poor people deserved better.

Left behind to do the burying, Simon felt grateful for the first time in a long time. He had no intention of ever meeting up with Lamar and his men in Silver Spur. He prayed Noah was long gone and had actually made a life for himself on the San Juan like the gal in Cheyenne said he wanted. Excitement for the first time in years filled Simon. Finally, he could do the right thing.

Or at least try.

He knew he would never be able to put the dark memories of what he had helped to do all those years ago in the Cheyenne village or the horror he'd been part of all the years that followed.

To keep himself sane, he had turned to drinking, whoring, and gambling. Ultimately, he knew it was a surefire way to keep him trapped on the road to hell.

But he did it anyway.

Now, here he was, standing before four newly dug graves on a lonely hill above the farmhouse, knowing full well his soul was being eaten up for everything he had chosen to do since 1878.

Well, no more.

He was sick to death of this cast of heathens he spent the last ten years with. Each man who had left the group was replaced with worse men. Men like Hyrum. The man had a sickness inside him, even worse than the others.

Simon tossed the shovel away, doubled over, lost his stomach at the side of the old cottonwood, and then kicked dirt over the mess.

The sun was a half-circle on the western mountains. It would be nightfall soon. He was bone weary not only physically but emotionally. He returned to the barn, mounted his horse, and rode west. It would take him several weeks, maybe longer if the weather changed, but come hell or high water, he would head back to the small border town of Willowby nestled at the foot of the San Juan. If he were lucky, he'd reach it before the others. Noah needed to know the danger. And Simon needed to clear his soul, even if it sent him to Hell! He had no doubt he'd end up there anyway.

Chapter Eighteen

March blew in with a blizzard of iciness along the higher elevations of the San Juan. Noah and Cora were pretty much housebound. The only one who had any freedom was Loka. He was gone off and on for days at a time.

"Every spring, he does this," Noah told Cora as he set his guitar aside after playing all morning. "It's mating season." He turned and studied Cora.

She had been running to the outhouse several times in the morning for the past week. He suspected she might be with child. She was sitting in a refurbished rocking chair he had fashioned for her and knitting a blanket for the foot of the bed. She had already made several pairs of socks and colorful caps for their heads.

She looked up and smiled. She was humming a tune. The yarn she worked with was spread over her lap, leaving several strands streaming down to the cabin floor.

"Umm honey, when did you last have your monthly bleed? We have been making love nearly every night for the past three months. Do you remember the last time you bled?"

She glanced up from her knitting; her cheeks were a deep shade of mauve. "Gracious Noah, why are you asking such a question?" She studied his face for a long while, then replied. "I'm not sure. I've just been enjoying not having the curse or the cramps that come with it. Is something wrong?"

Noah cleared his throat. "Nothing is wrong, but I think you might be pregnant."

Cora grasped her flat belly. "What makes you say that? Am I getting fat?"

He smiled. "No, sweetheart, I don't think you are getting fat. You've been losing your stomach every morning for the past week; I think it might be morning sickness. And your breasts are a little fuller, and your nipples are slightly darker. All signs of carrying a child."

"Oh, you really think so—a baby. And I thought I might be catching a flu bug or had eaten something that didn't agree with me. I've been afraid you might catch it."

"Well, if it's what I suspect, I can't catch this," he grinned. "Would you let me examine you? I've had enough medical background to be able to tell."

She set her knitting aside, "what do you need me to do?"

"Come over here, lay on the bed, and unbutton your dress." She did what he asked, but she looked dubious.

"Are you sure you don't just want to make love? You know you can any time you want to."

He took her hand and led her to the bed. "I always want to make love to you, but not right now. I want to examine you. Once she was settled on the bed, her clothing undone, he reached into his trunk, pulled his old medical bag containing his stethoscope, and approached her. Pushing her dress aside and lifting her camisole, he gently pressed the round disk against her belly to listen for a second heartbeat.

"Tarnation, Noah, that thing is freezing."

"Sorry, honey, I should have warmed it in my hands first. It's probably too early to detect an extra heartbeat. I want to make sure," he found he was right; he only heard one heartbeat. He used his hands and moved gently around her belly. She began to feel the heat of arousal move through her, and she giggled.

"Hold still," he grinned.

She did, but Lord, she loved his touch. Next, he checked her breasts, "are you a little tender when I touch you here?" he asked, running his fingers over the hardened tips of her darkened nipples. The sensual movements she was making beneath his touch had begun to arouse him.

"Umm, no," she whispered, "but your touch makes me crazy. Please keep doing it. In fact, I want you to kiss me."

"You are not making this easy. I'm trying to be serious."

"I'm very serious. Make love to me."

"You are insatiable. But then again, so am I," he chuckled.

"Is that good or bad?" she asked, a bit nervous.

"Very good," and he lowered his lips and took a nipple inside the warmth of his mouth. "I can see you will be a difficult patient." He moved his tongue, bathing first one breast and then the other before he moved up to her mouth, pressing his lips against hers, using his tongue to deepen the kiss as he partially crawled on top of her. When he leaned up to look down at her, Cora quickly began to lift his shirt.

Once she got it over his head, the rest came off quickly. "You don't have your long johns on today." She ran her hands over his naked chest, curling her fingers through the soft chestnut fluff of his breast muscles, then lower to his navel and the light dusting of masculine hair surrounding the indentation.

When she reached the waistband of his pants, she untied the front, tucked her fingers beneath the bottom half of his knee-length underwear, and pushed both articles of clothing down over his hips. He finished yanking them off the rest of the way. She reached over and wrapped her hand around his hardened arousal and moved up and down.

Cora rejoiced in the hardness she caressed and smiled when she heard him whisper, "I want to be inside you, fill you with my love," he half moaned, half pleaded. She removed her hand from him, and when she felt his stiffened sex brush against the silken triangle between her legs, she quickly guided him inside and welcomed him with her heat. In seconds, he was filling her as deeply as her body would allow. The sweetness hugged his length, causing him to groan against her ear. "Ah, Cora, I don't think I will ever get enough of you," he whispered, moving briskly within her.

She felt his climax the moment he released inside her and melted when she felt the pinnacle of her release match his.

Noah rolled off her onto his back and pulled her close to his side. "The next time you need to urinate, I want you to do it in that jar I put on the table."

"Gracious Noah, what a thing to talk about after what we just did for each other. Tarnation, whyever would you want me to do such a thing? For goodness sake, that's nasty."

He chuckled, "It's something I learned in Med school. It's called *Kyesteine Pellicle.* You let the urine sit for a couple of days; if a membrane, like a sticky film, forms on the surface, it's supposed to mean a positive pregnancy result. At least, that's what the medical journal says. I have never been able to test the theory until now."

"Then I guess this is your chance to try it. Okay, I'll do it; in fact, I need to go right now."

He watched her quickly dress, grab the jar and her coat, bundle up, and head outside. When they went to town in the spring, he would definitely pick up supplies to build a washroom with a commode.

Ten minutes later, Cora returned to the cabin. "Noah Harper, do you know how hard it is for a woman to pee in a bottle? Tarnation! Now, where do you want this? I need to wash up."

Noah watched her unladylike regard and chuckled. "Sorry honey, but it is the best way to get a result. If we are going to have a baby, it's best we know sooner than later. Put the lid on the jar and place it in the corner on the other side of the bed where it will be out of the way. Want me to get some water heated for a bath?"

"For now, I'll just wash my hands. But tonight, I'll want a bath."

"Me too. And everything that goes with it," he snickered.

Cora giggled.

The urine test didn't work, though Noah was still sure Cora was with child. He finally got her to narrow down her last menstrual cycle. As near as she could tell, it had been about a month and a half ago. Cora continued to get sick sometimes in the morning and other times in the afternoon. And that wasn't the only symptom. Her appetite had changed, and she barely ate anything, but when she did eat, it came right back up.

She was getting headaches and urinating more frequently; he figured she was probably seven to eight weeks along. He knew these symptoms were normal for some women. But he was frightened. Why hadn't he thought of any of this before they made love? They were out here in the middle of nowhere. It never occurred to him that he might deliver his own child one day.

The thought of a child was a blessing, and Noah felt sure he could deliver the baby. But still, he was worried. If there were any complications, well, hell, he didn't know. He began reading every medical book and journal he owned. The problem was that as each year passed, the medical field became more and more advanced. And there were too many things that could go wrong: breech births and cesarean sections. God, the thought of cutting into her made him sick.

The best scenario would be to find a way to get them to town as soon as the pass became clear of snow and mud. Even so, twenty miles to Willowby was not an easy route, and on foot, with the threat of more snow, the idea was nearly impossible for a pregnant woman. Cora was physically strong, but pregnancy took a toll on a woman's body.

Ah, Christ on a crutch, what should he do?

The only thing he was sure of was he never wanted to be alone again. She was such a part of him. He'd committed to her and had every intention of keeping it. He loved her more than he thought could ever be possible. And the child they made needed to be protected. But up here alone, if anything happened to take her or the baby from him, he would never forgive himself. Over and over, the fears and worries circled his brain.

"What are you looking so sour about?" Cora asked, looking up from her knitting.

Noah lifted his gaze from his books. "Not sour, just thinking."

"About what? Maybe I can help."

"Something you are probably not going to like."

Her pretty face turned into a grimace. "Then you just better spit it out."

"I think it will be better to wait until the baby is born before going to town. It will be early fall by then. It's a long trek, and we must make it on foot. And your morning sickness will probably get worse before it gets better. You will be further into the pregnancy when the nausea finally runs its course. I want you and the baby to be safe and healthy."

"I see. And you are worried it would be a strain if I go to town? And you are worried about leaving me if you go by yourself."

"Yes, if anything happens to you, it would kill me."

"Nothing's going to happen. Go and don't worry. I'll be fine, and I'll have Loka for company. I don't mind at all. There are things we must have to prepare for the child. I will be just fine if you go down by yourself. I'll miss you, of course, but there are things we will need. Take some of grandfather's money, buy the supplies, and maybe purchase a mule or a draft horse. Oh, and a wagon."

"But you've been sick. I hate leaving you alone."

"For goodness' sake, you told me this was a natural part of the process unless you were fibbing to me. I promise I can take care of myself."

"Will you promise to try and eat something even if it's just broth?"

"You know I will. It would be best to worry more for yourself; it's a long trip, especially on foot.

"How long do you think it would take?" *Christ on a crutch!* "I haven't returned to that town in over eight years."

"Grandfather was usually back in a month, but he had a friend down there with whom he spent time. If you go and come right back, I expect it will take a couple of days to get down, but quicker coming back up with a horse or mule and the wagon to carry everything. Maybe a week altogether."

"Any specific areas I should be aware of or avoid?"

"Well, it's been years since I went with Grandfather. I don't remember many difficulties—possibly the lower Narrows. With spring runoff, they can be treacherous. If you wait another month, you should be fine. By then, most of the runoff should be contained. Just keep in mind these mountains can be unpredictable. And stay away from any slot canyons. In the spring, they can be very dangerous. Hopefully, this morning, sickness will be resolved by that time."

Noah met her gaze. He was so damn proud of her. He got up from the chair he'd been sitting on and approached her. He took the yarn and needles she'd been working with, set it aside, and lifted her from the rocking chair. "Mrs. Cora Harper, I love you so much. His mouth crashed down on top of hers.

Cora swayed against the hard length of him. Her heart pounded in her chest like the crazy thumping of a hammer when he softly pushed his tongue inside her mouth, deepening the kiss. He splayed his hands across her back, down the sides of her ribs, and finally caressed her soft belly where their child grew. He lifted his head and gazed into her sparkly topaz eyes. "You'll start showing in a few months, and I can't wait to caress you here, knowing our child is growing inside you."

She lifted her hands and cupped them on either side of his face. "Tarnation, Noah, how I love you."

He smiled. "Want to go back to bed?" He was already tormenting her breasts, using his thumbs to trace over the hardened tips.

"Imm," she whispered and lowered one hand to stroke the hardness between his legs. "Let's do."

Simon finally made it to Willoby. He had been on the run for almost two months. So far, he had been able to elude the captain and his men. But he was sure none of them had forgotten him. He knew too much for them to let him go. He was pretty sure he was still ahead of them.

He also felt he was close to Noah. He needed to replace his horse if he was going to make the trip up the San Juan to warn him. He stood in the town's single livery and waited for the blacksmith to tally up his bill. In just a week, it would be April, he realized when he glanced at a calendar that hung on the owner's office wall.

To be on the safe side, Simon changed his appearance. He had added a few pounds, and though still slim, he was more muscular. Dressed more like a cowboy, he sported a short-cropped beard and mustache. His only resemblance to his old self was the silvery shade of his eyes.

He'd rented a room over the saloon and kept to himself. He didn't even attempt to spend any time with a sporting woman if there were any. The fewer people who noticed him, the better off he was, especially since he knew the captain and the men would soon be here. If he were lucky, he'd have a week before the others showed up and be long gone. A part of him was nervous about seeing Noah again, yet the other half was pleased to see his friend, even if it would be the last time.

Simon was positive he would be a dead man when all this ended.

"Hey, mister!" the burly blacksmith interrupted Simon's thoughts. "Are you going to be wantin' this other horse too? She's a beauty who will make a great pack horse and is partial to the Morgan you wanted to purchase. I just gave both horses a good rub down, clean-picked their hoofs, and just finished changing their shoes. They are both ready whenever you are. I'll give you a good deal."

"Sure. You got a saddle for sale?"

"Lawrance Chester has some good ones down at the Emporium. His prices are fair."

"Great. I'll go check it out. I need some supplies. Do you know if there are any maps of the area?"

"Check that with Laurance as well. He's usually well stocked."

"Thanks. I'll return in a few hours, and we'll settle up." Simon tipped his felt hat, headed down the street to the store the old man had told him about, and found everything he needed. The following morning, he was on his way, using the map. He had packed all his supplies on the extra horse he had purchased. The morning was sunny and filled him with hope. Something he hadn't known for years.

Captain Tamarin and the men had waited for just over a week in Silver Spur, the town the farmer mentioned. Simon never showed up. No one said anything, but they all knew Lamar's long-time riding partner had high-tailed it for parts unknown. He was a dead man if they ever caught up to him. They had already wasted too much time. The following morning, they packed up and headed southwest and back to San Juan.

April shone brightly in between all the rain showers. The snow was melting exponentially. The days were longer and warmer, with temperatures in the mid-forties to low fifties. Flowers were popping up in the meadows and on the mountainsides: Blue Columbine, Mule Ear, a yellow daisy-like flower, and bright red Paintbrush. Spring had finally shown her face.

Loka had been gone for several days, and Cora was getting concerned. The morning sickness had gone entirely, and though her belly was still small, it had begun to show a slight roundness, and her breasts were indeed fuller.

"You look more beautiful every day," Noah told her as they worked together to clean up after breakfast."

She smiled appreciatively, but her topaz eyes were filled with worry.

"What is it, sweetheart? What's got you upset?"

"I worry about Loka; he's been gone an awfully long time. He must be hungry."

"Ah, honey, like I said, he does this every spring. He won't starve. He is the best hunter I've ever seen, and remember, he still has a lot of wild in him and knows how to survive. I think he has a mate. You know wolves' mate for life."

Her eyes sparkled. "That's right. I remember my grandfather telling me that. He also told me that hawks and doves also do."

Noah grinned and pulled her toward him. "Yes, and so do most humans?" he whispered. Like the two of us, though, I'm glad to be human in this case. Animals don't make love like we do."

Her cheeks turned a delicious pink. He leaned down and kissed the tip of her nose. "After we finish cleaning up, do you want to take a walk? I think I know where Loka might be, and if he is, will that calm your worry?"

Her beautiful eyes lit up, "Yes, I would like to do that very much. I need to stretch my legs anyway. I feel like we've been cooped up here for months and months."

"We kind of have, but it hasn't been so bad, has it?" He leaned over, covered her soft lips, and felt the heat in her cheeks. Even after all this time, Cora still blushed when she thought of their lovemaking, and her precious look always thrilled him.

"No, it hasn't been bad; it's been wonderful," she smiled and shyly answered. "I do love making love with you. I love your body and the way you make me feel. But a walk would also be wonderful."

Noah grinned with mischief. "Then a walk we shall take." He leaned down and kissed her and caressed her breast, igniting her nipples to a hardened peak.

"Oh, yes," she whispered against his mouth.

"Oh, yes, what?"

"Yes, make love to me."

"There's nothing in this world I want to do more." He began to unbutton the top of her dress and pushed it apart, slipping his hand inside to cup her silky flesh. She took his free hand and led him to the bed. In minutes, they were both naked, moving hands and lips over each other's bodies.

More than an hour later, they were following the same path Noah had used the day he brought Cora back to the cabin after she had run away.

"If he is where I suspect, we must be quiet and hide. We can only watch."

Excitement careened through Cora. "You think he and his mate have pups, right?"

Noah took her hand and helped her over an outcropping of rock and tree roots. "That's exactly what I think."

"Oh, Noah, that would be so magical to see."

"I'm glad there are some things I can show you. But remember, we need to be quiet so we don't rile the female."

"You are taking me to the alcove Loka led me to, aren't you?"

"Imm," he lifted a finger to his lips.

Cora slightly tipped her head up and down in understanding.

There was a cluster of gamble oaks about fifty feet from the entrance. It was here they crouched down and watched. They could hear the whine of pups. The excitement created a sensation of butterflies fluttering in Cora's stomach. Her eyes widened with pleasure, and she took Noah's hand and placed it on her slightly rounded belly.

This time, his blue sapphire eyes glistened with surprise. He mouthed the word baby.

Cora grinned and silently moved her lips, "Yes."

The pups made another sound, and they could hear some rustling. In seconds, Loka moved up behind them.

Both Noah and Cora turned. The wolf had a look that said don't you disturb my family. With bared teeth, he let out a soft growl.

Cora shuddered. She had never seen Loka bare his teeth or growl at her.

Noah carefully pulled her against his body. "I think it's time to leave. The male wolf is very protective. I don't believe he would ever hurt us, but I understand he wants to keep his family safe."

When she glanced back, Loka was gone. Then she saw him moving inside the alcove.

Noah helped her up, and they headed back down toward the cabin. "You need to remember, my little angel. Loka is used to humans, at least me, and now you. His mate is wild, and humans are the last things she would want around her pups. To her, we are just predators. My guess is she has just given birth, and Loka ensures she won't be disturbed. We'll see him again in a day or two."

Cora looked at him with such love: "Thank you for sharing this with me."

Noah smiled, took her small hand, and led her back down the path. "When I first moved up here, I also worried about Loka being gone; he, after all, is half wild. He was all I had; it would have been extremely lonely if I had lost him. But obviously, he always comes back. In many ways, we saved each other's life."

"And I shall always be grateful. In about five months, we will have our own family to protect. Every time I think about that, my heart fills with joy."

Noah pulled his timepiece from his pocket. "It is still early. How does pan-fried trout sound for dinner?"

"Sounds wonderful."

"Let's grab our poles and head down to the stream."

That night, they enjoyed a wonderful fish dinner.

The following day, Loka visited, stayed for a few hours, and returned to the alcove.

Chapter Nineteen

Simon wasn't sure what kind of welcome he would get from Noah, if any welcome at all. Whatever it was, for the first time in years, he felt like he was doing something right, and the heaviness he had felt for so long felt just a little lighter.

Last night, he studied the map he had purchased. The trails up the mountain were primitive, but if he paid attention to the landmarks the map dictated, the trail was indeed possible even for a wagon. The map was old and had not been updated for at least forty years, and drawn by an old explorer, copied, and sold to those brave enough to make the journey. As in life, people, time, and places have a way of changing. He only hoped he could figure it out as he went. *No, I will figure it out!* He thought with determination. There was no other choice if he wanted to make things right.

And he did.

The map had directed him toward a narrow canyon. Water trickled down the center. He looked skyward; there were no clouds, just a Cerulean blue heaven. Thank God he'd be caught in a roaring river if it were to rain. Just another thing he had learned from the map he now folded and placed back inside his saddle bag.

He drew a breath. He had to find Noah. Not for the first time, he was glad he had snuck back to the saloon in Cheyenne the day the captain had spoken to the woman called Sugar. She was a bit more forthright with him than she had been with the captain.

He smiled as he thought of his luck and urged the Morgan forward, leading the mare buckskin with all his supplies as they continued to follow the trail. He didn't get more than thirty feet when he heard the horrendous screech of what he assumed was a mountain lion.

In the next few weeks, Cora felt the changes in her body. As close as they could figure, she was at the end of her first trimester. Her stomach had become a small, round, hard ball. Her navel began to stick out and look distorted. "Noah, I think something is wrong; my belly button looks funny."

Noah chuckled. "No honey, that is normal. Remember how I explained about the uterus and how it becomes a home for the child? It expands to accommodate the baby and, as a result, can push your stomach forward and cause the navel to protrude. I think it looks rather sensual. You are so beautiful, my sweet angel, and your belly button is very kissable; he leaned over and kissed the poking navel through her nightgown.

Cora giggled. They were lying in bed reading one of Jane Austin's romantic novels aloud. She felt a gentler story would be more comfortable for the baby to listen to than one of the horror stories she and Noah sometimes read.

She even requested he play lullabies on the guitar in the evenings, like Hush Little Baby or Pop Goes the Weasel, but when he played Yankee Doodle Dandy, she tapped her feet, and Noah picked up the pace. She truly believed the baby could hear them. But her mind kept wandering.

"Noah?"

"Hmm."

"Why don't you make love to me anymore? Do you think you'll hurt the baby?"

"No, sweetheart. I didn't want to make you uncomfortable. But if you want to, we can. The baby is protected by the amniotic fluid in the uterus and the uterine muscles." Do you want to? I've just been waiting for a go-ahead from you."

"I love your lovemaking, so yes, go ahead."

He gently closed the book he had been reading aloud, leaned over her, and gave her a deep, erotic kiss.

Cora reciprocated by sliding her tongue inside the warmth of his mouth. Their tongues began a swirling dance of mating, tasting, loving, and massaging as they melded together in the age-old bond of love.

He lifted her nightshirt, baring her breasts, left her mouth, and moved down, taking a sweet nipple inside his mouth.

"God, you taste so good he whispered against her moist skin. Her soft, love-filled sounds touched his soul in so many different ways. He could not imagine what his life would be without her. He moved his hands down her side to the curve of her waist, lower to her rounded hips inner thighs, and then up to the silky protection of curls. Cora caught her breath.

His fingers moved within the folds of her passion, kneading and manipulating the tender flesh, causing the moist nub of her desire to swell. God, how he loved the sounds she made, and he knew she was on the verge of an orgasm. She was warm, moist, and velvety when she lifted her bottom to meet his touch more fully.

Once her heartbeat slowed some, she began to do some touching of her own. She moved her hand between them, grasped his sensitive male hardness, and massaged him for several minutes. "I so love the feel of you," she whispered, blowing warm breath against him. "I want you inside me."

This time, it was him who was about to explode. He moved entirely over her and pushed the tip of himself to her opening. "Are you alright? I don't want to make you uncomfortable. God, you feel so good."

"I'm very comfortable, and you also feel so good. I love your body. And love the things it does to me."

That's all he needed to know. He moved deeper inside her and began to match her undulating hips as she pressed her hands atop his bottom and wrapped her legs around him.

Again, he kissed her deeply.

"Don't hold back she whispered against his mouth. Give me everything."

"He did, keening with pleasure as his climax spilled and comingled with hers."

The spring temperatures had risen; it was a beautiful day in the low sixties when Lamar showed up in Willowby, this time alone. What was left of his riders camped outside town. He didn't take the time to replace the ones he'd lost; he simply didn't want to be bothered. He was more concerned with getting his revenge. And now he could add Simon's betrayal to the mix. Though it went against his usual way of getting what he wanted, he came to town in disguise this time.

He was clean-shaven, wore wire-rimmed glasses, and dressed like the other men in town, wearing denim pants, a tan cotton shirt, and brown leather cowboy boots. A western-felt hat finished the look and topped his head. Lamar hoped this friendly change would bring him more information, so he dressed the part and came alone. The pants were stiff against his legs, and the damn shirt felt like starched burlap. He missed his comfortable Calvary uniform; even though it was well-worn, he had kept it in good condition.

He frequently tipped the brim of his hat as he walked the streets and asked questions. He knew how to look the part of a rancher, had been raised as one, and certainly killed enough of them. His lip curled in a sardonic half-grin though he remained pleasant to the town folk. He told them he was looking for his brother, who was needed at home. Their Pa was sick and dying, and how the old man wanted to spend what time he had left with his youngest son.

The town hadn't changed much from when he'd come last fall, and there was no difference when it came to getting information either. Still no luck. Before leaving Willowby to meet up with the men, he took a chance and spoke to the sheriff.

He introduced himself as Lamar Harper and asked about Noah. All he got were the same results he had gotten all those months ago. But the sheriff was all too happy to relate there had been a fire up on the mountain last year.

"Probably a lightning strike." The sheriff related. "There was an old mountain man, Elijah Franklyn, who lived in the same area. He might know something about this man you're looking for. Then again, he could have got caught in the fire and burned to death. He would visit town once a year for supplies, but we haven't seen him in quite some time. The few folks living up there are fierce people who like their privacy and don't cater to strangers. They mind their own business. And so do we."

Lamar was beginning to lose his patients. He already knew about the old man; after all, it was him who killed him and had his men burn the place down.

"The interesting thing is," the sheriff prattled on. "The old feller always seemed to be picking up supplies for two; it could be if your brother were hidin' up there, the old man was helping him. If you need more information, there is another gentleman who once lived in San Juan.

"His name is Silas Greenhand. He gave up the mountain life years ago. Now, he resides on a small ten-acre pig farm on the north end of town. If I were you, I'd check with him. He and the old man were friends, often played cards, and had a few drinks while Elijah was in town. But then we haven't seen Silas in a while, either. Sorry I don't have more information. I hope you find him. I have enough to worry about here in town and can't spare anyone to help. Our doctor just packed up and left last month. We got to find a new one and also a school teacher."

Lamar cursed with irritation the moment he left the sheriff's office. He untied his spotted sorrel, mounted, and rode out of town to meet with his men.

Somebody was going to die today.

Noah was packing up with Cora's help, preparing for the trip down the mountain to town. She handed him a stack of paper money. "Take this. I know you think it's mine, but grandfather left it for both of us, so don't be stubborn."

"I just worry if something…"

"Don't say it, Noah Harper. I won't allow anything to happen. Besides, there is plenty left if it is needed." She watched his mouth open for more argument and put her fingers over his lips. "Silence!"

He kissed her fingers and drew one inside his mouth, then grinned when he felt her shiver. "I wasn't going to argue; I was just realizing you are right, and there are things you need with this money you just gave me."

"We need," she corrected.

"Yes, we need. Hopefully, I can get a fair price on a small wagon now that we fixed up a place to store it."

They both had been working on a corral and a lean-to for the horse or mule he would purchase and bring back. He figured it would take him several days to get to town on foot, but the trip back would be much faster.

He still didn't like the idea of leaving Cora alone. But he knew she needed things for the baby, like material to make diapers and the tiny little clothes the child would need at least through the first year of life. Fresh fruit and vegetables, maybe a couple of chickens. He also needed to resupply his medical bag along with things that would help her when the time came for the baby in about five months. Loka had returned, coming and going throughout the day and spending the nights. That in itself made Noah feel better.

"I packed dried meat and fruit—two loaves of bread and jam. I wish I had butter; oh, Noah, do be careful. It's been so long since you were last in town. What if you get lost? Landscape changes. Things may look different. Maybe you should take Loka."

"Sweetheart. I'll be fine you gave me your grandfather's map. You told me everything you remember. Over the years, I have explored myself. It's not like I locked myself away from everything. I'll be back in about a week. You are what worries me most. I hate leaving you alone."

"I will also be fine. Remember, for years, I spent much of my time alone, especially when my grandfather went to town. I can shoot; there is plenty of food..."

"Come here and kiss me," Noah said.

She was in his arms in one forward motion, molding soft curves to the contours of his tall, lean body. She could feel his uneven breathing against the top of her head as he held her close, placing one large hand on her waist while the other explored the curve of her back from the shoulder to just above the soft angle of her bottom.

He kissed her forehead, then lowered his mouth and brushed her lips. A beautiful mouth he'd been attracted to from the first moment he laid eyes on her. The kiss was deeply sensual. Their tongues met in a burst of electric lovemaking.

Not one square inch was left untasted. Their heightened sounds of arousal mingled, becoming one. At last, they reluctantly parted. Only a fraction of an inch separated them. "I love you so much," he whispered against the moistness he had created on her mouth, then smiled. "If I don't get going right now, I won't go at all."

Grudgingly, she stepped away. "Promise me you will stay safe. Don't take any unnecessary risks."

"I promise, my little angel. I have too much to lose if I don't."

Loka chose to squat down next to Cora at that moment. His large golden eyes looked from her to Noah. "Take care of our girl, my friend," he told the wolf, grabbed his pack, and headed out the door with one last glance at the two most important beings in his life. The door quietly shut in seconds, and he began the lonely trek to town.

As Noah entered town, Simon found himself cornered in the narrow canyon by a very ornery-looking mountain lion. He carefully lifted his rifle and pointed it directly at the big cat.

But if he fired his Winchester, his position would be known. He didn't know if the captain and others had made it to Willowby yet. Or who else might be up on this mountain besides Noah? If any of them heard gunfire, the sound would alert anyone in the area; they had some unwanted company. It also might send Noah deeper into the mountain.

Carefully, with the least amount of sound, he led his Morgan and the buckskin back down to the mouth of the canyon, never taking his eyes off the lion. He secured the animals, and for a brief moment, he didn't move, just silently watched. Then he heard a thumping sound from the forest above the rock-face canyon. So did the lion. He turned and bound away, quickly disappearing.

Simon drew a sigh of relief—probably a deer or some other wildlife that would make good eating for the large cat. Before starting up the canyon again, he grabbed some jerky from his saddle bag. He took a long pull of his canteen, watered the two horses and waited for fifteen minutes, then mounted and headed up the canyon again.

He reached the top of the draw in the next hour. The mountain lion did not return. According to the map he purchased, he was halfway up the mountain; at least, he hoped so. He had already been on the trail for the past two weeks.

He watched the dark gray clouds in the distance and heard the soft crack of thunder. He wondered if the storm would pass by just as the others he'd encountered since leaving town. By now, it was close to evening. He'd spend the night and head out again in the morning. He cared for both horses, made a cover using a tarp he purchased in town, and hung it between two aspen trees. He laid out his bedroll, made a quick supper of bacon, beans and fried cornbread, and settled down for the night.

The next couple of nights were quiet and undisturbed but on the third night during the wee hours of morning, he was awakened by two very nervous horses. Their eyes and nostrils were wide with fear. Their muscles bunched tensely, significantly above the eyes, forming an upside-down V-shape. They were stirring up dust and stepping side to side, trying to escape their hobbles.

What the hell?' Simon mumbled as he reached for his Winchester and quickly rolled out from his bedroll. He cocked the rifle's lever into place, and without much ado, he moved to the frightened animals. The last thing he needed was to further their panic.

Quietly, he slipped up next to his morgan and spoke in reassuring whispers. He gently stroked his neck and muzzle. Once the mare detected the morgan had calmed, she also settled down. That was when he noticed the mountain lion had returned. He was only fifteen to twenty feet away and hidden in the thick brush. Simon's best guess was that the big cat was female. She probably had cubs nearby.

And she looked as if she were ready to pounce out from cover. No wonder the horses were a jittery mess.

Simon lifted the rifle and sighted in. He intended to frighten her away if he was able. He'd had enough killing for a lifetime, and he didn't want to make her cubs orphans. He didn't know if this was the same animal he'd seen a couple days ago, but it wouldn't matter; he had to save the horses. Forgetting who might hear. He fired.

Cora spent a restless night. She had become so used to the warmth of Noah's body that she shivered through the emptiness. Loka lay next to her, but it certainly wasn't the same. Lord, have mercy, she hoped Noah was safe.

She climbed out of bed, and Loka followed immediately. She opened the rear door and moved to the outhouse. Tarnation! It seemed all she did anymore was race to the outhouse to relieve herself but thank goodness the vomiting had stopped a month ago. The minute she stepped inside the tiny building, Loka also relieved himself on a tree trunk that ran perpendicular to the log side of the outhouse.

She wondered if Noah had made it to town and was on his way back to her.

He had been gone for a week.

Where had he spent the nights?

Was he cold?

Did he miss her?

God only knew she missed him. The baby fluttered in her stomach, feeling like the delicate wings of a butterfly. She reached down and caressed her belly. She was convinced the child was a boy.

Of course, girls certainly could be just as lively, she smiled. Her mother said she could be a handful when she was little.

There were so many times she had lived up here on the mountain, both with her grandfather and now Noah, that she wished she could have her mother to talk to. Some of the things that were happening to her body and things that would happen after the baby came would leave only questions another woman would know or answer. Noah was wonderful. He had taught her many things about her body. But he could never understand how it felt to carry a child inside him. No, there were just some things only a woman who'd been through the ordeal could help her to understand.

She stepped outside the outhouse and made her way back to the cabin. Loka dashed around the side of the building and joined her.

Cora reached down, fluffed the fur on his head, and scratched his pointed ears. "Want some breakfast?" she asked.

Loka made no sound, though he looked up and seemed to study her. His lips curled in what reminded Cora of a smile. And she grinned. "I take that as a yes."

She went to the smokehouse and retrieved some venison. She would make a stew for supper. This morning, she made biscuits. She sliced up some venison, placed the meat between the pan-fried bread, and poured a spiced flour gravy over the top. She shared her bounty with Loka.

Noah was making good time back up the mountain. The trip to Willoby took him three days. Cora was right. The town was undoubtedly more populated than when he'd first come. Not one soul recognized him. He was asked a few times where he was from. He made up a story and told everyone who asked he was passing through on his way back to Cheyenne. He got a few odd looks when he purchased the cloth for Cora, but no one asked or seemed to care as long as he paid in cash.

He indeed found a small buckboard and a sturdy mule at the livery. The livery owner, a middle-aged man with a salt-and-pepper beard, mustache, and thick eyebrows, told Noah he'd had more business in the last week than he'd seen in a month of Sundays.

"Really? Did other travelers pass through?"

"Only one," the owner stated. "Stayed a couple of days and moved on loaded with supplies and the two horses I sold him. He said he was headed up into the San Juan. Why any fool would want to do that is beyond my way of thinking. It's a dangerous place for a man alone. There are folks and wildlife up there who don't like company."

The information made Noah a bit nervous. He paid the livery owner and gathered his things. Though it irked him to use the money Elijah had left, he was thankful he had it. He loaded their supplies and began the trek back up the mountain without incident.

Over the years, with some of his exploring, he realized the map Cora had made him was close to his own intuitive exploration. He prayed she was doing well. He never realized when he finally fell in love, the emotion would hit him like a granite wall. If anything happened to her...well, it would destroy him.

Simon shot twice, once above the lion's head and again at the ground to the animal's right. He was ready for a third kill shot if needed, but the majestic lion did a turnabout and ran in the opposite direction.

Glad he didn't have to kill such a beautiful animal. Simon wasted no more time. He quickly packed, readied the two horses, and left the campsite the same way he found it, with no sign of human essence. God, he hoped this map was leading him in the right direction. This trip was undoubtedly taking longer than he'd first anticipated. All he had to go on was a wish for redemption and a dream of saving at least part of his soul. He hoped he would be able to find Noah. But hell, he could just as well be lost and heading in the entirely wrong direction.

He was probably out of his mind even attempting this foolhardy mission. Noah may not be anywhere up here. But, like the captain, he figured the old man the captain had killed was lying or protecting someone.

But this damn mountain range was twelve thousand square miles of rugged terrain. Home to hundreds of peaks over thirteen thousand feet high. The map only showed him passages to follow. Noah could be anywhere or simply nowhere.

At least the mountains were beautiful to look at. Lush green valleys that glaciers had carved out millions of years ago, leaving steep mountainsides and u-shaped canyons along with some of the most jagged and highest summits in the continental United States. It was an excellent place to make a life if one wanted to stay hidden and could handle the harsh winters.

Maybe if he did get lost, he could also make a home up here. He had nothing else. There was no home for him to go back to. His elderly parents had passed when he was just a young boy and long before he joined the Army. He was their only offspring. He spent his time in an orphanage back in Chicago from the age of six until sixteen. Then, he lived off the streets until he finally joined the Calvary in seventy-seven at twenty. If he had known then what he knew now he would have done things so differently. He shook his head, mounted, and continued his journey through the mountain pass.

Again, he wondered about Noah and how he'd gotten along these past years.

Chapter Twenty

Silas Greenhand was sitting in a rocking chair on the front porch of his small cabin just north of Willowby. The Morning sun had just begun to fill the sky and bring its bright rays across the pasture. Silas held a side-by-side Lefever shotgun, cocked and ready to go if necessary.

He anxiously watched as six disreputable men rode toward him. From what he could tell, each one appeared dangerous and ready to erupt. He sure as hell didn't need their kind of disturbance or conflict, and he knew with every fiber of his being they had both in abundance. He lifted his rifle and fired at the ground. "Not one more move if you want to live!" Silas ordered.

The riders stopped about a hundred yards from the porch, sending a cloud of dust and the pungent scent of animal dung swirling through the air. If one of you decide to get brave, he will get a load of buckshot in his chest!"

"Goddamnit!" Hyrum shuttered. "Another friggin' pig farm."

Lamar gave him a look of aversion, "Shut up!" He glared at the man on the porch and ground his teeth. " I don't want any trouble; I just have a few questions if you'd oblige."

Silas knew that could change in a split second, and he spat a stream of brown juice from the side of his mouth, and it landed on the dirt in front of the narrow porch. He never lowered his long-barreled shotgun. "Don't like company, and I ain't got nothing to sell, and I sure as hell ain't got no answers!"

"Well, now," Lamar glanced at the other men he rode with and grinned. He removed his faded black Calvary hat and slapped it against his dusty thigh. The frayed gold cord wavered in the breeze. "You, Silas Greenham?"

"Who's askin'?"

Lamar replaced the hat on his head. Though it goaded him to answer the old fart, he did. "Name's Captain Lamar Harper," he lied for the umpteenth time this day.

"Means nothing to me, and you don't look very military. I'd say that uniform you wear has seen better days. Who'd you steal it from." Silas exclaimed and spit another stream of tobacco juice. A medium-sized pig ran around the cabin with an earsplitting squeal, followed by an enormous hog.

The old man hollered at both pigs, and they soon disappeared around the back of the cabin until they were safely hidden in the rear. Silas chuckled, "It's mating season, and that sow is in heat. The big one wants a chunk of her." He spit again. "Like I said, I ain't got nothin' you want!" he growled. "I suggest y'all git!"

"Hyrum hissed impatiently and rested his right hand on the leather strap of his holster riding low on his hip. He nudged the chestnut as he rode a few steps forward. "I can end this problem for you. Just say the word."

Lamar held his hand up to stop Hyrum's killing spirit and forward movement. "He's just being a stubborn old man. He'll talk if he knows what's good for him. And if he doesn't, he's all yours, Hyrum."

"And that would be my pleasure, Captain."

Silas silently watched this troublesome bunch of roughnecks. He glanced at the man called Hyrum. He stopped, but he certainly didn't move back. He unholstered a six-shooter and kept it aimed at Silas.

"I was told by the sheriff in Willowby," the captain began. "You once lived on the San Juan and knew the old man he called Elijah Franklyn. The two of you were friends. After you moved down here, he would visit, have a few drinks, and play cards."

"Even if that were true, and ya can't believe a damn thing that foolhardy sheriff says. Elijah's dead now. Some blasted coward burned him out and kilt 'im."

Lamar stiffened, "the sheriff said it was a possible lightning strike, so what makes you think he was murdered?"

"Hmm, not likely. He had secrets like most men do. He didn't much like socializing, so he chose to stay hidden and alone. Had a family once, but they were all kilt in a raid years ago, right there in town."

"What kind of secrets?" Lamar demanded.

"Now that there is none of your business," Silas told him, spitting another stream of tobacco juice. "And even if I were to know what his secrets might be, which I don't, I sure as hell wouldn't share them with you. Silas smirked and tightened the grip on his rifle.

"I'm looking for my younger brother," Lamar said, quickly losing patience. "He's supposed to be up in the San Juan. I thought the old man would know him. I was told he came down once a year for supplies in town, and it appeared he always bought enough for two. Thought maybe he might be helping out my brother."

Silas knew exactly why Elijah bought for two, though he answered with, "wouldn't know anything about that. He did come off the mountain once a year, spent a week or two in town, and we had a few drinks and a few good hands of poker. Got grouchy when I beat him," Silas chuckled. "But beyond that, I wouldn't know what he did when he returned home."

"Christ almighty Capn, are you believin' all this bullshit?"

"Shut up, Hyrum!"

"The hell I will!"

The pig chose that moment to dash around the cabin again with one of the loudest squeals any of them had ever heard. Hyrum fired. The pig dropped, wiggled a bit, then didn't move.

"Hot damn bacon and pork chops for all!" A young golden-haired man snickered with delight.

Hyrum turned and looked at him with an evil grin. "Damn right, Sean and I'd say mighty good eatin' for the next several weeks."

"Hey! You, sonsabitches! That's going to cost you fifty dollars!" Silas demanded.

"You don't say," Hyrum sneered. "Well, to my way of thinking, you just offered us that squealing pink pig."

Silas fired his rifle; dozens of buck-shot beads scattered across the yard—a few whizzed by a couple of the men at Lamar's rear. Two horses danced carelessly back and forth across the yard, stirring up dust. A third horse raised on his hocks, screeched with fear and ran off, knocking his rider to the ground. Another man turned his mount and chased after the runaway horse.

"That's it, had enough of this shit," Hyrum spat. "Ain't gonna find out nothin' from this old geezer. He lifted his Colt .45 and fired. The bullet knocked the old man back against the exterior wall, and then he toppled forward. He fell and landed on the porch floor and didn't move.

"Sonofabitch, Hyrum!" Lamar shouted. "Half the town will be coming out here now. The man was well known. Now, here we are again with no answers. Maybe I ought to just shoot you, you useless piece of shit!"

"You could try!" Hyrum growled at him, but I'm the better shot. "I joined up for the excitement of killing and ravishing the female population. Maybe I should shoot you, and then we can all forget your Noah Harper revenge. How 'bout it, Captain, you ready to die?" Hyrum gave Lamar a sarcastic grin. "And now that I've had time to think about it, maybe good old Simon had the right idea by going out alone." Hyrum cocked his pistol for the second time. An ear-shattering report cracked through the air.

But it wasn't Lamar he shot at. He aimed at the bone-dry weeds that made up the sod-covered roof. The spark from the bullet created a flame that would quickly consume the rickety old building. He holstered his gun. "Now we're done here!"

Everyone except Lamar shouted with glee; his glee came when he sidled his mount next to Hyrum's dun sorrel. Before Hyrum had the chance to even notice, Lamar swiftly reached and grasped the man's six-shooter from the holster, held it by the barrel, and used the butt end to swing the heavy weapon against the side of Hyrum's head. The crack was hard enough to knock Hyrum off his horse and onto the ground.

Hyrum looked up at Lamar in shock before he passed out.

"Next time, you take it upon yourself to do whatever you please without consulting me," Lamar barked. "I'll do more than give you a swipe across your head. I'll kill you without a second of remorse. He flipped the barrel and grasped the grip, pointed the gun at each of the men. "And that goes for the rest of you. If you don't like the rules I set, then you can stay here with a bullet in your head and burn in the fire along with the old pig farmer."

"Yes, Cap'n," he heard in unison.

"One of you help Hyrum back on his horse." Damn, he was aching for action. Maybe Willowby was the place to start. "Let's head to town and release some of this killer energy we all seem to have!"

Woohoo!" Though their reply wasn't nearly as boisterous as usual, they agreed in unison as one called out. "Female beaver, here we come!" Dust flew over the yard as the six men galloped from the yard and toward town. One of them had been tossed over his horse, unconscious.

Silas Greenhand, though in tremendous pain, had been playing dead. His roof was already in flames. He crawled from the porch to the yard, whistling for his mule grazing out back.

Cora missed Noah something fierce. She hoped he was safe and on his way home. She climbed out of bed. It was still very early in the morning. The sky was gray. Once again, sleep had eluded her for most of the night.

She yawned and stretched as she made her way to the outhouse. Very soon, the sun would split the sky, spreading its golden brightness over the treetops surrounding the cabin, leaving a beautiful, nearly cloudless morning and a late spring sky as blue as Noah's eyes. According to the outside thermometer, it was sixty degrees. "How about some fish for supper?" she said to Loka. "If we go now, we can be back in time for breakfast. The wolf made a soft howling sound.

"Sounds good to me, too," she told him." If I'm lucky, I might catch enough to add to the food storage in the smokehouse." As she bent down to give Loka a scratch between his pointed ears, she felt a pull on the lower side of her abdomen, not the dull ache of a monthly cramp but sharper. Seconds later, it disappeared. Sweet Lord, was something wrong with her or the baby? Loka seemed to detect her fear and gave her a wet tongue on the side of her cheek.

Cora stood and clasped her lower back. How would she know if something was wrong? The only thing she was sure of was this was a different feeling. Tarnation, she hoped Noah would hurry and get home. She didn't want to do this pregnancy stuff alone. Then she remembered reading in one of Noah's medical journals about how the ligaments connected to the uterus would stretch in the early stages of pregnancy, part of preparing the body. Sort of felt like a side ache she sometimes got. Growing pains, her grandfather said. She felt relief. The pain had not returned, and everything else seemed fine.

She grabbed her fishing pole, and she and Loka headed for the stream.

When she returned an hour later, near seven, holding three fat trout, she heard the distant sound of gunfire. Or was it the crash of thunder? No, the sky was clear of storm clouds for miles.

Loka glanced up at Cora, and she could swear it was a look of pity. All thoughts of filleting and smoking the fish were flushed from her mind as she watched Loka take off through the forest at a dead run. *Oh God, oh God!*

Noah stopped to make camp about two-thirds the way up the mountain and about a half day's ride from Elijah's burned-out cabin. It was getting late. He had been pushing all day. Both he and the mule were exhausted. He'd stop here for just a few hours and wait for dawn. He could use a couple of hours of sleep and trying to get up the last leg of this journey in the dark was foolish.

He figured this would be his last stop. He should be home by tomorrow. He laid out his bedroll under the protection of a craggy outcrop of rock. Dug a small fire pit and made coffee. After finishing up the last biscuits and venison Cora had made for him, he poured another cup of coffee, changed his mind, tossed it into what remained of the fire, and crawled into his bedroll. Sleep took him instantly.

He was startled awake hours later. What the devil! He had been having one of the most erotic dreams of his life. He and Cora were making passionate love, and she was touching his naked body in all the places he craved. He was as stiff as a steal rod.

Hell, he wanted to return to the dream, but real life was so much better, and the sooner he got home, the sooner she would be in his arms. Still disoriented from sleep, he jerked himself to a sitting position. Something wasn't right. He tossed his bedroll aside, yanked his boots on, and reached for his rifle just as a pinkish morning sky began to glow. In moments, the sun would be over the jagged cliffs at the eastern edge of the canyon.

For a few seconds, he paused. Everything went deadly quiet. He listened momentarily before leaving his campsite. A thunderous crack of gunfire came from below his position. Then another. He quickly gripped the old Spencer more securely and covertly moved toward the unexpected sound he estimated was about a mile away—had someone followed him after he left town?

There were no more shots, only a gentle breeze blowing through the trees and the soft sound of water flowing from a narrow creek. Who the hell was up here? He knew a few others lived on the mountain, but the only other human he'd ever encountered was Elijah. And certainly not down this low.

Thinking about what he was about to do was probably foolish, but he needed to know who was up here, and if they were dangerous, he wanted to lead them in the opposite direction. He prayed Lamar and his men hadn't returned. He checked his rifle for ammo. It was fully loaded, and he began to walk down a narrow path at a near-silent pace.

He made it a mile when he saw a lone man with two horses, and he was getting ready to move out. Something about the man looked familiar. Quietly, Noah stayed hidden in the thick scrub oak. Over the years, he had learned to move with nearly no sound. He visually checked the surrounding area.

The man was alone. He had a gentle way with his horses, and when he started to mount a black Morgan and grasp a lead rope connected to a female buckskin, Noah set his Sharps down came up behind him and wrapped his arm about the man's throat, yanked him back, knocking him to the ground. The horses nervously stumbled though they remained where they were. The two men rolled in the dirt for several minutes. Finally stopping, Noah straddled the man and pushed the tip of his hunting knife at the man's throat. "Who the hell are you, and what are you doing up here?" he demanded.

"I'm looking for someone," Simon nervously answered but found it difficult to stop staring at the angry-looking man and the very sharp knife directed at his neck. "Maybe you know him."

"We keep to ourselves up here and mind our own business. Which is what you should be doing." Noah glared into the man's cloud-grey eyes. He felt a familiarity as he glared at the man's face and eyes. Recognition funneled through him like the hot edge of a saber. Yes, he knew this face. Memories of a long-ago past washed over him—the pain, the betrayal, and an overwhelming loss of friendship that could never be mended. But Noah didn't want to give this man any quarter and certainly didn't want the man to know he knew who he was. "Who the hell are you?" he barked.

"My name is Simon Mason." Though Simon was sure Noah knew precisely who he was, he continued. "I rode with a man called Noah Harper while serving in the Calvary a little over ten years ago. I'm here to give him a hand. He has enemies that want to see him dead. Do you know of him?"

Noah took a hasty swallow and left his knife on Simon's neck! Judas! If Simon was here, that meant the captain wasn't far behind, or maybe he was already here and hiding in the brush. No, Simon was alone. And Noah trusted his instincts. If the captain had been here, he would have taken charge right out front. Then what about the shots he'd heard? *Who was shooting? And why?* He asked pushing the tip of his knife slightly deeper, though drew no blood.

"There was a mountain lion ready to attack my horses I fired to scare him off." The knife released a tiny bit but never left.

"This country is full of them, there isn't anything up here to interest you. I suggest you pack up and leave the mountain and head back to town." Noah barked.

Simon squinted up at the man who had been his friend. "We were friends once, me and Noah but I imprudently turned my back on him when he most needed me."

That did it and Noah growled his discontent. "In fact, Simon," he began with a derogatory expression of fury and again pressed the knife to Simon's throat this time drawing a dot of blood. "You left him to die and rode out of that village and never looked back."

"I'm looking back now, and if Noah will accept my heartfelt apology and allow me to help him, he might save himself and possibly help me to keep a portion of my soul. At least what's left of it, I'm sure Hell's fire will soon see me burning for my sins."

"You think I should help you with that?" Noah spat with indifference. "Where's the rest of the men, including The Lord Tamarin himself? Why don't you come out, Lamar," Noah shouted, "and get this over with!" He yanked Simon up to his feet, forcing him to release the lead rope he had been gripping in his right hand. Then hauled the man over to a narrow aspen trunk, where he used the lead rope and shackled him. Finished, he went back for his rifle. He moved about ten feet from Simon, squatted down, and kept his Sharps pointed at Simon.

Simon blinked and shook his head. How could he convince a furious Noah that he was alone? Here to help him. "You are as stubborn as I remember," he finally said, blowing his hair out of his eyes. "Look, I know you don't trust me and don't want to believe a thing I say, but I've come up here alone. I left the captain and his men months ago, and there's a good chance the bastard is also looking for me. The men he now rides with are the lowest kind of vermin God ever set on this earth. Not to say I am any better, though I didn't take part in a lot that's happened over the years, I never did anything to stop it either. Noah, I'm sure the captain is close behind. If we're lucky, we will have a week at most."

"There's no we if there ever was. You made that decision years ago. Give me one good reason why the hell I shouldn't just kill you?"

"Because you are not a killer, and frankly, after everything that has happened since that day in the Cheyenne village, I no longer fear death. It's what I deserve."

"So, you've become a martyr. Is that what you are telling me?" Noah swore in disbelief.

"I've done things and seen things I never should have. No, not a martyr. Just a fool who certainly should have acted differently starting that day in the Cheyenne village."

"For your sake, I wish you had. You knew I still lived, yet you joined Lamar and the rest."

"If I had given any indication you still lived, it would have been like signing your death warrant. You know that as well as I do."

Noah knew Simon was right, but it still galled him that the man had chosen to ride out with Lamar and leave him there alone to die anyway. And he would have died if it hadn't been for Loka.

Simon interrupted Noah's thoughts and his recriminations. "Do you remember a sporting gal in Cheyenne? She worked in a place called The Kingman. Pretty blond, her name was Sugar. You played guitar there for a couple of months?"

Noah turned slightly pale though made no outward sign. "What about her? I played guitar in many saloons; several pretty sporting girls worked upstairs in any given drinking hole throughout the west."

"She remembers you. According to her, you did more than play your guitar. On occasion, you would spend a night or two with her. Whether true or not, she remembered you very well and was full of information about you. She said you got a little tipsy one night and told her of your plans to go south and live alone in the San Juan above the small town of Willowby. The very next day, you were packed up and gone. Do you remember now?"

Noah made no comment.

"To make a long story short, Lamar got the same information before I did. He hurt her pretty badly, and because of what he did, she was angry and all too happy to share that information with me in just a little more detail. Even in the business she chose to make her livelihood, she cared about you and believed that I told her the truth about giving you warning and giving you help."

Still, Noah made no sign that he believed him and remained silent.

"Noah, you need to prepare; Lamar will stop at nothing until he gets what he wants. And damn it, I want to help you. I'm done with all the killing and torture Lamar and the man partake in. His biggest mission in life is to make you pay for what you did during the court martial trial! He wants you dead, and not an easy death. And he has murdered several over the years who tried to help you in the beginning. I swear to God, I did not help him in any way, but I also didn't try to stop him. You've got to believe me. I know him, and I know what he's capable of. The men he runs with are worse. They have no provocation or conscience. They just kill, pillage and rape the innocent."

Simon seemed to be telling the truth. Noah could certainly remember the day in the Cheyenne village and all the bloodshed committed under Captain Tamarin's orders. He still had nightmares. But trust Simon, that step was too much to ask. He had Cora and their baby to think about. He heard a warning growl from behind him. He knew it was Loka, but he did not look back. He kept his vision, and the barrel of the Sharps pointed at Simon. There was fear shining in Simon's eyes. It was more than the old Army rifle pointing in his direction. His face became a sickly snow white.

"Noah at your back...a wolf..." Simon choked out and glanced at his Winchester, securely tucked in the rifle boot attached to the saddle on the tall fifteen hand Morgan.

"Make one move, and you're a dead man." Noah hissed.

Simon went utterly still. "Didn't you hear me? There's a wolf at your back, and it looks like he's ready to take a chunk out of you!"

Noah raised one hand but remained silent.

In seconds Loka joined his friend, though he never took his big golden eyes off Simon. He stopped at Noah's feet and remained motionless.

"Good Lord, you have a wolf for a pet. Is he the same one you had at the fort all those years ago?" Simon shook in awe.

"Not a pet but a friend and the only one who stood by me when you left me for dead in the Cheyenne village. He will attack if you make any sudden moves." Noah looked down at Loka. *What the hell was he doing here? He should have stayed with Cora. She needed his protection.*

Noah lowered his rifle and yanked Simon to his feet and gave him a shove forward. "Start walking. Try anything stupid, and my friend will tear you limb from limb.

Simon silently nodded.

Noah grasped the reins of the two horses and led them all up the mountain path right behind Simon. When they reached his camp, he ordered Simon to move beneath the outcrop of rock he had used to make his bed under last night. He then gathered his things and placed them back in the wagon. He tied both of Simon's horses to the rear.

Simon did as he was told without argument but never took his eyes off the wolf.

Noah reached into his pack and tore a piece of paper from the map Cora had drawn him. He jotted a few words down, curled the paper in a tube, and wrapped it in leather strips. Finished, he turned to Loka and placed the note in the wolf's mouth. "Cora, go home!"

Loka whined but quickly backtracked on a lightning run back up the canyon.

"Cora?" Simon questioned. "Is that the wolf's name?"

Christ on a crutch! Noah inwardly cursed. He did not answer but said, "You had better not be lying to me, Simon."

"I wouldn't lie. You were the only person I could ever call a friend. I realize I turned my back on you all those years…"

"Don't want to hear it." Noah wasn't sure what the hell he was going to do with Simon. The only thing he knew for sure was that he couldn't outright kill him unless he had to. So far, the man had shown no sign of aggression. He seemed to be sincere. But then he'd seen such behavior before. What had Lamar done to Sugar to get her to spill the beans? But furthermore, he should never have drunk himself into oblivion and spilled his secrets to her. Talk about stupid!

Once everything was packed up, he ordered Simon into the back of the wagon. This time, he tied his ankles and had him scoot to the rear just below the wooden seat. He climbed into the driver's seat, released the brake, and began the trek home. He still wondered how he was going to deal with Simon.

And protect Cora.

Chapter Twenty-One

Cora was beside herself with worry, hearing the shot fired and watching Loka take off. She could only pray Noah was all right. She'd entered the cabin about two hours ago. Trying to calm herself, she pulled out her knitting needles and yarn. She would make another pair of booties and a little cap for the baby.

A scratching sound came at the door sometime later. Loka! Cora set her knitting aside and went to the door. The moment she opened it, Loka came in. Something was in his mouth and he dropped it at her feet.

"What is this? She bent over, picked it up, and quickly unwrapped the leather binding. A note from Noah, she immediately recognized his handwriting.

Cora, my love,
I should be back soon, but I warn you, I am not alone. I am unsure if I can trust this man who is accompanying me. I once knew him many years ago. I will explain further when I get home.

For the time being, he is unaware of you. I know this won't please you, but I need you to go to the hiding place we fixed up for you in the shed. Please stay there until I call you.

I love you, Noah.

Noah was correct. This didn't please her one iota, but she loved and respected him. She would do what he asked of her. But who in thunderation was he bringing up here? Someone he knew years ago. She chewed her lower lip with worry. What did all this mean? Had he met this person in town? But who would he know in town? And what about the gunshots she heard this morning?

There were too many questions. Loka looked up at her, licked her hand, turned, and ran out of the cabin and back down the path toward her grandfather's old place, hopefully to Noah. Right now, he needed Loka more than she did.

She gathered her knitting supplies—some nuts and fruit to snack on and a jug of water—and descended the pathway to the shed. They had created a corner for her to use where a stack of crates, lumber, and a menagerie of other items would hide her if anyone but Noah came to look for her.

She was grateful they had chosen this section of the shed. There was a small window with cheery curtains, a comfortable chair, and end table, and a narrow sleeping pallet lay before the small table. Weeks ago, they decided to fix the corner if she needed it. She placed her items on top of the table to the chair's right and waited. Every few minutes, she checked outside, peering through the slit in the curtains that covered the one window.

The town of Willowby hadn't seen such troubling activity in years. The last time anything came close to this kind of horrendous disturbance happened more than a decade and a half ago when about twenty renegades attacked the town, shot up the place, and killed some of the citizens. But all that was before Jim Adderly had taken the position of Sheriff only three years ago. Willowby was still small. Only one saloon was located just outside the residential area and away from the good folks and families who lived within the town's limits.

The saloon was called The Last Stop, a small place with only one level. Men came to play cards and have a few drinks. Two young women who worked there served drinks to the cardplayers and danced with the cowboys while music filled the place from a self-playing Pianola. The business certainly could not handle the influx of wild and out-of-control men who had burst through the doors yesterday morning. They had come to town to raise hell.

And hell, they raised.

They created numerous fights to break out, cheated at cards, and used the only two women who worked there. Each man took a turn with the girls. They had not been hired for that kind of work. No one cared. They were both hauled to the back storage room and forced to pleasure the men. All this was going on before Jim even got there to stop them. Zeb Waters, the bartender, had finally been able to sneak away, but to where nobody knew. The way Jim figured it, the old guy's job wasn't worth getting his head shot off, so he ran. People were getting hurt, and he was determined he wouldn't be one of them.

Willowby still had no doctor. And the townspeople were too afraid to step in and help the injured. According to the residents, the sheriff was paid to protect and remove any ruffians who showed up to cause trouble.

After Jim had been sworn in to replace the old sheriff who had served for years and died unexpectedly three winters ago, Jim thought this would be such an easy job. After all, the town was relatively quiet and filled with God-fearing people. Even the train that stopped for water to refill the steam engines hadn't brought trouble like this. Most of the passengers didn't even bother to get off the locomotive. They just waited while the train's engines were taken care of, then moved on to bigger towns along the route.

But today was different. It began earlier yesterday morning when Al Shiver was fishing down at Lone Creek and heard the gunshots at Silas Greenhand's place. The frightened man left his gear behind and hightailed it to town and the sheriff.

The Sheriff hadn't even had time to head out to Silas's place before the town was inundated with trouble. He was completely outnumbered. He had threatened the men who'd taken over the saloon to leave town or get sent to jail. They didn't listen; they just laughed at him as if he were some fool they could efficiently deal with. And deal with him, they did.

Now, he was forced to sit in one of his jail cells, locked up since last evening. God only knew what they had done throughout the night. Gunfire once again exploded down the street. He could hear riders gallop past his office. One bullet shattered the glass in the front window. It would have caught him in the arm if he hadn't laid low on the floor.

A woman screamed somewhere outside, then a second. What the hell was going on? More horses ran past in a blur. This time, they were riderless. Someone must have opened the corral gates and freed the horses from the livery where they were kept for sale or rent. The action would also prevent anyone from chasing the outlaws down and would take hours to round up all the horses for any posse. And Jim doubted anyone in town would have the guts to ride with him.

In the next hour, everything became quiet. The jailhouse doors flew open and banged against the wall. Louise, one of the Saloon girls, stumbled in. Her lip was bloody, and what little clothing she had left was torn to shreds. "They are gone, but they left Carla in pretty bad shape. She needs a doctor. Oh Jim, what are we going to do?" She grabbed the keys dangling from a peg on the wall behind the sheriff's desk and quickly unlocked the cell door.

"One of those men was the same one who came in the day before yesterday looking for his brother." Louise's whole body began to shake. "But let me tell you, he was a changed man from the one he portrayed. Did you recognize him when you came to stop them from wrecking the place?" She didn't wait for an answer. "Oh God, it was horrible. Me and Carla are not those kinds of girls. We were hired to wait tables and entertain with our dancing and singing. Not what those men wanted of us. But they got what they wanted anyway. Dear God, Jim, they raped us over and over again." Tears streamed down her face.

Once Jim was released from the cell, he quickly stepped out and took Louise in his arms. "I'm so sorry, honey. Take me to Carla, and let's see if I can help. I finally found a doctor, but he won't be able to get here until next week. Did any of them say what they wanted?"

"A good time was all they'd say. We tried to explain that this was a nice town…." Tears slipped down her face. "They just laughed and said they had found what they wanted. And they took and took."

Silas Greenhand chose that moment to fall through the open doorway. "They killed my sow and set my place in flames," he said before he collapsed, blood spilling from a wound in his upper chest.

Jim glanced out through the door. A mule was loosely tied to the hitching post. How the man had even mounted the animal was a shock to Jim and another set of problems.

<hr />

"How have you been since last I saw you?" What an idiotic question, Simon thought. How would anyone be after hiding for all these years? But he asked anyway. One of them needed to start saying something, anything.

The question irked Noah. "Why don't you just shut the hell up! There certainly is nothing I want to share with you."

"You really hate me, don't you? I don't blame you. I hate myself most days."

"Let me put it this way: I don't hate you. It takes far too much emotion to hate, but I sure as hell don't like you. At one time, I believed we were good friends. However, that all changed the morning the Cheyenne village was decimated."

Simon had no answers, right or wrong. And even if he did, he knew it would make no difference to Noah. "Where are you taking me? If you mean to end my life, do it now. God only knows I deserve it."

Noah silently swore. He didn't know what he was going to do. If there were an inkling of truth to Simon's warning, it would be foolish not to take heed and even more ridiculous to rid himself of the man. But *Christ on a crutch*, it sure was tempting. "Act like a man and stop feeling sorry for yourself. I certainly don't pity you. Long ago, you decided to ride with Tamarin. I don't give a damn how you feel about it now or what any of your reasons were back then. I'm not interested in having a conversation with you! The time for any explanation is long gone."

Through the rest of the morning, both men remained silent. Elijah's burned-out cabin was close. They should be there in the next hour. They would stop and rest the mule, and Simon's two horses also needed water and relieved of their burden. He glanced back at Simon; it appeared he'd fallen asleep. Noah clicked his tongue and slapped the reins against the mule's back, urging the animal at a faster clip and closer to what was left of Cora's old cabin.

And closer to home.

The more Cora sat still, the more nervous she became. The waiting was making her crazy scared. There had to be something she could do. She stood up and moved to the door of the shed. She heard a soft rustling. Something was moving across the yard. Her heart sank with dread. She softly reclosed the door, moved to the side of the window, and lifted the curtain to peek outside.

Tarnation, nothing but a dad blame family of squirrels racing across the yard, dashing up a tall gamble oak next to the shed. One by one, they leaped to the next tree and then the next. A doe and her fawn also moved through the yard, heading toward the stream. Mercy, she felt like an idiot. She needed fresh air, so she stepped back outside with a sigh of relief.

Loka was waiting at Elijah's cabin when Noah and his wagon pulled to a stop in front of the rubble. He jumped down and went to the wolf. Squatted down. "You are supposed to be with Cora," he whispered. "Go, she needs you more than me."

Loka glanced from him to the wagon and gave a mulling sound.

"Go!" Noah commanded.

Simon raised higher up against the wagon's back beneath the seat. He saw the wolf and watched Noah bend down, seeming to be conversing with the creature. He looked worried, and Simon wondered what was going on. There was much more happening than what met the eye.

Was Noah protecting someone? If so, who? He watched the wolf turn and head back up the canyon. Simon began to study his surroundings. They were stopped in front of a burned-out cabin, and on closer inspection, he recognized it as the one Lamar had ordered the men to burn last fall. And though Simon had not been a part of the killing and destruction, he had been there. watching in the shrub with Earl and two others. Again, he glanced around. "What are we doing here?"

Noah watched Loka return home and turned swiftly to glare at Simon. "Don't you want to see the murderous scene you were a part of?"

Simon turned pale. "Look, I know you want to believe I took part in this, and sure, I was here waiting with two others in case we were needed..."

"That's guilt enough. You killed an old man who never did a thing to hurt a single soul. Even if you never pulled the trigger, you are guilty by association. Just as you were in the village that day."

That was true enough, and Simon regretted it more than Noah or anyone else could imagine. The things he had witnessed over the years would never leave him.

Revulsion filled Noah's face as he walked to the animals. First, he released the mule from the rigging connected to the wagon and led him to the stream at the back of the property. Then returned to do the same for the two horses that Simon had with him. He lifted the saddle off the

Morgan, removed the packs from the buckskin, and tossed Simon's gear into the back of the wagon along with his saddle.

Without a word, he moved to the stream, leaned down, cupped his hands into the icy water, filled them, took a long drink, washed his face and neck, filled a canteen, and quickly returned to the wagon. He tossed the canteen to Simon, who caught it with his tied wrists using his lower arms.

While Noah and Simon were leaving Elijah's burned-out cabin, Lamar and his men were waking from the night of revelry they'd had in Willowby. They camped at the foot of the San Juan's, hidden inside a red sandstone box canyon. Even for this time of year, the canyon was lush and green thanks to the narrow stream from an underground opening in the northwest corner.

But Lamar fought a hangover like nothing he'd had in years. Maybe he should start to slow down. After all, he was in his late forties. Most men his age were already married and raising a family. But hell, that kind of life was never meant for him, and he couldn't deny he'd had a splendid time last night tearing up that little one-horse town.

He also had to admit that the little gal called Carla was the best poke he'd gotten in years. However, there wasn't much left of her when Hyrum finally got his hands on her. When he thought about what Hyrum had done to her, it made him sick. Damn the man! Before all this was said and done, Lamar vowed Hyrum was going to be as dead as Noah. He would personally see to it. But for now, he needed the sick-minded sonofabitch. Not only was he the bloodthirstiest of the bunch, but he was also the best damn tracker Lamar had ever worked with.

"That sure was one hell of an evening we had last night, the best we've had in a long time. Oooeee!" Eric shouted with glee. "Are we going back in tonight?" he directed the question to Lamar. "The town is ours. The look on that sheriff's face when we locked him up in his tiny jailhouse was more fun than what we did to that old man with the pigs. What was his name?"

"Greenhand," Charley shouted with glee," he lifted his coffee tin in salute. "The dumb pig was mighty tasty, too."

Lamar glared at Hyrum. "We might have been able to have a few more nights in the town if Hyrum hadn't friggin' ruined it for us. What the hell is wrong with you?" Lamar cursed. "Why didn't you just get your poke and leave her be? Did you have to ruin her, you selfish bastard? We all could have had more fun for the next few nights."

Hyrum laughed. "And this comes from one of the most selfish men I've ever known. How many of them whores did you hurt in Cheyenne? Or Denver? Then there was Miles City!"

Lamar scowled. "There is a time and place for everything. They had the information we needed. And I had to convince them, but I sure as hell didn't ruin any of them."

"Information you needed, you mean. This is your friggin' quest. You and your death wish for Harper! Me, I'm here for the fun. And that woman gave me plenty! Not only did I get a poke. And several at that. I got to have fun with my skinner, and you know how I like to carve when I'm finished with the pokin'. I was making up for lost time. I might not have if you hadn't stopped me from using my skinner when I had that sod buster's woman. So, I figured I was due for some entertainment in town!"

Lamar just shook his head with disgust. "Sometimes I think you ain't even human. And if I'd given it more thought that day on the prairie, I would have shot you along with the sodbuster and his family. Until this mission is complete, keep your cock and your bloody knife to yourself!"

"Yeah, Hyrum, what the hell?" Eric snorted and tossed the remains of his coffee in the dying firepit.

"You all got your poke, so quit your bitchin'?" Hyrum gave them all a disparaging look. "At least I waited till last."

Lamar, sick of the whole bloody situation, bellowed out. "Pack up! We are heading up the mountain to the old man's cabin."

"What fer Capn'? Nothin's left."

"If I'd wanted your input, Charley, I'd have asked. Now pack up!"

With a few shrugs and grumbles, the men did what Lamar ordered. An hour later, they were moving out from their hidden canyon. And closer to Noah, he hoped.

The following day, they encountered a small ranch, and Hyrum licked his lips in anticipation when he saw a pretty little dark-skinned woman step into the barn.

Chapter Twenty-Two

Noah made it to his cabin about two hours after leaving Elijah and Cora's burned-out place. He was still undecided about what to do with Simon.

Cora was waiting with Loka just outside the shed. Over the last several months, her thick black hair had grown a few inches longer and reached her shoulders. Today, however, she had the thick strands pulled off her neck and held in place with her mother's hair combs. She was so pretty, and if it weren't for Simon, he would have leaped off the wagon and run to her, gathered her up, taken her to the cabin, and made love to her. Naked skin to naked skin.

Loka glanced up and gave a quiet buff sound, and Noah watched Cora turn and head back inside, though the wolf remained outside. He glanced over his shoulder at Simon. He didn't seem to notice. In fact, he looked to be sound asleep with his hat pulled down over his face. He pulled the brake on the wagon, climbed down, and unhitched the two horses and the mule. In minutes, he led them to the corral he and Cora had built; then, he quickly moved toward the shed.

Cora was sitting in the chair when he opened the door. Her knitting implements were spread around her on the floor at her feet. She stood and ran right into his arms.

"Tarnation, Noah, I've been so worried. Who is this man you said you were bringing with you?" But she didn't get a chance to question further when she felt his lips move across her face. "God, I've missed you." He captured her mouth and slipped his tongue inside, giving her a hardy, desire-filled kiss, all the while caressing her slightly rounded stomach.

After a few moments, when he stepped away and she got her lusty emotions under control, she chastised him. "What's going on? Who is the man?"

Before answering, he had a question of his own. "What were you doing outside? You were supposed to stay out of sight?"

"You try sitting in that dad-blamed shed. It's stuffy and getting hot!" She huffed, resting her hands on her hips.

"Ah, come on, it's not that bad. Just admit you were getting antsy." He tickled her under the chin.

She growled. "Instead of questioning me, tell me, Noah Harper, who did you bring up here?"

"Oh Lord," he grinned. "She's using my full name; she must really be angry."

Cora tightened her hands more securely to her hips and glared at him. "Well?"

"His name is Simon Mason."

"You mean the one who betrayed you. I'd certainly like to give him a piece of my mind." She began to step around Noah.

"Oh, no, you don't, you little spitfire." He pulled her back and wrapped his arms around her. "According to Simon, he stopped riding with the other men months ago."

"And you believe him?" She glared up at him with curiosity.

"So far, he seems to be telling the truth. And he appears to be very remorseful. He was never good at lying, so I'm inclined to think he's telling the truth. I didn't want to take any chances with letting him loose, especially around you, until I'm absolutely sure.

"So far, he doesn't know about you. Loka is out there guarding him. And at the moment, he can't do much. I bound him up in the back of the wagon. If he tries anything, Loka will stop him. He claims he's here to warn me about those same men who attacked Elijah and burned your cabin. He insists he wants to help me. He definitely was alone. Caught up to him several miles below your old cabin."

Cora's full lips stiffened to a narrow line. "Well, I'm telling you right now if you think I'm staying…"

"If I thought you would stay in here, I would probably insist. But I knew you wouldn't. And you are right; it is stuffy here. You could have opened the window. He wrapped his arm around her shoulders, and they stepped outside.

Simon pushed his hat up using his bound wrists. They were stopped again. But restrained as he was, he couldn't lift high enough to see where they were. And that wolf, Noah called Cora, was growling at him as the animal squatted on the edge of the wagon bed. He wouldn't have dared to move even if he could. His stomach ached with fear. "Noah!" he croaked. "Your wolf, Cora, is back. And it looks hungry!"

Cora's eyes turned to two large, looking saucers. Then she grinned. He thinks Loka's name is Cora?"

Noah chuckled. "When I first saw Loka tearing up the dirt to get to me, I ordered him to return and said two words: Cora home. Simon heard that, and he assumed it was the wolf's name. I just let him think that."

"I see, but it is funny."

Noah kissed her on the cheek. Why don't you go back to the cabin, and I'll take care of Simon."

"Take care of him? Tarnation! She swallowed with worry."

"I'm not going to hurt him, but for now, I don't trust him around you. If he has been lying and the other men find out about you…" he shook his head. "Damnit, Cora, you and our child are too important to me. Can you just let this go for now? And do what I say."

Without another word, she gathered her sewing, yarn, and crochet needle and headed back to the cabin.

"Cora," Noah whispered over to her. "I love you."

She gave him a look over her shoulder. "I love you too. I'll go and make something to eat. Unless you want me to help unload the wagon? And it looks like a mighty nice wagon. But I thought you were only getting one mule. Where did the two horses come from?"

"They belong to Simon. And he will help me unload."

"I see." She turned away and made her way back to the cabin

What the hell was going on? Simon nervously worried. He could swear he heard the distinct sound of two sets of footfalls. And the sound of two voices. The wolf Noah called Cora was still glaring at him and growling with bared teeth. Good God, maybe this hadn't been such a good idea to come up the mountain looking for Noah. But he knew deep down that he needed to warn his old friend no matter what it might cost him. He couldn't let Lamar follow through with his plans. He heard Noah approaching the wagon, issuing an order to the wolf. "Down!" That was all he said.

The wolf turned to the sound of the voice command and leaped off the wagon's back end. Noah came into view. An Army-issue Colt Peacemaker was tucked inside a holster at his right side. He lifted the pistol free and pointed it toward Simon. "Scoot up to the end of the wagon, and don't do anything stupid."

Lamar and his men were riding single file through the rugged landscape at the foot of the San Juan Mountain range. Evening was coming on, and they would need to make camp for the night.

Hyrum was still new to the country; the first time he'd been through was back in the late fall when they killed and burned out the old man's cabin. And he was none too happy about the heat this time around. He was miserable and made no secret of it.

"I thought you said it would get cooler as we moved higher." Hyrum blasted one curse after another. "It's May, for Christ's sake. It should be cooler. Just when in the friggin' hell is that supposed to happen?"

He had heard over the years about the Godawful southwestern desert and what it was like in the summer, but it wasn't summer yet. This land between south Colorado and Utah along the Continental Divide was damn miserable. Beautiful to some, filled with nature's sand-blasted red, cream-white, and yellow sandstone, intermingled with ever-present black lava rock, but the friggin' sun glared down and baked the black jagged surface, making everything feel ten times worse.

"Goddamnit, Lamar!" Hyrum complained yet again. He never referred to the captain by his title on purpose. In his opinion, it gave the man more power to browbeat the men. And that was the last thing Hyrum wanted for himself. The rest of them could kiss Lamar's ass if they chose, but he'd had enough of the arrogant bastard to last a lifetime. One of these days, Hyrum would take that power and make himself the one in charge. He removed his hat and used his kerchief to mop up the sweat from his forehead and run it through his wet hair before he clamped it back on.

Lamar ignored him, and not for the first time he questioned his sanity. When they were up here at the beginning of winter. The weather was much cooler. In fact, damn right cold. But he'd be damned if he'd allow Hyrum to get to him.

The dislike between the two men ran both ways. And Lamar knew at the end of this, one of them was going to be dead. They moved into a rock-shaded box canyon two hours later. It was times like this that Lamar missed Simon. He had a calming effect on the ranks. But the coward ran off. He would be another in a long line of killings Lamar would continue to commit. He thought of what he'd done over these years since leaving prison. It hadn't been pretty, and he figured it would get uglier before it was over. Maybe he was leading them all to hell after all. And that was just fine by him.

※

The town of Willowby was in mourning. Left with a huge mess to clean up, a shot-up saloon, and broken glass in several buildings around town, including the sheriff's office. Two people had died that day. Carla, the girl who'd taken the most punishment, passed the following day from the extensive beating that involved internal injuries.

What the hell those men did to the poot girl made Jim nauseous, in fact, he'd lost his stomach the moment he laid eyes on her. Silas Greenhand, the old pig farmer who lived a few miles from town, had also dropped dead from the shot he'd taken out at his place. Thankfully, he could precisely describe the same hoodlums who'd ransacked the town before he died.

Even with all that had happened, the young sheriff Jim Adderly couldn't form a posse. Not one person would volunteer to ride with him. As far as any of them were concerned, this was the job of the U.S. Marshall. But he wasn't due to arrive for two weeks. By then, the likelihood of ever finding the culprits would surely be a lost cause.

Damn, what a mess. The only saving grace was that he had several decent descriptions, including his and Silas Greenhand's. Silas had pretended to be dead for all the good it did him, and as soon as the outlaws rode out after setting fire to the man's eclectic house, Silas had been able to mount his mule and get to town. However, the bullet ripped through his chest. How he ever made it this far would remain a mystery.

From what the old man told Jim, the men were looking for someone; Elijah Franklyn had ostensibly been helping. Who might that be? Jim had no idea. The old man came to town once a year for supplies. He paid with silver coins. He minded his own business, only staying a few days in town and spending the rest of his time with Greenhand out at his place or playing poker at the saloon. So, whoever he may or may not be helping would remain a secret.

Rumor had it that back about fifteen years ago, there was a child who had lost his family during a raid on the town. His whole family had been killed. The older man had taken the child away. However, the kid was never heard from again.

Jim entered his jailhouse through his attached room at the back, where he spent his time off-duty or when he didn't have a prisoner to watch over. And that was seldom, just the usual drunks on Saturday night. On top of his desk was a stack of paperwork. He figured it was time he went through it. The top of the pile consisted of tax collection notices. Beneath this were wanted posters and a message from the Governor. The message he opened first and discovered had been posted over a month before.

Lamar Tamarin and a list of at least seven others took up the space on the first piece of paper—the second held descriptions and drawings. Eight posters were attached. Eight faces.

A Captain Lamar Tamarin, Hyrum Raintree, Eric Bradley, Sean Bradley, Charley Stephans, Earl Silverman, Jacob Salter and Simon Mason. According to the paperwork, four of these men were Ex Calvary and were court marshaled over ten years ago. Lamar Tamarin had spent two years in Leavenworth.

All of them were wanted up north for killings in and around Chyenne and several families who lived on small farms outside of Denver. Each man had a thousand-dollar reward attached to them. As Jim studied the posters, he realized he didn't recognize Simon Mason or this Jacob Salter. The two men had either kept out of sight or had never been at the saloon. Probably dead. The other hellions spent all night and half a day tearing up the town and saloon.

The aftermath of the attack had been severe. Two were dead, and the town torn apart. Though it pained him, he guessed it could have been worse. But Carla, he couldn't get what remained of her out of his mind. The blood, the pain. What kind of animal did something like that?

The door pushed open; two men stepped inside. "Louise just packed up and left town on the stage." They said in unison. "If you still want a posse, we're volunteering. They were both good girls; we all understood they were there to look at. Or dance with, serve our drinks, maybe steal a kiss or two but never overstep the bounds of decency. Not one of us would have ever done what those men did. What do you need us to do?"

With relief, Jim looked up and met both of their serious faces. "I'm glad to hear that question. Have a seat, and we will make a list of things we will need. There is a reward, and you two are welcome to it if we are lucky enough to catch those animals."

"Ain't doing it for the reward. Hell, whatever money is to be made can go back into the town's coffers for repairs."

Jim nodded his agreement. They began to make plans, and Jim filled the men in on the information he'd learned from the Governor's message and shared the pictures that had been sent of the criminals. He also talked about what he'd learned from old man Greenhand and the direction the killers may have taken.

They all agreed to meet here in the morning. Maybe there were a few brave people left in town after all. Jim gave a grateful sigh.

Noan holstered his gun once Simon reached the end of the wagon and then ordered him off. Once the man's feet hit the ground, He undid the shackles.

Simon stretched and took a few steps back as he suspiciously watched Noah. "Are you going to trust me now?"

"Nope, but at the moment, I don't have much choice, it would seem."

"I don't blame you. And I know you don't believe me, but I swear I only came to warn you about the men and help any way I can."

Noah shrugged. "You can help me unload this wagon."

"Who were you talking to?" Simon asked as he lifted a crate from the wagon and placed it on the ground.

Noah didn't answer. When all the supplies were on the ground, they carried the animal feed to a lean-to. Other items were stacked near the back doorway to the cabin. The remainder they took to the shed, where Simon noted a chair sitting in the corner by a single window. Beneath this was a sleeping pallet. The large space had enough room for a man to sleep inside.

"Who sleeps out here?"

"You will until I figure out what to do with you."

"I see. I have some eatable supplies in my packs. You are welcome to take them into your cabin. I have coffee, bacon, flour, cornmeal and beans. Since I'm your prisoner, you might as well get some use out of them. Unless you plan on starving me to death."

Again, Noah was silent.

The cabin door opened, and they heard items being pulled inside.

"Stay here," Noah ordered and left Simon in the shed. "Honey, let me get the stuff inside."

"Don't be silly. I can start putting things away. I have coffee ready, a batch of biscuits, and stew left over from last night. There is enough to feed all of us."

Simon was intrigued by the sound of a sultry female voice. He stepped to the doorway and looked outside. On the narrow porch connected to the back of the cabin, he saw one of the prettiest women he could remember ever seeing. She wore a blue and white gingham dress with a full skirt, a white lacy collar, and long straight sleeves cuffed at her wrists and matched the material of the collar.

Her deep, ebony hair was pulled back from such a beautiful face; it made Simon catch his breath. She was petite and stood several inches shorter than Noah. He couldn't help but watch as Noah protectively embraced her, caressing her belly. Simon wondered if she was going to have a baby. A part of Simon envied Noah, while another was happy for him. He deserved all the goodness he could find.

If only he hadn't let Lamar intimidate him all those years ago, he might have been able to have a happy life. He turned from the doorway, thinking about Seely, the sweet, petite blond he should have made a life with. He remembered the tears in her cornflower blue eyes as he walked away from her and left with Lamar. How foolish he had been.

Noah made his way back to the shed. *Judas!* he hoped he hadn't messed up things by bringing Simon up here. I suppose you saw that," Noah said as he stepped back inside the shed. Simon's back was to him, and he was separating his packs from the rest of the items they had already taken to the shed. "You do anything to hurt her, and I will kill you!"

"She's lovely, Noah. I would never hurt her or you. My only wish is that I hadn't left my own happy life behind and rode out with Lamar all those years ago."

When Simon turned around and faced Noah, tears of regret filled his eyes. And for the first time in the last twenty-four hours, Noah knew Simon had been truthful in everything he had told him. She has food ready. Are you hungry? I know I am."

Simon nodded, grasped his food pack, and followed Noah to the cabin. The scent of coffee, biscuits, and venison stew filled the cabin.

Cora eyed the man who followed Noah inside. He wore a well-tended beard that covered his jawline. His hair was the deep color of burnt umber. His eyes were a silverish shade and appeared to have witnessed too much in life.

Yes, there was a sadness in him. His facial features held a rugged, outdoorsy look. Not as handsome as Noah, but attractive. Slight crow's feet at the corners of his eyes and down swept at the edges of his mouth. He was at least six feet tall, maybe an inch or two shorter than Noah's height. "Ma'am," he said and tipped his hat before removing it.

She stepped closer to Noah, gazing up at him. "Would you bring one of the trunks over for an extra chair?"

"Of course," he tightly wrapped his arm around her, resting his hand on her waist and turned her toward Simon. "Simon Mason, this is my wife, Cora."

Simon's eyes widened with surprise. "Cora!" he repeated. "But I thought…"

Cora grinned and stepped to the door, letting Loka inside. He gazed at all three of them and gave off a growl when his eyes rested on Simon. "Loka, be nice," Cora said to the wolf. "Loka is our friend," she informed the man.

"I see," Simon gave Loka a nervous look and turned to Noah, who was grinning.

"Please have a seat," Cora told the men and placed a plate filled with biscuits on the table along with a jar of blackberry jam and began to scoop up the stew into bowls.

Simon sat and looked around the small cabin. The place was simple: a couple of trunks, one double-size bed, a small pot belly stove, and a massive fireplace with a trammel in the open firebox—a colorful braided rug on the plank floor at the bottom of the bed and another lay before the prep area in front of the sink. He noted the guitar hanging on the wall. "You still play?" he asked Noah, who remained silent and continued to eat.

"Oh yes, he is very good." Cora supplied.

"I agree. He entertained our unit in the evenings while we were on patrol." He took a spoonful of stew and gave her a delighted look. "This is wonderful."

"Thank you. Have a biscuit." She instructed. "This is blackberry jam." She pushed the jar toward him. "It's one of Noah's favorites."

He lathered a spoonful onto the biscuit.

Loka chose that moment to plop down on the floor before the fireplace hearth.

"A pet wolf, good Lord Noah, how did that come about?"

"He is not a pet as I told you earlier but a protective friend. Maybe if you would have helped me out that day in the Cheyenne village, you would know," Noah growled the accusation, said no more, and continued to eat, covering his biscuit with jam.

Simon swallowed and nearly choked on the mouthful of biscuit.

"Loka saved Noah's life after the soldiers left him to die," Cora answered the question.

Simon glanced from one to the other. "I guess Noah's told you what happened that day."

"He has told me. And how he survived for the years after?"

"Change the subject, Cora,"

She looked over at Noah; he was beginning to sound like that ornery snow monster he'd been in the beginning. Her stubbornness flared slightly. "Noah, you are being rude!"

He temporarily remained silent, then slammed his cup on the table, sending water droplets across the surface. "Not a good subject while eating." He noted the hurt in her amber eyes and reached beneath the table, caressing her thigh. What the hell was wrong with him? She was only trying to be polite. They never got company and he was acting like a jealous fool.

"True, I guess," she admitted. "But just remember you brought it up to begin with." He didn't argue; she was right."

"I'll just wait outside," Simon told them.

"Stay right where you are, and finish eating," Noah barked, and the sound caused Loka to stand and glare at his human counterparts. Noah caught the irritation on Cora's face and what appeared to be a scowl on Loka's. He quickly added. "Please. Then, to Loka, he said, "lay down."

Cora delicately changed the subject. "Do you play an instrument?" she asked Simon.

He cleared his throat, "I play the harmonica."

Oh, that's wonderful. My Grandfather played. Do you have it with you?"

"Yes, ma'am, I play it for my horses when we make camp. It calms them."

"Maybe one of these evenings, you and Noah can play together. I love music."

"Are you about done eating?" Noah directed the inquiry at Simon. "I'd like to finish putting supplies away." He stood abruptly, wobbling his chair.

"Simon shoveled another spoonful of stew into his mouth, finished his biscuit, stood, and said, "I'm ready whenever you are." He looked down at Cora. "Thank you for the food, Mrs. Harper; it was delicious."

She smiled, "you are welcome. Noah stormed from the cabin, stood on the narrow porch, and held the door open. "I'm ready," he grumbled.

They spent the rest of the afternoon organizing the shed and bringing the household supplies into the cabin, where Cora began to put things away. She placed the material for the baby's clothes and new shirts she would make for Noah, along with yarn, thread, and sewing needles inside the extra trunk Noah had built for her.

She smiled; he had even thought of getting her some lace, satin ribbon in different colors, and enough material so she could make a new dress or two—soft flannel for diapers and nightgowns for the baby. In fact, he had gotten her everything on the list she had given him. She was so excited and couldn't wait to tell him how pleased she was.

That evening, after a supper of roasted grouse hen, potatoes and carrot, and berry pie for dessert, she politely asked the men if they would play some music for her. "But maybe you both are too tired. You made a long trip up here, and you've been working nonstop for hours."

"Another time, honey," Noah pleaded. He wanted so badly to have some alone time with her.

"Did you fix a spot for Simon to sleep?"

"Yes, ma'am. I have a nice pallet. I brought you my travel supplies. I have some bacon and beans and coffee."

"Ooo, bacon. It's been a long time since I've had any. I'll cook some up for breakfast. One of these days, Noah and I would like to have a milk cow. All the things we could make with her milk. Butter, cheese, and when the baby gets older, we will have fresh milk."

So, he was right; they were going to have a child, Simon realized with a smile. Though he knew Noah wouldn't believe him, Simon was pleased Noah had found happiness. The love these two shared was a come-to Jesus' moment. "Well, thank you again for the wonderful meal. I am pretty tuckered out, so I will head to bed. Did you want to restrain me for the night?' He looked to Noah.

Cora also looked at Noah. "Nope, Loka will keep watch over you."

"All right then," he said with an anxious edge. Then I'll see you in the morning."

"In the morning," Cora repeated.

Noah and Loka followed him to the shed. Once Simon was inside, Loka lay down in front of the door. He would remain there all night.

Cora was still seated when Noah returned. There was hurt in her topaz eyes. And he knew he'd put it there. He stepped in her direction, and she held up her hand to stop the motion.

Chapter Twenty-Three

"You need to explain your behavior, Noah. I haven't seen you act like this since I came here looking for you. I understand your anger and your mistrust of this man. But I am on the outside looking in, and if you recall, you and I didn't trust each other initially. We both thought the other was making up stories. This evening, I had the opportunity to study Simon. And I believe he carries such guilt, an inner sadness that only regret can give." She covered the berry pie she had made and carried it to the counter.

"I feel he is telling you the truth. I know you don't believe him, but my feelings are strong. Give him a chance." She turned back to him. "Ah Noah, if I didn't know better, I'd swear you were jealous. You have no need ever to feel that way. You are the only man I will ever love. And you should very well know that."

Noah swallowed. "I know what you say is true. But it's so hard, honey. I have waited all my life for the kind of love you've given me. I guess I'm selfish that way. And when I watched you be so friendly I got scared."

She went to him, pulling him close. "I love you so much. You are my everything. I don't want to lose what we have. For now, let's listen to his warnings. Everything inside me says he's here for a positive reason. He knew how angry you would be, and yet he came anyway." She reached for his hand and raised up on tip toes to brush her lips against his.

"Those men who murdered my grandfather were determined to kill him no matter what. It made no difference if he told them what he knew about you or not. He sensed this from the beginning, so he sent me hiding beneath the cabin in the room I made myself. He knew if they knew about me, I wouldn't have a chance of surviving, and the Lawd only knows what they may have done to me before they took my life. It is also why he sent me to you. And thank God he did."

He tightly pressed her against him and lifted her chin, lowering his lips to hers. The kiss was filled with love and need. His tongue met her in a rush of warmth as it mated with her own. "Ah, honey, what would I do without you? I need you more than you need me. She could feel the emotions clear to her toes.

"You are wrong; we need each other to make us whole."

"I promise to speak to him first thing in the morning. I wasn't willing to listen to him earlier, but I will if it means he can help us."

She smiled and unbuttoned his shirt and longjohns, running her hands across his bare skin and watching his soft chest hair curl around her fingers. "I want you so much I can hardly breathe."

His mustache tickled her cheek as he moved back to her lips. "All I've thought about the past week is having you in my arms and being buried in your warmth."

"Me too," she whispered against his open mouth, moved down, pressing her lips against his nipples, using her tongue to swirl around from one to the other, all the while unhitching his pants and sliding them down his hips and thighs to pool at his feet on the cabin floor.

Her skin was like silk and velvet when he undid the buttons of her dress and touched and tasted her with his tongue. Her breasts were like globes of softness, her nipples exploding in hardened arousal when they filled his mouth. He bathed her in warmth with his tongue and listened to the beautiful sounds she made as he suckled and gently reached down between her legs.

They stood before each other, naked, excited, and filled with an unadulterated need for each other. He began to back her toward their bed, and once there, he lifted her, laid her down, and quickly joined her. Neither stopped the kissing or touching as they shared the need and mutual love.

Cora murmured and arched toward his mouth and hands; when he moved his fingers through the folds of moist feminine flesh, she cried out. "Please…Noah, I want you inside me. She spread her legs, reached down, wrapped her hand around his smooth hardness, and guided him to the place of joining, hot and slick.

The moment he entered her, she grasped his bottom and tucked him inside in one fluid motion. She climaxed almost immediately, and he quickly followed suit. Still connected, he plundered her lips, slipping his tongue to meet hers. They began exploring and igniting their body's passion again—this time at a much slower pace.

Dawn would be approaching in a few hours; the skyline showed the first signs of light cresting the canyon wall. The wind-blown sandstone surrounding Lamar and his men had already begun to show the sparkle of the approaching sun.

Two of the men had been up most of the night, playing cards, drinking to excess, and listening to the horrendous sounds of Hyrum and the dark-skinned housemaid he'd taken captive the day before.

They'd been moving slower since leaving the small town of Willowby. With each day that passed, the territory they traversed became rougher. Passages were becoming narrower and more challenging to ride through.

Lamar had forgotten how rough the terrain was. They had to stop more frequently. Damnit, he wanted this whole ordeal to come to an end. He'd given up ten years of his life, and for what? He had never come close to capturing Noah in all that time. He always managed to miss the bastard by a week or so. His thoughts became disrupted when he heard Charley's accusations.

"Why you somebitch! You cheated!" Charley pulled his Colt from his holster and aimed the muzzle at Earl's face.

Unaffected by the threat, Earl roared with laughter. "What the hell did you expect? "We are thieves, marauders, and occasional killers, after all!"

"Maybe, but I thought we were also friends." He cocked the hammer spur back with a hard clicking sound.

The laughter became louder. "What is it they say? Oh yeah, there is no honor among thieves."

The other two men, Sean and Eric, stirred, rolled over, and continued to snore.

"We'll just see about that, you somebitch!" Charley hissed.

"Would you all shut the hell up? We got to head out in two hours, and some of us are trying to get some sleep, and that is tough enough with this damn heat!" Lamar shouted out. He knew the men were bored and itching for excitement. This whole situation was turning into one immense pain in the ass.

He had hoped to avoid the ranch he'd seen yesterday when he scouted ahead with his spyglass. They had already left too much bullshit behind, especially after the altercations with the old pig farmer and the destruction in Willowby. But in the end, he decided it would be wise to let the boys have some fun and blow some steam off with someone else rather than themselves.

Hyrum was already hard enough to control. And the rest of them were beginning to listen to the sick bastard more as time passed. But Lamar just couldn't let go of his vengeful thoughts regarding Noah. The man had to pay.

"He's a cheatin' somebitch, Capn' He deserves to eat a bullet. And why the hell are you yellin' at us? Hyrum over there is making enough racket to wake the dead with that halfbreed house girl he grabbed yesterday. All night listening to that is enough to drive a sane man crazy. Maybe he's the one we should shoot! Right Earl?"

"Damn right, the selfish bastard! Then again, after he's done with them, there isn't much left."

"Why don't ya all go bang yourselves!" Hyrum shouted out with glee and grinned down at the pretty woman. She reminded him of that Carla gal back in that one-horse town they shot up at the beginning of the week.

"Jesus Christ!" Lamar hissed. "You can all kill each other when this job is done. Put your frigging guns away and get some sleep. And Hyrum, Goddamnit, tone it down, for Christ's sake!"

"Ah, shit!" Charley swore and angrily tossed his cards down, spilling them across the rocky ground with a handful of coins. He took an angry swallow of whiskey but nearly choked when the exploding sound of Hyrum's gunfire pierced the hot night air.

"Jesus H Christ, Jim, look what they did to the Galaherger's family. I ain't never seen so much blood. The wife and two daughters. Oh, God..." Skeet turned and tossed his breakfast into a nearby sagebrush. Jim watched Pete, the other man who rode with them, turn pale as snow. He joined Skeet and shared the sagebrush. Minutes later, the two men stood, wiped their mouths, grabbed their canteens, and rinsed the bile away.

Jim figured they would return to town, leaving him alone in this search. They had been the only two who'd come forward after Willowby was ransacked. They were brave men, but this was way beyond bravery.

"I suppose you both want to go back now?" Jim asked, feeling hopeless.

"No, sir. We've seen this kind of thing before. But that was back in the days toward the end of the war. We were only eighteen and rode under the command of William Anderson. The men nick named him Bloody Bill. Those men left a lot of bodies in their wake.

"Pete and I were sure glad to be reassigned to Fort McKinney and even signed up for another six years in early seventy-two. However, that also turned out to be no kind of picnic toward the end. There was the battle at Little Big Horn, and thank God we weren't a part of it, and then two years later, the massacre in a Cheyenne Village. We were out on patrol in the opposite direction when it happened. By the time we got back, it was all anyone talked about. All the men involved were court marshaled. And the captain who led them was sent to prison. He blamed one of his men who survived for testifying against him and the others."

Pete interrupted. "They all thought the man was dead when they'd left him behind in that bloody Cheyenne village. But he survived. Made it back to the fort with a wolf, if you can imagine." He glanced over to Skeet. "Hey, you remember what that soldier's name was?"

Skeet thought for a moment. "It was a bible name, as I recall." Then he blurted out, "Noah!"

"Harper?" Jim interrupted as he studied both men

"That's right," Pete agreed.

Jim began to understand more about the reasons the man had gone into hiding and why the outlaws were searching for him.

"Poor bastard had tried to object to the horrible acts happening in the village. But no one would listen. After the damage they had inflicted, they all rode out, leaving Noah behind, assuming he was dead."

"That was their mistake. He was beat up pretty bad but alive. The doc at the fort fixed him up." Pete shook his head in disgust. "Skeet and I were released from our service before the trial began. But the stories that were told were enough to make a man's skin crawl. It's just been a long time since we've seen or heard of this kind of thing. And now this blood bath! Just give us a minute, sheriff, and we'll get through it."

Jim nodded with gratitude. "I think when you're up to it, we should bury these poor folks and head up to Marble Canyon and make camp on the outskirts.

"Yes, sir."

"We will meet up with Harald Long Tooth, a half-breed negro who used to scout for the military years ago and is familiar with this territory—been livin' up here for the past fifteen years. He's a hermit, was married once, but lost his wife and two sons during that raid in Willowby when many others were killed. Left town and never looked back."

"Let's get these poor folks buried. Skeet said.

Two hours later, they were heading toward Marble Canyon but stopped when they heard the echo of gunfire—first one shot, then another. Dust kicked up on the ground about twenty feet ahead of them. "Lord God," Pete shouted.

Noah untangled himself from Cora's shapely legs and arms, which were lovingly wrapped around him. He rose, trying not to disturb her. She looked so peaceful, and he knew she needed to rest after their night of lovemaking. He moved over to the sink, bathed quickly, shaved, and pulled on clean long johns, pants, and shirt. Socks and boots came next. Once dressed, he stepped outside, quietly closed the cabin door, and walked the short distance to the outhouse. When he returned, he started the coffee.

Cora smiled and stretched as she watched him fill the coffee pot and pour in the aromatic beans she had ground yesterday. The blanket that had covered them through the night slipped down to her waist, exposing her naked upper body and a pair of full breasts that displayed darkened nipples the color of deep mauve. "Good morning, husband," she said with a sensual grin.

He spun around, "I'm sorry, I didn't mean to wake…" he stopped midsentence. She was so beautiful, even with the redness on her soft skin caused by his three-day worth of whiskers. "Does it hurt, honey? I should have shaved."

"Huh, what do you mean?"

"Your breasts, do they hurt from the burn my whiskers left."

She glanced down at her nakedness, blushed, and pulled the blanket up. "Umm, no, I like the feel of your whiskers. They tickle and make me feel so close to you when you kiss and caress me with your lips and tongue."

He swallowed, "just the same, I should have shaved. I don't want anything to mar your soft skin. I have some salve for the burns." He moved to his trunk and pulled his medical bag free. He had the healing cream in seconds and sat on their shared bed.

The scent of coffee filled the cabin and mixed with her unique feminine sweetness. He lowered the blanket and began to rub the medicine into her skin. The burn marks were not only on her breasts but also stretched down across her stomach. *Judas!* He felt like an oversexed heathen.

Cora gave an aroused intake of breath. "Ummm, husband, unless you want to return to bed, I think I better apply the medicine myself."

Noah gave her a crooked grin. "Feels good, does it?"

Her cheeks stained an attractive pink. "Too good," she admitted. "And I need to get up, visit the outhouse and wash up. Maybe tonight we can fill the tub. I've only given myself spitz baths this week and would like to soak."

"I could use one too. I will check on Simon; he had better not have betrayed us and run off to inform Lamar and his men of our whereabouts."

"Noah, you promised to give him the benefit of the doubt." She reached for the container of salve.

Noah shrugged with a non-committed lift of his shoulders.

She knew he was trying, but he was so stubborn. "I'll start breakfast once I clean up." She pulled her chemise over her head as she spoke, stepped into her dress and shimmied it up, quickly buttoned the front, and finally jammed her stocking feet into her shoes. She raced out of the cabin to the outhouse.

"Hold up, honey, let me check the area.

"For goodness' sake, Noah, I got to go."

He grabbed his rifle and followed her. When she finished, he led her back to the cabin and headed for the shed where Simon was supposed to be.

Simon heard the shed door open and watched Noah step inside.

"I see you are still here."

"I don't know how I can be much clearer. I'm here to help. There's no way I'm going to run off."

Noah shrugged. "Time will tell."

"You fixed this place up nice for a jailhouse."

Noah glanced around. "I fixed it up for Cora to hide in case she was ever in danger, and I could not help her."

"How did you meet her? Was she one of the gals in a saloon you played at?"

"Hell no!"

"Ah, sorry, I meant no insult."

"She was the granddaughter of the old mountain man you, Lamar, and the other men murdered."

"I told you I had no part in any of that. But I am guilty for not trying to stop it," he sadly admitted. "I am glad they never found her, or she certainly would be as dead as her grandfather and worse.

"Some of those men Lamar chose to ride with...God, it was bad—the things they did to women. I am so glad they knew nothing about your Cora. You're a lucky man. She is beautiful and very devoted to you. If I had only listened to my conscience, I would have settled with my own pretty little gal and probably had a couple of kids by now. You have to know what I did to you, and keeping company with Lamar and his gang is one of my biggest regrets."

"So, you say. I brought you some clean water," Noah stepped back outside and returned with a large washing bowl of water and a pitcher. Clean up, and come up to the cabin. Cora is making breakfast, and there's a pot of coffee."

"What did you do with my saddle bags? I have clean clothes and my toiletries inside. them."

"In the corner below the shelves. You have ten minutes." Noah turned and stepped back outside, closing the door behind him. He prayed he was doing the right thing. He returned to the cabin and the woman he loved and would protect with his life.

Chapter Twenty-Four

"Hold it right there!" Came a gruff-sounding voice. "One more step, and I'll blow your brains out.

Jim, Pete, and Skeet pulled the reins of their mounts and came to a dead stop. "It's me, Longtooth, Jim Adderly, Willowby's sheriff. I'm here with my deputies. "We just want to talk."

"Ain't got nothing to say!"

"Did you hear what happened in town a few days ago? Or what went on at the Galaherger's place?"

"Nope! Now get!"

"It's important. You need to know for protection, and we could use your help."

Longtooth sure as hell didn't like being bothered with what happens in civilization. He'd had his fill years ago, but he also knew the sheriff wouldn't come all this way if it weren't necessary. He could remember when the man was just a boy and friends with his youngest. No, this must be important. "Dismount and leave your weapons behind, then come forward. And be quick about it!"

Jim inclined his head to Pete and Skeet. All three dismounted. The closer they came to old Longtooth's camp, the more remote the place became. Surrounded by dried oak brush, willow, gamble oak, and juniper added to the rocky seclusion. The smell of sage and boiled coffee filled the air.

"It's been a long while," Jim said, holding a hand out for a friendly shake.

Longtooth ignored the extended hand and moved to the firepit.

Pete and Skeet sat down on a circle of red sandstone surrounding the pit. Inside, a smokeless fire burned.

"Get to the point. Say what you got to and forget all the dilly-dallying around."

"We are hunting a murderous gang. They leave death and blood wherever they go. They claim they are looking for a man. His name is Noah Harper. We need to know if anything unusual is happening up here."

"There is always something going on, and I learned long ago to mind my own business."

"These cutthroats have committed atrocities worse than what happened sixteen years ago in town when you lost your family. They need to be caught. If they are not, you could lose all this privacy you have built for years. I have informed the United States marshal authorities, but they can't get anyone out here for at least two weeks. The same goes for the Army. If you could give us a hand, we can take care of the problem ourselves, which would be better for you and everyone else."

Longtooth remained silent, and Jim and the men waited. "I suppose you want me to do some scouting."

"We would appreciate any help you can give us."

"Noah Harper, you say? I heard Elijah Franklyn was helping someone up at his place. Now he's dead, and probably the same is true of whoever he helped."

"We believe," Jim added. "These men are responsible for that killing. The leader, a man named Lamar Tamarin, was once in the military and was responsible for the slaughter of a Cheyenne village back in '78. He travels with some of the men who served with him." Jim glanced from man to man but focused the most on Longtooth.

"Noah Harper is the one who turned them in and testified against them. Most were court marshaled and let go, but Lamar Tamarin was imprisoned for the deed. He was released after two years, has sworn vengeance, and has been searching for Harper ever since. Over the years, they have left a trail of blood wherever they go. I received the wanted posters last month, but Lamar no longer looks like he did in the poster when he came to town, and no one recognized him. He used a different name and claimed he was searching for his long-lost brother."

"And you believe this Harper fellow is hiding up here?" Longtooth asked with a scowl.

"Yes."

Longtooth became quiet. He scratched his bearded salt-and-pepper chin. His hazel eyes, more brown than green, appeared deep in thought as he studied Jim. He'd known Jim for years and, frankly, liked him when he'd come to spend time with his sons. "Elijah and I were friends for many years. He had his secrets, but I never asked, and he never told. He also lost his family during that raid: a daughter, her husband, and their child. All right, I'll help. What do you need from me?"

"We'd like your scouting expertise if you are willing. I've never been any higher on this mountain than we are right here. I am unfamiliar with what's beyond."

"Well then, that's the answer I needed to know. Let's make a little trouble of our own."

"We welcome the help. Mind sharing that coffee?" Jim gazed at the pot with longing.

"Help yourself. I'll be ready here in a minute." With that said, Longtooth stood and moved through a cluster of shrubs and into a hidden sandstone hollow—an opening no one had noticed until now.

For the following week and within a mile's radius, Noah, Cora, and Simon prepared for whatever attack would come from Lamar and his men. And none of them doubted that it wouldn't come.

Snag traps, holes dug and hidden with branches, pine needles, and leaves to camouflage the trap. One misstep and down they'd go.

They strung a wireline and once struck, it would trigger a wall of spikes to pop upwards with an explosive sound of cracked wood and fallen debris. Any forward movement would come to an abrupt halt and possibly mortally wound man and horse alike. The main point was that whatever they did would make enough racket to alert them of the danger.

Simon explained more about the men Lamar paid to ride with him. "Hyrum, who joined them about a year ago, is a bloodthirsty rapist and murderer. He enjoys bringing horrendous pain to his victims, especially women. His sexual appetite is beyond anything I've ever seen. The thought of them getting their hands on Cora…I can't think about it, let alone talk about it. We need to stop them any way we can before they have a chance to get to her," Simon could already feel the bile creeping up to his throat. "Can she shoot?"

"As well as I can with a rifle."

"That's good. I was thinking it might be safer for her in the cabin. She could hide beneath the bed and keep Loka with her."

"She and I already discussed that. She argued and made a valid point that makes sense. She would not have any mobility. And if she needed to shoot, it would bring more harm than not. With the recoil and the loudness of firing the weapon, she could be hurt along with our baby."

"She is a handful of fire, isn't she? You are a lucky man. I truly wished I had listened to my conscience and stayed with you that morning in the village."

Noah looked at Simon; part of him still didn't fully trust the man, but he had done everything he had promised. Still, needing help from him was infuriating. He had to swallow his pride because he did need him, like it or not. Cora had to stay safe. It went against everything he thought or felt, but he asked anyway. "If I don't make it off this mountain and you do, please get Cora down to town. I haven't had contact with my family for years. As far as they know, I'm dead. And as far as I know, they could be gone also. But I do have two sisters. Promise me you'll get Cora on a train and send her to them. I know they will welcome her.

"Of course I will, but I'll be honest, you have more chance of surviving than I do. I've been feeling like a dead man walking for the past ten years. But I give you my word."

They heard Cora's voice coming across the way and through the trees. "Supper's ready."

"Keep this between us," Noah implored and watched Simon nod his compliance.

Both men moved to the creek and washed before heading to the cabin.

"What the hell's wrong with Hyrum?" Charley asked. "He's been in a piss poor mood since we packed up this morning. Hell, look at the fat lip he gave Earl and all 'cause he asked him to pass the coffee pot."

"He's a psychotic lunatic; that's what's wrong with him." Both Sean and Eric spoke at the same time. "No conscience, nothing to stop him. Jesus! Why does the Cap'n keep riding with him? He only leaves one mess after another. And he's going to get us killed."

"That's true. I ain't never seen a man who loves killing and torturing more than Hyrum." Earl broke in, moving fingers across his swollen lip. "It just ain't natural. I mean, I've done my share of the killin' and having a good time with the women, but unnecessary torture, no sir!"

"You know the captain's rules, no witnesses. If Hyrum wants to take things further, so be it. You had a good time! He had his. Are you two willing to stop him?" Charley hissed. "I know I ain't."

"But…"

"Put a cork in it, all of you. I'm sick of hearing it." Lamar growled, sounding like an old grizzly. *But they were right. Hyrum was out of control.*

"What a bunch of crybabies." Hyrum chuckled as he sidled his horse next to Lamar's.

"You could use more self-control, for Christ's sake."

"Why? I'm getting so much enjoyment! It's what life is all about. You know what they say: live in the moment. And I plan to live in every single one."

"Not when it puts the rest of us at risk." Lamar pointed toward the distant mountains. "I want to be up there by nightfall. There won't be any more stopping for entertainment."

Hyrum gave him a snide grin. Time would tell which one of them would emerge a winner in this power struggle, and Hyrum loved to win. He jerked the reins to the left and turned back to the men, chuckling. Yup, that day was close.

***

The supper consisted of smoked trout, potatoes, and carrots. Cora used the corn meal Noah had purchased in town to make fried corn cakes. For dessert, she made apple cobbler out of spiced canned apples, sprinkling a coarse sugar coating on top as it baked in the Dutch oven. The cabin was filled with delightful smells as the men entered, followed by Loka. She knew Simon was still a little nervous around the wolf, especially when he'd shove his nose against him and sniff his scent. "Loka! Leave the poor man alone," she scolded.

Loka backed off but didn't move far. He plopped down on the floor before the tiny stove and patiently waited for his evening meal, which she immediately gave him. He gobbled it all down in nearly one gulp. He went to his water bowl, drank his fill, and scratched at the door. Since Simon had been here, the wolf slept outside, guarding the place and giving protection each night.

Quickly, Cora accommodated him and opened the door, "protect! She ordered unnecessarily. Closed the door and placed the platter of meat and boiled vegetables on the table. She filled the men's mugs with fresh coffee and gave herself chilled, sweetened tea. She saved any coffee drinking for the morning now that she had the makings for tea.

"Everything looks great, honey," Noah smiled.

"Sure does. You are an excellent cook, Cora.

"Thank you," she softly said.

The men spoke to her during the meal about the day's activities. "We are about as prepared as we can be. I've hauled the comfort items you wanted up to the alcove. And I don't want any argument; Loka will be with you."

"I still don't like hiding away, not when I can help. You know I shoot as well as you."

"I know you do, but you can help by being a lookout. If you see anything out of the ordinary, you can alert us.

"Like what? What in tarnation am I supposed to see? The place is well out of view, hidden in thick shrubs and trees. I can do nothing or see anything from up there; you know that very well! You are just being your usual stubborn self." She expostulated with obvious irritation.

"Talk about stubborn!" He growled back, glaring down at her. Loka will be with you. You know his senses are powerful tools. He can see, smell, and hear the things you can't. Simon and I can't be in the same place at the same time. It would defeat our purpose. This way, we have four sets of eyes, giving us all a better chance."

She knew he was right.

"Please, honey, do this for me." I need you and Loka to be our eyes and ears. You can fire a shot if you think Simon and I should be aware of something. Loka will protect you with his life. Please, honey, I can't do what I must and worry about you. Stay in the alcove with Loka."

She gave both men a meaningful look. "I suppose that could help. But I still think it would be better if I were with you." She took a fork full of food, quietly chewed and swallowed. "What if Loka got hurt or killed? Remember my grandfather when he tried to stop those monsters? Thunderation, Noah, if anything happens to you!"

"Ah honey, we have placed dozens of traps circling the cabin in a mile radius. Not to mention the traps we've sent to get up to the hollow and all the noise makers we've added. There will be so much racket; there is no way they can get here covertly once they pass the mile radius. At the moment we have the advantage. They don't know I've been warned about them. And most importantly, they don't know about you. Or that we have Simon's help."

They could try and convince her all they wanted. But she had her own ideas of staying safe, which didn't consist of hiding under a bed or staying in some hole in the mountain. She'd hid when her grandfather ordered her to. And look what that got. No, not this time. She dropped the subject, knowing it would get her nowhere. "Can we have some music tonight? I still haven't heard Simon play his harmonica."

"Sound travels long distances up here; I'm not sure that would be wise."

"I know. I guess I wasn't thinking. I just thought since we were inside that maybe..."

Both men watched her crestfallen expression.

"I suppose just for a little while, it wouldn't hurt."

"I'll go get my mouth organ," Simon offered.

"Mouth organ?"

Noah chuckled. "That's what he calls his harmonica."

Excitement filled her beautiful topaz eyes as she cleared the table, stacked the dishes for washing, and filled the dishpan with hot water and the soap flakes. Simon left to get his harmonica, and Noah helped her clean up. By the time Simon returned, everything had been cleared away and washed.

Cora sat in her rocking chair while the men readied their instruments. Fascinated, she watched Simon move his mouth organ back and forth across his lips while blowing into it. He started playing a Stephen Foster song called Oh Suzanna, and Noah quickly joined him with the guitar.

She tapped her foot to the rhythm. "I know this one," she told them with pleasure. Standing, she glided around the small space and began to sing. *"Oh, Suzanna, don't you cry for me. I come from Alabam with a banjo on my knee. I'm goin' to Louisian, my true love for to see."* She giggled as she moved in a two-step and continued to sing out.

Noah, exhilarated by her excitement, began to sing out with her as he played. *"Oh, Suzanna, don't you cry for me."*

Cora danced with each man for the next hour as the other played on. Her pretty face was flushed with joy when she finally sat back on her rocker. Simon slipped his harmonica into his shirt pocket and said his goodnights as Noah hung his guitar on the wall.

"Thank you both so much!" She grinned. "I had a wonderful time." The minute Simon was gone, she threw herself into Noah's arms. "I missed being held by you with your guitar pressed against my body as we danced."

"Is that so?"

"Yes, she leaned into him and gave him a kiss, which he deepened immediately and backed her toward the bed and began to undress.

Lamar and his men were on the move for the next three days, this time without the encumbrance of any women. By midday of the third, they were at the burned-out remains of Elijah's old cabin.

"Where to now, Cap'n?"

Lamar studied the surrounding area. "Now we split up and search. That old man knew Harper; I feel it in my bones. So, the traitor can't be far from here. Remember, you are only looking for a sign. Nobody, and

I mean nobody, does anything except make the sound of a hawk in flight like we talked about. Have you got it? If we hear your warning, we will get back to you. Otherwise..." Lamar pointed to a grove of trees in the distance. "We will meet up there, say, in two hours."

Everyone agreed. Yet Hyrum held a look of rebellion that worried Lamar, and he wasn't about to let him go rogue. "You're with me, Hyrum. Let's move." An hour later, everyone heard the cawing sound of a hawk.

Hyrum spotted the tracks, and they led up a narrow canyon. "Looks like they were pulling a travois or some kind of sleigh. The grooves in the ground are deep. Whatever was hauled was heavy. Someone who knew the old man even took the time to dig a grave and bury him." Hyrum jerked a finger at an old, gnarled tree near a lean-to and a crude marker beneath it some twenty feet to the left of them. They quickly rode over to it.

Lamar spat with vehemence. Thanks to his loss of patience, he'd ordered the men to leave before they had all the facts. Maybe it was time to give up this payback he felt he had earned and had been looking for since his release from prison. Nope, he would never give up, not until either Noah or himself were dead.

Charley, Earl, and Sean rode up at a fast gallop and joined them. Eric followed only seconds later.

Noah and Simon made one last survey of the traps they'd set over the past week. Everything seemed to be working proficiently. Both men knew it was only a matter of time before Lamar and his cutthroats would surround the place. "I'm still nervous about Cora's safety. Her pregnancy is still in the early stages, and I don't want her or our baby hurt.

"Do you think she will stay hidden in the cave we fixed up for her?"

"To begin with, but at the first sound of gunfire, the stubborn woman won't sit still. I know she'll grab the rifle and come to help."

'What about Loka, won't he try to stop her?"

Noah's face filled with concern. " He's as stubborn as she is. He would give his life for her. He would also follow her anywhere, even into Hell, if he thought she was in danger. I can see them both racing down the mountain path."

"She loves you, Noah. Make her promise to stay put."

I won't use our love to blackmail her. She has a mind of her own, and in her place, if I thought for one minute she was in danger or needed my help, I'd go through hell to get to her. She is instinctual as well. Both she and Loka will refuse to be cornered no matter the danger. If caught, they will be at the mercy of Hyrum and the others. Well, you get the picture. Loka is just as protective of me. Do you remember how he showed up when I first came across you? He was supposed to remain at the cabin with her, but he sensed I needed him more. You know how that turned out."

"Yeah, I remember that growl and those Godawful sharp teeth. You are right; if Lamar and his men saw hide or hair of him, they'd just shoot him. And Cora..."

"Kind of like you would have done had I not taken your rifle," Noah stated with a frown.

Simon gave him a look of understanding. "Yeah, just like that. Only I would have tried not to hit him, only scare him off."

Noah nodded, "I believe you, and over these past ten days, you've proven you don't like killing anymore than I do. Maybe in time, you will find some peace."

"I already have, thanks to you and Cora. No matter what happens, I will never forget what the two of you have done for me."

"I will admit that with each day that passes, I see more of the man I used to know. The first few years I was up here, it took some getting used to. But now I have found more peace than I ever thought possible. The best of it has come since Cora came into my life. She has given me a love I thought I would never know and shown me how integral and precious life is. When I wake up each morning and see her lying next to me, it's like the greatest gift I could ever receive.

"Loka won't leave her side. If she decides to leave the safety of the hollow, he will accompany her as long as he senses she needs him more than I do. So, I pray we can keep all this under control. The thought of what they would do to her before they killed her scares me to death, especially now that you've told me about Hyrum's sick preferences. They won't just kill her; they'll do much worse. God, I pray we can win this battle. I need to stop all the running and hiding. Make a connection with my family, and I can't until all this is over."

Simon thoughtfully studied Noah. "They never knew anything about your family. Your military and personal files, we were told, were lost. In everything we shared in friendship, I don't remember you speaking much about your family other than they were farmers. I always assumed you had lost them the same way I did mine. I swear on my life, I did not say anything to anyone about what we shared."

"Doesn't much matter now. They have found out where I am."

"I've been as honest as I can be with you. Though I participated in some, it was mostly witnessing. I've made the decision when all this is done, and Lamar is either dead or back in prison; I mean to turn myself in. And you should take Cora and return to your family and the beautiful farm the two of you told me about the other night. Start a life, maybe finish your medical schooling, and have a legitimate practice. You were damn good, Noah. Don't let it go to waste."

"We'll see; I'm not sure what I will do now. Plenty of small towns in the West could use a doctor. This will be a decision Cora and I will make together, but I certainly will let my family know I'm alive, and they will be grandparents, though I'm sure by now they already are. My sisters would be married with families of their own. Let's walk out to the ridge and check the valley. If they are coming, that's the way they'll get up here. I can't explain it, but I feel they are close."

"Maybe you have some of Loka's sense. But I agree they are close."

"I figure they have reached Elijah's burned-out cabin. If that's the case, they will be here soon. Several trails lead away from the area; picking the right one might take a while if we are lucky. But that's a long shot at best."

"I know I wouldn't have found you if you hadn't found me first. However, as much as I despise Hyrum, I must admit he is a good tracker."

"And I wasn't careful about covering tracks when Cora and I went down to get her things. I hope I didn't make it too easy. I don't need anyone else to lose their lives."

"They are killers, Noah. They would have done their worst no matter what."

"This is the way they came, all right, and it don't seem they were in any hurry either. Spent some time here," Longtooth grumbled.

Together, the four men gazed down at yet another destroyed homestead. At least this time, there were no bodies. On closer inspection, they realized the place had been abandoned probably decades ago.

"Well, if there is one thing I kin say about them, they are leaving a trail any idiot could follow." Longtooth gave Jim and his two deputies a look that said they were the idiots. "Looks like they are moving toward old Elijah's place. "I'll take you that far, and then I'm done. You're on your own. I'm returning to my canyon where I belong."

"I understand," Jim told him. "We appreciate you taking us this far."

A scowl was Longtooth's only response.

They made the steep climb up the canyon, and by late the following day, they could see the remnants of the old mountain man's cabin.

"There is a mess of tracks up here," Longtooth motioned to the ground. The closer the four riders came to the cabin, the more they could see the sign moving off in several directions. "Let me check out a couple of these paths. Then I can tell you the one they took." Longtooth spat a wad of tobacco juice on the ground and rode beyond the grave that held Elijah Franklyn.

Noah and Simon saw movement on the outskirts of the valley below. At this distance, with the naked eye, they couldn't be sure if it was an animal or man. They were still miles away. Noah's cabin was well hidden by large boulders, a thick line of ponderosa, and aspen now full of unfurling buds that would turn to heart-shaped leaves. They seemed to sing as the mountain breeze fluttered through the branches.

Watching the movements in the distance, Noah sensed it was a group of men. It would be only a matter of time before his home of the past eight years would be laid bare to the marauder's vision.

The cooking fire had not been stoked since breakfast hours ago and would only be lit again this evening if all was right. They planned to have a cold lunch, alleviating any smoke in the air. The traps they set certainly weren't foolproof, but they would slow anyone down and make enough noise to let them know how close the intruders were.

Simon lifted the spyglass he carried from a leather case at his side and telescoped it out. Careful to keep it from reflecting the sun's glare, he studied the movement. "It's them! You might want to get Cora up the mountain." He slid the brass scope back in place. "If we're lucky, we may have an hour," he turned to give Noah a look of concern, but Noah was already gone.

Chapter Twenty-Five

"Cora, I need to get you up to the hollow. Those men have cleared the tree line and are now in the valley; it's only a matter of time before they find us."

"No, I don't want to hide away. If I'm to die, I would rather be with you."

"Honey, we've talked about this. I can take care of myself, and I have Simon's help. You need to protect our baby. I couldn't live with myself if anything happened to the two of you."

"Now you sound like my grandfather. He kept me out of sight, and look where it got him. He's dead!"

Noah saw tears begin to crest her lashes, though he knew she was desperately trying to keep them in check. He moved to her and pulled her into his arms, pressing her tightly to him. "Please," he begged. "The hollow is hidden. No one but you and I know about it, not even Simon. Do you remember where we placed the traps?" He could feel her bobbing her head against his chest.

"I remember. I'll go, but if I feel like three guns are better than two at any time, I'm coming back down to help."

"I swear, between you and Loka, I have never known any two beings more stubborn. Grab the rifle. I've put enough of your needs up there; you should be fine. I'll walk with you halfway. Then I have to get back here to help Simon."

"If I lose you, I might as well shoot myself. I can't bear to see another person I love die."

Noah kissed the top of her head. "Let's pray that doesn't happen." He stepped back and looked deeply into her eyes. They were such a beautiful shade of topaz and held a depth of emotion that made what he needed to say next the hardest thing he ever would say. "If this doesn't work out the way we hope and both Simon and I are killed, it would indeed be better if you take your own life. From what Simon has told me about these men, especially the one he calls Hyrum, ever get a hold of you..." he swallowed thickly and nearly choked.

"Well...a quick death is better than the pain and horror he would put you through if he were to find you. So please, stay hidden. I will do everything in my power to keep myself alive."

He lifted his Colt single action from the leather holster on his right hip. "Take this with you. I won't need it. It would be best if you have it. Your grandfather's rifle I put in the hollow won't do you much good if caught off guard and trying to fire in the brush. You won't have time to sight in and fire a second shot; you'll need the pistol."

"I have a much better aim with this," she reached into the trunk she used and pulled free a mean-looking slingshot.

"How come I haven't seen that before?"

"Frankly, I had forgotten about it. It was the first thing I learned to shoot before my grandfather taught me to fire a rifle. And I am very good at it, rest assured."

He studied her with admiration. "I don't doubt it. You are always full of surprises." This time, he lifted her chin and kissed her deeply, meeting her explorative tongue with his own, giving her all the love and fire he possessed. When he lifted from her, she looked well kissed and hungry for more, just as he was. "We need to move."

She agreed, quickly discarded her dress, stepped into her pants and a long-sleeved shirt, and grabbed her slingshot, tucking it inside her waistband.

Noah reached for his own Sharps rifle, opened the cabin door, took her hand, and signaled Loka to follow, which he did without hesitation.

Hyrum aimed his pistol through the obstruction of trees and brush. "Up there, I can make out a cabin. We got him!"

Lamar joined him at the top of the broad valley. "I can't see anything. Where are you looking?"

Hyrum pointed. "Right up there, nestled in that grove of pine. What the hell, Lamar? Are you blind? The damn thing is as plain as the big nose on your face."

Lamar ignored the insult for the time being. The cabin was so well camouflaged that Lamar had to squint to make out the framing of a small cabin. The thing was made of logs that blended in so well with all the trees that once you saw it, it stuck out like a sore thumb. "Damn, Hyrum, you know as much as you drive me up a tree and piss me off most of the time. I got to admit, you have the eyes of an eagle." He tapped him on the back between the shoulders, "well done."

"That's what you pay me for," Hyrum snidely remarked. "But don't ever touch me again, you somebitch!"

Lamar just grinned and motioned Charley to come forward, pointing to the small structure hidden in the landscape. "Take Earl and check out that cabin." Charley nodded but never got the chance to get Earl's attention as a bullet ripped through the ground at the side of Earl's chestnut stallion. The animal screeched with fear and reared up on his hocks, sending his rider off the back and onto the ground with a heavy splat. "Sonofa..."

"Looks like he knows we're here," Hyrum unnecessarily said, humor dancing in his words and look.

Another shot, this time knocking Earl's hat to the ground and sending his horse running back in the direction they had come from. Sean shouted as another bullet ripped through the air. He held onto his hat and guided his mount back several steps. "What do you want to do, Cap'n? We are sitting ducks out here in the open."

"Grab Earl and go after his horse, then take cover in the trees and follow the valley's eastern side where I told you and Eric to go. Then split up, ease your way up the hillside, and each of you come in from a different direction."

"Yeah! What he says, you dumb shits." Hyrum laughed, gave Lamar a look of disgruntled amusement, shoved his spurs into his horse's underbelly, and rode straight for the ridge, firing his Smith and Wesson.

"Hyrum's loco; that's all there is to it." Earl picked up his hat, poked a finger through the hole in the felt, slammed it back on his head, and swung up on the back of Sean's gelding. They rode hell-bent for leather toward the runaway mount.

Lamar shook his head and ordered Eric to follow in the same direction Hyrum had gone. For the moment, the shooting had stopped. He gazed over at Charley and ordered. "You're with me. Let's finish this. And when we are done, I want Hyrum dead."

"Sure thing, I look forward to it. Have always hated the bastard!"

The explosion of gunfire reverberated through the mountain as Noah returned to the cabin. They were already here. He pulled his Army Colt from the holster and circled the cabin's perimeter. Cora was right; he had more mobility with the handgun. The smell of gunfire filled the air. He looked for Simon in the thick tree line.

Nothing.

Carefully, he made his way along the side of the building, then toward the ridge where they had seen the riders coming in. Two more shots rang out. A rustling in the brush to his right. He swiftly moved in that direction. "Simon, that you?"

Silence.

A loud crash came next. Someone hit the trap in the ground they had dug with the spikes. He heard the screech of a horse and moved in that direction. Reaching the spot, Noah saw a riderless horse halfway down the deep hole. The animal was in horrific pain. Both his forelegs were broken. Regretfully, Noah needed to put the animal out of his misery. It was a shame the horse was a beautiful, dun gelding with black and white speckles. "Who in their right mind would have galloped through this thick forest? I'm sorry," he spoke to the horse as he pulled the trigger.

"Hyrum would, he doesn't give a shit about anything but himself. That was his horse." Simon stated as he emerged from the thicket. "I sent a few warning shots, which all of them ignored. Earl and Sean started moving up from the valley's eastern edge after they caught Earl's spooked horse. I'm sure they will be headed this way soon enough. Lamar and Charley are coming in from the opposite side and heading toward your cabin. Eric followed up along the ridge, the same direction Hyrum bolted in. I was going to follow them, but then I heard you. Did you get Cora and Loka settled?"

Noah silently nodded. But he worried about the direction Hyrum and the other man took. *Christ on a crutch,* Cora was up there. Another crash came from behind them about a hundred yards from the cabin.

"That's got to be either Charley or Lamar. They stayed out of my range."

"Tell me again about Hyrum. I'm not too fond of the fact he may be heading toward Cora's hiding spot."

Simon gave Noah a fearful look. "He's a psychopath and capable of the ugliest and most vile atrocities I have ever witnessed from any man. I would have killed him, but I couldn't get a clear enough shot."

"The only ones I know are Lamar, Charley, and Earl," Noah admitted. "Have no recognition of any of the rest of them."

"Like I told you, most of us who started with Lamar are either dead or opted to desert. And most of those men were killed when Lamar and Charley caught up to them—hung for desertion. Charley has become as bloodthirsty as the rest. I wish I'd had the balls to get away early on, even if it meant my death. Death would have been far better than what I witnessed over the years.

"We started with twelve original riders from our unit—one by one, most of them were killed or, in Lamar's mind, deserted. Either way, they ended up dead. There was one in El Pueblo that got shot by a whore he cheated out of payment. I don't know if you remember Jacob Salter. He was lazy, good for nothing. No one liked him, and no one was sorry he got himself killed." Simon lowered his gaze to his hands grasping them together tightly in shame.

"After that, only four of us were left: Charley, Earl, Lamar, and myself. The other men Lamar hired as time moved on were the worst bunch of men I've ever seen. None of them had any respect for life. Be glad you never knew Hyrum; he's the worst. Lamar found him in Denver along with Eric and Sean, brothers who make their living as card sharks and extremely quickdraws. Involved with several shootouts and always came out the winners. Damn, Noah, I wish I could express my..."

"Not the time for regrets. I'll check out who fell victim to that last crash. I think it was where we placed spikes. With disgust, Noah mumbled. "Out of all this damn mess, I feel the sorriest for the horses.

※

Cora heard the shots at least three. Seconds later came the deafening sound of two traps being triggered. The cacophony of noise echoed through the air and circulated inside the hollow of sandstone. A shudder of anxiety crashed through her. Minutes later, nothing. Too quiet. She glanced over to Loka. He was alert, his teeth bared, and a low growl emerged. She shifted her vision to the circumference of the alcove. She felt strongly that the wolf was warning her.

They weren't alone.

"What is it?" she asked in barely a whisper. Again, she glanced back at Loka, but he was gone. Gone! Oh Lord, where? The only entrance was before her; he certainly had not left that way she would have seen him.

She grabbed her knapsack, filled with first aid items and snacks. She checked to ensure her slingshot was still tucked into the waistband of her pants. At the last minute, she remembered her grandfather's rifle and slung it over her shoulder. Several stone barriers were at the rear and would give her a hiding spot. Tarnation! She needed to move; if she didn't, she would be exposed. And she certainly couldn't leave by the front entrance. Quickly, she moved to the rear. At least back here, she could still have a decent view of any intruders. And a clear target to use her slingshot if she needed it.

Once behind the shelter of the rock, she leaned down and stuffed the bag with sharp-edged stones. The jagged outcroppings that stood like sentinels at the rear would make a good cover, reminding her of the jagged growth you'd find in a much deeper cave as she made her way toward them. For the umpteenth time, she wondered where Loka had gotten off to. How did he get past her without her seeing him? For a minute, she thought she saw a shadow.

Staying in the darkest part of the hollowed sandstone, she pressed her back against the wall to the left and inched her way to the rear. Once there, she quickly realized the wall wasn't a wall at all; it was a mere illusion. A large slab ran the rear length and stood free, covering a pathway she never knew existed. Why hadn't she noticed this the last time she was here? She should have done some exploring.

She peeked behind it—another unseen surprise. A very pale stream of light was coming in from somewhere ahead, shadowing a narrow pathway of four to five feet in circumference. On the sandy ground were several prints. Animal prints. She followed the path for about ten feet and came across the dim light's source. Shrubbery covered a small opening and blocked the daylight from coming inside, though there were enough tiny openings through the branches to let a small amount of light in.

If you didn't know about this, a person could look straight at it from the outside and never realize it was blocking an entrance. Feeling foolish, she hadn't explored the last time she was here, but she'd been so annoyed with Noah, tired and hungry, all she could think of was what she could do to survive. Clearly, Loka knew of this opening, and that's how he got the wood inside the last time they were here. But why had he abandoned her now?

She peered through the camouflage of brush and saw Loka waiting. Filled with relief, she crawled out into the fresh air, caught a breath, and carefully followed Loka's sure-footed steps around the stone path toward the front entrance. The wolf stopped, turned, and nosed her thigh in warning. She heard a man's voice.

"Why lookie what we have here!" Hyrum licked his lips and stepped from the sunlight into the sandstone hollow. Cora laid the rifle aside, grasped her slingshot, loaded one of the rocks from the knapsack, and took aim. She didn't have to be told; she knew this was the horrible man Simon had spoken of when he didn't think she was listening. Loka gave a soft growl.

***

The deadly sounds of traps set throughout the area began to explode into a jumble of horrific noises. Yet, the blended sounds that crashed through the mountain held an organized precision of order. One by one, they were triggered. It reminded Lamar of a well-run unit of trained soldiers. Maybe he had never given Noah enough credit.

"There are traps everywhere!" Charley exclaimed. "Jesus, the trees here are so thick you can't see more than a few feet in front of you. I suggest we hobble the horses and go on foot."

Lamar agreed. There was no sense in harming horses; they would need them. The only positive was when they caught Noah. There were plenty of trees to hang him from. And hang him, they would. Maybe torture a while for the hell of it. The thought pleased Lamar, and knowing Hyrum was an expert at inflicting pain made him almost giddy. "I wonder if anyone's seen Hyrum after he broke free of us and rode up the hill?"

"Hell, if I know, the man's insane," Charley grumbled. "At the moment, it's best to only worry about ourselves. This forest is so thick with growth it's all I can see, and they are scratching the shit out of me every time I step past one. And still, I can't see the friggin' cabin, can you?"

Lamar stopped and studied the landscape. "He had help!"

Charley glared at Lamar. "Or maybe he had more military know-how than you ever gave him credit for."

Lamar didn't care for the insult and backhanded Charley. But he had to admit that he had already wondered if he were honest with himself. This certainly wasn't the Noah Harper he remembered. "I'm not going to buy that. Someone warned him," Lamar pushed another bristly pine bough aside. Then, as if a light lit up in his mind, he ground his teeth together and swore. "Simon! *Had to be Simon.* That whore in Cheyenne gave him more information than the bitch gave me. I knew I should have killed her after I got what I wanted. She was protecting Harper!"

Charley wiped his bloodied lip and narrowed a gaze when he turned back to the captain. "When would she have done that? She was beat up pretty bad, and as far as I know, Simon never had alone time with her."

"The sonofabitch figured it out! He probably went to her when I sent him back to town for more tobacco and whiskey for the road. He was gone long enough to get what I wanted and speak to her. A week later, he lit out and left us a man short."

Charley removed his hat and absently scratched his forehead, shook the broken pieces of pine branches from the felt rim of his hat, and slammed it back on. He had come to hate Lamar but, for the moment, pretended otherwise. "Most of the time, we are a man short with him along anyway. He was useless when it came to the festivities we liked to play. He kept to himself and constantly wallowed in some melancholy or another. My guess would be he was too big of a coward to do anything but run!"

Lamar couldn't argue. He had only initially pressured the man into coming along because he was part of the original unit. The excuse he'd been using for years was no longer viable. Not realizing he spoke aloud, he said. "In the beginning, he had a calming effect on some men." Realizing what he just admitted, he clamped his mouth shut in a straight line of irritation.

"Those men are long gone, Cap'n. Now he's just plain useless, and me and the boys have often wondered why you've kept him around all this time. He ignores the rest of us and keeps himself separate like he's a step above. He's become the biggest cowardly *Milk Sop* I've ever known. Frankly, I never missed Simon Mason after he skinned out. But you take Earl, Eric, and Sean; they are all good ol' boys."

It galled Lamar to have his foolish decision about Simon brought to the forefront. And if he didn't need Charley, he'd put a bullet in his brain.

Charley noticed the anger building in the captain and swallowed his fear as he added. "I didn't mean nothing by that captain." He could taste the fury building inside Lamar and wondered what payment the captain would make him suffer for being so outspoken. He'd already given him a bloody lip. He quickly tried to justify his words. "I just meant I think you are right. The bastard found a way to warn Harper. Remembering back, we all knew he and Noah were close friends. It's the only thing that makes sense to me." However, anything more he meant to say quickly died on his tongue when more gunfire shattered the silence.

"Let's move!" Lamar barked the order.

Cora watched the gruff, ugly man step inside the cave. At first, he just looked around. "So, this is where you've been hiding. Should have known, good place for cowards." He began kicking at the cold firepit, sending ash and skeletal remains of old logs throughout the hollowed-out red rock. He noted Cora's stash of feminine clothing on her makeshift bed. He moved in that direction and tossed the bedding against the wall. He dumped her clothing, food, and sewing supplies across the dirt floor.

"Well, well, Harper, you're not alone. You got yourself a woman, and you're hiding her up here. Now things are gonna get mighty interesting." Hyrum chortled in delight.

The sound of his laughter made Cora cringe. She wasn't sure if she should use her slingshot or move to a safer place. More shots came from below. She heard someone shout. The ugly man inside turned back to the entrance and pulled a pistol from a low-riding holster on his hip.

Cora caught her breath, loaded her slingshot, and released a rock. That's when he saw her and fired.

A man Noah didn't know had been stabbed by one of the lower spikes forced up when the wire was triggered. He cautiously moved to the trap. The man was dead. There was no horse in sight. Possibly sensing danger, the horse came to a dead stop and dumped his rider into the spikes before he ran off.

"That's Sean." Simon's voice emerged from the thick line of oak brush that had begun to fill in after winter. "I don't know what happened to the horse he rode. Eric just left him like this and started out on his own, but he didn't get far. He is up the hill tied and gagged with a broken leg. He'd been ordered to follow Heber but got caught in a snare. He won't be a problem. Lamar and Charley are moving toward the cabin. Probably there by now. I haven't seen Hyrum or Earl, but according to Eric, Hyrum was still headed higher up the mountain. They all were ordered to find you and meet at the cabin in two hours. With or without you. Preferably with you. No matter what condition you might be in as long as you were alive."

Simon checked his timepiece. "The two hours are nearly up. What do you want to do?" Then his face paled. Charley had moved out from his hiding place behind the thick-trunked pine. He was only two or three feet from Noah's rear, which he quickly eliminated. He reached out rapidly and grasped Noah's neck before Simon could give a warning. He shoved his Colt against his back, pinning him at a standstill.

Simon raised his gun and pointed it at Charley. "Looks like we have a standoff. You can't shoot us both without getting yourself shot. Then again, I'm told you've been ordered to keep Noah alive. But if you move your gun to shoot me, you have him to contend with. And if you kill him, you have Lamar to contend with."

Charley laughed. "I have my bone to pick with this coward. Lamar has made his choice, and I've made mine." He glared back at Simon. "Have you forgotten how good I am, old friend? He Roughly yanked Noah back and grasped him by the throat, this time cutting off his oxygen, pressed the side of the colt against Noah's neck, and fired. The heat and sound of the blast caused Noah to buckle and fall to his knees.

Noah could feel the blood from where the bullet had grazed his neck and knew it blended with the blood that oozed from his ear. The gun report was so deafening he feared his ear drum was punctured.

Horror struck Simon's face as he grasped his upper chest and fell backward, muttering, "I'm so sorry!"

"I bet you are, you Goddamned deserter!" Charley sneered down at Simon's still body. He quickly tied Noah's hands behind his back, grasped the top of his shirt, and yanked him up. Placing the gun against his cheek, he whispered with humor. "Howdy Noah, have ya missed me? The captain is right interested in seeing you again." He then blew a sharp whistle, sounding like the cry of a hawk, alerting the others that he had his captive. He shoved Noah forward and forced him down the path and through the trees toward the cabin.

Chapter Twenty-Six

Cora watched the stone she'd let loose slam against the side of the man's head. He grasped his wound. The shock caused him to fire, the bullet hit nothing of consequence.

"Sonofabitch! He cursed. "What the Hell?" Blood was already trickling down the side of his face. Dazed and caught off guard, he wildly fired again. This time, the bullet crashed uselessly into the rock wall, sending shards of sandstone exploding outward and prickling his face, adding to the pain. With a curse, he collapsed on the ground.

Survival instinct took control; Cora looked down at Loka and motioned him to follow. Both moved into the thick protection of trees. She knew all hell was breaking loose below from the sounds that reached her.

She hurried shuffling through the thick mountain trees as she descended the path. She knew she didn't have much time before that hideous man followed her. She carefully checked all the snares they'd set along the hillside. She would probably never know how that man she'd left back at the hollow sidestepped the snares as he made his way to the hollow, but it didn't matter; he had found a way. She reached the midway point and found Simon lying motionless on the ground. He'd been shot just below the shoulder near his heart, and he was bleeding heavily.

Dropping to her knees, she pressed two fingers against his neck below his jaw, as Noah had taught her. Simon had a heartbeat. "Can you hear me?" She asked.

His eyes slowly opened. "Cora, he's in trouble. We need to help him."

She reached into her knapsack, pulled free a wad of soft bandaging material, and pressed it against his wound.

"Forget that. Just help me up."

"If we don't stop the bleeding, you'll die from the loss of blood."

Simon grasped her hand. "I'm a dead man already. While I have life left, we need to help Noah. Forget about bandaging me. He's been taken to the cabin. They are going to kill him. Now help me get to my feet!"

As if Loka understood every word, he ran through the trees and toward the cabin. "Loka, get back here!" Cora hissed the order. "Oh mercy, he's going to get himself killed. Simon, if you plan to help me, hold still. I need to fix you up! She pressed a thick square of bandaging on the wound. This time, he did not argue.

Jim Aderly and his two deputies, Pete and Skeet, cleared the tree line at the valley's edge. The sounds of gunfire echoed loudly from the hill beyond.

"Should we split up?" asked Pete.

"I believe we are safer together," Jim told them. He lifted his spyglass and peered through it. "No one's guarding the hillside." He shoved the tubular field glass back into his saddle bag. "Let's move. We will keep to the tree line in case we need cover. Someone up there is going to need our help. And God help them if it's the men we've been following."

Noah's throat and neck felt like they had been wrapped in barbed wire, and he couldn't hear a damn thing out of his right ear. Charley constantly shoved him, causing him to trip. He tried pushing back, hoping to knock Charley off guard, but Charley only applied more painful pressure to his cheekbone.

"Keep that up, old friend, and I'll kill you. You see, I don't give a shit what Lamar wants." He shoved Noah again.

In the next few minutes, Noah again fell forward face down, but this time, when he glanced up, he was staring at a pair of scuffed boots—Lamar Tamarin's boots, which he used to kick Noah in the jaw. Everything went black. His last thoughts were of Cora and their child. Was she safe? Had they found her? Oh God, how would he get out of this and protect her? "Go get the horses," he thought he heard Lamar tell one of the men. Then, nothing as thick, heavy blackness consumed him.

Cora reached inside her knapsack, removing more bandaging and a small antiseptic container. "The bullet is lodged beneath your collarbone. I need to stop the flow of blood. Hold still." She covered the wound and tightly wrapped Simon's shoulder with the padding and wrapped it around his shoulder. "You are as weak as a babe. I'm afraid if you move, the bullet will slip and bury itself in your heart. You must wait here," she told him with determination. "I can handle myself. I've been doing it most of my life."

"This is different, Cora; these men are killers. You can't go alone, and Loka can't help you; he'll just get himself shot. I'll be fine. There's nothing wrong with my legs, and my shooting arm is uninjured. Just help me get close enough so I can have a good aim. Can you retrieve my Colt?"

She did so. The gun was lying half covered in pine needles. She brushed it off, slipped it inside his holster, and helped him stand. He gazed down at her. "What did you think you would do on your own, Cora? You can't stand up to those men by yourself, and then there is Hyrum; if he sees you and gets ahold of you, trust me, you will wish you were dead!"

"Is he an ugly man with tobacco-stained teeth and bowed legs?"

Simon gazed down at her. "You've seen him?"

"He found my hiding place. I got him pretty good with my slingshot and knocked him out cold, at least for a while. What happened after I left, I don't know."

Loka came back through the brush and trees. He stared at both Cora and Simon. A look Cora had become familiar with these past months. "Loka wants us to follow him."

Simon glanced from one to the other of them.

Cora smiled. "You'd have to live with him to know.

Though Simon was weak, he stubbornly managed to stay on his feet. They made it within fifteen minutes, only a few yards from the cabin. Though they remained hidden in the bush, what they saw frightened the devil out of both of them. However, they quickly recovered, and Simon fired his Colt. Cora pulled back her slingshot and let loose.

Noah wondered if his jaw was dislocated. The last thing he remembered was Lamar kicking him with the heel of his boot. He couldn't open his mouth or utter a word even if he wanted to, and he didn't; it was just a waste of energy to try. These men had only one thing on their minds: punishment, like ten years ago. He knew he was in bad shape. Simon was most likely dead...and Cora...? Dear God, was she safe with Loka?

He found himself tied in a sitting position on a horse's back, and the prickly feel of a noose hung about his neck. Someone was above him in a tree, looping the rest of the rope over a sturdy willow branch. Using his peripheral vision, he glimpsed a slight movement in the thicket to his right, but he couldn't tell who was out there.

Instantaneously, all hell broke loose. A shot was fired, and the man above him fell from the tree. The rope he'd been working on in the tree above fell uselessly to the ground. Lamar and Charley pulled their six-shooters from their holsters and checked the surrounding area. Then Charley dropped like a Croker sack filled with rock. The horse Noah sat on nervously lifted, leaning back on its hocks, came back down hard on his forelegs, and bolted. Noah was trapped. There would be no escape tied as he was to the horse. Like it or not, he was about to have the ride of a lifetime.

This was the scene Jim and his two deputies came upon, four men. Two were lying on the ground unmoving, and another was tied onto a very frightened chestnut gelding who reared up. A noose dangerously surrounded the man's neck. But in the time it takes to swallow, the nervous horse dropped down on all fours and sped off through the thick, tree-lined terrain, taking his captive with him. The other man, who came to town looking for his brother, was already mounted. He rode in the same direction as the man and the runaway horse.

"I'm going after them," Jim informed Pete and Skeet. You two check those two on the ground. If they're alive, bind their hands and tie them up back to back against the hanging tree." After issuing his order, Jim reined his horse around and followed both the runaway animal and the man in pursuit.

"Come on, Pete, we best get started." Skeet started to walk over to the man who had fallen from the tree. "This one is dead," he rolled him over on his back. "How's the other one? Is he still breathing?"

"Yup."

"Then let's get him tied up before the sonofabitch wakes. Then we'll drag them to the tree and double-tie them together like Jim wanted."

"Hell's fire, Simon, the horse Noah's tied to just took off. I need to help somehow. She began to stand.

"There is nothing you can do. Let the other three who just rode in take care of it."

"Who are those men, Simon?"

Simon was finished. The exertion of the hike they'd taken down the hill and what was left of his strength was used to shoot the man in the tree to prevent him from tightening the noose around Noah's neck. And now he was entirely done in. "I'm not sure," he told her with a wave of pain. "But I think one of them is the Sheriff from that town at the bottom of the mountain. I remember seeing him several times when I stopped there for supplies. The other two are probably his deputies."

"Willowby?"

"Yes, I believe that's the town's name."

Cora briefly studied the sheriff before he followed Noah and the man called Captain. "He is not the same man I remember as a child. But if they are here to help, I thank the good Lawd."

Simon leaned back against the thickened tree trunk and closed his eyes. He breathed heavily, and Cora wondered how he'd even made it this far. His wound still bled. Loka again disappeared, but now he followed the runaway horse. Fear overwhelmed her; not only was she losing Simon, but the horse Noah was bound to was galloping dangerously through the trees. And now Loka raced off after them. The man Simon identified as Willowby's sheriff barked orders at the two men with him before he disappeared into the trees and followed the other riders.

Charley came to and reached for his gun. Cora lifted her slingshot and fired another rock on target. Charley collapsed once more.

Hyrum pulled himself up from the ground. Western sun filled the hollowed-out sandstone as it poured in from the wide entrance. Goddamnit, bested by a woman! He picked up his handgun, left the cavern, and followed the woman's trail. Before she knocked him out, he could have sworn he saw a large gray wolf with the woman. But that couldn't be right. The blow to his head from whatever she shot at him must have caused more damage than he thought. Blood dripped into his left eye, and he decided he must be seeing things as he hastily swiped at his eye with his bare hand.

The shooting had stopped. Everything was eerily quiet. He didn't like it. He should probably get a horse and escape. Let the idiots he'd been riding go it alone. But the damn woman was too tempting? She was all alone. And she showed grit. He sure as hell couldn't resist that. Wherever he was going, she was coming with him.

Licking his lips and grinning, he descended the hill and followed the tracks she had left behind.

The feminine tracks weren't the only ones. Wolf signs were everywhere. He shivered slightly. He hated wolves just as much as he hated sodbusters.

Cora was bent over Simon, trying desperately to help him, but there was nothing more she could do. A tear slid down her cheek. He had fallen into the darkened abyss of unconsciousness. She stood, turned, and began to move toward the hanging tree. Once she arrived, she heard someone moving close behind her. Had Noah somehow gotten away? But that thought dampened the moment she was viciously grabbed by the back of her shirt, painfully flipped around, and forced to face the man she'd left in the hollowed sandstone cavity. Seeing him up close made her stomach sour. Nervously, she glanced around the wooded area, hoping to see an escape route.

There was nowhere she could bolt to freedom. Sweat began to trickle between her breasts.

Hyrum again spun her around, this time in the opposite direction. He savagely shoved her between the shoulder blades. "You want to live you'll do what I tell you. Now move!" At the hanging tree she caught a glimpse of the deputies pulling the two motionless men away and swiftly disappear through the trees. Hyrum never noticed them. He was so intent on her.

Once he had her out in the open, he grasped a handful of her hair and yanked her back against him. With his right hand, he used a knife against her throat. "No lousy bitch bests me!" he ground out against her cheek, then stiffened when he heard the deadly growl from his rear. He unconsciously loosened the blade from her neck and turned. Loka stood not more than a few feet away. His fur stood as if electrified, and his sharp teeth were bare. Saliva dripped from his mouth; his prominent yellow eyes were wide with a killer's fury. He looked like death.

He hadn't deserted her after all.

Hyrum released Cora and threw his knife at the wolf. The wolf was gone before the knife met its target. The knife wabbled as it struck the ground and buried several inches in the damp soil.

Cora used the opportunity to give the man a hard shove and began to run.

Hyrum stumbled and quickly righted himself. He fisted the back of her shirt, tearing the cotton material and popping a few buttons free. He licked his lips. This was going to be enjoyable.

She lifted her hands to her chest.

That's when Hyrum noticed her slingshot and yanked it out of her trousers. "There won't be any need for this thing," he laughed. "You are mine." He tossed the slingshot aside, knocked her hands away, and tossed her to the ground, bringing his crusty lips and yellowed teeth close to her mouth.

His breath was rancid. Cora turned her head in a rush and screamed.

Everything seemed to explode in the next few seconds. Loka crashed through the shrub and leaped up on the man, knocking him off Cora.

Hyrum couldn't move; he was paralyzed with fear as Loka held him down with his powerful body. His growl was the most vicious, frightening sound Cora had ever heard from him. He was drooling from his enormous fangs. He could rip out the man's throat in a matter of seconds if she didn't stop this. But should she? This was the man she'd heard so much about. This is the man who had taken part in her grandfather's death and burned their cabin to the ground. And this was the man who had defiled and slaughtered many women.

Hyrum tried reaching for his holstered gun, then realized he couldn't get the weapon with the wolf holding him down and trapping him. He had been so intent on catching the woman that he never noticed the wolf's return. And like an idiot, he had not retrieved his knife. The damn thing still stood upright in the dirt. He considered himself a brave leader, but nothing he felt now was heroic. This was a friggin wild wolf who wanted to kill him. He tried pushing the animal off. The drooling, angry beast wouldn't budge. Loka took a chunk out of Hyrum's lower arm, and Hyrum screeched out in pain.

"Get him off me, woman! You stupid bitch he's..." his words were cut off as Loka pounded his paw on the man's throat, cutting off his air. Everything went black for the next few minutes.

Cora had never seen Loka this deathly ferocious before. She knew she needed to stop his behavior, but the order froze in her throat.

There was someone else behind her. "Don't move, young man," the voice cautioned. "I'll take care of this."

She could hear the rifle lever click into place. She quickly turned to him in a panic. He aimed straight at Loka. "Run Loka!" She screeched.

He did.

Cora turned back to the man with the rifle. "Please..."

Ready to fire, Pete felt the woman jerk his arm, sending his shot wild when he pulled the trigger.

"No!" she shouted in desperation. "Don't shoot the wolf; he is my friend and protects me. He just saved me from being raped and murdered by that dreadful man on the ground."

The bullet skimmed off the trunk of an aspen. Pete lowered the rifle. And glared at who he thought was a boy.

He was she. And she was desperately trying to hold the front of her shirt together.

Pete studied her, then over at the wolf escaping into the woods. "Friend, huh! And who is this?" Pete pointed the rifle down at the bleeding man, who lay unmoving.

"I know he was one of the men who killed my grandfather last fall. I think his name is Hyrum."

"What's your name?"

"Cora Harper."

"Any relation to a Noah Harper?'

"He's my husband, and these men were here to kill him. Oh God, he could already be dead!"

"If he's the man those men were going to hang, he's alive. Got away when the frightened horse he was tied to bolted off in a mad dash."

Fear struck Cora in the heart like the rip of an arrow. She swallowed with panic. "Don't you see this is no place for a frightened horse to run through blindly. Noah is still in danger. "I need to go after them!" she reached down, grasped her slingshot, and shoved it into her waistband.

"The sheriff is following him and the other who's called Captain. It's safer for you to stay here."

"You say the man called Captain followed Noah. Dear God, he's the one who wants my husband dead."

The sheriff will get them. Who's the dead man up on the flat?"

"Dead man?" In her fear, she had forgotten about Simon. She turned to make her way back up the hill.

Pete reached out and grasped her arm. "You don't want to go up there; it isn't a pretty sight. His throat has been slashed. Who is he to you?"

He was a friend of my husband. Oh God! Oh God! He's dead?"

"Yes, ma'am, I'm afraid so.

She felt the accursed tears come but couldn't stop them. There was nothing more she could do for Simon. "His name is Simon Mason. He soldiered with my husband back in seventy-eight." She couldn't think about that now; she needed to help Noah. "My husband," she began and looked up, seeing the man's tin star on his shirt pocket. "Which way did he go?"

"Ma'am, you can't help. Probably just get yourself killed. You are better off staying here. The sheriff knows what he's doing. "My name is Pete. I'm one of Sheriff Adderly's deputies. The other man with us is Skeet. We've been chasing these men ever since they left Willoby in devastation. They created an awful mess down there. We lost some good people." He reached down and removed Hyrum's revolver from the holster.

"Hey, Skeet," Pete shouted out. "Come over here and give me a hand. We have another to haul back to town. "This here lady is Missus Harper."

"Who?" Skeet looked at Pete, as he came through the trees scratching his head, and repeating, "who?"

Pete swung around. Cora was already halfway up the hill. "Damnit," he hissed. "I better go after her. Can you handle this?"

"Sure, no problem. But who were you talking about? What lady?"

Noah knew someone was following him. Good or bad, he couldn't say. He couldn't turn his neck enough to check over his shoulder, not with the noose tied about him. And not trussed up the way he was. He needed the flexibility of his hands, which was impossible because they were bound at the rear. The only thing holding him on the horse were his knees and thighs pressed to the horse's barrel who refused to slow. It took every ounce of Noah's strength to stay seated.

He was quickly losing this battle. The wild run was zapping both him and the horse. He knew they'd both be killed at this ungodly speed.

Whoever followed had now ridden to the side of him, reached out, and grasped the reins, finally slowing the horse. "Easy boy," came the man's gentle voice. Within a matter of seconds, the wild-eyed stallion slowed the pace. Noah had no idea who had just brought the horse down to a slow walk, but he breathed a sigh of relief and only prayed it wasn't Lamar or any of his men. "You all right?" The man asked as he came into Noah's vision.

This was a new face. Noah nodded; Some of his hearing had returned, though his voice was still gravelly. The man was close to his age. "Who are you?" he asked, eyeing him with suspicion.

"I'm Sherrif Jim Adderly from the town of Willowby. You Noah Harper?"

Noah ignored the question. "My wife, she's all alone. She needs my help. They'll kill her and worse if they find her. I have to get to her."

"They are a deadly lot, that's for sure. They've been dropping bodies all over the countryside." Jim removed the prickly noose, dropped it to the ground, then started on the bindings wrapped around Noah's wrists at the back and those imprisoning him to the stirrups. "Let's get rid of these bindings, and we'll look for your wife."

"I'd be grateful, sheriff."

Jim met the man's eyes with empathy. He hated to be the one to say it, but the words had to be said. "I got to be honest with you, Mister Harper, if those men got ahold of her, she's probably dead. Looks like they weren't too kind to you either." He helped Noah from the skittish mount and handed him the spare gun he carried.

"It doesn't matter what they did to me. I need to get to my wife. She's four months pregnant."

Jim gave Noah a look of understanding. Another rider moved out in the open. The sound of a horse's knicker mingled with evergreen shrubbery bobbing in the cool San Juan breeze and grabbed their attention. Noah had a pretty good idea who it was. He gripped the gun the sheriff had given him.

Brutal laughter precipitated the sound of Lamar Tamarin's voice. "Looks like the end of the trail for you boys. We might have us two hangings on this day."

"And who would do the hanging, mister?" Jim slowly turned to face the man. It was the same man who'd led the raid and the killings in town. "Your men are all out of commission. Would seem you are on your own." Jim stepped away from Noah whose back was to Lamar. "You planning on murdering the law this time?"

"What law? Is that what you call yourself?" Lamar continued his demonic laughter as he pointed his Colt, already cocked and ready, but didn't get the chance to fire accurately as the clamorous, ear-splitting sound of rifle fire echoed through the canyon. His bullet went feral.

Noah used the disturbance to his advantage and cocked the weapon the sheriff had armed him with, turned, and pointed the gun at Lamar.

Lamar had already recovered, clicked another bullet in the chamber, and pointed the weapon directly at Jim. His thin lips split into a chilling smile as he glowered at both men. "You know what you've just done, sheriff, you've armed a wanted criminal," he lied."

"The only criminal I see here is you and what your men are capable of and have surely done, Captain Tamarin. Now, drop your weapon! Your poster says dead or alive! I'm obliged either way. You and your men have left enough death and blood to fill the whole of Colorado territory."

"You're finished, Lamar," Noah added, keeping his eyes and gun on his nemesis. If Lamar's weapon weren't aimed directly at the sheriff's heart, Noah would have fired, but the chance of Adderly getting shot in the process stopped him. Instead, he used his words as a weapon.

"And you know it." Noah spat. "Sure, you might get lucky and shoot us both. But then what? You've spent the last ten years hunting me. You have broken hundreds of laws to do it. If you are captured, you'll spend the rest of your life in prison, or a firing squad. If you manage to avoid that, you'll run like you've forced me to since the Cheyenne village and the farce of that military trial? Trust me, it isn't any life you'd want to live. You could kill me, but what do you have after that? Your reason to keep going will die with me."

Years of insanity flashed in Lamar's eyes. "Doesn't matter," he spat. "The way I see it, it's me or you." Lamar thought about what his bastard father would have done in this situation. It didn't take much thinking he knew what he had to do. He had two guns pointed at him. He was dead anyway. There would be no life for him at the finish. Noah was right about that. He knew what he had to do. He wouldn't go alone. He pulled the trigger.

Noah and the sheriff fired at the same time.

Jim was hit in his upper arm and dropped his gun.

For several seconds, Lamar stared at them like a comical clown that had been resurrected at a country carnival, then drooped sideways and slid from his horse, looking more like a snake trying to slither back to his grassy hiding place. He landed on his back. A hole the size of a ten-dollar silver piece bloomed scarlet on his forehead. Ten years of running, hiding, and never staying in one place long had ended in those few seconds. Just the way Lamar had lived since boyhood. Out by violence.

"Sweet Jesus!" Jim swallowed tightly. "How'd you do that? I thought we were dead men." He grasped his arm and fell to his knees.

Noah held onto the pistol and moved toward Lamar and kicked the man's weapon out of reach. No doubt Captain Lamar Tamarin was dead. He left him and went to the sheriff to check his wound. The nervous horse he had been tied to started running again. No one paid attention.

"I have medical supplies back at my cabin. I can fix you up. But right now, I have to find my wife. There is another man out there; he's even more dangerous."

"Worse than this one or those other two back at the hanging spot?"

"Yes, he's worse. He enjoys hurting women and then slowly rapes and kills them."

"I've seen the results and the after-effects take a strong constitution." Jim admitted and reached out for Noah's hand. "Help me to mount up. You can ride the other horse this man rode in on. God only knows where the skittish animal you were on went."

"Hold on a minute," Noah ripped a section of his shirt, tore it in strips, and tied it tightly around Jim's arm. "You were lucky the bullet just grazed your arm. It's a deep graze that will need stitches, but this binding will help slow the blood flow. Thank the Lord for all Lamar's meanness; he was always a lousy shot, though to hear him tell it, he was one of the best."

"Are you a doctor?"

"I joined the Army before I finished Medical school, but I'm a trained medic."

Jim nodded. "Why were those men after you?"

"It's a long story, and I will gladly explain, but I need to find my wife right now." As if in agreement, the eruption of another gunshot blasted. Noah helped the sheriff onto his horse and then mounted Lamar's. Both men returned to the shallow clearing where Noah had almost been hung.

Chapter Twenty-Seven

Hyrum was good at playing possum; he had done it many times when he needed to hide or fool someone into thinking he was submissive. Today was one of those days. The moment the wolf released him, and he was able to catch his breath, he opened his eyes and ignored the pain in his arm where the Goddamned wolf bit him.

When the deputy approached him, he grabbed Hyrum by the arms and began to drag him toward the horse that held Earl and Charley. Hyrum seized the opportunity and kicked out with a force that allowed him to gain his feet quickly, yank on the unsuspecting deputy's lower legs, and swiftly knock him off his feet.

"What the hell?" Skeet gasped. His head felt like it had just split open when he hit the rocky ground.

"What the hell is right, you Goddamned hick!" Hyrum grasped the man's gun out from under him and shot point blank into the center of Skeet's chest. The body began to convulse.

"Nobody pulls one over on me! Not some stupid deputy and certainly not some mealy-mouthed woman!" She might be dressed as a boy, but nothing she wore would deter from the fact that there was a female body beneath the masculine clothing.

He thought of all the enjoyment she would give him once he got his hands on her. She had spirit! The sound of gunfire further down the hill pushed his thoughts aside. Charley and Earl were tied on the back of one of the horses. The woman and the other deputy were gone. He could hear that bloody wolf growling from somewhere in the tangle of trees. To add to the problem, he heard a rider coming in. He pulled the bodies from the horse, mounted, and spurred the gelding hard, forcing him into a fast trot as he moved into the densely pine-scented forest. There would always be another day for him to find entertainment.

"I'm sorry about your friend, Mrs. Harper. He had lost so much blood we would have never gotten help to him fast enough to save him."

A tear rolled down Cora's cheek. "I know you are right. I feel bad. He tried so hard to be a good man in the end. He saved my life and Noah's, too, when he shot that man out of the tree."

Pete helped her over loose shale splattered over the hillside and led her to where he'd told Skeet to drag the third man. "I told you I need to help my husband."

"And I told you you're safer here. The sheriff knows what he's doing. Please, Mrs. Harper..." The argument ended when they cleared the thick evergreen shrub and heard yet another shot fired. They saw that the two men were no longer tied to the horse. They both were lying on the ground. The horse was gone.

"Jesus H!" Pete shivered in fear. "Skeet!" he shouted. "Stay here!" he told Cora as he rapidly returned to the hanging tree.

Cora heard someone riding in before she could see him. She prayed it was Noah and that he was all right, but trepidation gripped her. What if it were the other man they called Captain? And Noah and the sheriff were dead! She anxiously watched the tree line where she heard the sounds and readied her slingshot.

Relief flooded her when she saw Noah and the sheriff riding into the small clearing. She clasped her hand to her chest in relief. Noah was climbing down and helping the sheriff dismount when she reached the two men. "Thunderation, Noah!" She wrapped her arms around his waist and rested her head against his chest. I have been so worried, so afraid I had lost you." When she looked up to meet his eyes, she saw one eye black and blue and swollen. His ear had dried blood in it. A swollen jaw and a raw-looking rope burn that circled his neck. She gasped.

"I'm slightly banged up, but I'm fine, honey. It's you and the baby I'm concerned with. Are you all right?"

Cora never got the chance to answer when they all heard Pete yell out. "Sonofabitch, that monster killed Skeet! Never should have left him alone!" All three of them raced to Pete.

"What happened?" Jim knelt next to Skeet's body. "Everything was under control when I left to chase down the runaway horse and the man who called himself Captain."

Tears were in Pete's eyes when he looked at Jim and then at Noah and Cora. "The bastard must have been faking. When I left to help the lady, I thought he was unconscious. Oh, sweet God, Skeet, I'm so sorry."

Noah glanced at Cora, "Hyrum?"

With tears in her eyes, she sadly nodded. "He also finished off Simon. Cut his throat."

But everything was forgotten when they heard the loud crash of heavy tree branches snapping. The sound thundered and echoed through the forest.

Noah looked at Cora with concern.

She knew it was one of the traps they'd set. Part of her hoped it was Hyrum who got caught in it. "Let's Go!" She began to move down the incline. All three men followed, though Noah grasped her hand inside his and led the way to the trap.

Hyrum was feeling pretty damn good about himself as he guided the bay gelding between two tall Ponderosa pine. He never saw the hidden wire stretched beneath the overhang of tree limbs as he kicked the horse into a canter. The wire snapped against his chest with enough force to break the branch and cause the wire to whip around his upper body, yanking him backward off the horse. He hit the ground so hard it knocked the wind out of him. Pain shot through his arm from the wolf bite when he found himself flat on his back and tangled in yards of barbed wire. He couldn't move and could barely breathe. The horse he'd been riding was completely unharmed. Took a few steps forward, glanced back at the trapped man, and gave a nicker that sounded more like laughter before he trotted off, leaving the man in misery.

Hyrum couldn't even curse when he heard someone approaching—actually a few somebodies. The one who called himself Sheriff, the other deputy, and Noah Harper, the man who had caused all the years of fuss for Lamar and the rest of them, circled him. To the side of Harper was that damn woman. And sonofabitch, if she weren't wearing a Cheshire Cat smile.

"Looks like the bastard caught himself in a shit pot load of trouble, wouldn't you say?" Pete looked at the others. "And I can rightly say it is well deserved. The bastard just killed my best friend!"

"I couldn't agree more," Jim said. "In fact, I think he might have some scars to take to prison with him." Jim sneered down at Hyrum.

"Why don't you all shut up and help me out of this!" Hyrum bellowed the moment he caught his breath.

"I don't know about that. How you're trussed up will make it much easier for Pete and me to get you back to town. And you will be nicely wrapped up for the United States Marshall when he hauls you off. What do you think?" Jim glanced at the others, who seemed filled with a sense of humor. "In fact," Jim continued. "I left word in town for the Marshall to follow us up here; we'll probably meet up with him halfway down."

"You can't just leave me like this. There must be some law against cruel and unusual punishment."

Jim winked at the other three but narrowed in on Noah. "I don't suppose you'd let me use your wagon to get the dead and two living men back to town.

Noah wrapped his arm around Cora's shoulder. "Of course, however, I would want it back before winter." They both looked at Jim and Pete. "You are both welcome to stay the night and head out in the morning with your prisoners."

"Thanks, but I would rather be done with this post-haste. Some outraged people in Willowby want justice. We might find ourselves hanging these two live ones. But I would be obliged to have the loan of your wagon. "I'll return it to you long before the summer ends."

"Hold on a minute," Pete interrupted with a severe downward frown that said more than words ever could. "I don't want Skeet anywhere near these muderin' egg suckers!"

"No worries, Pete, I wouldn't disrespect him like that. We'll tie him to his horse and take him back that way."

Pete nodded, satisfied with the decision.

Loka chose that moment to show himself. "Great, Scott!" Jim gasped.

"That's what I thought when I first saw him," Pete told the group. "Mrs. Harper says he's a friend.

As if Loka sensed they were speaking about him, he moved toward Noah and Cora, nudged them apart, yawned, showing his elongated fangs, and plopped down between them. Jim and Pete looked thoroughly bemused as they watched.

By early evening, all the men were gone. The living outlaws secured along with the dead. Sean and Eric were the first two to fall victim to the traps. Sean had been spiked, and Eric was found later with a puncture wound and a broken leg when his horse had run mindlessly into the large hole concealed with sticks, grass, and pine needles. He died slowly and painfully, just as his horse would have had Noah not put the poor animal out of its misery. Earl, who'd been shot out of the hanging tree. And lastly, Lamar Tamarin, the leader and the one who had started the whole fiasco of revenge.

As promised, Skeet was separated from the others.

Jim, Pete, and Noah used some of the wire that bound Hyrum to contain Charley. If either tried escaping, the wire would bite into their unprotected skin, limiting their movements and keeping them confined. Jim figured it was payment for the murders they had committed, the torture of families, and the horror they had perpetrated in town.

Charley finally regained consciousness from the blow Cora had given him with her slingshot, and Hyrum, who never stopped whining about his predicament, were both placed below the seat on either side of the wagon. Pete held his rifle aimed at both

At Simon's request, he remained on the mountain and was buried amongst the trees behind the cabin. He had no family to inform about his death. Noah had been his only friend.

Later, when they were alone, Cora cleaned up Noah's wounds. He had her put a couple of drops of isopropyl-alcohol inside his ear in case of damage to the eardrum and salve on his neck. She brought a bucket of icy water from the spring house, dipped a cloth, and placed it on Noah's eye. She filled the hip bath for him. Though he didn't need her help, he let her wash him, knowing it would make her feel better, not to mention how good it made him feel.

"I wrote a letter to my family, and I gave it to Jim to post for me in town," he told Cora as he stepped out from the tub and let her wrap a towel around his waist.

"You did?"

"Yes, it was way overdue. I let them know I was alive and well. And my reasons for staying away all these years. I also told them about you and the baby we're expecting, and we would like to visit them in spring."

"Oh, Noah, that's wonderful. I'm sure that will please them."

He pulled her into his arms and kissed her deeply. "It's been a long day; let's go to bed." He reached down and caressed her rounded belly. The baby fluttered against his hands. He stepped back and looked at her with wonder. "Did you feel that?"

Cora giggled, "Of course I did; after all, the baby lives inside me, at least for a while."

"Yes, ma'am, he does." He let the towel fall to the floor. Let's get you undressed so I can introduce myself."

She complied with haste. Within minutes, they were both naked as the day they were born and tucked into bed. Noah reached over and caressed Cora's breasts, teasing her nipples with his thumbs, then his lips and tongue. "You are so beautiful, my sweet angel."

She sighed, filled with love and arousal, as she reached down and began to caress him, enveloping the velvet hardness of him.

Loka grunted, moved to the large fireplace, turned a few circles, plunked down on the floor atop one of the braided rugs, and rested his head against his front paws.

They both chuckled at the wolf but gave no further thought as they took their time, making love with lips, tongues, hands, and bodies, leaving nothing untouched or unloved. And when Noah slipped inside the warm, honeyed sheath of her body, he smiled when he heard her moan with pleasure.

Epilogue

Emilia Ayn Harper was born in late October. She weighed nearly seven pounds. Even though the labor was hefty, Cora was a trooper, constantly reassuring her nervous husband that she was okay. But Noah was scared and berated himself for not getting her to town for a real doctor. He fussed and worried. He couldn't stand the pain he watched fill her face each time she had a contraction. After twelve hours of hard labor later, their beautiful daughter finally came into the world.

The little girl was a mixture of both of them. She had blue eyes, and though Noah explained that all baby's eyes looked blue when they were first born, Cora insisted they would remain blue. And they did. At six months, her eyes were a beautiful sapphire blue just like Noah's—and dark wavy hair like her mother's.

Once again, Loka disappeared, making his own family, they assumed. He'd been gone for weeks. They trekked up the mountain to the hollow to share their babe with him, it was empty—no sign of him or his mate or any pups. "Looks like he and his mate found a new spot, Noah whispered. Just as they turned away to head back to the cabin, they heard the baying sounds of a wolf.

They turned just as Loka appeared at the back of the hollowed-out alcove. He slowly walked up to them, sat back on his haunches, and quietly studied the three of them. After several moments, he made a soft barking sound, stood, and circled his human friends, rubbing up against their legs.

"He's saying goodbye, isn't he?" Cora sensed with tears in her eyes.

"I believe so. He has always been intuitive and knows we are no longer in danger, and we want to move on with our lives in town. He has returned to his natural way of life. As I once told you, wolves mate for life. The males also help raise their young. Minutes later, Noah's words were proven.

At the rear of the hollow, they could see a beautiful black and gray female watching. She let out a lone call to her mate. Loka turned to look back at her and returned his own howl. In the distance, somewhere outside the cavern, they heard several wolves calling. With one last longing look up at Noah, Cora, and the baby, Loka turned and raced back through the cavern meeting the female. Both animals entered the hidden pathway and raced toward the rear entrance.

Cora squeezed Noah's hand. "I will miss him," She turned to her husband tears dripping down her cheeks. He gently pulled both she and baby into his arms.

"So, will I. I would never have survived after being abandoned in that Cheyenne village or in the years that followed had it not been for him. A large part of him is still wild, and he needs to make his own life," Noah whispered and gazed toward the rear entrance. "He would have struggled had we taken him into Willowby. But there were tears in his deep blue eyes when he spoke again.

"I've decided to continue my medical schooling. Helping you birth our child, I realized I need to learn much more. When I'm finished, Willowby could use another doctor."

"That's wonderful, and I could help you study while learning some things myself."

"I would very much enjoy that, my little angel."

By the spring of the following year, Cora and Noah decided to leave the mountain. They made their home on the outskirts of Willowby. Noah had applied for medical training in a small private school in Boulder, Colorado. There were only a few students. He began his studies and discovered he could do most of it from home, only taking the train twice a month to turn in his homework. The doctor in town was familiar with how the school was run and took Noah on as part of his training. He was a quick learner, and Doctor Robert S. Snow was happy to teach the much younger man all he knew. Doctor Snow found Noah very knowledgeable and easy to prepare for his degree.

Willowby was thriving and a very different place than Cora remembered. After years of negotiation, the town finally got a railroad spur equipped with a small station and a brand-new telegraph office.

They had learned the two men Sheriff Adderly had arrested, Hyrum and Charley, had been released to the Marshal out of Denver and taken to the territorial prison, where they would both spend the rest of their lives.

Early one Monday morning, six months after their arrival in Willowby, the Denver Rio Grande stopped briefly at the railroad spur. Two tall, slender women disembarked from the passenger car and stepped onto the platform. They looked identical in face and body build, though both dressed very differently.

Cora was headed into town for her by-monthly trip to the General Store. The first thing she noticed as she steered the buckboard around the depot was the two women standing side by side with their luggage on the wooden walkway at their feet. They were twins, and Cora wondered if there was a possibility they might be Noah's twin sisters. Excitement began to swirl through her. Could it be them? She adjusted her grip on the reins, connected to the harness, brought the single draft horse to a stop, and pulled the brake. She lifted her young daughter from the large basket on the floor and climbed down to the dusty street.

She had to know if she was right. Noah would be so happy if these women were indeed his sisters. He had never heard anything back from his family after the sheriff sent his message over a year ago, and he figured they were all lost to him.

Cora eagerly stepped onto the platform, carrying Emelia in her arms, and moved to the two women. "Excuse me," she said, getting their attention.

Both women looked at her curiously, then down to the beautiful little girl she held in her arms. "Yes," both women answered at the same time.

"My name is Cora Harper, and I was wondering..."

"Cora Harper? Good gracious, are you our brother's wife?"

"If Noah is your brother, I am his wife." Excitement filled Cora. "We had a letter sent a year ago and heard nothing from his family. We assumed they were all gone. We had given up hope of ever seeing any of you. Gracious, he will be so happy to see you both!"

"A year ago?" Maddy said with shock and glanced at her sister Alley. "Why we only received Noah's letter a month ago. And look at you; you've already had the baby and got your figure back. Why it took me nearly a year to even be able to fit into my regular clothes. You are so lucky." Maddy caught a breath and longingly gazed down at Cora, and the little girl snuggled in her arms. "She is adorable. May I hold her?"

"Of course," Cora handed the child to Maddie, who happily cuddled her. "Her name is Emilia," Cora told them.

"After our mother, how wonderful she will be so proud."

"Then your parents are well?"

"Oh, yes, other than Papa's arthritis. And Mama won't leave his side." Alley chuckled, "even though he told her to stop babying him."

Emilia giggled when Maddy hugged her again. "You are so pretty, just like your mama."

"And look, she has Noah's blue eyes and her mother's dark hair. Oh, Cora, she's precious," added Alley. "Let me hold her," she pleaded to her sister.

Maddy handed over Emilia and glanced at Cora. "Anyway, that's why we chose to come for a visit. It's been so long since we've seen Noah. We just had to see him and wanted to meet his family."

"We did send a letter to let you both know we were coming," Alley admitted. "But I guess you never got it." I hope it won't be too inconvenient that we showed up unannounced!"

Cora's smile lit her face and filled her amber eyes. "I usually only make it to town every few weeks to pick up supplies and check the mail. I'll bet your letter is at the post office. But it doesn't matter. This is such a wonderful surprise; Noah will be so pleased. He has missed his family so much. When we heard nothing back, we were afraid something might have happened. We planned to take the train sometime this summer when he has some free time from studying. He wanted to show me where he grew up and hoped some of his family would be left."

"He's continuing his medical studies; that's wonderful news," Maddie told her.

"Yes, he also works with the town doctor for on-the-job training. When he finishes his studying and testing, he would like to start his own practice."

Emilia began to fuss, and Cora relieved Alley. "She's probably hungry and needs a change."

"We won't impose; we arranged to stay at the boarding house for the next week. And we don't want to keep you from your errands."

"Don't be silly. This is no imposition. However, getting rooms at the boarding house was a good decision. Though we would love to have you, our home is tiny, and you will be more comfortable at the Willowby Boarding house. They are building a hotel on the east side of town; it should be finished by fall. Tell you what," Cora continued. "I will drop you off at the boarding house so you can get settled. I'll finish shopping and pick Noah up at the Docs in two hours. I'll take care of Emilia, and we'll meet you back here and have supper together. Lawd, he will be surprised and so delighted to see you."

"Sounds grand." Both Alley and Maddie leaned down and kissed Emilia on the cheek. They all climbed into the wagon and headed to the Willowby Boarding House.

That evening, they dined together. The sisters filled Noah in on all that had transpired over the last eleven years.

Maddy and Alley stayed for a week with a promise to keep in touch as they boarded the train for home.

Cora and Noah added another girl and two boys to their family in the following years. They made yearly visits to the farm Noah's family owned and continued even after his parents passed on. He was always grateful he could reconnect with them in their last years and that they had the chance to know his children.

Noah finished his medical training a dozen years ago, and his practice thrived. They built a larger home with plenty of room for their family of six. He and Cora's love for one another never wavered, and they proved it when they held each other in the night and deeply kissed and caressed, making love as easily as they did when they were younger. As the children grew, Noah played his guitar each night after supper, and they all took turns dancing with one or the other. They had a splendid life filled with love, laughter, and comfort.

They never saw Loka again, but they knew he had been free and happy for the rest of his life—a life he was meant to have.

One night, years later, they lay in bed. They heard the sound of a wolf in the far distance. Of course, after all the time that had passed, they knew it couldn't be Loka, but the beautiful sound warmed their hearts and filled their bodies with the love of warm memories.

"You don't suppose it could be one of his pups....?"

Noah ran his fingers across her lips. "One never knows. But you and I will always feel the spirit of his love and protection. Just as we always did from the beginning."

Made in the USA
Monee, IL
18 February 2025